THE MODERN ART OF DATING

Bennett Joshua Davlin

CENTERED AMERICA PUBLISHING GROUP

OTHER WORKS BY BENNETT JOSHUA DAVLIN

BOOKS FICTION

MEMORY
Penguin Books U.S., Random House Australia, Blanvalet Germany, Sony Books Japan

DREAMSPACE: Escape C19
Centered America Books & Various Foreign Publishers

UNION 57
Centered America Classic Books

MAJOR MOTION PICTURES

THE MEDALLION
Sony Entertainment & Columbia TriStar Pictures

MEMORY
Warner Bros. & EBE

BOOKS NONFICTION

HOW TO WIN THE WAR
THE PLAN TO SAVE THE U.S.A.
Centered America Books

SAINT MICHAEL STOOD UP
China Is Gog
Centered America Books

GOD'S GUIDE TO THE END OF THE WORLD,
WHEN EVEN YOU CAN BE SAVED
Centered America Books

THE MODERN ART OF DATING

Bennett Joshua Davlin

CENTERED AMERICA
PUBLISHING GROUP

CENTERED AMERICA PUBLISHING GROUP
Published by Centered America Books
A Publishing Division of Davlin Productions, LLC
269 South Beverly Dr. Suite 537 Beverly Hills, CA 90212

THE MODERN ART OF DATING

This book is an original publication of Davlin Productions, LLC

PRINTING HISTORY
Centered America Books trade paperback edition / August 1, 2024

An application to register this book for cataloguing has been submitted to the Library of Congress.

ISBN 979-8-9881466-1-2

PRINTED IN THE UNITED STATES OF AMERICA.

10   9   8   7   6   5   4   3

For my friend, actor, & fellow auteur,
Dennis Hopper

ACKNOWLEDGEMENTS

I thank my wife for agreeing to grace the cover of this novel. This tale was inspired by a dark deed attempted upon a *Maxim* model and yours truly decades ago at a high-profile rockstar's birthday celebration. We managed to safely escape as we were with my friends who looked after us. The next day I began seeing this novel and its movie adaptation playing out in my mind; so this tale literally wrote itself from that event.

This novel is dedicated to my good friend, the acclaimed writer, producer, and director Dennis Hopper whom I had the honor of directing in a film; Dennis loved this story. My management firm at the time, Michael Ovitz's AMG tried to sell the book for me back in 2000, but it was deemed by my Penguin and Random House editors as too controversial to print at the time. Still, it was passed around by many Hollywood creative executives for years furthering my film and TV career. More than a few studio executives still regularly text and even send pics of them rereading its dogeared manuscript; now they can possess a proper, bound copy.

I'm grateful to my teachers from the *Episcopal School of Acadiana, Tulane University, London's Kings College* and *City College, Tulane's A.B. Freeman School of Business*, and *New York Film Academy*. I'm also indebted to *TheGreatCourses.com* which allowed me to continue learning since graduate school.

I thank the late Buckley Norris and the former studio head Dan Melnick for showing me the ropes in town. I also thank my late, dear friend, the TV creator Glen A. Larson, who loved this twisted tale.

I thank my entertainment attorneys Robert A. Darwell and Phil Rosenberg.

I'm deeply appreciative of *Blanvalet, Random House, Sony Books, Centered America Publications,* and my other publishers worldwide for translating and printing my work in various foreign languages.

And I thank my dedicated readers and film fans for making it all possible.

Let's rewind time back to Hollywood 1999
before LGBTQ took over.
When people could speak their minds,
men were men,
women were women,
& movies were

BIG

Taking The Gods

"It is no great accomplishment to hear a voice in your head. The accomplishment is to make sure it's telling you the truth."

<u>Anonymous</u>

One

Three of them are naked.

Hair golden against hunter green felt. You break them down, finding fault. But these three are perfect . . . etched faces, modern day works of art. We stuff Mona Lisa's half-assed grin in the back of *The Louvre*, but hang beauties like these on every magazine cover in every checkout line in the free world. A glimpse of art as you fish for loose change and discount cards. The faces, heroin half-starved--so surgically crafted that you don't ever expect to see them in person. No, they live amongst the clouds.

And who said Greek mythology was dead?

So you peer down at the visages of these three women. What is it about them? You know that faces are just cartilage, muscle, skin, and hair lopped onto a bony skeleton. Then you wonder, maybe it was those Disney cartoons you were reared on with blonde bombshell Cinderellas and Betty Page-like Snow Whites? Or Barbie with her torpedo tits that defy gravity and her inhumanly proportioned hips? Like an Aldous Huxley novel, did nursery school forge your definitions of beauty?

She giggles back at you.

Eyes half crossed and a bleached white smile—then the sudden rush of fear. You've never met this woman before--she could scream! Alert the neighbors! Then the cops. . . next thing you know, you're grabbing your knees, taking it from a huge black guy named Luther who raves about momma's Chicken Jambalaya while he tickles your stomach via your rectum.

But don't worry.

Tonight, she's not doing that kind of yelling.

The three bodies rest beneath the sulfuric haze of the pool table lamp. Your eyes slowly trace their way across their bodies. It's strange—like living in some kind of porno film. It feels odd in a way that escapes words. So you focus on the brunette. She smiles back at you, eyes sparkling.

How did you get to be the lucky man?

You vaguely remember it had something to do with Nazi silverware, Pinocchio's Step brother, velvet party invites, Swamp Invader video games, and nature shows. Tonight you'll hitch a ride on Apollo's chariot. And up amongst those Olympian clouds, you'll frolic amongst these goddesses like a kid in a fucking candy store. You will defy all taboo, all laws, all things created to confine your true instincts. Derek was so right about that. But--

No.

It's ridiculous to think that you can understand this snapshot in time. You're just going to get lost on the wild ride. To understand, we have to go back to the beginning. Be warned, because as we go, you'll refuse to believe that we're alike. You'll label me an anomaly. You'll struggle, squirm, and look for any way to distance yourself from me.

But you'll be lying.

Because one thing will gnaw at you from the chasms of your mind—one truth to deny with all your will. For as you huddle behind your shield of hypocrisy and lies, you'll be peeking around the outer edges . . . just a little-- like a morning commuter rubber-necking charred bodies on the freeway's shoulder.

Careful now.

You've been poking around that shield for three pages. So let's just cut the bullshit and step down that dark path together. Forget about self-help books, fictitious rationalizations like men being from Mars and women from Venus. Let's really do some self-exploration. You know you want to. Because my name is Cullen Gersh. And you and I, my friend, are very, very much alike.

The Wild Kingdom

"Know then thyself,
presume not God to scan,
the proper study of mankind is Man."
-Alexander Pope (1688-1744)

Two

My religion is TV nature shows.

With remote in hand, I watch The Animal Planet Network, African antelope stumbling across a muddy creek—click—PBS, the graceful Cheetah running headlong across sun drenched savannahs in a hundred mile long courtships—click—Discovery Network where the chickens cluck out a basic language of five unique sounds. Some turn to the heavens for the meaning of life.

I look no farther than *The Learning Channel.*

It's as if the Universe concealed the answers to existence within Amazonian army ants marching under triple canopied jungle—click—a dying Hippo laying in torrent of waters as a tiger bites into his flesh and--

"Cullen, you said you'd turn it off?"

I glance down.

Her head passes in and out of my range of focus. . . heavy grunts of constrained breathing. Veronica has long reddish brown hair which sweeps out along the pillow, framing her fine features and pale skin--imagine a young Nicole Kidman with bigger tits. She's great. She's decisive. She knows what she wants.

Which is why I love her.

But my hips are getting really tired.

She digs her nails into my back—not in ecstasy, but irritation, "I don't need to watch wildebeest mating right now," she suddenly flips me over and gets on top. For some reason it reminds me of when I first met her in New York. Two years ago, when I was still in graduate school at NYU.

A friend invites me to a big entertainment attorney's party. Imagine one of those million dollar industrial lofts where decorators are paid untold sums to peel the paint, rusticate the wood floors—and give it that just right, squatter feel. Now fill it with Tisch drama school types— girls with exposed midriffs swaying to house music. . . a dread-locked D.J. with the prerequisite nose ring, perspiring over dueling records. The place smells like Scotch and stale beer. The sudden cacophony of laughter as a gay black man in a white ascot strokes his cat. . . alright, you get the picture.

People often reminded me of different animals. When I think back to my alcoholic mother padding around in her slippers and bathrobe, I'm reminded of the three-toed sloth. . . that animal that sits in trees and only comes down to the ground once a month to take a shit. At this party, I turn to my right where the finance guys— the herd of identical antelope--laugh it up in tiny estuaries of patterned Holland & Holland shirts. To my left, a handful of mini Kafkas cackle like hyenas, stuffing Swedish Meatballs and the last drops of free Glenlivet down their turtlenecks.

I never fit in.

Which is why I flee to the tiny balcony. I see her instantly and my heart races—that lighthearted feeling you get when you see a stunning woman. . . her profile silhouetted in the blinking neon light of the falafel shop across the street. Cobalt blue light flashing against her face. If I were a screenwriter, I'd write:

```
EXT. LOFT BALCONY — NIGHT

CULLEN, tall and dark, turns to VERONICA,
mid 20's. The sound of party chit chat and
music in the background.

                VERONICA
        You're     an      artist..
        aren't you?

                CULLEN
        I'm     gonna'    be     an
        entertainment       lawyer
        soon--which  is  kind  of
        close.

                VERONICA
        (eyes him for a beat)
        So what's your story?

                CULLEN
        I'm moving out  to  the
        coast next fall to work
```

```
at         ITM-International
Talent-
```

VERONICA
```
I know it.
```

It's like the start of a romantic movie, isn't it?

As we date, I start to notice a new dimension to my nature shows. Stuff like: "The Male Sperm Whale takes his mate for life," the august narrator's voice set against the magnificent whales cruising through azure water, "if one dies, the other will soon follow. . . almost as if their souls intertwined."

And it hits me.

I am the whale.

And I know what I have to do.

We're at her uncle's ski house in Killington. . .fire blazing in a stone hearth. We're wrapped up tight in a purple Patagonia fleece blanket, the tag rubbing against my tail bone as snow falls silently outside. The kind you see in those Time Life "The Music of Christmas" commercials.

"I love you," I whisper.

Her eyes take on that dreamy quality as she answers, "Ditto."

We roll over and make passionate love by the hearth. And it was only much later that I realize the truth. Veronica's an actress--she craves the spotlight. In that ski lodge, it's not me she loves.

It's just the moment--

"Who's got the best pussy?" Her face moves in and out of my range of focus as she rides me.

Don't know about you, but I don't enjoy verbally stroking people on the merits of their genitalia—no matter how good it is, c'mon, we're not shopping for meat. So I merely grunt, pretending not to hear her--

which is kind of ridiculous when you consider that her face is only a couple of inches from mine.

"Who's got the best pussy in LA!" she demands, legs hanging over my shoulders.

"You do," I whisper into her ear.

Yeah, like you wouldn't say it.

My comment breaks the dam, a river of sexual energy coursing through her, "Oh wow!" she stares up at the ceiling. This signals that I have exactly thirty seconds before she kicks me off her. Veronica claims it all tightens up after an orgasm.

Yeah . . . right.

While she waits for me to finish, she shuts her eyes, not knowing what to do. After all, everybody climaxes together in the movies. I guess in a small way, we're all like her, choreographing our kisses and embraces from films and TV. But she's a master at it. As I finish, I know she's running some *Elton John* soundtrack in her head. When it comes to sex, Veronica has more rules than a Japanese tea ceremony: lights properly dimmed, the Swedish foam pillow correctly placed under her head, *Brookstone's* sounds of the ocean playing on the stereo, our bodies cleaned and positioned just right in her four-poster bed.

Ever look at yourself doing it?

Ramming back and forth. Legs splayed all over. Perspiring stomachs suctioning against each other, making those loud farting sounds. Not much different from two pigs rooting in the mud. But Veronica takes breaks--wipes sweat away like a makeup artist tending to a close up. You'll never hear those farting sounds or--

"If you're not going to finish," she gripes, "you can do it in the bathroom."

Alright, so she seems weird. But this is just one snapshot in our life together. How about if I looked at you through one moment? You might form some pretty general opinions. Veronica's got more dimensions than this. For instance, when my Mom died last year, she drove me home, made all the funeral arrangements--was there for me when I was weakest. If you're sick, she'll drop everything to help you. She's like that. Compassion is her strong point. And when things are going good, she can be a little self-involved.

Just listen to her now as she lays in bed, chattering on about this part in a stupid *Pert* hair commercial she's never going to get--"Shoots in Fiji in a few weeks," she tells me how they don't give you any warning. They just call and poof! You're as remote as Brook Shields in *Blue Lagoon*. Veronica always talks about ads and commercials and films she never gets.

"But I could never leave Pooh Bear," she kisses her stuffed Pooh Bear, tattered and wrinkled from a lifetime spent in her company, "he's my little Rhett Butler--never spent a night apart."

Don't know about you, but I get creeped out when she talks like this too. She's had that animal since she was a kid. Takes it to the ski lodge, on vacation, everywhere. Despite all this, I feel this light sensation in my chest, a wonderment at her sweet smell. It's true, I don't like my job, life after college isn't what I expected, but she's here—and it's almost enough. I scan her *Gone With The Wind* posters—hard to miss them plastered all over the walls. She loves that film. On the night table are framed photos, snapshots documenting her life: high school cheerleading photos, family pictures. In one, I see her dad, this stodgy investment banker. . . even in this photo taken at the Cape, dressed in tan slacks and a white polo shirt, he stands solemn faced, holding his beer—

A beer, not a bad idea.

Fumbling through shelves of non-fat cottage cheese and chilled Oreo cookies, I grab the last of the six pack. Suddenly, I hear a voice narrating my every move:

"After the male human engages in his mating ritual, he will either sleep or seek out nourishment such as beers, potato chips, or the TV remote control," I stop in the living room. Veronica has one of those massive entertainment centers you only find in fraternity dorm rooms. I pick up the *Bose* remote, testing the weight, peeking through the open bedroom door to make sure she's asleep.

She usually passes out quick.

So I quietly turn on the TV. *The Learning Channel* is running crap on the Titanic—click--*The Discovery Network* has a show on alligators and crocodiles for "Predator Week"! Did you know there are only two places the alligator is found in the world? American swamps and China--of all places!

I sit on the couch, sipping beer, watching the show. I'm not the stealthy alligator, eyes above murky water, surveying prey. I am the whale. I am content. For you girls, here's a secret: guys often grow bored with their women. In college I realized that when guys feel weak, they become little babies in need of a woman to coddle them. Instead of a mother you have a wife. But when they're feeling strong, they often feel different. Is that why I love her so much? Because of the ungodly school debt or the fact I'm still bunking at her house and can't afford my own place? Is that why I keep wanting to give her my grandmother's wedding ring tucked away in the *Allan Edmonds* shoe box on my side of the closet? This is more than fear.

I really love her.

I sip the Sam Adams like a sperm whale siphoning plankton from the briny waters of the sea. Veronica will make a career of acting and I'll continue at ITM. Not bad for a poor kid with a barbiturate addict as a mom and a dad who died when he was eight. In a few years, I'll have the first down payment on that house in the Palisades.

Veronica will have a breakfast room with a view of the sea. She loves the sound of the surf. It all seems so simple. Yet unknown to me, everything I worked for will soon be gone. Replaced by evil and fire.

Because I was about to get an invitation to hell.

Three

I am a slave to ITM.

International Talent Management. . . sounds like some Bolshevik propaganda program. If you drive by our Beverly Hills office, your eyes are drawn to a glass arcade surrounding our very own *Calder* sculpture…it's the thing that looks like a twenty foot red soup spoon about to fall off a round, blue ball. If the sun is just right in the sky, you can peer through the wall of green glass and see talent agents, jackets draped over their chairs, ties loosened, as they march around in their wood-paneled offices, chatting on their wireless headsets.

These are the proverbial dealmakers of Hollywood. Their well-known clients are paid sums greater than the G.N.P. of most African nations to sit in a trailer for most of the day, smoking too much pot, venturing out to utter a few lines in front of a movie camera. Meanwhile their ITM agents collect a ten percent commission on all of these deals. Now look closely, do you see me through the glass negotiating with my trained verbal skills, reviewing contracts with my NYU acquired legal expertise? Of course you don't.

Because I'm in the fucking basement.

"I need that damn package upstairs now!" Claryssa cries out from a distant corner.

Search me out through the line of interns sorting mail. I'm the one in the corner filing mail into the wall of pigeon-holed slots. A virtual stream of envelopes, interoffice memorandums, and scripts in gold ITM liners passing through my hands.

The young freckled kid in his early 20's standing next to me is my summer intern, "Claryssa asked if you'd handle this," then he's off and running back to his corner.

Glance down at the package—three manila wrapped envelopes tied together with black string. Why am I handling this? Peering beyond the envelopes, I eye Claryssa across the room as she berates an underling. "Get that fucking package up now!"

Claryssa is five six, curly brown Jew-fro hair with a thin, round face. She has that rapturous Russian Jewish quality. . . beauty with an edge. In any other city Claryssa would be stunning. In LA she's just OK, lacking the surgically sculpted cheekbones, and ridiculously bleached teeth. A hundred years ago I could imagine Claryssa handing out fliers for the Bolsheviks on some Moscow street corner, toiling for the *dictatorship of the proletariat.* In the information age, she's down here. And when the revolution comes, you don't want her knocking on your front door. She's tough and she's smart. She went to Harvard undergrad and Harvard law.

Preparation H, she calls it.

Claryssa and I are friends. Beyond this tiny basement hovel, other law graduates work grueling hours, buy BMW's, author corporate briefs, get married at The St. Regis, act as junior on depositions, and refurnish rambling Connecticut farm houses.

Claryssa and I deliver the mail.

My days consists of shuffling envelopes in pigeon holed slots, picking up agents' kids at Beverly Hills High, retrieving boxes, returning cars for agents who had a little too much blow and booze with their hooker at La Dome the night before. Sometimes one of the junior agents upstairs lures a female studio exec or assistant into phone sex. ITM's got this expensive phone system. Sometimes twenty agents might be listening in to a juicy call--

I cut the string.

Each package is addressed to a recipient's name in thick black Marks-a-lot. I sort the first envelope into its recipient slot without a second thought, but the pigeon hole isn't large enough for it. The corner rips and I see red velvet. In a windowless room of proletariat gray, you take notice of bright red glowing like a blast of sunshine. I carefully draw the torn envelope out of the hole.

I'm a little intrigued. In all my time I've never seen a velvet correspondence. I reflect on the magnates of the industry who made their name in the mail room by steaming open letters and perusing their contents. Glancing to my right, I can almost imagine David Geffen leaning over my workstation, steamer in hand, ready to go. I pull back the tear, studying the red velvet envelope...elegant cursive writing covers the front of it in sweeping white letters which read:

WANT TO SIN IN HELL?
OPEN ME NOW

"Break time," Claryssa's voice sounds over my shoulder, sending me stuffing the envelope under my desk.

We take all our breaks together.

After all, Claryssa and I are the veterans of the mail room--been there longer than any of the others. She was already here six months when I arrived and the word is that she's about to be promoted to the talent coordinator's desk. We break into the building's alley. . . a submerged walkway framed by concrete and a tall wooden fence. Above us, through creeping fingers of tree branches, sunlight warms my face. I like it here. I hear birds in the distance.

"What a day," she whispers.

I turn away from Claryssa, watching a thin line of tiny ants gathering up parcels of a discarded potato chip around my Allen Edmond wingtips. Carefully they carry the tiny morsels along a thin military convoy running from the gap to the edge of the wooden fence. Claryssa suddenly steps back, crushing a dozen or so of them under her heel.

"You see the envelopes?" her eyes widen.

"Yeah. What is it?"

She explains that a week before I started last year, they arrived--three envelopes for the three chief partners. The old mail room interns had seen them the prior year too. They told her that they went out each year to the top agents and studio types.

"Is it an invite?" I ask.

"Who knows?" Claryssa shrugs, "whatever it is, it's happening this weekend," she fishes into her purse for a cigarette and then smiles devilishly, "a friend of mine at CAA heard it's an orgy. . . maybe like that scene in *Shampoo*?"

I struggle to imagine the three stodgy, senior partners at ITM, all thinning hair and flabby waists. I can't even imagine them on the toilet let alone engaging in an orgy, "Probably just a bunch of industry types kibitzing about film grosses," I shrug it off.

"Just another ridiculous indulgence," she grunts.

See. I told you she's taking down names for the revolution. Then she gripes about the biz, "People out here are just fucking awful."

I look down at the line of dead ants in the wake of her last step. A quick rush of fear. It only lasts a second or two, just feelings and emotions. If we break it out into words—it sounds a little like this: I'm training to be one of these people. Look at my clothes. I bought this suit at *The Men's Warehouse* on Wilshire with the little money I had left after I sold the Nissan. The wool glistens because I press it with a towel and an iron. I can't afford dry-cleaning. School debts hang over me like an angry weight. Will I ever get out of the fucking mail room? And why did I eat a Twinkie for breakfast. Ugh, I can feel the fat growing around my hips.

When I look up, God's light is gone.

"Slot those invites," she drops the cigarette over the dead ants, snuffing it out with her heel, "then Mo Simon's got a special job for you."

"Not Mo," I gripe.

Mo Simon is the world's biggest asshole—one of the three senior ITM partners. He addressed me once. I was coming back from lunch. He was leaving with some big movie director. I open the door for them, just to be nice. Mo stops and criticizes my door opening abilities. He felt I should have swept both doors open for them.

With a wink Claryssa tells me I have to pick up a package at *Hermes*, "It's probably for his mistress."

Fast forward five minutes:

"You sure you wanna do this?"

Eddie, the black security guard cringes as he surveys the polished fender of the car. I silently nod my head and shut the door. The key turns. The British racing green Aston Martin DB-5 starts, engine purring. The leather seats are cream with elegant, hunter green piping and a mahogany dash that smells like an Edwardian study. Near the emergency break is a photo of Mo Simon, soft and bald, sitting amongst his soft and ugly wife and daughter. Carefully, I push the peddle.

The car cruises out of the lot.

It's like floating on air. I cruise down to *Wilshire* and prepare to turn onto *Rodeo*. Opening the sunroof, light beats down, warming my face. At the corner stands two beautiful blondes in skin tight stretch shirts with *Diesel* dyed blue jeans—the kind with the purple tint—and big BCBG shopping bags dangling from nail polished hands.

Let's take this in slow motion, shall we?

Their sunglasses drop, crimson lips purse. Two sets of blue eyes following me like fans at The U.S. Open. I am the ball—well, me and the Aston Martin DB-5. How funny first impressions can be. To these two women, I'm not the gentle, kind, loyal whale. I'm the suave, mid-twenties lion in shirt and tie, driving my sleek sports car around the corner. I'm wild--

I'm the lion.

I'm still supercharged when I arrive at *Hermes*. Quickly I stuff the orange and black boxes in the trunk. Then I decide, why not. I deserve a quick cruise through

Beverly Hills. But storm clouds gather as I glide up to *Cannon Dr.* and back. It's starting to rain. So I hightail it back. With paper towel from the garage bathroom, I wipe down any trace of rain droplets and return to my desk. An hour later I get the call--

I'm in deep shit.

Claryssa warns me that I've been summoned to Mo Simon's office. I wait in the hall that smells like popcorn. Someone must be microwaving in the lounge. Through his open doorway I spy a screenwriter sitting in a chair in front of Mo's glass top desk. How do I know this guy's a screenwriter? Because he's wearing military fatigues and a t-shirt that reads

"If You're Pompous And You Know It, Clap Your Hands"

He catches me looking at him.

He reminds me of a wolf, cutting with those intense eyes set under a serious brow. He looks pissed off. But there's something very confident about him. I turn away, listening to his voice. It takes me a moment to place the accent . . .sort of English or maybe Scottish—it's a clipped accent, but natural too:

"Thanks for meeting with the meeting," he says.

"Last time I saw you was at your Dad's Christmas party," Mo replies out of view in the doorway, "so what do you have?"

"It's sort of a reality based film, no real script, it's organic," continues the screenwriter, "in the vein of *Truman Show* meets *Cops*—"

"Sorry Derek," Mo stops him in mid-sentence, "before we get into this, I need to see this nutless wonder for a sec. You don't mind, do you?"

"Aye, knock yourself out," the screenwriter stands.

We cross each other as I enter. He smells like my father's cologne. Then I'm looking at Mo as he turns red-faced, screaming at the top of his lungs, "Gersh, you're a fucking crack addict, do you know that?" he slams his hand across his calendar, "have you seen my trunk? A junkie could've packed those boxes better. What? Did you never take geometry?"

Let's mute him out and spare ourselves the irritation.

The mouth, the foul coffee scented breath as he sends tiny bubbles of spit across the papers on his desk. Without the sound, I realize Mo Simon has a very wide, flat mouth and a shiny bald head—reminiscent of the albino lemurs of southern Madagascar. The round head is framed by the Plantronics headset and the loose collar of his cream, herringbone weave *Ascot Chang* shirt which I picked up for him. C'mon, put a hairless cat in this guy's lap and you've got Dr. Evil.

He bounces gently up and down as he berates me.

The new craze at ITM are these big rubber balls trainers use in gyms. Some high paid ergonomist told all the senior agents that sitting on them instead of regular chairs would take stress off their—like you really care. Anyway, Dr. Evil stops bouncing on his great blue ball. Leaning over his mahogany desk, he repeats himself.

I better turn the sound up again--

"Gersh," he points to a black and white picture on the wall of the gray haired Morris Lepke, founder and patriarch of *ITM*, "in 1921, Mr. Lepke founded this firm with principles of strength and intelligence. But you just don't get it…do you?"

"I guess not," I reply. It doesn't matter that I'm a Columbia and NYU law school graduate. I am a pledge in this new fraternity. I'm simply going through the hazing.

Mo looks up at me again, "You're a sparrow's fart from being fired--"

One of his four phones rings.

He finds the correct one, snapping on an ear-set--the type that wraps around the head. Then his mood changes as quick as a hypoglycemic girl riding a double *Starbucks Mocha Latte*, "Tom! So good to hear from you," he presses the mute button, schizophrenically flashing coffee stained teeth at me, "what the fuck are you still here for shit-trap?"

I step back from the desk.

"How's Australia?" the mood changing again, "shoot going well? Getting' any? Really. . .so tight it hurts? Nice," I'm in Romper Room, watching the lemur bounce his ball in a hundred eighty degree turn. Now I'm staring at the back of his bald head bobbing up and down in front of the autographed *Hunt For Red October* poster against the back wall, "Of course, I'm jetting out to Sydney tomorrow. Now Tom, I don't do this for just any client."

I gesture to leave when my eyes focus on the lemur's bronze sculpture of John Wayne resting on the corner of the desk—the kind of crap "The Franklin Mint" sells you with promises of a future increase in value. Jesus, this town is tacky. Resting under John Wayne is a photo of Mo's ugly daughter and a stack of freshly delivered mail. Then I see it! The manila envelope! I see the message winking at me again:

WANT TO SIN IN HELL?
OPEN ME NOW

This time I can see a date poking out of the tear in the envelope: "**August 28th**". I glance back at the lemur's calendar spread open on the desk--gone for the next week to Australia. The date on the envelope is for this weekend. Glancing through the open doorway, I see no one, the screenwriter isn't even lingering in the hall. In my mind I imagine a young David Geffen, boldly holding his pocket steamer, urging me on. He knows what I want.

I pocket the invite. Stuffing it under my jacket, I can't wait to race to the bathroom to open it. On the way out, I bump into the screenwriter who's entering the office. He pats me on the chest, tapping a hand against the concealed envelope. I smell the fleeting scent of my dad's cologne and see my life pass before me—this screenwriter knows Mo. I've been caught. I'll lose my job! But he just leans close and whispers:

"Going to be one hell of a party."

Four

“**W**hat's this?” Hal winces.

Hal Rosenberg has a flat, wide face like somebody hit him with a frying pan. His gray eyes are set wide around a hooked nose, framed in a flowing sea of stubble-less skin that gives him an almost angelic quality. He's five ten, thin and soft, and a doctor--third year internal medicine resident at UCLA. As for his clothing--

You'd think Hal stepped straight out of a Gap ad. In all the years I've known him, Hal wears the same thing: green Gap cargo pants, a black Gap V neck sweater over a white Gap t-shirt, Gap socks, and Nike high-tops. This is his uniform. From a deep pocket of his cargo pants, he produces a bottle of Purell sterilizing lotion, wiping his hands clean. Which is why he always wreaks of rubbing alcohol.

"Want to sin in hell?" his gray eyes scan the outside of the velvet envelope as he reads aloud, "open me now."

Hal seems a little transparent to you because he is transparent. He really is just a Gap ad, simply filling the background shot. He is the idealized, new millennium man. The one you always forget is there. He never asserts himself to anyone or anything—I've never seen him kiss a woman though he still claims he had a girlfriend during our first semester in college. Sophomore year, I check her out--turns out she's a lesbian. They just hung out and drank a lot of coffee. Because he's the soft shouldered type that every woman extols as the perfect man, but would never think of sleeping with. In college, we filled endless hours questioning his sexuality. And although I've no idea what's going on in his head, he is the most kind-hearted, trust-worthy friend I have.

"I was thinking," Archie drawls in his Tennessee accent, "next week, we could have our get together at a frozen yogurt stand--more women there than the Barneys Hanger Sale. And I bet you they're all fit."

Hal scoffs, "How can you say that?"

"If they're not healthy, they'd be eating at *Baskin Robins*," he answers in a matter of fact voice, "and the yogurt couldn't cost more than what--a buck? That's our meal ticket, baby."

"Yogurt melts," I retort.

"Man--I tell you," Archie stares dreamily into space, "can't look at a hot woman these days without thinking about jumpin' her."

"I just read that men will be going extinct," Hal mutters, "in the future it'll be only women."

"Damn," grins Archie, "I wish I was there."

Archie Joe smiles. The Chinese American looks like a model when he smiles. He hails from Memphis where his parents own a Cantonese restaurant—I ate there once--not bad. I recommend the Sweet and Sour Shrimp. Archie went to Duke on scholarship. We were study partners in law school. With spiky black hair, he has a surprisingly angular face—Archie is good looking. Back in New York, he was the ladies' man--the guy who broke plans because a new female friend suddenly dialed him up.

Archie still pins Sports Illustrated Swimsuit Calendars on his kitchen bulletin board. Still garbed in his preppy get-up, a Men's Warehouse pinstripe suit and striped regimental tie, he looks like he belongs back in Manhattan and not in the Beverly Hills El Torito Mexican restaurant.

Do you see us?

Over near the far window overlooking Camden Ave. We're the ones sitting in the corner on those high stools, making dinner out of the free nacho chips and salsa. Notice the three warm, half-filled Corona beers, rings of condensation around the bases--that's the price for this free dinner. So until our bellies are full--

we're gonna take these beers real slow.

Every Thursday, we have this late night get-together. Because out on the West Coast, these are my buddies. Hal is my closest friend in the world. I've gotten to know Archie a lot better since he got transferred out here. On the stool next to Archie is a thick pile of screenplays. Archie isn't in the entertainment industry. He works in Prudential's derivatives department, reviewing contracts for traders—or some crap like that. In New York, the business card alone could easily get him laid. Out here "A Piece of The Rock" makes the eyes glaze. Like everyone else, Archie takes a great interest in the entertainment business now. He even subscribes online to *Variety*. And he loves doing my coverage. Which is great. Because I detest them.

Coverage sucks.

Authors or screenwriters slave away for years on a screenplay or book--like this one for instance. The project gets sent in and is quickly bounced down to the mailroom underlings—those shmucks from the last chapter. These college interns and friends of friends pass judgment on these projects.

These acne faced kids and wannabe writers critique your great American novel or screenplay in 3 page long commentaries dripping with pseudo intellectual lines like "the characters are strident", or using words such as "tepid" and "jumbled" in their descriptions. This coming from kids whose idea of high literature is reading *The Wizard of Id* on the can. As you can tell, I don't like anything about coverage. Which is why I'm happy to let him read.

"Guys," he puts down one script, laughing, "catch this--Geppetto is lonely now that Pinocchio's moved on. So he carves a piece of wood from the stairs and makes Pinocchio's step-brother! Get it," he cackles, "PASS!" The script drops to the floor with a loud thud.

The clan of waitresses in the corner glance up. The place is mostly empty by now. Happy hour is over and we're just milking the chips. They used to stand over us, arms akimbo, asking if we were ever going to order that second beer? Now they just gather beneath the sign that reads "Tipping isn't a town in China."

We can't afford a tip.

We're all underpaid. My job sucks, but when I think of working too much I just think of Hal. His dad was a leading manufacturer of bras, but lost it all a few years ago. Now Hal gets his ass kicked at UCLA--seems like the guy's on call at the hospital every night, working until he almost passes out. Just look at those blue rings under his eyes—he didn't used to have those. Archie's not too happy either. He's got some boss he calls "The Bitch." She overheard a comment he made about her when he first started and has been gunning for him ever since. We drive beat up Chevettes and broken down Hondas with ripped seats and air filters that stink like piss. We buy our clothes at Men's Warehouse and clearance sale racks at The Gap. Besides me, they have no girlfriends—Hal might not want one. And with crushing Visa card debts, Archie can't afford it anymore.

"When are we gonna start looking for an apartment?" he asks as he peruses another script.

"Soon," I settle them down.

The two of them are looking for a new apartment because they can't afford their old ones. I'm supposed to live with them in the new place, but I wonder what we're going to get? The places they're passing on are pretty damn cheap. But I don't need to worry about all that now.

After all, this is happy hour.

We're content to stare at the three muses. The three women across the street. Peer real close through the window, you'll see them: a Latino, a blonde, and a brunette sitting at the window of the cigar bar across the street.

Yeah, those three.

They're there every Thursday night too. For months we've watch them hook up with different guys, always driving away in some fellow's fast car—like a living cliché played out before our eyes. A month ago, Archie worked up the guts to walk across the street and introduce himself. Hal and I watched him from the safety of El Torito as the three Amazon nymphs--I nicknamed them that, stuck their noses in the air, laughing him away. That's pretty tough.

Now don't get me wrong, but c'mon, that's no way to treat people. Anyway, that was the last time I saw Archie hit on a woman, even though he talks about it all the time--

"Is this an invitation?" Hal studies the velvet envelope, taking a big swig of beer.

"Hey, what are you," Archie cautions, tapping at his beer, "some big spender? I don't have enough for a second round. Do you?"

"Take it easy," I mutter.

Hal opens the envelope, revealing a velvet covered greeting card. Laying it on the table, he carefully runs his fingers across the velvet card as I caution, "It was a pretty big letdown. And I stole the thing—could've cost me my job."

"I like the naked chick," adds Hal, but the comment doesn't seem genuine when he says it. . . like a child pretending to be a grown up.

"Naked?" Archie peers over his script.

One side of the card is covered in a stylized portrait. Like those Vargas paintings in Playboy. It's of a skimpily clad woman with devil's horns and a pitchfork slid seductively between her exposed legs. She smiles. The other side reads:

**THE ANNUAL BALLET OF CHESTNUTS
SATURDAY, AUGUST 28TH 8:30PM
1136 HACIENDA AVE.
B.Y.O.D.**

"B.Y.O.D.?" wonders Hal, "Bring your own. . . date?"

I shrug without an answer, adding, "I looked up Hacienda Ave. It's in Sherman Oaks—"

"The Valley, ugh!" groans Archie from behind his next script.

"What's a ballet of chestnuts anyhow?" Hal wonders aloud.

"I hate ballets," I gripe.

"It's not a ballet at all," Archie fires off in a matter of fact voice, the script still concealing his face as he says that "in 1501, the Catholic Pope Alexander VI presided over a Vatican banquet for priests. A dude named Burchard documented the whole thing. Candelabras were placed around the room--chestnuts scattered on the floor holding fifty courtesans," he lowers the script, winking at us as he adds, "them be the ho's for you simple boys."

"So what did they do?"

"Catch this. The floor was filled with chestnuts. Then all the priests and wealthy dudes started screwing, cracking the chestnuts with their bodies. The Pope and his daughter, Lucretia, watched from a table, distributing gifts to the guests who fucked de' most bitches."

Hal and I stare at him incredulously, wondering if he's bullshitting us again. He reads the suspicion in our faces and shrugs, "C'mon guys, I was a history major," he taps a finger on the invite, "and I don't need to be that to know that I'm in."

"People don't have orgies anymore," Hal scoffs, "I mean--there's AIDS and Herpes and Hepatitis C—just to name a few of the possible side effects."

"And if you don't get off the porch you'll never leave the house?" Archie's reply makes little sense. But he doesn't care. He just smiles, "Ooh, I get hard just thinking about it."

"That's bullshit," Hal rolls his eyes.

"Honest, I really am hard…feel it," Archie grabs Hal's hand.

Hal jerks it away, "I was talking about the party! Guys it's probably a gay mafia thing."

"What's wrong with that?" Archie blows a mocking kiss, "Hal, if I were gay, I'd love you, Gap boy."

Hal grabs the back of his sweater, "I bought this at Banana Republic."

I decide to end the party talk, "I probably couldn't even get us all in."

Archie peruses the invite, "It doesn't specify how many guests you can bring."

"And I'm going to pretend to be Mo Simon?" I wrangle.

"There's no name on the card."

"There will be on the guest list."

"There's gonna be a lot of names," Archie brushes my concerns away.

Then I remember, "Besides, Saturday I promised Veronica we were going for a romantic dinner."

"Look," Archie points at the Amazon bitches across the street chatting up two tall Persian-looking guys, "I'm tired of being outside looking in."

I must admit, I am intrigued too. I did risk my job to get this velvet card. And I definitely can't afford another dinner. My Capital One Cards about to get shut off. I remember how Mo's Aston Martin felt—the two girls with their BCBG bags staring at me—I was the lion. I want to be the lion again. My mind flows through visions of what the party might be like. I imagine Hugh Hefner in his robe, the whole Mansion, blue pool and grotto, naked women with long stemmed martini glasses--all situated between a Walmart and a Krispy Kreme, because hey, we're talking about The Valley.

"Yeeha! We are goin' to party!" Archie drops another script in the Pass pile and stands up in his stool, chanting loudly, "Party! Party! Party!"

Hal drops his head, embarrassed.

From the corner, the waitresses really give us the evil eye.

Five

Veronica and I don't go to dinner.

C'mon, cut me some slack. I can barely afford a croissant. And don't say I'm a cheap asshole. If I had the funds, we'd be dining at *Little Door* right now, eating— well. . . whatever kind of food people eat at *Little Door*. Why am I even telling you this? Maybe because Veronica's flashing the evil eye at me as we drive down

The Ventura Freeway. I feel sweaty and stressed. She's pissed off because—

"Turn left," Archie sticks his head between us.

Archie and Hal ride in the backseat. Arch directs us from his Thomas Street Guide, cradled thick as a bible in his lap. Sticking his head between Veronica and I, he smiles straight, white teeth, "Isn't this romantic? Just the four of us out on a Saturday night."

"Stick to the directions," I bark back.

In the rearview mirror, I notice the edge of Hal's hawk nose poking out from behind my seat. He doesn't look happy—but he's never happy around Veronica. She thinks he's in love with me. She says he's jealous whenever she's around--but she doesn't like any of my friends.

If you saw the three of us now, you'd think someone had died. Archie and I are decked out in the one black shirt we own. Sporting imitation *Diesel* jeans, we wear the same black, wing-tip shoes from the office—in the dim club lights, no one notices. Luckily, Hal's Mao suit of Gap apparel is mostly black. As for Veronica, she's clad in skin tight black jeans and a tank top.

"Cullen, dude I don't want to be rude," Archie wrinkles his nose in my rearview mirror, "did somebody piss in here?"

"It's the air filter," I make my voice firm. To be honest, I don't even smell it anymore-- been meaning to give the car a service when I have the money.

We turn off the freeway.

Now it's official. We're in The Valley. Remember that cheesy strip mall in your town that they tried to turn into the bingo parlor? Imagine endless streets filled with them, punctuated by Taco Bells and Beirut-style tenement housing, tin foil plastered across all the windows. Why do people do that?

"Turn right," Archie instructs with the seriousness of a bomber pilot, "we're here."

I glance out the window.

It's a defunct Kentucky Fried Chicken, letters hanging off the building. The windows are boarded. The Colonel shut off the lights here a long time ago. Just as we're about to bicker, I notice someone standing in the shadows near the old drive-up booth.

Flash my lights.

We sigh, realizing it's just a Gay Bear. Clad in black leather jackets and biker boots, Gay Bears are Schwarzenegger-like giants who man the front doors of LA clubs. With lists in hand, they decide who will pass the velvet rope with the intensity of a Nazi doctor sorting new Auschwitz arrivals. I roll down the window and take a look at him: smooth, stubble-less faces are their trademark, free of all fats and lipids. They're Gay Bears because—

Well. . . straight guys can't look this groomed.

"Come for the Colonel's secret recipe?" the Gay Bear puts a thick forearm against the car.

I flash the velvet envelope. He hands me a Xeroxed sheet, "Have a good time."

The gang gathers around me, eyes on the Xerox. It's a copy of a map of Hollywood. Which is all the way back over the hill.

"What is this," mutters Hal, "Treasure Hunt?"

Let me save you some time.

Remember the map of the world from *Raiders of The Lost Ark*. The one with the red line charting Indy's progress around the globe. Now imagine one of those lines crisscrossing all over Los Angeles. Because we hit two more seedy locals with two more maps. We're covering more of the hills than a redneck on a celebrity house tour.

It's almost midnight.

The Honda's hot with perspiration. I can't turn down the windows because it'll mess up Veronica's hair. And I can't turn on the A.C. because the piss smell will kill us all. So we sit in this moving steam-room, defrosting the fog off the windshield. The map leads to a neighborhood called *Mount Olympus*, a swank subdivision of multimillion dollar homes high in the Hollywood Hills. A security guard stands at the entrance of the street. One flash of the velvet invitation and we're ushered through as he adds, "Should turn on your defogger."

Thanks. . . like I'm a fucking idiot.

Then we see it.

Think of that gated English house from *Dynasty*.

Fill the yard with tents, flicker strobe lights in the windows of the house—and drop a hundred or so guests in the dimly lit front lawn. Don't forget the elegant gate, because that's where we are.

Locked out.

"The stars are not in your favor," this South African Gay Bear tells us. Flexing his biceps, the leather of his jacket crinkles. I can't stop looking at this tiny tuft of hair just below his lower lip.

"Dude," Archie points at me, "this guy really is Neil Simon--"

"Mo Simon," I correct him.

"Could be Simon Le Bon for all I care," The Gay Bear screws up his eyes, adjusting his headset, "and he ain't on the list either," he licks the tuft of hair, "and if you ain't on the list, ya just don't exist."

Veronica leans in close to him like Cat Woman--chest out, tits standing to attention under her skin-tight black top, "Isn't there some way. . . maybe you could let just us two in?"

"That is not an option!" Archie turns to me.

"Cullen, this is ridiculous," Veronica's imploring me.

"Cullen?" the bear interrupts, "Cullen Gersh."

I nod my head yes. But he's not buying it. Only after I show him my driver's license does he grin, "You're on the list."

I'm on the list?

How the hell is that possible? Did Mo somehow not leave? But why would he trick me? Then I see the wolf's glare. It's the screenwriter from Mo Simon's office. Clad in jeans and a T-Shirt that reads "Show Me Your Greatness", he greets us, kissing Veronica's hand, "A pleasure to meet you all. I'm Derek Van Horn."

Although she fights to conceal it, her eyes are ablaze. She's impressed. In that same clipped accent, he introduces himself to Archie and Hal. Archie hands him a card with his handshake. Derek reciprocates with a card. Then he wraps a casual arm around my shoulder as we walk up to the house, "I hoped you'd show up," his skin still smells of my father's old cologne. Peering into my eyes—his look is so intense I turn away, "Thanks for not saying anything to Mo about the invite."

He pats me on the back "C'mon, he's a fucking asshole."

Now we really are old buddies.

Derek opens the front door and--

Wow.

Remember all the Hustler letters that begin with, "I never thought it would happen to me, but—"? Well, I'll spare you the clichéd sexual analogies, pulp magazine adjectives like "gushing fluids" and "torrents of exploding juices". We freeze. Big strobe lights flash on and off—the quick hint of a grand piano pushed against the far wall. The air is hot--smells like latex condoms and sweat. In the center of the room is. . . well. . . maybe Archie sums it up best:

"Dude," his eyes open wide, "that's a whole lot of people fuckin'."

An orgy doesn't look like what you think. . . it's not all bodies on top of each other, limbs moving in syncopation like a barrel full of snakes. It's more like a bunch of little clubs—groups ranging from one to five getting it on. Among these faces I see studio development executives, a few famous feature film actors and actresses. . . men going down on women. . . condom wrappers. . . women going down on women. . . hips flailing. . . perspiring backs rising and falling. . . tons of vibrators. . . one guy with his hand up this chick's ass. . . and chestnuts scattered everywhere.

I clam up.

What the fuck have we wandered into? I feel like that time I bungee jumped during spring break in college. I leap off the platform--the world rushes at me—too quick, too fast for words—

"The rain has come!" Archie prances around in a circle like an Indian doing a shaman dance.

Hal glances at me, stubble-less upper lip raised, the hint of pearly white teeth—that look of fear. Then I eye Veronica, her mouth agape, eyes darting everywhere, taking it all in.

With a devilish smile, Derek ushers us down the hall. Through French doors, I peer into an elegant salon where a beautiful blonde—tall and Nordic with Playboy perfect breasts, crouches on all fours. Behind her this old, hairy guy rides her from behind--his other hand reaching around her front. Four video cameras mounted around them, project their image on TV screens surrounding them like a sun dial.

"The *voyeur* room," Derek turns, pointing to a half opened door. Through the crack, I see only a blue neon light, faint hints of bodies, "the enema room. It's b.y.o.d. on the diapers--"

"So that's what that means," mutters Hal. He glances around as he nervously cleans his hands with his tiny bottle of Purell, the scent of sterile alcohol in the air.

Derek points towards the ceiling, "Up there is the anal, vibrator, and foot fetish rooms. . .the attic's the cave--"

"What happens in the cave?" asks my breathless girlfriend.

He turns, winking, "Very primitive stuff."

Derek leads us to the pool area.

By this time we're wide-eyed kids who've wandered into some strange adult ceremony. Clinging to a tiny stone bridge arching eight feet over a steaming Jacuzzi below, our bravado is gone. Chlorine fills the air. Rave music blasts. I scan the yard--stragglers wandering to the tennis court, people rooting on the lawn like pigs, a drunk guy on a pool-chair—we're the only clothed people here.

Archie nudges me, "Look down, dude—beats the shit out of watching the Amazon bitches."

Below us, a tall, skinny sitcom star whose name I won't mention is busy fucking four Playboy centerfolds positioned along the sides of the Jacuzzi. How do I know they're Playboy centerfolds? Because he takes great pain in arranging them by the order of their months—January, March, June, and September, as he screams at his passed out buddy that, "I'm juss'gonna fuck around this year."

Turn to Derek who wears the distant smirk of a spectator. Those probing eyes. He's so strong, so confident. Below us the sitcom actor transitions from winter to spring.

"You guys all old friends?" Derek asks.

"I'm fucking around this year!" enthralled with his wit, the actor repeats his one liner--voice echoing through the pool area.

"Yeah," I answer.

"Why'd you come?"

"I dunno," I feel his eyes on me and glance down at the sitcom star who digs deep into March, "maybe the mystery of seeing what others can't."

"Presents," yawns Derek, "are always more interesting when they're wrapped."

I realize the sitcom star's passed out buddy is his agent. How do I know this? Because the drunk guy wakes up, slithering towards the Jacuzzi where the winds of March blows. Now they share the girl, the agent high five'ing his client as he screams, "We've taken the agent client relationship to a whole new level."

"Strange," observes Derek, "we explore the inner depths of our intellect, discourse about nature and the human condition, but hang our sexuality along with the skeletons in the closet. People have to be drunk just to go in the closet--"

Flash—another one of those moments. I see myself throttling Derek Van Horn and tossing him into the Jacuzzi below.

Derek flashes a knowing wink, "You just thought about hurting me."

I'm rendered speechless. But before I can say anything—

"Derek, baby!" I turn, hearing the guttural, course Bronx accent.

Facing me is a fat guy, mid 50's, hairy belly hanging over what appears to be a giant diaper or Depends Undergarment. The little hair remaining on his pointed head is frazzled, sticking out from either side like flared elephants ears, "How ya doin, kiddo?"

I realize I've seen this guy in Variety. A sudden gust of chlorine fills my nose, making my eyes water.

Derek introduces me, "Meet Irving Hershberg, feature film producers and your host. Irving, Cullen is a friend of mine. . .agent trainee at ITM."

"ITM?" he looks like a Chinese pot-bellied pig as he flashes a mildly impressed smirk and readjusts his diaper, "juss talked to Mo Simon last week—classy guy."

"What were you looking for?" I realize this guy is the big-shot cartoon producer on the Disney lot.

The Pot Bellied Pig doesn't seem very interested in talking about it, "An animated sequel—shit like Snow-White II or The Aristocats Go To New York."

Flash--I see the handshake—selling the script, launching into the partnership ranks at ITM, "I have a solid scripted sequel to Pinocchio," I stammer, "it's his step-brother actually—big family demographic and. . ."

Step back for the wide shot. So I'm standing on this bridge, making kids cartoon shop talk with a fat guy in a diaper as people fuck all around us and the sitcom star moves into one of those Hollywood moments that seem screwed up when you first move out here, but now it's become normal.

Irving tires of the shop-talk when he notices my girlfriend, "Who is this Gilda look-alike?"

I introduce Veronica.

Freeze.

Now look at her expression. The moment she hears the word "producer" this shit- eating grin appears faster than a Pavlov's dog at a Texas barbeque. Notice how the lips curl at the end? That's her mom's cocktail party face. Come on, she's at an orgy for Christ's sake, talking to a fat guy in a diaper!

"You're an actress?" Irving asks rhetorically.

"Well. . . I've only been out here six months—"

"We should take a lunch—"

"Sure—that'd be great!"

"I'm fucking around the year!" the actor screams again--the joke's gotten real old.

I stare at them. I'm not a jealous guy, but my girlfriend doesn't like anyone. And here she is, taking a lunch invitation from this fat bastard. Irving tells an anecdotal story about his last film, his finger brushing across her breast. Alright, it was brief but--

He touched her fucking tit!

Resting on the banister of the bridge, Derek Van Horn watches me. I feel naked and fight to conceal my feelings. Finally Irving is pulled away by a woman in a business suit--some assistant who says Irv needs to say hello to a well-known actor whose name I already told you I won't mention.

Walking away, Irving's eyes are still locked on Veronica's—like they're speaking in some telepathic language known only to producers and actresses. He moves away, never turning from her as he mumbles, "send me over the script," but he isn't talking to me.

It's time to go.

"I can't believe you!" she screams.

We're back in her bedroom. My eyes dance across the living shrine to "Gone With The Wind." Veronica jabs a finger in my chest, eyes red and angry, "I can't believe how you dragged us out of there. He was just talking—is that a crime? He's a big producer—"

"C'mon, the man was wearing a diaper."

"Why do you have to be so judgmental?" she opens her mouth—for those of you without Method Acting girlfriends, this is the dramatic depiction of grand revelation—like Moses communing with the burning bush, "this is about your insecurities, isn't it?"

"What?" Jesus, this is like talking to a dog.

"Darling, you don't need to be afraid," she strokes my cheek--her smell intoxicating, "I love you. The fact that I might lunch with a funny fat man is nothing. I'll tell you where we're eating if you want—"

I nod no.

Maybe she's right?

I'm being crazy. Forgive me, but this town--this life gets to you. I hate jealousy too—a disgusting character trait. We fall into her bed and make love. I smell the sweet scent of her body--the clean smell of the sheets. In my mind's eye, I reflect back to the first time I met her— a beautiful face set against the blinking lights of that New York falafel shop--a perfect moment.

And I love her.

I'd be nothing without her. As I roll over, her beautiful red hair in my arms, I lay in a half dream sleep where I fish the screenplay out of Archie's pass pile, type out a wonderful ITM coverage, and hand deliver it to a diaper clad Irving Hirschberg. We sit in his voyeur room, TV screens all around us. On the TV screens, I watch him flip madly through the script--adjust his diaper—and shake my hand, grinning, "I'll buy it." As I bask in victory, I notice a final TV, the entire screen filled with two probing eyes, staring right at me, reading every thought in my mind--

As Derek Van Horn probes deep into my soul.

Six

"So who is Derek Van Horn?"

"Hah," laughs Claryssa, lighting another cigarette, "just a member of one of the richest families in town. Worse than entertainment types--Van Horns' veins run blue."

"Blue?"

Claryssa explains that there's a whole click of wealthy families in the city that have been here for almost a hundred years. In LA years, that's like tracing your lineage back to the time of Christ. They're all Protestants and keep to themselves, "Like that country club on Wilshire-- right on the rim of Beverly Hills," she explains, "no Jews or entertainment types allowed. That's their stomping ground."

"How do you know all this?" I ask.

"Newspapers always in the bathroom," she's embarrassed as she confesses that, "sometimes I read the social page."

A gust of wind rushes down our alley, the sound of leaves scraping across cement. It's still morning, the sun hasn't reached our alley—dark gray with a slight chill. Claryssa performs a little dance step—feet clicking across a puddle of black tar, remnants of the ants she crushed last week. Since it's her first day upstairs in the talent coordinator's office, we steal only one break together.

"Ya know," she muses, "should' a' been a dancer," she mockingly thrusts her arms out in a tango like move, head swept back.

"Who's his dad?" I press.

With a frown, she stops dancing—the tone hinting that she almost doesn't want to talk about him, "Made his money in rain gutters I think. Ever notice how really rich people get rich off weird stuff, like the racks they stack gum on at the grocery store?"

She drops her cigarette on the ground, staring down at it. "Mo's been trying to get into The L.A. Country Club for years. Hip-pocketed Derek to get in with his dad," hip-pocketed is when an agent informally reps a new, untested client without dropping paper—signing a contract. "Derek's gone around town on a few pitches, scripts—nothing sold," she snuffs the cigarette out with her heel, "stay away from the Van Horns."

"Why?" I ask.

I imagine her answering with one of her regular quips like: because they're another one of those rich fucks. But her eyes just glow with intensity, that powerful Claryssa stare—the Proletariat pig about to deliver a rousing revolutionary speech in Tsarist Russia. But she says nothing, simply walking towards the door. "C'mon, I gotta lot of calls to make."

I can't sneak out until two o' clock.

It's my first day as head of the mail room. So I'm busy. Besides my new supervisory tasks, I spend my morning reading enough of the script to type out a flattering coverage for "Pinocchio's Step-Brother"—it got excellent marks on dialogue, content, and characters—go figure. At the entrance to the Mount Olympus community, another rent-a-cop eyes me suspiciously from his patrol car. I flash the gold ITM envelope and he nods knowingly.

C'mon, they're all aspiring screenwriters.

I park along the street, walking towards the front gate, my blood rushing. Fantasies race through my mind—the sale of the script--I'll fix that piss-stenched air filter—no, screw that, I'll buy a whole new car. And I'll take Veronica to The Little Door, wines and foods and desserts and music and making love all night.

The front gate is open.

I stare up the drive of the Dynasty House—manicured lawn, box hedges, and a yellow Bentley convertible parked at the front door. It's hard to imagine that this was the same home from The Ballet of Chestnuts. Walking up the path, I feel the hood of the Bentley, still warm—Irving probably just returned from lunch.

The distant sound of music echoes in my ear.

I ring the doorbell—nothing. I ring again and finally knock on the door--my hand taps the door open. I guess they don't bother to shut their doors in Mount Olympus. The echoing sounds of atonal music assaults my ear--like Schoenberg, atonal rhythm--the rapid clanging of piano keys. Pretty impressive, huh? Alright, I confess, Veronica gave me this box set on the history of music. I used to jog in Central Park.

"Mr. Hirschberg?" I call out.

No answer—just that music.

I expect to leave the script with the maid, but no maid in sight. I can't just leave it in the foyer. I wonder if I should just go back to the office and have it messengered later? No. Irving must be home, his car's out front, the piano clanging, he's probably getting a music lesson—clang! Clang! Clang! Crossing the foyer, the music grows louder. I didn't realize how stripped his house was for the party—there's all kind of antiques and ornaments now—the framed movie posters of Irv's films--an academy award and two Golden Globes rest in a glass case near the bathroom door.

"Mr. Hirschberg?" I call out, "anyone home?"

Clang! Clang! Clang—fuck atonalism, this music is awful.

I turn the corner and—

Oh fuck.

Irving—the little potbellied pig, stands at the grand piano, pants at his feet—clang! Clang! Clang-- bare hairy ass pumping—clang! Clang! Clang—as he tosses another body up in the air, her ass banging on the piano keys— clang! Clang! Clang—her head tilted back—clang! Clang! Clang--red hair spilled across the glossy black piano—

Veronica?

Slow motion.

The rush of gastric fluids burning up my insides. His back to me, her head tilted away, they don't see me. The dam breaks, I vomit all over Irving's carpet. The ITM envelope falls out of my hands landing on the marble floor with a—crack!

Veronica glances up, eyes wide.

She stops fucking on the piano.

The potbellied pig fucked my swan.

Time speeds up again:

Irving's bald, pointed head whips around, eyes wide at the puddle of puke, "You asshole, that's an antique Hopi rug!" he doesn't even care that it's my girlfriend, the woman of my dreams, that he's fucking--

"Cullen!" screams Veronica.

Fast forward.

Remember the bungee jump—too fast for words— too fast for thoughts? Stumbling, falling against one of the movie posters—it crashes apart on the floor. Need air. I'm outside--the world is too bright, the paint of the Bentley blinding me. I lean on the fender for balance, vomiting again—puke on the black asphalt driveway, splattered droplets on the front bumper—brown on yellow. No more music. I hear Irving and Veronica screaming in the house.

Oh shit, I've got to get out of here!

Driving.

La Cienega—Sunset Blvd.—Pico—I just drive. Remember the promo on Hawaii Five O' or Miami Vice? All quick jump cuts of shit that doesn't make sense. . . like some massive tidal wave--the flash of cars and stop lights, pedestrians and school crossing guards, Irving was fucking my baby!—Olympic Blvd.—Venice Blvd.—San Vicente—roll down the window, sunny, mid 70's, her ass clanging against the keys—Texas Ave.—Barrington Ave.—Lincoln Blvd.—shut my eyes at a stoplight, I see

Irving's wizened old penis penetrating her beautiful red pubic hair—ugh! The intersection of Sunset and the Pacific Coast Highway--trying to pull over and swallow my vomit back down. A valet opens the door. I'm at Gladstone's Restaurant where I had my only nice meal with Veronica in LA—Sunset to the P.C.H.--did I drive here on purpose?

Leave the car with the valet—a gust of wind--he says something—too fast to understand. Irving fondled her bare breasts--Gladstone's a seafood restaurant overlooking the ocean—she was the love of my life--tumbling, drawn to the beach, rush of surf and water—I see her looking up at him as she sucks his dick--the sun's setting in the distance. A great orange disk streaking purple and pink across distant clouds and calm ocean—he fucked her over and over and over on that piano—the scene looks like a postcard it's so mockingly beautiful—she moaned and kissed him, tongues intertwined--today should be earthquakes, fires, and riots, but it's just ANOTHER FUCKING SUNNY DAY IN LA!

Cold.

Time slows back to normal, except it doesn't feel normal—it feels too mellow, too slow. Things take shape—thoughts form. Look down, I'm standing in the surf up to my shin. I've ruined my only pair of black wing-tip Johnston and Murphy shoes. I'm cold. Surfers carry boards out of the ocean, ogling this strange guy in a pinstriped suit, standing in the sea. I wish the ocean would carry me away. Flash—the thought of sinking into murky waters, ending this whole existence thing.

But I'm too much of a pussy to kill myself.

Collapse on the sand, shiver and cry. Flash—the thought of Irving fucking Veronica--my stomach turns knots—no, there isn't a word for how it makes me feel—like someone pulls out my intestines through my mouth.

Tears trickle down my face. My lips quiver and I cry and I weep and I sob--

"Sir," I turn to see a young blonde waitress in her mid-twenties. She smiles at me? Is she trying to help me? "I'm sorry sir," she winces, "this is a public beach, but you're kind of disturbing the patrons," she winces, pointing behind me.

I turn.

All these bibbed families have stopped eating their late afternoon meal, sitting frozen--forks stuffed with lobster held halfway to their mouths. Little kids cry, staring out the window, tears flowing down their faces. All eyes peer through the windows of Gladstone's at this pathetic weirdo sitting in a wet pinstriped suit, sobbing like a child.

I'm a homeless person to them.

I gather myself and leave.

In days of Indian summer, the sun hangs forever.

Picturesque over the horizon for hours, it doesn't set until nine o'clock. It's all orange light in Veronica's apartment as I pack my few personal effects—clothes, toiletries, my sleeping bag and *thermarest*—into the military duffle bag. I push out the thoughts of them together. Hate fills my soul now. I think of pissing all over her bed or stealing her Gone with The Wind posters. No, that would only give the little bitch pleasure.

I loved her.

I was going to be her whale.

Here's a confession, maybe I wouldn't have even become an agent if it hadn't been for her. In law school, I entertained thoughts of becoming a writer, but I can't write worth shit. I think back to my fantasies of us. There was this one particular fantasy that stands out--the two of us in an elegant sports sedan, maybe a BMW 7 series. We're older, driving through Connecticut or Vermont, classical music playing, winter snow on the ground. No kids in the back seat, they've all grown up. Just Veronica and I driving. And I turn to her and she's old, all wrinkles and gray, but so beautiful and. . .even as I think about it now, the hate leaves and the tears come as quick as a menopause hot flash.

I'm going to cry again.

Wipe a tear away, catching the reflection of my face in the mirror—red flushed cheeks, disheveled hair, tie undone. I never even called the office after lunch. Turning, I steal one picture of Veronica from her dresser. I don't choose the one with the two of us at the Cape. I pick the one of her laying back on grass, smiling at the camera—just like a movie star. Just to be spiteful, I think of taking her beloved Pooh Bear. Then I decide just to steal her Gone With The Wind commemorative jewelry box.

How hollow movies are.

They definitely don't show you this shit.

Hey, at least I didn't steal her panties like some pervert—

I hear the door open. Heart skips a beat. Why did I linger so long? Footsteps in the hall and then she's there—just a girl now—not my beautiful, graceful swan, "I'm so sorry," her eyes are glassy and red. She drags herself in. I want to reach out, to hold her, but I wonder, is this another act? When she was strong with me, was she playing Sally Fields in Places in The Heart? Scarlet O'Hara when Tara fell to ruins? Was her compassion merely a scene study?

Anger surges.

"You fucking whore!" rage—I explode, "—had to be Monday. One salad and you're flat on your back--couldn't even wait until Tuesday!"

"Just who do you think you are?" she barges in, eyes cast away from me as she storms her way to the dresser, quickly taking off earrings and a necklace, "you were there before you even got off work."

I stand over my military duffle bag—all the possessions I own on this planet--thump—thump—goes my heart—the quick flash of her face in the blinking falafel shop light—thump—thump—there goes my life—thump—thump—all because she spread her legs for—

"You just don't understand," she spins around angry.

I'm speechless. . . searching for words.

Energy ebbing from wobbling knees--she sits on the edge of the bed, "I put up with all your whining about your job." This is a new tune, something I've never heard before. "You can't afford your own fucking apartment, so I let you stay here. I carry you on my back," she hunches over like Quasimodo, "carrying you all the way out to the West Coast. I know your dad died when you were young and your mom—"

"Don't you dare talk about my parents. You fucked the diaper boy!"

She wants me to lash out, because it's a role she can play—the angry lover, "Irving is an Oscar winning feature film producer!"

"Sure," I toss the military duffle over my shoulder. Conflicted feelings--she was there for me when my mother died. She took care of me when I was sick when--

"I have a career too, you know," she adds.

The hot rush of rage, "Just stay on your back. I'm sure you'll make it."

Crash! A porcelain cup explodes on the wall near me--barely missed my head. A barrage of words—unmanaged emotion, she learned this at Playhouse West, "You're a fucking worthless joke."

Just keep walking.

"And don't you think you're better than me, Cullen Gersh! You and I are the same," her words echo off the walls as I cross through the bedroom doorway, "what's your day like? Picking up agent's kids at school, packing trunks, delivering mail--at least I only have to fuck them once. You do it all day all week—all year."

I turn, "Maybe you could give me some pointers on that."

"Take that back!" teeth gritted.

"Fucking whore."

Enraged, red eyes blazing. It would be so much easier if she wasn't so beautiful—so clean looking--so perfect even as she berates me, "Get the fuck out of my apartment you penniless shit. You think you're better than me? I'm gonna make one call and Irving will make sure you never work in this town again! YOU'RE FUCKING FINISHED!"

Keep walking.

I'm exhausted after my fight with Veronica.

Hal's on call at the hospital. Archie has enough problems working overtime with his bitch of a boss. I don't want to burden anyone. Then as if the Universe finally acknowledged my sorrow, it begins to rain—droplets of water beating across my cracked windshield. I realize I haven't eaten all day and pull into McDonalds. The drive-through line is long. I park, racing to the restaurant. But it only has an open air eating area of booths gathered around a tiny cubicle building. It's raining hard and I'm instantly wet. In the corner, a bum rants and raves about the government.

Reaching the awning, I gripe, "You'd think McDonalds can afford a roof."

"It's a Mini-Mac," the female Mexican clerk stares blankly at me—with the face of a horse. She hands me my order from the dry protection of her semi-portable cubicle.

"What?"

"This is a Mini-Mac," her lips barely moving as she speaks in monotone, like Mr. Ed chewing on grass, "a satellite McDonalds. Want full service? Go to the full-service McDonalds on La Cienega," she stresses the word McDonalds and prepares to slide the glass closure shut, "until then, thank you for choosing Mini Mac."

It's six o'clock when I return to ITM--feels like I left this building a million years ago. Combing back my hair in the rearview, I try to appear presentable. I got food poisoning, that will be my story. On my way in, a security guard turns to me:

"Mr. Gersh," he eyes me cautiously, "you're wanted upstairs."

"Sit down, Cullen?"

This guy looks like a mole, with two massive eyes. I've never seen him before. With tiny hands he readjusts his narrow, frameless spectacles. Clad in a drab gray suit, he ushers me into one of the chairs in a cramped third floor conference room--the type they use for meetings with new, hip-pocketed talent.

The mole stares me down, "From Australia, Mo Simon contacted the senior ITM partners earlier today with some very serious accusations. A matter involving theft of mail, lying about Mr. Simon's identity, trying to sell a script as a trainee—"

Normally I'd mute him off.

But I'm just too tired to bother. After all I'm not even listening, why should you? Let me sum it up. This guy is one of the labor lawyers ITM employs to properly fire trainees—because once you're fired, you have to be treated with kid gloves. Hot heads like Mo Simon might say something stupid in a meeting like this one. This joker, on the other hand, will wish me luck, give me my final paycheck, shake my hand goodbye, and instruct security to quietly make sure I'm out of the building in twenty minutes. If they follow me around, it's too obvious and embarrassing and I could sue for millions.

What the mole's not saying is that Mo Simon's assistants have already called everybody in town and black-balled me out of the biz. And I'm not just talking about being an agent. I won't be able to get a job at any entertainment firm from Bloom Hergott to that fat guy with a wart on his chin in Anaheim who fixes D.W.I.'s, but claims to be in the biz because he got his cousin a dancing gig as a Pocahontas at Disneyland. And forget New York too—or the book biz. Mo Simon's drum is heard on both coasts. As for practicing law outside of the entertainment field, I've never taken the bar for any state. I was going to be an agent, not a lawyer. Just to pass the bar will take months of work--

I stand up, sparing us all the trouble, "You can send my personal belongings to me when I have an address. I'll leave the building now."

By six thirty, I'm no longer head of the ITM mail room.

Tears trickle down my cheeks. I never cry. I thought Veronica was mine—that our souls were intertwined and communally owned. But the bitter truth is that you own no one, you have no one. Look at me, shielding my face with my hand as I weep like a baby. The rain's stopped-- sunset blinding me through my rearview mirror. The light making the cracks of my fingers light up white hot.

I remember a sunset with my father. Five or six years old, we're deep sea fishing in Virgin Gorda, Bitter End Yacht Club visible in the distance. The boat rocks, "Look for the green flash, Cullen," he points at the setting sun as we head towards land, "it's that last flash of light left by the setting sun and it turns green."

I rock with the boat, the smell of sea salt, fish, Coors beer, and my dad's cologne. His cologne--like Royal

Musk mixed with Old Spice. . . his cologne. . . his cologne. As if the hand of fate had cast it, I notice a card resting in the passenger foot-well. It reads:

DEREK VAN HORN
SCREENWRITER

There's a phone number below it. Archie must have dropped the card on my floor. It's fate. My father's cologne. . . the smell still lingering in my mind. I don't know why, but I pull over at a phone booth in front of the Ralph's Supermarket on Olympic Ave.

And I call him.

Seven

"**Y**ou look like shit warmed over."

The wolf is clad in jeans and a t-shirt that reads "I Luv Animals, Cuz They Taste So Good". He dries his hands with a rag. From the narrow street carved into the side of the Hollywood hills, I knew this place would be awesome. Frank Sinatra croons "It Was A Very Good Year" as he leads me inside. I see the CD spinning on one of those fancy, wall mounted Bang & Olufsen stereos.

The front room spills into a loft styled room. . . hardwood floors trailing into wall to wall glass overlooking the city. It's the same view you get in a window seat on an airplane taking off from LAX. A sea of lights flicker back at me, the grid-like paths of the streets—reminds me of a giant microchip on fire.

"I was just cooking pasta," he flips vermicelli from one of those fancy Calphalon pots Veronica wanted for her birthday. I feel wobbly. Derek sees this and puts the pot down, walking over to an elaborate bar of cut marble and wood where he pours a vodka shot, handing it to me. "Purely medicinal."

"Thanks."

I shoot it.

Derek serves me pasta in a porcini reduction sauce. I nibble at it but I'm not really hungry. My intestines are still distended with tension. With quick glances, I study the furniture--like modern art, industrial metal and appointments of cut glass. . . the clean look you find in shops on Robertson—a lamp made out of poofed rice paper resting on a silver triangle—stuff no one can afford. Then it hits me.

It's quiet here.

In Los Angeles, where more people are crammed into less space than anywhere else on earth—except maybe India or some fucked up country, it's always noisy. But high up in the hills, I hear the wind brushing along the glass wall. . . the crackle of Derek's fireplace--not that cheesy gas burning type that comes standard in LA apartments, but the real thing. His place is big. A stairway in the center of the living room spirals down to an entire lower floor I haven't even seen. Through the glass I see hints of a pool with one of those disappearing edges, so it seems like the waters is falling over the side.

After we eat, he leads me through a doorway into a game room with a massive pool table and Carlsberg Beer lamp overhead—and he has the original Centipede arcade game! In the corner, I bounce pool balls around the table as we speak. It's easy talking to Derek Van Horn, intense eyes--the only thing he's focused on is you. I can't explain it, but I still feel like he's my best friend. I tell him the events of the day-- pool balls rolling across green felt.

"Can't date the talent," he grabs the eight ball when I'm done, sending it off into a side pocket, "they're all wackoes."

"How did you get your accent?"

He sets up a pool shot with two balls and lines his cue stick between stern fingers, "Watched a lot of Monty Python videos," he flashes that intense look--you don't know whether to laugh or—"just kidding," he hits the ball and turns to me, smiling. It's the first time I've seen him smile, "was sent to Eton when I was eight."

And I don't just do the talking. Derek tells me how his ancestors came out to farm in the early 1800's: "Before the movie industry or even the 1850 gold rush was a thought in anyone's mind, they made their fortune in orange groves that used to cover what's now greater Los Angeles. Then they got into real estate speculation and oil."

"I heard it was in making rain gutters," I say.

He laughs and proceeds to tell me that he was an only child, graduated from Duke and decided against his father's will to do the one cardinal sin: to enter the ever hated film industry. He doesn't spell it out--but he got some type of inheritance to buy the house because his dad refuses to support him and he hasn't sold a single thing.

"Aye," he nurses a snifter of Armagnac as we sit by the fireplace, "Mo set up meetings, but I've gotta say-- they just don't make them stupider than film development people. Nowadays, people don't even need writers."

"They always need writers and lit agents to manage them."

"It's all reality. No story—no substance. I'm looking for some great neorealistic film, but we've pushed the envelope so far, there's nothing left to shock you. We've seen naked lesbians on TV and pedophiles on film. We grow bored with the most amazing special effects. Audiences crave COPS--to see real criminals arrested by real police or Jerry Springer—real white trash goin' at it because they fucked the same cousin-- want to believe that wrestling is real and politics fake."

"The way you talk about it," I sigh, "it sounds like one big snuff film."

"Darkness is in everyone," Derek's eyes bore into me, "the sick, perverted concepts on screen are the same ones we stuff in the back of our minds. You'd like to kill Veronica right now—wouldn't you? You'd like me to kill her. I'd do it."

I don't bother answering his joke. So he changes the subject asking, "If you had total freedom, what would you like to do with your life?"

"I always wanted to be a writer," I think back to that kid writing stories and I feel like I've failed. Then I lighten the mood by adding, "don't know if I could entertain all these sick thoughts though."

"You thought about hurting me when we were at that party."

I don't bother denying it, "How did you know that?"

"That's why you're an agent trainee and I'm a writer," he raises his glass in a toast, "out of social contract, we restrain ourselves as a culture, but it still lingers—the raw, primal energy. We ignore politics and focus on watching others go wild-- football players clashing on the field, strippers fucking on the stage, gunmen in news briefings, movie actors slaughtering rooms of people," the fire dances with his eyes as he leans close. I smell my father's cologne, "every great writer has to get in touch with that primal instinct. If you don't feel it, how will the audience?"

"Sometimes there's mystery in not showing something," I sip the Armagnac, feeling his eyes upon me, "but just hinting at it."

He gives me a wink and I sense a devilish underside, a razor's edge to this man, "I think you want to enter the dark side. That's where those thoughts come from. After all, you crossed the gates and entered that party."

"That's true."

"Happy you did?" he's painfully blunt.

"If it wasn't Irving, I guess it'd just be the next guy. At least I learned about her now rather than when we're married. It hurts so much. I wish there was no passion."

Derek glances at his watch—one of those multi-dial, handmade Patek Phillipe's you see in Cigar Connoisseur Magazine, "once I took a house in Majorca for break—"

"Where's Majorca?"

"An island off the east coast of Spain. I was there with my girlfriend, making love all day. Her friend joined us for a week. My girlfriend was always impressed with the way I had screwed her. One night after one too many bottles of Rioja, she asked if I'd fuck her friend. I had sex with both of them."

"Sounds awesome," I raise my glass to him.

"Not really," he stares into space, an almost sad look, "our relationship was never the same. Somehow we'd taken something filled with passion and lost it. But at the same time we'd opened doors in ourselves that none of us really wanted to peer down—as if the Universe concealed the answers to existence along that dark path and in knowing the secret, we would all lose our high-mindedness, our illusions of being lofty."

A long silence.

"What the fuck are you talking about?" I ask.

He chuckles, "I don't know--sometimes everything seems so complex that I want to just shoot myself dead. I see it as clearly as your violent little outbursts. I'd do it too if it could somehow benefit somebody or something- -suicide is so damn selfish."

"On that note," I set my glass down, "time I hit the road."

Derek laughs, refresh his sifter at the bar, "Where do you have to go?"

"Well. . ."

"I have four bedrooms," adds Derek, "just stay here until you get back on your feet," he picks up the phone, dialing a number.

"No, I can't impose on you like that."

"Seriously, you could move in."

"Can't," I explain, "I'm going to move in with Hal and Archie in a new place."

"The guys from the party," he says, a thoughtful look filling his face. Then he grabs a portable phone from the table, dialing a number as he confides that, "I've been going out of my mind here—need human contact, a roommate—inspiration!"

"But you barely know me."

"We barely know ourselves. And this place is safe," he points up at a little black sphere mounted to the ceiling of the room—just like those glass half-globes on department store ceilings. I glance down the hall and spot another sphere on the ceiling, "security monitors in every room. The former owner was a security nut, even found a 9mm pistol tucked under a hollow floorboard--not a safer place in town."

I scoff, "But I could never afford—"

"If you don't want to feel like you're imposing, I'll charge you an unreasonably small rent, say three hundred dollars a month. You pay when you have the money. I'll even draw up a nice little rent document and you can sign it. Very legal."

"Why are you being so nice to me?" I ask.

"Because you're considerate enough to ask that question."

It's all happening so fast.

I feel so close to this guy who smells like my father's cologne. He's upbeat, confident, strong--I almost feel it rubbing off on me. I need to go to the bathroom. He leads me downstairs, showing me the three spacious bedrooms, bigger than any I've ever seen in LA. There's a fourth door, a metal one with a numeric key lock.

"What's that?" I ask.

He still holds the phone to his ear, obviously on hold, "My bedroom--a lot of expensive stuff in the house, so the added security and--" the caller on the other end answers because Derek winks at me and speaks into the phone, "yes, I want three special types sent over pronto. . . thanks," he hangs up.

"What's that about?"

"Calling some women over."

"Hookers?"

"No, actresses. With some inheritance money, I bought part of a casting agency. I go through the book of head shots--pick a few every so often—just to relieve the stress."

"Thought you said don't date the talent."

He winks, "Ah, but never said you couldn't fuck em."

Fifteen minutes later the doorbell rings.

We're upstairs in the living room. Derek greets them at the door. I hear the click of high heels on the wooden floor. From out of the darkness, he guides three beautiful red headed women into the living room. They're like swans—perfect 10's with slender waists and bosoms almost bursting out of black, skin tight dresses.

He smiles to me.

He thinks this is his way of trying to help me. But I'm not going to superimpose Veronica's face on these beauties. I demurely say no. Derek grabs one of them, pulling her ample breast out of her dress, running his fingers along her nipple. But I don't feel like a man now. I feel like a little baby, a child. And sex is the last thing on my mind.

I say no and excuse myself downstairs.

Lights dance through my bedroom window.

The well appropriated city grids of Los Angeles flow into the horizon. . . a sea of humanity spaced within well planned system of streets, electric lines, and sewage systems. In the distance, jets take off and land from LAX. It's late. The sounds of Derek and his three women—the rushed breathing—the moaning and sighing—have long since stopped.

I can't sleep.

I realize that what I thought was a dark picture over the dresser is actually one of those wall mounted, high definition TV's. I turn it on, the picture sharp and bright—click—click—click—flipping   through   the channels until I stop at The Animal Network's special on Rhinoceroses.

Just a rerun.

It's that time when the rest of the world shuts down. Muting the Animal Network, I lay naked on the bed--eyes following the distant lights of jets taking off and arriving at LAX. I hear the soft breeze. Yes, I think I'll move in for awhile. Although I fight it, I reach into my duffel and pull out the stolen picture of Veronica—that's the way I want to see her.

Cradling the picture to my chest, I weep.

Sounds pathetic, huh? Well think of all the pathetic things you've done, but never told anybody—bet it's a lot worse than this. So I lay there, cradling my swan, not knowing if I should scream or cry, staring at the twinkling sea of lights, feeling cold and alone. I shut my eyes beckoning to sleep, but it doesn't come.

I think how broke I am—have to find a job, any job. I toss and turn for hours—vacillating between wanting to hurt and wanting to control Veronica, and weeping in her lap—then dawn's light breaks in the eastern horizon. It's like living in one long day. This is how I spend my first night as a resident of Derek Van Horn's home.

Then the sound begins.

Eight

Tap—tap—tap—

It echoes through the house--must be an old mechanical typewriter hidden behind Derek's numerically locked bedroom. Tap—tap—tap—ding—I hear him slam the mechanical paper shaft back to center. Derek is regimented. All day Tuesday, from seven in the morning on, the rhythmic tapping and dinging of the machine--

regular and punctual as an orchestral movement. By the late afternoon, after a full day of Animal Planet and Discovery Network nature specials, I can raise my finger every twenty eight seconds for the--

Ding!

Then—tap—tap—tap—Derek is hard at work. I think to call Hal and Archie. I know they must be worried about me, but somehow I just can't face them. I remember that I left my diploma back at the office. I call security and give them my address so they can ship my stuff. Then I feel like being alone.

I drive to my Mini Mac.

Sitting in my outdoor booth, sunlight on my face, I nibble at an Egg McMuffin and hash brown, wondering what happened to those old apple pies in the deep fried pockets? I'm groggy from lack of sleep. The grizzly bum in the back corner screaming at his imaginary friend is not helping my headache. My mind wanders. . . wonder what Veronica's doing. . . sucking Irv's dick probably. . . buying clothes. . . hanging out at a bar . . should I take the California bar. . . should I hang myself in my bedroom? Nah, wouldn't do that to Derek. I'd rather drive my piss-stenched Honda off one of those high cliff roads near his house.

Hell, probably just land in somebody's swimming pool.

I imagine my funeral, a sparse affair. Veronica clinging to the coffin, tears flowing, so grief stricken that--flash—she's sprawled across her bed, raising the pistol to her mouth. Pan away from the gruesome scene and simply see blood splatter across those tacky Gone With The Wind posters--droplets of crimson and black.

But no. She'd just love it if I died, finally have some dramatic cross to bear--collapsing over my coffin, beating her breasts, recording the moment as an emotional catalyst, storing it away for a human condition exercise in her drama workshop.

Then it hits me.

A moment of clear lucidity. I stop, Egg McMuffin halfway to my lips as I scan the restaurant. . . the squirrelly kid waiting in line, the bum behind me, the RPS delivery guy at the payphone, the smell of cooking grease in the air—all the boring details you normally ignore as you wolf down your breakfast and head out to work. The thought takes shape. Novelists and drama types like Veronica sit in studies, espousing the human condition. . . lone Mallory fighting for his life atop Everest. . . a passion filled Juliet taking her life for love--exaggerated, dramatic movements where someone always dies. That's just escapist fantasy. It isn't what life, what being human, is all about.

The human condition is here--at Mini Mac!

The human condition is that depressed guy over there at the table. . . a double hamburger please. . .worrying about your Visa and MasterCard debt . . . super-size those fries. . .hours squandered in front of the TV watching Friends. . .is that Coke for here or to go. . .running the shampoo bottle under the shower to get a little out more because you keep forgetting to buy a new one. . . the boring crap, the endless dribble, is the human condition. We are all the human condition!

Veronica's tailored her life within this grand illusion. What I craved at ITM, mixing with the movies as if it would make me cleaner, better—is ridiculous! It's like someone's lifted away a veil and opened my eyes to reality! Fuck the Aston Martin DB-5, fuck the dreams I had, I'll live here, feet planted on the ground, firmly resting in the real world. Just then, a gust of wind blows through my Mini Mac. An open newspaper lands on the table. I grab hold and see it—like fate. Just read the ad:

MAKE BIG MONEY ON THE INTERNET
CALL NOW!!!

And that's how on Wednesday, I wind up here.

Do you see me? It's my first day. In the back corner of the large room filled with rows of cubicles, broken down computers. I'm the gray eyed, sallow faced one that looks like he could fall asleep. Because I barely slept last night too—all nightmares and cold sweats. I answer the ad, hoping for a legal consulting gig with some hot internet start-up, vision of I.P.O.'s dancing through my head. But this isn't that kind of company. I yawn and hit the button on my phone. You're watching me take my first call as a technical support agent for Alpha Systems Software.

So why didn't I have to take a training seminar?

C'mon get real. When you're computer's frozen and you pay $30 for tech support, do you really think you're speaking to a highly trained professional? Why would a highly trained professional do this fucking job? You were conversing with the guy who in the old days sold aluminum siding and encyclopedias over the phone.

Just look around.

Emaciated chain smoking Mexicans who look like a pack of wild dogs. . .that overweight black woman scratching her caboose ass as punctually as old faithful. . . the squirrel like chick with thick glasses and pig tails— c'mon, pig tails! It's not 1970. You could sell tickets to this thing--a circus of the strange and forgotten. Hunched over our computer terminals, we type in your complaints, reading verbatim what the computer spits back at us.

In the first hour, I'm already frustrated with morons calling in because Swamp Invaders From Alpha Centauri keeps freezing up their CPU. Shutting my eyes, I imagine pimply faced teenagers and pedophile stalkers in overcoats, fat and unkempt, as they bitch over their phones, cursing at me:

"This fucking game is so cheap that—"

Click.

I start hanging up on them. You know how they say your call might be monitored to assure customer service? Bullshit. What the company does monitor is your speed and efficiency at handling the calls. Because I'm hanging up on all my callers so often, my efficiency rating soars through the roof.

By Tuesday I'm promoted.

I'm now a supervisor, handling special calls and hanging up on them. I'm one of the most efficient supervisors in the place. Hey, it pays. I get to be alone and almost don't have to talk to anyone. I entertain the thought of bringing my law books here and prepping for the California bar between sporadic calls. I don't have to interact with anyone. I squander my free time staring at the sound tiles covering the wall. Time slows down when you've barely slept in three days—like stretching silly putty out in a long string. Hey, if you hadn't slept in 3 days, it'd make sense to you.

I sign Derek's rent document.

He complains that I didn't bother to read it. I assure him I did. But the truth is, I skimmed it—hell, not only the small print, but even the big print just looks blurry.

The rest of the week becomes rhythmic.

Tap—tap—tap—tap—ding! I hang up on people— return home to the same lyrical sounds day after day. At eight o'clock, Derek opens his iron door and we prepare dinner—tap—tap—tap--I lay there at night as the visionless nightmares awaken me, not even remembering what's so frightening—tap—tap—tap—ding! The question begs an answer, what the hell's he working on?

One afternoon I arrive back early. Derek, wearing a T-Shirt that says "Don't Fuck With Mr. Zero", stands on the green felt pool table, tools and screwdrivers at his feet. He fiddles with the black security system unit in the ceiling. In his hands, he holds a tiny black box with a glass face. Upon seeing me, he shoves the unit up into the plastic housing and out of sight.

"What is that?" I groan.

"Motion sensor," he snaps the black plastic globe over it, "damn thing broke. Had to buy another, costs a bloody fortune."

I take the opportunity to ask him what he's working on: "Is it a book?"

"No," he chuckles, "but if it all works well," he finishes screwing the housing back and rubs his hands together, "it'll be my greatest story."

That evening during dinner, I nibble on the rosemary Dijon mustard lamb chops he's prepared. They're so beautiful that I don't tell him I abhor rosemary. Hell, I barely taste it. This lack of sleep has robbed me of my taste buds.

"Cullen," Derek's eyes tear into me with seriousness, "mate, you haven't slept in almost four days."

"I'm getting a little shut eye."

"I hear you rolling around half the night. I could get tranquilizers--something to calm your sleep down."

Sleeping pills—flash—my mother padding around the kitchen, pumped up on barbiturates, unable to deal with my father's death. An addict. I'd rather be dead than relegate control to some pill, "No drugs," I stiffen, insulted, "won't touch them."

"Maybe if you called your friends or—"

"No. I'm fine."

I retire to my room, pretending I'm going to sleep. I hear his footsteps down the stairs, hid numeric locked door shutting and then--tap—tap—tap—tap—ding!

These invisible nightmares are killing me. What the hell is he writing? I toss and turn, afraid to go to sleep, eyes focused on the tiny black motion sensor monitor in the ceiling. The animal show on the flat TV casts against the tiny, black globe—like staring through a fish-eye lens. The rhythmic typing fills my ears. Is it a book? A movie? I remember when I met him. He was pitching an idea to Mo Simon. Wow, that seems like years ago:

"It's sort of a reality based film, ya know, in the vein of Truman Show meets Cops—"

What could the story be about?

It's got to be voluminous by the speed he's typing. Hey, I aspired to be a lit agent, c'mon I'm supposed to be intrigued by this mystery. So I lay there, my fifth sleepless night. The lack of real sleep is driving me mad! Dark rings form under my eyes. I start to see strange shapes out of the corner of my eyes. My mind shuts down and then starts up—thoughts rushing through me and then slowing down to a snail's pace. I'm always in a cold sweat now, heartbeat raging like it'll explode through my chest. One sound bathing my very senses—tap—tap—tap—tap—ding!

What the hell's he working on?

On Tuesday night, I mope home early, staging a false exit out of my bedroom at 7 o'clock, trying to catch him on his way out, to glance inside at the room. The numeric lock clicks--the door opens. I catch another hint of the red flag hanging on the back wall—weight-lifting dumb-bells on the floor--a disheveled bed—

"Hey," he smiles, shutting the door, "didn't know you were home."

"Got in early."

We dine on scallops in a port reduction sauce washed down with a Louis LaTour Corton-Charlemagne. I'm no longer talking. I sit, eyeing him with a stare filled smirk. Derek fills the conversation, telling me how he learned how to cook at *Escoffier Culinary School* in Paris during a summer break. After that he was addicted to the art. Beethoven's 9th Symphony plays in the background as--

The doorbell rings.

Derek offers, but I go to open it.

"Buddy!" Archie grins, arms wide.

Archie's wearing that same smile your long lost cousin flashes when he finds out you won the Powerball lottery. Fear grips me. The same fear that caused me to evade my underlings in the mail room, to shut off all communication with the outside world.

It's been safe here.

I've been living in a solitary cubicle, sleeping in a solitary house in the hills, traveling in my solitary car like Captain Kirk beaming down to explore some new planet. I'm not alive. I'm a ghost. The sight of Archie standing in the clean Formica foyer makes everything inconsistent with the surroundings. Like at that shop at the mall, where they superimpose your face on the cover of Biker Magazine.

"Thought you'd have Hal with you," I try not to grumble.

"Oh, he's parking the car—parking's a real bitch up here," his eyes scan the room, "been worried about you man. Didn't return any of our calls," he suddenly sees the loft room at the end of the hall—jackpot! "whoa—this is the Mac Daddy pad!"

"What are you doing here?" I ask.

"Buddy," he grimaces as if I should already know the answer, "we're moving in!"

Nine

I lay alone in my bedroom.

Through my wall of open windows, airplanes glide in regular patterns through the twinkling, night sky. The evening air smells fresh and cool. Carried by the breeze, I hear footsteps on concrete as Derek tours them through the pool area.

"Fab place," compliments Archie.

"Really beautiful," adds Hal.

"Thanks," Derek leads them on, "and I have the rent agreements for you to sign."

"Shit," jokes Arch, "I'd sign my soul over to live here. Just show me the dotted line."

He invites them to live with me because I told Derek I promised to live with them. He did this so I would stay. Then why do I feel jealousy at their presence? I'm not gay. Why do I hate them here? Is it simply that I tried to escape my entire life, to wash myself clean, to reemerge a man with his feet on the ground, a solid job, no longer aspiring for that dream world of movies—the world that the dreamy eyed kid saw when he escaped his own fucked up life so many years ago? Or is it just the nightmares driving me mad? I push the pillow over my face, a dry anguished scream. I'm so fucking exhausted—I just want to go to sleep—one night where I can sleep more than two minutes.

"Are the bedrooms down here?" asks Hal, his voices trailing away.

I toss and turn. An hour later I hear bedroom doors closing as they go to sleep. Then again the tap—tap—tap—I find it comforting now—like the buzz of an air-conditioner. I feel the cold sweat of my body soaking into the sheets.

"Cullen," Hal opens my door, hesitating for a long moment before he sits at the edge of my bed. He's so kind, so nice, it's impossible to be upset with Hal. I roll over, examining his thin, hawkish face. He's taken off his black V-neck sweater, just his white T-shirt which makes him look out of sorts, "you alright?" he furls his brow, "Derek says you haven't slept since you got here."

"I sleep, it's just a lot of nightmares."

"What kind of stuff?"

"I can't really remember," I sit up on one elbow, "how'd you guy's get here anyway?"

"Archie exchanged cards with Derek at the party," Hal stresses the fact that, "Derek called us. We were all worried about you. Derek wanted us to come over, to meet with you. Archie told him how we were tied up having to move out of our places. So he offered us a place to stay for a few days--thought it would help you if we were around. Really nice guy . . ." his voice trails off-- then, "he said he offered you sleeping pills?"

"You know how I feel about that crap."

"Yeah," another long pause, "I want to make sure you aren't mad. I mean--we came to help."

"I know. I'm not mad," I lie, "sorry I didn't return your calls, it's been hard to--"

"Try to rest," Hal's in Doctor mode, surveying his patient—and that expression on his face. Do I look that bad? "I finish my rotation tomorrow and get off early. Why don't we go for a drink? I'll pick you up from work."

I hesitate. A drink? In public?

"I start my trauma rotation in Mexico day after tomorrow," he sighs, "won't see me for the next two months. So let's do tomorrow night, alright?"

I lie again and nod, "Sure."

I just want him to get the fuck out of the room.

The next night, Hal drives.

It was another sleepless night. Drenched in cold sweat, I run a hand through my greasy hair. . . brain speeding up and slowing down—cars and lights and people streaming by at the speed of sound—red streaks of brake lamps against La Cienega Ave. Then everything freezes and starts all over again. We're headed up Sunset Ave. In a normal city, a friend wouldn't take a person like me out in public.

In LA, I'll fit right in.

"Where are we going?" I ask, eyes plastered to the windshield.

"Somewhere we can talk," Hal doesn't like confrontation. He'd fiddle with a tape-deck radio if he had one--but his car is a broke down Chevy Celebrity *sans* radio or air conditioning/heater. So I sit in the silence of this moving conglomeration of plastic and rusty steel, breathing in stale, warm air.

I shut my eyes, peeking through eyelashes.

Ever try that? The world looks like shades of colors warming your eyelids. Your mind conjures up curious shapes—really curious if you haven't slept in a fortnight. I think I see an ice skater in a cape of fire, dancing elegant circles, arm spinning—

"What are you doing?" Hal asks.

Silently transfixed by this fiery figure, only one thought fills my head: I just want to go to sleep—just for a moment, a few seconds. I will not become my mother.

"Look at that accident," mutters Hal.

Open my eyes. Someone's driven their BMW right into one of those concrete bus benches. The car's plowed up over the supports, front end smashed, windshield shattered, engine smoking. I shut my eyes again, watching the light dance across them--

"You getting out of the car?" asks Hal.

We're here. Told you time isn't flowing right these days. Ding-ding-ding—that door is ajar warning goes off in my ear--sounds like Derek Van Horn's typewriter broad strokes. The air is cold. I open my eyes. A Mexican valet holds the door open. I notice The Greenblatt's Deli parking sign and realize Hal's taken us to this tiny club on the backside of Sunset called North.

"Just one drink," adds Hal, mist rising from his mouth. He glances uneasily at the long line waiting to enter the bar.

Let's take a minute to educate you--consider this your LA nightlife tutorial. See those guys waiting to get into the bar? Those are the penguins. I'm not joking, a bunch of white guys clad in all black ensembles--from Banana Republic cheap to Prada ridiculous. Their hair's cut the same way, bodies buffed the same way, even their stupid strut is the same—they pick up these new trends in GQ and Details Magazine—the only thing they read. So telling them apart is like discerning a single waddling penguin from the pack of thousands on some white, Antarctic ice flow.

You'd almost get a chill if it weren't for the penguins' female companions. Their dates are all the same—22, 23 years old, been in LA six months, and go figure, they want to be actresses. They're all clad in stretch fabrics, hair dyed platinum blonde, collagen injected lips, breasts that defy Newtonian physics, and as anorexic as an Ethiopian on a hunger strike. Basically they're a set of massive fake tits propped up on spindly, stick legs. Yes, these are the flamingoes. For those of you from Iowa, flamingoes are the pink, tropical birds from that Miami Vice promo.

Now in the liberal LA sexual climate, the mating rituals between the penguins and flamingoes—birds from two very different extremes, can get quite confusing. If two penguins are together, there's a 50/50 chance they're buddies or gay. If the penguin has more than one flamingo around him, it's either because:

1. **The penguin is gay and out with his platonic flamingo friends.**
2. **The penguin is straight and one or more of the flamingoes is bisexual.**
3. **The penguin and the flamingo are both bisexual.**

4. **The flamingo forgot which penguin she's with (hey, penguins all look alike), and she's up for new experiences.**
5. **Or all of the above.**

The collection of identical birds stand as still as concentration camp prisoners--waiting to be sorted by the two Gay Bears at the door, arms crossed, golden list on the stool beside them. The birds never challenge them. Why? A bear fighting a bird—even if the bear's gay, you can imagine who wins that fight.

Hal fears we won't be able to get in. Then he'd have spent $4.50 in valet fees for naught--and you know how broke he is. I walk boldly to the head of the line, subtly flashing my ITM business card. They give trainees these nameless cards when you're hired--a perk, carte blanche for entrance into any LA club. I'm not stupid enough to give those up. The Gay Bear examines the ITM logo and glances up at me. I try to conceal a yawn.

He nods us in.

North is like a tiny ski lodge.

Start with dark accent lights, a pinch of hip music, add a sweeping staircase, stained glass, a long copper bar and booths. Now mix in a hundred penguins and flamingos, add a dash of the odd blue jean clad wanderers, garnish with two Gay Bears--and you're ready to drink.

Weaving between crowds of laughter and drinks, for the first time, I realize that the bar is actually a basement room with only a fire door leading out onto Sunset Ave. The frosted, stained glass windows are artificially back lit. If you broke the glass, you'd see a brick and mortar wall. Just as I think this, I see her:

She's striking.

She's not a flamingo. The face and hair look real. . . breasts aren't falling out all over the place. Tall and fit, she has that sleek linear body with normal sized, well-proportioned breasts--beautiful like golden silk falling along her back, framing milky white skin, high cheek bones and a stern, well-crafted nose. She could be some Viking warrior, like the Valkyrie chick from all those Wagner Operas. Clad in black leather pants, a silver G Gucci belt, I make a double take--she's wearing a tan sweater. A burst of color in an otherwise black world. Her hand rests on the bar, fingers tapping against the copper surfaces. Two guys move away from her, leaving a space at the bar. I herd Hal into the gap as I tease, "Sure you don't want to go to El Torito?"

"I got paid today," he sighs, "can afford a round," the loud music makes him uncomfortable. Hal always puzzles me. Why the hell are we here at this trendy club anyway? Hal hates clubs.

"What'll it be?" asks the bartender, big and brawny—a Gay Bear filling in for someone else.

The urge to sleep overwhelms me. But I know there's no way that's going to happen--

"Two Anchor Steams," Hal orders, handing the bartender his Visa card, cautiously adding, "we'll close the bill out."

I swing around, perching my elbows against the bar, surveying the tide of black and spandex as I ask Hal, "So what's up?"

"You're undergoing trauma," he says. No shit. He wavers and gains strength, "it's affected your sleeping pattern. Now no one's ever died of sleep deprivation, but you've got to take some medication."

"That's what they told my mother and—"

"You're not your mother, Cullen. Take it once--sleep this thing off."

The flash of my mother, waking up from a dreamy sleep--she doesn't even know the day of the week or even my age. Calling out for medication, I walk into her bathroom, everything's big. I stand on the sink in order to open the medicine cabinet. A wall of orange vials without tops, because I have so much trouble opening them.

"Hal, I'm ready to go."

"At least drink your beer," he moans in the faint voice of someone who's overstretched his boundaries. Then he takes a sip of his beer, a drop or two landing on his black V-neck sweater, glistening on the polyester, cotton blend.

Still facing away from the bar, I grab my beer, kicking back the first couple of sips. I can't actually let beer flow down my throat. I have to suck at it like a baby with a bottle--I know, it's weird. And I could never beer bong in college.

My eyes glance at the booths devoid of people, a small "Reserved" sign resting on each table. It's sort of the same as Mo Simon's Aston Martin DB-5. That reserved sign says I may get into the bar with my ITM card, but I'm definitely not in the club and—

"Excuse me, asshole!"

It's the Viking girl, brow scrunched, pissed off, jabbing a finger at me, "You know, I don't need every asshole rubbing against me," I look down. My elbow is barely touching hers. Glance around the bar, slave-traders afforded Africans more space on their boats than we have at this bar. She smirks, "fucking prick."

It's that same smug look Veronica flashed me.

"What's your problem!" I explode—days of rage and insomnia rushing through me like a pot boiling over, "I wasn't trying to touch you—we're all crammed together."

"Well then," she rolls her eyes, "why don't you cram against your little gay buddy and leave me alone."

Now she's getting nasty--picking on poor Hal. Others take note. I waggle my finger in the air, just to make a point, when—

"Slow down, buddy," the Gay Bear barkeep leans over the bar, slamming a restraining arm against my chest. Just about knocked the wind out of me. C'mon, like I was going to hit her! I've never hit a woman in my life and I'm not about to start with this stupid bitch.

I stick my hands in the air, making the surrender signal, "Fine," and I move Hal between us. The Gay Bear stalks away flashing the look that cautions: one more time and you're out. With shaky knees, I try to make small talk with Hal, finishing my beer as fast as I can so we can leave. A minute later, she glances back at me again and I spin my finger near my ear—flashing her the crazy sign. Fuming, she rolls her eyes, disappearing into a corner.

"Are you feeling OK?" asks Hal with an amazed look.

"What do you mean? I haven't slept in two weeks—"

"I know. But don't you feel like you could go to sleep. . . now?" he fidgets with his hands.

"You trying to hypnotize me, Hal?"

Hal looks puzzled. He studies my empty beer on the bar, glances at his own beer, half full. I never know what this kid is thinking. The Gay Bear hands him his credit card and receipt, muttering, "Two Anchor Steams--seems to be the drink of the evening."

Slowly, Hal turns to his left.

He's staring at the spot the Viking bitch occupied a few moments before--her Anchor Steam bottle still rests on the bar, three quarters empty. Hal stops signing his tab, his hand's shaking, "Oh no."

"What?"

His head shoots around, those wide set eyes scanning the back corner of the club. Then as quickly as a Wimbledon spectator, he turns eyeing the other side of the bar. My eyes follow. The Gay Bear is on the other end, chatting it up with a flamingo--smiles and breasts hanging out—Hal grabs me. I've never seen this look before.

He's so serious, "Come with me to the bathroom."

So I'm thinking Deliverance.

Is this going to be the night? Am I to be Ned Beatty, squealing like a pig—can you believe an actor did that? Is Hal going to drag me into some stinking stall and profess his undying love for me? His hand tight around my arm, he drags me towards the toilets. But he leads me to the woman's bathroom. The door's locked. Hal shoots a quick look out of our alcove, staring around the bar. Music's pumping, people lost in conversation. No one notices us.

"Do you think you could break down this door?" he asks.

"What?"

"Just do it!" he screams--I've never heard him scream before.

I throw myself against the door, the way they do it in the movies, "Aw shit!" I think I broke my shoulder. The door rattles. But the lock doesn't give way.

Hal pushes against the door, but to no avail. He's much smaller than me. Turning to me, he grunts, "Do it again!"

Nursing my wounded side, I aim my foot near the doorknob and kick. The door rushes open and I freeze.

"Oh wow," I gasp.

The Viking bitch is passed out on the floor.

Arms spread, she lays facedown, head at the base of the toilet. I wince. That's where the last drop always falls. Dumb bitch must've just gotten too drunk and passed out, I muse. But Hal's treating it like the end of the world.

"Oh shit! Oh shit! Oh shit!" he pushes me into the bathroom, trying to shut the broken door behind us.

"What's going on?" after all these sleepless nights, I don't need a mystery.

But all I get is this hyperventilating: "Oh shit! Oh shit! Oh shit!" then he gets an idea and slaps her right across the face--

"What the hell are you doing!" I cry.

Her eyes open, eyeballs rolled back in her head. She's semiconscious. He tries to maneuver her head over the toilet, but she's too big. He turns to me, pleading, "Help!" As we position her head over the toilet, he jabs his finger into her mouth, pressing down on her tongue.

She starts vomiting into the toilet. I turn away. Hal keeps choking her with his finger until she's dry heaving. He flushes the toilet and rolls her over again, slapping her.

"Will you stop it!" I cry.

She didn't even feel the slapping--isn't even reacting to the slaps anymore. This launches him into another "Oh shit!" spasm.

"Wait a minute," I piece things together, "you knew she'd be here?"

"It was an accident--an honest accident."

"What was?"

He stuffs a valet card in my hand, "Don't have time to talk about it here. There's an emergency exit right outside. Get my car from the valet-- bring it around to Sunset?"

"You want to kidnap this girl!" I'm flabbergasted. I mean, I know he's never been with a woman, but this isn't exactly the way to break in. What is he even--

"Just do what I ask!" he shakes me, eyes wild, "I'll tell you everything in the car!"

I stop the broken down Chevy Celebrity on Sunset.

I can't believe this is happening. The fire door bursts open--Hal trudging across the sidewalk with the Viking bitch covering his sloping shoulders--she's bigger than him. He's trying to get her in the car, but with his small frame, can't quite open the door. A bum in front of Greenblatt's Deli watches us with curious eyes. Real professional. Glancing around for cops, I race out, opening the door, wind blowing back my hair as I lay her down in the back seat.

This is madness!

Hal leaps into the driver seat, accelerating the car before I'm even inside. I hop in the back, landing on her as I shut the door. I'm about to lift my head up when I hear police sirens ring out. Oh fuck! I'm going to the poky. The sirens grow louder, red and blue lights dancing through the interior of the car. My heart drops.

I can see it now.

I'm in this jail cell, slumped over on all fours as Luther rides me from behind slapping my ass every few seconds, muttering, "Bet'cha them Hollywood types don't give luvin' like this."

The sirens pass us.

The LAPD black and white races by, turning on Crescent Heights, racing down the hill. I'm so lightheaded, I can't move—hands shaking like a Parkinson's victim on amphetamines. I take deep breaths, trying to regain control. Then I smell this sweet scent. My nose is plowed into the Viking girl's silky blonde hair.

I'm lying on top of her.

I hop off, cutting the top of my head on the burned out overhead, ceiling light. Scared shitless, lightheaded, and severely tired, I crawl into the front seat. Hal, hunched over the wheel, turns off Sunset, navigating us up into the dark Hollywood hills. There's lots of yelling now:

"What the fuck is going on!" I finally scream.

"I was trying to help you!"

"Help me? By kidnapping that woman?"

"Alright," he finally says, "since you wouldn't take sleeping pills, I drugged your beer with a benzodiazepine—"

"You did what?!"

"A tranquilizer."

Flash—the image of me, turned around, studying the bar. Hal reaches over, dropping the tiny pill into my beer bottle, fizzing as it dissolves in the beer.

"It was scentless, tasteless," continues Hal, "the carbonation of the beer helps it dissolve quick. The idea was you'd get sleepy and—"

Flash—me becoming really tired. I put a hand to my brow, amazed that I might actually fall asleep. Hal credits it to the beer, helps me to the car. I collapse in my bed and sleep for two days.

"But," adds Hal, "I fucked up."

Flash—the three Anchor Steam bottles. All three of us, me, Hal, and the Viking bitch—all crammed together. The Viking bitch accidentally takes my beer.

"Oh shit," there's no time to even berate him. We're two guys driving around the Hollywood Hills in a beat up car with a passed out girl in the backseat, tranquilizers running through her system, and--

"What should we do?" asks Hal.

He knows we have only one solution.

"What the hell is going on?" cries Derek.

He's wearing a black T-Shirt that says "The Beatings Will Continue Until Morale Improves." Hal and I lay the Viking Bitch across the pool table in the game room. My head cracks against the Carlsberg Beer lamp, sending sweeping light swaying back and forth.

She opens her eyes. The first time she did this, I nearly had a heart attack and dropped her in the driveway. But her pupils just dance around, red lips gurgling tiny bubbles of spit--muffled words. Then a silence punctuated only by Derek's Centipede and Space Invaders games in the back corner.

"Just calm down," I add.

But there's just more screaming:

"Fuck all that," barks Derek in his clipped accent, "kindly tell me how this drunk chick wound up on my pool table."

"It was a mistake!" Hal's on the verge of tears. He's practically emptying his tube of Purell into his palms, rubbing them together—the smell of rubbing alcohol floating through the air--

"Hal tried to tranquilize me at the bar," I explain, "with—"

"It was a benzodiazepine," interjects Hal, rubbing his hands.

"What type?" asks Derek.

Hal hesitates, a fresh layer of sweat on his forehead, "Flunitrazepam—I forced her to puke and thought I saw the pill, but I must've been mistaken."

Hal and Derek share a strange knowing glance. Then Derek's pieced it all together, his frame visibly shrinking, "Have you lost your mind bringing her here? I'm from a high profile family. If she wakes up, she'll think we shagged her—"

"Who's your Daddy! Who's your Daddy!!" an ecstatic voice. I turn. His briefcase falls to the floor. It's Archie, tie loosened, standing in the doorway, just home from work. "Whose birthday is it?" He thinks she's a hooker.

"This isn't a fucking joke," cries Hal.

"I know. She's a hotty!" he can't take his eyes off the Viking bitch, "definitely worth the credit card debt."

The alcohol fumes burn my eyes, "Will you put the fucking Purell away!"

Hal tucks the bottle into the pocket of his Gap pants.

"So what do you propose?" Hal asks us.

So we're deliberating over the unconscious girl with about as much order as the last chopper out of Saigon.

"I gave her a 1 mg dosage for someone who weighs his weight," Hal points at me, "she'll be out for," glancing at his watch, he runs a mental calculation, "at least 16 hours."

"That ain't till about noon tomorrow," adds Archie.

"And she'll have no memory of this?" asks Derek.

"None," Hal's definitive on this point, "probably no memories up to thirty minutes prior to ingestion either. Chances are she won't even remember Cullen or I or when I drugged her beer."

"Then it's easy," concludes Derek, "drive her down to the city and dump her now before anything happens."

"Dump her!" exclaims Hal, "where?"

"I don't fucking care where—a park bench--someone's yard. Anywhere but here!"

"No," Hal nods, "she could get raped, robbed--we'd be responsible for it."

Derek can see that the sight of the girl unsteadies our nerves, "Let's take this into the kitchen."

So we gather around the elaborate marble and zinc kitchen island with this oven that cooks with this bright light that—like you care right now.

Derek stresses, "Hal, you're responsible for her. I didn't ask for her to come here."

"Well for now, this is where I am so—"

"Take her back to the bar," suggests Archie.

"The bartender saw us," I interject, "Hal used a credit card—they've got a record of his name that could be traced back here."

"All the more reason to get her the fuck out of here!" thunders Derek.

I interrupt, "There must be some middle ground," my insomnia ridden mind races, "we could leave her on a skyscraper roof. Who the hell ever goes on a skyscraper?"

"Insomnia boy," adds Archie, always trying to be humorous when he's nervous, "how are you gonna get her past security guards in every skyscraper in town?"

"Plus," adds Hal, "in a half drugged state she could wander off the roof," he takes a deep breath, "we'll just have to let her wake up here--confess the whole thing."

"Are you out of your mind!" Derek screams with a force I've never before heard, "you said the girl was a bitch. And she's gorgeous and drugged. She's going to wake up, look at this place, hear my last name, and see dollar signs and police bars. Even if we got off, at best, you'll all be on Jerry Springer and I'll be stuck with the multimillion dollar lawsuit!" He crashes his fist atop the marble island, "get her out of here now!"

"No!" objects Hal with a spine I've never seen before.

Derek storms out of the kitchen.

"Alright," Hal's relieved now that he's left, "the only decent thing is to let her wake up here."

"Wait a minute, bro," Archie raises his hand, there is no more humor to this scene for him to play with, "I love you Hal, but I ain't goin' to jail just because you screwed up. Derek's right. I'm not saying we do—well—what he wants us to do and dump her on a bench. But her waking up in here is not feasible."

"What are you intimating?" asks Hal.

"I'm not intimating anything. I'm saying that the press would go nuts over this. We're not the brothers in Compton, shooting and raping. This is a bunch of pussy ass white boy, rapists. I do not want to make the cover of USA Today with that epitaph."

"So she wakes up here," demands Hal.

"If you care so much," adds Archie with the interesting point, "drive her around in your car all night and confess to her when she wakes up."

"And if I get pulled over, the cops'll never believe me."

Archie rebuts, "Get her a hotel room."

"We'll be seen," frowns Hal…

We squabble for another few minutes, considering outlandish ideas like breaking into North and leaving her in a janitor's closet. Then about deserting her in some secluded spot in the Hollywood Hills when Derek reenters the room.

"Everybody shut up," Derek comes into the kitchen, devilish eyebrows pointed down again. Casually, I look down and feel my knees wobble. He's zipping up his blue jeans, "I just fucked the bitch," he drops a condom in the kitchen trash can for all to see, "SO GET HER THE FUCK OUT OF HERE!"

Stop time.

Stop it all.

Backtrack, erase what we just saw and heard. Jesus, I think I might vomit. The muscles in the back of my neck turn to concrete--like a weight pulling at my shoulders. But time won't stop this time. The clap of Hal and Archie's footsteps echo as they race to the game room. I'm following. But it's not like I'm here. I'm staring down a long hallway, watching these events unfold in the distance as we reenter the game room.

"Holy shit," this exasperated exclamation is the best Hal can manage, "holy shit."

The poor Viking girl lays on the pool table. Her leather pants hang off her leg—I turn away. Let me tell you, it doesn't look like those air-brushed shots in Playboy or that stash of internet porn shots hidden on your hard drive—this is the real thing!

I fall over, dry-heaving.

"Aiighh!" Hal attacks Derek, arms flailing.

Deafly, Derek lunges an arm out, catching Hal in midair, slamming him backwards on the pool table. Derek is all red faced, eyebrows squinted, the razor's edge out for all to see. Through gritted teeth, he sputters, "I didn't ask you to bring her here. But I am making you take her away now," his hand tightens around Hal's neck, "get it?"

I'm in shock.

He tightens his grip. Hal's arms flail. Then choking, he nods out a Yes.

Derek releases him, silently walking back to the living room. Through the open door, I watch him pour himself an Armagnac. An after dinner drink! Who the hell have I moved in with?

We drop her off at The Jonathan Club.

It's a ritzy club overlooking the Santa Monica beach. The idea was Archie's. Prudential hosted some kind of July 4th party there last year and he went for the free drinks. Hal and I drive alone, covering the Viking girl with a beach blanket in the trunk of his celebrity. It takes forever as we drive down Sunset and a series of back roads, our pulse jumping with every turn.

Under the light of the moon, ocean breeze in my face, we quickly smuggle her through the parking lot and along the sandy dunes. The club has this outdoor pool area. After a quick survey for guards, I hop the fence and open the gate. We lay her out on a pool chair, panties on, leather pants buttoned up. On a side table, I position two empty martini glasses and an empty bottle of Tanqueray—I dump the contents of it in the sand.

As I'm about to leave, Hal lingers behind, "She looks almost too formal."

"What?" I can't believe this shit.

"I mean--look at her arms," I turn. Her arms are gathered in her lap, head slumped over, blonde hair obscuring her face from view, "she looks so sad," adds Hal, "so alone."

"Fine," I take her arm, laying it out across the side table. Then I place her other in her lap, wrapping fingers around the long stemmed martini glass.

"Oh," adds Hal, "make sure the gin is within reach so--"

"Fine," I put the gin bottle next to her feet and even open a can of olives we brought—those extra touches are ever so important. So she had too much to drink, spent the night with some A list power-broker at this A list club.

"Do you think we should check her wallet, at least get her name?" asks Hal.

My first instinct is to say I don't want to know her name. But it makes sense. Maybe we could even call her from a pay phone, make sure she's alive and--

A dog barking.

My heart freezes. Hal's eyes open wide. Faster than a Pink's double chili-cheese dog passing through your bowels, we're out of there--in the car, racing away. Relief sinks across my face as Hal navigates us back towards Hollywood. We're no longer connected to the Viking girl, I tell myself. It's like it didn't happen.

"I learned yesterday that I'm doing my trauma rotation down at UCLA's clinic in Mexico," mutters Hal, "going to be gone for eight weeks," rubbing his sore neck, he gives words to my other thoughts, unspoken sentiments lingering in my mind:

"He raped her, Cullen. He raped her and he has to pay."

A new pressure falls upon me. Now I don't even want to go back to my home—to face him. How did I get caught up in this mess? Derek Van Horn raped the

Viking girl--the thought sickens me. As we cruise back up Sunset towards that lavish home set high in the Hollywood Hills, I know something has to be done about it. I don't know what it will be, but I'm a good guy--I do the right thing. Something must be done. I know, deep in my heart, the Camelot Years in the Hollywood Hills are behind us and--

Nothing is ever going to be the same again.

Part Three

Clan Of The Cave Bear

"Those who do not sometimes go outside the rules, never get beyond them."

-Gianlorenzo Bernini (1598-1680)

Ten

The Viking Girl haunts me.

The newspaper says nothing today. From the shock of the night before, I can't even conjure up her face--just the one image: head slumped over, blonde hair falling into her martini glass. I cut another piece of the rib eye, cooked well with blue cheese on top--the way I usually like it. Tonight though, the steak and Bandol wine fade to tasteless gray. I steal a quick glance at Archie and Derek. It's as if the tension in the air has a tangible weight, pushing our heads down towards our plates.

In this new atmosphere I don't know what Archie's thinking. We're friends, but he's that type you only know on the social spectrum. Our conversations never run deep—the idle chatter of dinners and drinks. There are glimmering hints of his education, but his interests aren't far reaching beyond having a good time. Right now Archie attempts to conceal his nervousness underneath a happy go lucky façade. Look at his lips, the thin smirking grin. But his eyes reveal the tension. As he chews his meat, the end effect just makes him look stupid.

I think back to last night:

"Damn you!" Hal screams, beating against Derek's door.

I've never seen the kid raise his voice, let alone threaten someone. Maybe this is some other side of Hal that I've never seen. Or perhaps his show of bravado is merely because Hal knows he's leaving tomorrow and that tonight Derek won't open the metal door. For the only response to his fists and big words is the—tap—tap—tap—ding! of Derek's typewriter. I try to shower off the cold sweat, but it won't go away. The tension only aggravates my insomnia. . .laying in bed all night, I realize that for now I am a prisoner without money—Jesus, why can't I sleep? I resolve to leave next week when I get my first pay check from Alpha Software.

Before the sun is up, I hear his Celebrity start up—he leaves for Mexico. He's on a brutal trauma rotation, on call every other night. I remember the last time he did this. For two months, I won't see him.

That evening I go into the game room. I can't tear my eyes off of the pool table. I feel nauseous and leave. But to Derek, we're just one big happy family in a house in the Hollywood Hills. During dinner, as I chew on my succulent steak, I feel certain Hal will call the police. I know him—the way he thinks. We'll all be dragged into a crime that only one of us perpetrated. I study Derek's face, elongated and distorted in the reflection of my dinner knife. Only then do I notice it--

There's a swastika on the edge of the knife!

At first I can't believe it. I glance at the spoon and fork, each one bearing the insidious mark. Holding up the fork, I study the scratched lines and mutter aloud in disbelief, "What the hell is this?"

A gray faced Archie stops eating and turns at me.

Derek takes a sip of his wine, "What's it look like?"

"Like silverware props from Hogan's Heroes." I can only hope.

"It's the Nazi High Command's silverware."

Archie shoots a familiar glance at me. This is the final straw. We've suddenly bonded together. Derek stands, calmly carrying his plate back to the marble island in the open air kitchen as he tells us this story:

Flash--imagine a guy resembling Derek, but dressed in US Army get-up. This is his grandfather who he explains is a lieutenant with The 101st Airborne, Easy Company, during World War II. They liberate Berchtesgaden, Hitler's mountain hideaway--all high ceilings and million dollar views. The staff and help have fled the place, leaving it as empty as The Shining. So liberate simply means that Derek's Grand-Dad and his soldiers buddies bust in, looting everything in sight. Old Grand-Dad nabs the silverware from the private dining room.

Archie holds the fork by the end, treating it like that monkey in Outbreak, "You sayin' this the same fork Hitler ate with?"

"Yes," Derek rattles off in a matter of fact tone, "along with Luftwaffe Reichsmarschall Goering, General

Heinz Guderian, Propaganda Minister Goebbels, SS Reichsfuehrer Himmler--among notables. I'm sure there were many others."

I'm thinking the same thing you are: can't wait until next week to move. This guy's a fucking loony, ready to blow at any time. I'm already trying to decide if I'll sleep in Griffith Park or on the beach until I get paid—down near the Jonathan Club seemed real nice.

"It's just silverware," adds Derek.

That's it. I speak, "I know you've graciously invited us to stay here, but has it occurred to you that maybe me being Jewish and Archie being Chinese too--might—well, maybe we could have used other utensils?"

Derek's expression is still frozen. Like he's the only one in the room who can't smell something, "I have some plastic silverware from an old barbeque."

Archie explodes, hopping out of his seat, an accusing finger in the air, "This is some fucked up shit. I've been eating off Satan's fork."

"C'mon, the fact that he was a great communicator with a monstrous message does not make him Satan."

"What does it make him?" I wince.

"He was a pioneer of propaganda. Adolf Hitler was the first person to grasp the influence of mass culture, herding the masses into formation with the radio and—"

"We don't need a lecture right now," my anger takes control.

"He was a human being. They were all humans," adds Derek, "humans have capacity for anything. A great propagandist could talk you boys into doing anything, he could rationalize any concept or blackmail his followers with the lives of those they loved--"

"I don't care professor!" explodes Archie, "I don't want to eat on his silverware. In fact I don't want to stay here—nothing's worth this crap. Even if this place is free."

Silence.

Derek sighs, cupping his two hands in front of him. He's using that power again. I feel his eyes probing into me, "Why don't we get to the point. You think I did something criminal last night--"

"Damn straight," Archie interrupts.

But he isn't talking to Archie. He's talking only to me. He wants me to side with him, but how is that possible? He continues, "My family is a pillar of society--a recognizable name. They may not be my favorite people, but I would never allow them to be dragged through the mud because your stupid, spineless friend--"

"Did you have to rape her?"

My question hangs in the air.

"I did what I had to do," he continues to stare straight at me. But I refuse to turn away, "I didn't create the situation, I resolved it. C'mon Cullen," he throws up his hands, "she was on Flunitrazepam!"

Hal told me it was a benzodiaz-a-something. Flash--I vaguely recall Derek asking some question about the drug and Hal calling it something with an H. But I still don't see how this figures into anything?

"The drug Hal used is illegal in the United States," explains Derek in a smug, forceful tone, "not even mentioned in the Physician's Desk Reference--have to smuggle it in from Mexico or Europe at the risk of facing jail time."

"How do you know what tranquilizer he gave her?" asks Archie.

"Kids from LA know their boutique drugs. He told Cullen benzodiazepine, but that's the group of drugs it belongs to," explains Derek, "I asked him which specific drug--in his nervous state he confessed to me that it was Flunitrazepam. He was nervous enough to tell, but still cautious enough not to use the more common name."

"What name?" Hal's the nicest guy in the world. He could never be so insidious.

"It's called Rohypnol," Derek answers, "nicknamed Roofies or Rufinol."

I vaguely remember hearing something about Roofies—a date raping story on 20/20 or CNN--bunch of fraternity guys drugging some chick and--

"Who made you the doctor?" Archie furls his brow incredulously.

"I knew a little but," Derek grabs a stack of papers from a drawer in the kitchen island, spilling them out on the table, "this is what I was doing last night while Hal banged on my door."

Glance down--a bunch articles he's downloaded off the internet. Archie and I scan the headings of the pages, bold black print exploding: "ROOFIES", THE NEW "DATE RAPE" DRUG OF CHOICE--NEW DRUG, 10 TIMES MORE POTENT THAN--ILLEGAL DRUG ROHYPNOL LINKED TO DATE RAPES AND—"

I scan the scattered pages as Derek continues, "Rufinol is a potent tranquilizer similar to valium, but stronger--"

Kristin, A University of Minnesota sophomore, awoke after a night of dancing downtown nightclub with bruises all over her body and no memory of how she got them--

"It's tasteless, scentless," adds Derek, "you would never have known there was a 2 mg dose in your beer until—"

--a 2 mg dose in one beer put a woman flat on her back in a moaning state of carnal bliss, to waken with no memories of the previous night, wondering what the heck happened--

Flash—the image burned into my mind--the Viking Girl collapsed on the pool table, eyes opening, lips moving, gurgling spit. She wasn't asleep, but she wasn't awake. Why would Hal want to give me something like that? It would never put me to sleep.

Often times women have no recollection thirty minutes prior to ingesting the drug. They are found in cars without clothes on and can't remember anything except feeling violated.

"So with all the drugs available at his hospital," asks Derek, "medications any insomnia ridden intern could legally procure—Hal chose this insidious, illegal drug?"

Until recently there has been no way of detecting the drug's presence in cases of sexual assault, and few confirmed victims have been identified--the use of Rohypnol in sexual assaults—

C'mon, Hal would never try to drug me.
But Veronica claims he gets jealous when I'm with her. I remember his brooding stare in the car ride to the Valley. And I did confess to you that I never know what's going on in his head. Maybe in my weakened state, he thought he could—no, Hal isn't here to defend himself. This is ridiculous, "How do you even know he really used Roofies?"
"Found it in the trash," Derek slams the massive, half-filled bottle onto the table, bigger than any medicine bottle I ever saw in my mother's cabinet. Through clear orange plastic I see little round pills. I glance at an

illustration of the pill on one of the internet sheets—it's a match. I turn the bottle around, reading the label:

ROHYPNOL 2 MG DOSAGE
QTY: 200 tablets

Holy shit.

I mean there's enough tablets here to rape a whole sorority--or gay bath house for that matter. It's half empty. Now don't start thinking about those times I kind of blacked out when Hal and I were drinking in college— that has nothing to do with this half-filled bottle of. . . the most insidious. . . illicit. . . date rape drug on Earth.

Jesus, my ass already hurts.

Maybe Derek has a point? Maybe Hal loves me, couldn't control himself and-- hey, that still doesn't excuse Derek for raping the poor Viking girl. It doesn't change anything! But, somehow, for some indescribable reason--it does.

"Hal had only one reason for keeping her here," presses Derek, "he knew she'd ingested an illegal drug and if discovered in a urine test, he'd go to jail. He needed time for it to work out of her system. That's why he wouldn't risk taking her outside."

"Why?" I ask.

"Because Rufinol vanishes from the system quickly. When the Viking chic awoke, he would tell his story, claim it was some other sleeping pill and it would be too late to test it. But she'd still wake up in my place and probably sue all of us—"

"And," Archie completes the thought, "Hal wouldn't go to jail."

"Exactly! Which is why I had to do what I did," Derek never says the word rape--somehow it's becoming more palatable to us—a sacrifice, like he took a bullet to save us, "it was the most expedient method. It raised the stakes--forced him to dump her."

Derek stands up. I'm no longer thinking of Derek Van Horn--no longer thinking of running off to Griffin Park either. I'm seething with anger--anxious to beep Hal and confront him. But no, I have to think this thing out--confront him in person: face to face.

"Now," Derek fuels the fire, "you do what you feel's right. I'm inviting you to a charity party my parents are throwing—plenty of press there. You still feel I've done wrong, it'll be the perfect forum to expose me. Just don't forget, we leave at eight."

Eleven

This insomnia's killing me.

Just look at me now, dialing Hal's beeper number in my cubicle. My finger moves so slowly—like I'm watching them on an NFL slow motion replay. Jesus Christ, how long have I gone without sleep? Hey, don't be upset, I've lost track of the days too. I think today is somewhere between Wednesday and Friday. Forgot my watch at Derek's, so I think it's sometime between five and six. Soon, I'll just say that my age is somewhere between 25 and 30--

That was an insomnia joke.

I start laughing. The big, black woman in the next cubicle steals a quick glance at me. Look at her expression--do I really look that screwed up? I'm sweaty, shirt sticking to my body. Hell, I'm even busy today, hanging up on my tech support callers as I try to beep Hal.

But no response.

I imagine Hal operating, covered in blood up to his elbows--quick jump cuts like in E.R.—I.V. lines set—people screaming—Hal in the middle of it all, saving lives. Yeah right. Probably butt-fucking the unconscious vasectomy patients in pre-op. Suddenly all the sweet, quiet aspects of his personality seem so insidious, every one of his silent, brooding moments, an opportunity for suspicion.

Look at him.

Clad in his Gap outfit in this artificial scene in my mind. What's the Gap thing all about? Dressing like the masses--trying to fit in. That's how Dahmer dressed while he was making chop suey out of his Korean neighbors— well, I know they were definitely foreigners. When you think about it, the real wackos are always the straight laced types.

They were so quiet, everybody says.

As if there's a place in your high school year book for "Most likely to be an anal Rufinol rapist". Hal's quiet too. Think I'm being paranoid? Imagine you have an old acquaintance who's stashed away enough Rufinol to rape the entire principality of Liechtenstein.

Wouldn't be so composed, would you?

Dialing his number into my pager for the fifteenth time, I tap my fingers against the cubicle desk, waiting for him to call. The phone rings—I'll save you the grief. It's some Swamp Invader asshole—click. You'd think they'd figure out this software's shit. Anyway, enough about work. Hal doesn't calls me back all day. I go home, lay awake in bed, hoping they'll forget about me.

But Derek drags me to the party, "C'mon, be good to get out for awhile."

The Party is at The Beverly Wilshire Hotel.

It's a really nice place just around the corner from ITM. If you can afford a room there, I highly suggest it. The walls of the grand ballroom are lined with mirrors, reflecting the mishmash of guests back at each other. If you look at just the right angle through the mirror--looks like the guests and tables of food and wine continue into infinity, a never ending cocktail party where--

"You must be Cullen. I'm Derek's mother," I turn. Mrs. Van Horn is a lioness-- thick, blonde hair that poofs out like the old Jackie O hairdo, framing her entire face. What you really notice is her prominent, square jaw— cosmetically altered skin drawn tight. She looks like she's ready to bite into antelope on the plains beneath Kilimanjaro. Her hand is bony, but firm in mine. It happens again! Flash--I see myself cracking her across the face.

I fight to hide the violent image.

"Derek told me you were feeling ill," I must look like crap, "but we're so happy you could come," she turns to Derek, "I'm going to steal this one away for a moment," before I can say no, the lion's dragged me off into the tundra of suits and smiles.

My weird violent thing ends. Mrs. Van Horn navigates me through the lavish gathering. The smell of mixing perfumes fills the air. She chatters on, "You should try this herb they sell at Whole Foods--sleep like a baby. You do shop at Whole Foods, don't you? Oh, it's so fabulous. Of course my husband hates organic stuff—meat and potatoes man. Everything's black and white with him--hates these get togethers, locked away at the house right now. And your father? I'm sure he's—"

She could keep this up all night.

It's like watching someone play handball by themselves. She doesn't listen to anything, but continues serving out words, knocking the conversation back and forth on the wall. All that's required of me is the nod of the head. Guiding me into the vortex of the party, through crowds of older doctors, execs, and philanthropists, the momentum of her lips increase--like a jet engine preparing for takeoff, "I don't know why Derek moved into that house of his—huge place--when he moved last month--said it was just horribly big for one person and it's so white and minimal and—"

"Last month?" I interrupt.

You'd think the world ended. I've broken her train of thought. She's frazzled, can barely nod out a yes. Didn't Derek say he'd been in the house for awhile? It's almost like—

"Darling!" a tall, gaunt man in a velvet smoking jacket rushes up to us. He smells like those scented French soaps they give you in hotels. His sidekick is a nondescript Gay Bear in tight leather pants and loose fitting, ruffled shirts: the type pirates wear. The chattering continues. I step backwards, testing the waters. Nothing happens. . . take another step back and another--

I find myself in a corner, wedged between a fake fichus and the wet bar. I drink glass after glass of champagne, mildly shaken by the cacophony of the room--

"Buddy," Archie discovers me, "I think if we have enough guns, we could shoot our way out."

"Mrs. Van Horn would talk you to death first."

"Get in touch with Hal?"

"Hasn't answered my beeps."

Archie raises his eye, the look of suspicion, "Been thinking all day about it. I'm not saying I agree, but what Derek did, makes sense," I nod, sipping the last of my champagne. Archie takes this as a sign of my complicity and continues, "I mean--it's not like the girl'll even remember. She'll think she had drinks with some bozo and wound up at the beach."

Archie's reassuring comments send me into a cold sweat. Thoughts race, mere sensations. If we give them words they sound like: am I like the Viking Girl? Has Hal violated me before? I stop sipping the champagne. I feel ill like--

"Sorry about the party," Derek discovers us, "I confess--invited you because I can't take it alone. But we've made our appearance. Let's blow this place," he has a bottle of champagne in hand, "I feel like partying."

That's how we wind up here.

Look around. Have you ever seen so many penguins and flamingoes in one place? Dave Mathews blasts in your ears. These are the most beautiful women you've ever seen, lounging on gigantic mattresses like some Arabian harem--standing under the massive flower pots as big as something out of Alice In Wonderland.

There's no roof over your head.

It's all stars and open air. Sauntering up the staircase full of waddling penguins, I turn, admiring the blue pool framed against windows overlooking the city. This is the veritable Mecca of LA pretension, the Vatican for all Gay Bear protectors of the velvet rope, the most impossible bar to get into in the world.

Sky Bar.

Although I've softened with Archie and Hal's reappearance, I'm still not hot on public places. But I've never been able to get in here—the curiosity to see it kills me. After a minute, I'm ready to go. Like everything in Los Angeles, it's just an illusion. C'mon, the place is a fucking pool bar for the Mondrian Hotel, the big white skyscraper towering over us.

Derek ushers us up to what looks like a massive tree house, an open air bar with a timber roof. Flamingo waitresses show off their massive tits and midriffs over sarongs concealing spindly legs--for those of you from Nebraska, a sarong's a Fijian skirt. The place is packed, a sea of black leather and blonde hair. Of course, the manager knows Derek and escorts us to a reserved table.

"Wow, look at that," Archie mutters as we sit.

At the next table, holding court, is a group of the most beautiful women I've ever seen in the city. A conflation of perfect faces, perfect breasts, perfect black jeans and stretch fabric ensembles. They laugh, casually eyeing everyone except for us.

My cellphone rings.

It's Hal. Derek and Archie eye me as I stand up, taking the call downstairs where I can hear him better. I find a corner alcove. A huge mirror reflects my face back at me as I cradle the phone close to my lips, "Why didn't you call all day?"

"I was in surgery. Did you talk to Derek?"

"Yeah," I try to quell emotions, "wanted to ask you about that drug?"

"What?" I hear voices in the background calling to Hal, "look, I gotta get back to the O.R. I'll call when I get off tomorrow--"

Click.

Frustrated, my head spins when I return upstairs. At the top of the stairs I bump into a dark haired girl in a black leather jacket. She has a mole on her cheek like Marylyn Monroe. With startled eyes, she glances at me before continuing downstairs.

I've had enough of this evening. At my table is a round of beers. I tell Derek I'm going home. A drunk Archie barely nods as he eyes the nymphs at the next table. Derek grabs my hand, firm grip, asks me to wait-- the wolf eyes studying me, wondering what happened on the phone.

"Nothing," I assure him, "didn't get to really talk," and I escape his grip, "I'm going home."

After I leave, things get strange.

Let's rebuild the events from what I hear later. But we're going to have to do a little guessing to fill in the blanks. Maybe Derek thinks I left because Hal and I are going to turn him into the police? Maybe he's just testing the waters? Maybe they're just drunk. Because he orders another round of beers and then shots of tequila. Archie's loose--top buttons of his shirt open, talking, laughing. I imagine Derek pointing to the table of girls:

"Go on," he coaxes Archie in his clipped accent, "how many times you going to be sitting like this--next to women like that? Go say something."

Derek's ordered a few rounds because Archie needs a little more alcohol to dull his sensibilities. Then the switch happens. Archie stands up, runs a hand through spiky hair, strutting over to the table. They ignore him, talking to their waitress as he stands over them. Fear grips him. He turns and Derek flashes him the thumb's up.

The waitress leaves.

Archie sighs, "You girls look bored," he drawls in his best Tennessee accent, "thought I might buy y'all a round of drinks," he scans the empty glasses, "looks like three martinis and a Vodka cranberry."

Silence.

Restrained smiles, eyes downcast, staring away from him. But a drunk Archie isn't leaving until he gets a response. The response probably sounds something like this:

A brunette amongst them in jeans and a black stretch top, shakes around the ice in her empty Vodka cranberry, "Well—like, we just ordered another round."

"Why don't I buy one after that? Give us some time to get to know each other."

"I wonder," her words sting like icy daggers, "what would ever make a funny, little Asian guy like you think that your smirky grin's going to open our doors?" the other girls giggle at Archie, "I mean, why don't you run back to your little Chinese friends and leave us big, white girls alone."

The entire table's laughing now. The laughs and grotesque cackles rip him apart. His head spins. He stands there like a child, unable to move, afraid his wobbly knees will give way as the pain shoots through his heart. He's tired of his life, of this place, of meeting carbon copies of the Amazon bitches, of being laughed at and embarrassed. But you couldn't tell any of that. From the outside, Archie's still smiling because that's what my friend does when he's hurting.

The party's over.

Restraining emotion, he carefully negotiates his way back to his table. Once away from the spotlight, rage burns through his veins, eyes watering below a feverish brow, "I could kill that fucking bitch!" he explodes, "that fucking whore—could slit her throat. Why is this city filled with a bunch of fucking bitches! I mean you've got to have money and cars and all that shit just to get treated like a fucking human being!"

Derek pats him reassuringly on the back, "C'mon, we all get shot down--"

"Not that way!" Arch pulls away, "I mean—I've never met women like this—fucking bitches," he wishes he were back in New York, where you don't need a job in entertainment to get respect, where the Prudential business card and regimental tie means something. He's tired of sipping his one beer at El Torito, tired of his bitch boss, tired of being broke. The process has taken days and months, but he's almost ready:

Derek places the pill on the table.

I imagine it resting against the dark wood table--a tiny circle only the two of them can see. Archie's anger vanishes. With glassy eyes, he laughs because Archie always laughs when he's shocked, "No way," he thinks Derek must be joking with him.

"Said you wanted to slit her throat. Why not this?"

"So I can be in the same boat you're in?" Archie has a moment of lucidity through the drunken fog, "don't worry--I think you did the right thing, but--"

"Fucking bitches," adds Derek, "the brunette was the worst—a total cunt."

"C'mon, you're talking crazy."

"It struck me when I was reading the literature," continues Derek, "it's not like rape. Remember when you were a kid in school? You fanaticized that if you could stop time, you'd stare up all the girl's skirts? It's just like that."

"You're nuts," Archie's sure he's just joking.

Derek's dead serious, "Let fate take over," he holds the pill in the air, "drop this in her drink—see what develops. If she passes out at the table, she's had too much to drink and nothing happens. If we get her alone, we spirit her out of here and you," Derek merely winks, "mate, next thing she knows--she wakes up at the beach."

Derek glances over to the other table. The group of girls glance up at Archie for a moment and snicker. They're laughing at him. His hatred seethes. Derek's words start to make sense to him.

Then Derek sees something, "Fate's deciding the matter--let's go."

He hops up. Archie rises too, heading to the exit. Looking back, he realizes Derek isn't there. He scans the bar and spots Derek working his way through the sea of bodies in the back corner. Only then does Archie notice the waitress, tray of Martinis over her head. Derek is taller than the girl and takes his time finding the red Vodka cranberry amongst the Martinis.

Slow motion.

The pill falling free from his hand, flipping--tumbling as it lands in the Vodka cranberry. It sinks through the ice, dissolving like an Alka Seltzer commercial. Speed up—the waitress continues pressing through the crowd. Derek leaves the tree house.

Flash—the flamingoes continue chatting, flirting with a fresh group of penguins. The brunette takes a sip of her new drink as someone tells her a joke--

Flash—three of them go downstairs to the bathroom. The drugged brunette feels suddenly ill, woozy. While the other two snort lines in the stall, the brunette wanders outside for fresh air. The wolf is waiting, smiling as he grabs her hand. Her brain's slowed down, she tries to react as he draws her close to him.

"How're you doing," he lays her down on one of the massive couches, leaning over her, caressing her cheek.

Her two friends come out of the bathroom. Derek kisses her long enough for them to finally decide she's gone back up to their table--

Flash—she's muttering nonsense as he practically drags her along the alleyway to the front door. A group of patrons pass this guy and his drunk chick—one of a hundred they've seen tonight--

Flash--exiting through the front door, he pulls her confused face close, kissing her as he says, "I know darling--let's get you to sleep," the two Gay Bears at the front door even smile at him--even seeing her face.

I hear them come in.

The front door keeps opening and I never hear it shut. Archie laughs. I roll over, praying for sleep. Through my window, LA glimmers in a sea of lights. I've become used to the view, staring at it until the sun rises in the eastern horizon. I lay there for another ten minutes and then--

"Whoa!" I hear Archie explode in a spasm of giggles.

What's going on up there? I follow the voices up the staircase. It's dark in the living room. I see lights coming from the open door leading into the game room. As I push open the door, I hear breathing.

Freeze.

Archie's still wearing his shirt, pants and shoes discarded—bare ass flexing as he pumps back and forth, arms planted on the pool table. Hanging around his bobbing thighs, I glimpse a girl's limp legs.

"What the fuck are you doing?" I scream.

Archie's head turns, eyes glassy and bloodshot—he's totally fucked up. I race to the pool table. A drunk Derek's passed out against the Centipede game. The girl's laying on her back, naked, exposed breasts, a line of pubic hair merging with Archie's sweating abdomen. She moans in carnal pleasure as he leans over, sucking on her breast as he rams in and out of--

"Have you lost your mind!" I rip him off her.

His head cracks against the Carlsberg Beer lamp. As if hypnotized, her eyes follow the swaying light. Archie turns around, throwing a drunken swing at me. I dodge it. Derek awakens, wiping weary eyes.

"You let him do this?" I scream at him.

Before Derek can respond, Archie explodes, "SHE'S A FUCKING BITCH!" he covers his face with one hand, pointing at her with the other, "I am so sick of this fucking city! It's so fucking. . ." tears form in his eyes.

He's drunk and stupid, cradling his face in his hands, collapsing on the floor, "she was laughing and--"

Ding dong.

The doorbell. My heart skips a beat. The screaming stops. The doorbell rings again. The drunk girl brushes her hand across her thigh, giggling, the only sound in the whole room.

Derek shoots to his feet. He knows what I'm thinking, "Nobody noticed us leave," he adds, "Archie got the car and picked us up."

Ding dong.

Standing in my boxer shorts, my mind's racing. I hear the front door open, feet moving across the living room floor. We want to move, but we're paralyzed with fear.

It must be Hal.

"Well move her!" Derek whispers, breaking out of his trance.

There are no closets, no other doorways to spirit her out of the game room. A half-naked Archie and Derek try to drag her behind the pool table. Hal won't notice, we'll--

"Aaiighhhhhh!" it's a woman's scream.

And I'm turning, thinking the girl woke up! We're all going to jail. But she's still drugged, eyes staring dreamily up at the Carlsberg Beer lamp swaying through the air. Then I turn to the doorway and almost pass out from fear. Holy shit.

It's Veronica.

Twelve

"**W**hat the hell's going on!" cries Veronica.

Late take stock of this moment. I'm in my boxer shorts. Archie and Derek hold a naked, drugged brunette by the arms and legs. Archie's pants sit at his ankles--his flaccid penis and condom hang in the dark haired girl's face. Definitely not the way you want your mom to catch you.

Time speeds up--

"I-I," Veronica stammers, standing in the doorway, "came to get my Gone With The Wind jewelry box—"

Flash—The Gone With The Wind jewelry box I stole from her. How did she find me? Shit. I gave ITM my address to deliver my things--an easy phone call for Irv to make. Flash--my life flashes before me. Veronica may live in a dream world, but she's no idiot. I can already see that jail cell at the Federal Correctional Facility as--

"She's a stripper," offers Archie in a feeble voice.

"You're not exactly the best liar," Derek drones, admitting the futility of the lie.

The drugged girl laughs.

"What's wrong with her?" Veronica's teeth rattle.

"Nothing!" I cry, "just get out."

"She's drugged," then she repeats it again as if her mind didn't register it the first time, "she's drugged!" and a smug grin fills her face "when the police find out, you are fucking over, Cullen," she turns, ready to race away.

Pure reaction.

Feet flying, I race after her. The living room is dark. She bumps into the kitchen island. I dive out, tackling her to the ground. Feet scamper around us--others enter. Fuck! Something hits me hard in the head—the clang of metal against bone--blood streaming into my eyes. I force her hands to the ground and hear something metal thud against the wood floor.

Archie, unable to find the light switch, turns on the kitchen island's oven. It uses red heat lamps to cook pots and the room's suddenly bathed in orange red light—the way it looks in Hell. Through blood, I see Veronica fighting for her life, trying to break my grasp. Teeth clenched, she's kicking. I've bled across her stretch top, speckles of blood on her bare midriff.

Archie leaps in behind me, holding her legs, "Shit!" he cries, "bitch kicked me in the face," but he manages to hold her legs down, wrestling them to the ground.

"Have to ruin me!" I slam her wrists against the wooden floor, blood burning my eyes "have to ruin me!" I'm screaming—barking—rage rushing through me, blood splattering all around. I see the skillet on the floor, my blood on and around it. In the red light of the stove, the blood looks black and murky. I suddenly remember the smug look she wore only minutes ago, the sadistic pleasure at the completion of my downfall.

"What're you gonna do?" she grunts, teeth bared, "drug me? Rape me?"

She knows I could never hit her. She knows me as well as I know myself—knows that sooner or later Cullen Gersh, the nice kid, the studious lawyer, the agent want to be, will let go of her hands—and she'll march out of here. But she doesn't know the bitter insomniac who's lost everything including the gift of sleep.

Other footsteps--Derek races up the stairs into the living room. Where was he? Sliding along the floor, he leans over her--blood obscuring my vision.

"What the fuck are you doing!" she screams and then a grunt.

My hands turn to concrete, holding hers down. Shut my eyes. Think about it. Derek won't kill her—won't hurt her. How the hell am I going to get out of this mess? He's trying to force something into her mouth. Gritting her teeth, she growls like a dog.

She tries to free her hands. By now my palms are sweaty and wet with blood-- hard to hold on to her skinny wrists. She suddenly coughs and gags. Glance around his head. Derek pinches her nose shut, forcing her to open her mouth to breath—then he stuffs the pills between her teeth and clamps her jaw shut. It's a death struggle like the tiger and the dying hippo just to keep her mouth closed. Twisting, kicking, she finally gags, swallowing it. Then her mouth opens wide, chest heaving as she takes in deep breaths. Derek watches, making sure she didn't hide the pill in her lip. Just look at her face. You can tell she swallowed it.

"What did you give her?" Archie asks.

I turn to Derek, reading his expression. He doesn't need to say it. He gave her a Rufinol. Turn back to Veronica. In the red light, her eyes are wide. She stares at me, tendons and veins stressed, ready to burst through the skin. Does she think she's been poisoned? Archie gets off her legs, leaning against the kitchen island.

Derek rolls off her, chest heaving as he reaches atop the cabinet, pressing a dish-towel against my bleeding forehead.

"What'll happen?" I inquire, feeling Derek's hand through the blood soaked cloth.

"She'll get woozy."

"But she'll remember!" adds a fearful Archie, still naked below the waste.

Flash—remember the scattered internet articles:

Often times women have no recollection thirty minutes prior to ingesting the drug. They are found in cars without clothes on and can't remember anything except feeling violated.

"She lives alone, right?" Derek speaks of her as if she isn't here.

I nod yes, the dishrag still pressed against my head—a wincing pain.

Veronica makes her desperate plea to me, "Don't let them kill me. . . Cullen. Please, don't let them kill me," I feel for her and then remember the smug grin she flashed at me only minutes ago. She's already getting groggy--

amazing how fast this thing works. A haze covers her eyes.

With his free hand, Derek reaches into her pants, pulling out her Tiffany key ring, "We'll drive her back to her place, tuck her in bed. If the articles are right," he takes a deep breath, "she won't remember coming here. . . memory lapse, that's all."

"Jesus Christ," Archie moans, "Jesus Christ."

Once she realizes we're not going to kill her, that we're conspiring to simply rob her of her memories, her fear returns to anger. As illogical as it might seem, she threatens us. You know how women can be: "Fucking bastards," she eyes us in the red light, like she's burning our faces into her memory, "I'll remember--remember all of this. Cullen, you are . . .you are. . .you--"

Thump—thump—goes my pulse in my forehead as I study her in the red light of the oven—thump—thump— remember the way her face first looked in the pulsing neon sign of the falafel stand—thump—thump—her eyes glaze—thump—thump—how did everything get so twisted?—thump—thump—her mouth opens wide— thump thump—now she's staring through me.

"Is. . . is she out?" Archie whispers.

"Yeah," I release my grip.

Her fingers curl open in her hands.

I just lay on the kitchen floor.

After awhile the bleeding stops. The dishcloth makes a tearing sound as I carefully pull it away, trying not to rub the scab open. With a careful finger I get sick, feeling the small crack in the center of my forehead. Maybe I should get stitches? I'm woozy.

Derek carries Veronica into the game room. Then in the red light of the stove, I watch him carrying the brunette to his car. Will he leave her on the beach? He returns, silently marching through the kitchen. I follow

him into the game room. The lights are off, shades shut--
only the dim lights from the Centipede and Asteroids
video games illuminate the room.

"I put Archie to sleep," sighs Derek, "going to drive
the brunette down to the beach. I'll come back for
Veronica. Rather get caught with just one than two."

Look down. I barely see Veronica. I remember that
she was clad in diesel jeans and a black, stretch top. I
can't see the clothes in the darkness. Reach out, running a
finger along the stretch top, feeling erect nipples. My
head spins. I'm disoriented from the head wound.

"You alright?" he asks me.

"What if she remembers?" I ask.

"We're going to jail," adds Derek in a matter of fact
whisper, "take it up the ass from a big black guy who'll
rave about Momma's Jambalaya," amazing how
composed he is. Derek touches my shoulder, making sure
I'm a team player on this one, "what're you thinking?"

You don't own anyone.

That's what I'm thinking. When I was a teenager, I
thought after you had a woman's love or her body, you
owned her. I used to believe my girlfriend would carry a
mark on her--that even though I was gone, she would
always somehow belong to me.

But it's not like that, is it?

Strange how we have trouble recollecting all the
people we've had sex with? You'd think we'd remember
them clearly—like some police lineup. But we don't. You
might say marriage is permanent, but c'mon—it's just a
long term lease. People die or divorce and go on with life,
taking new lovers. Hell, if they do spend their lives
together, they don't even know what the other's thinking-
-living in a sea of silence, never aware of the dark
fantasies lurking beneath them. As much as we might

want to be, none of us is the whale. I don't know what we are. Maybe, just--

Human beings.

We've got these huge brains that entertain thoughts wilder than just eating and procreating. We construct symphonies and computers and fret about happiness and fear and being alone. We get violent for no reason and jealous and angry. I don't think it can all be summed up in a one hour Animal Planet special. My mind swims, a wincing pain in my forehead.

Standing in my boxer shorts in this dark game room, bathed in the meager light of the Centipede video game, I feel cold, isolated from everything I've ever loved. Peering down at Veronica's silhouette, I can think only of what she did to me, trying to control me—to destroy me because she can't face what she's become. Maybe the lack of sleep and the head wound has made me crazy.

Tears.

Fired from ITM—sleepless—becoming some worthless technical consultant—and that isn't enough is it? No. She needs me in prison. Hell, she'd have me dead if she could. I hate Veronica—hate her more than anything on the earth. If I wasn't such a conditioned creature, I could hurt her now. But I'm not . . .I'm decent. Then why am I entertaining this thought—not a surge of nondescript energy like those violent spasms—this is a well-crafted fantasy.

"I know what you're thinking," Derek whispers in my ear.

Does he? Staring off into the blinking screen of the Centipede game, I feel the trail the tears leave on my cheeks. I can't believe what I'm feeling—what I'm thinking! Like some primordial Id, some invisible force possesses me now--my hands shake as I stare down at her red hair on the green felt table.

"I'm going," Derek leaves.

I'm alone.

I want to feel Veronica naked one more time.

I imagine the red hair against the green felt. Hell, I'm just rationalizing now, playing games with myself. In the darkness I pull off her top, unbuttoning her bra, the breasts falling free. They feel different now in my hands. My head swoons. Reaching around I take off her shoes, listening as they thud against the wood floor. No thoughts, I just continue, unzipping her pants, it's difficult to pull them off her legs. She moans in the darkness. I have total control over her now. I've fantasized about controlling her for the past two weeks. And now I've taken her soul, her very body from her. We've all entertained such thoughts.

But I've found a setting to carry them out.

I feel a stinging in my throbbing forehead. Pull off her panties, drawing them down her smooth legs—feel the patch of red pubic hair. . . flat abdomen. . . supple breasts. She lays naked and prostrate before me in the darkness—like some concubine of Kubla Khan's. Shit, I'm sure that guy must've had some concubines.

Stick a finger between her legs.

She's wet.

"Ugh," she moans in pleasure through the soupy smile--this little whore who fucked Irv Hirschberg—this little whore who tried to destroy me—this little whore who robbed me of my sleep filled nights.

The hate rushes in like the tide--all consuming. I feel around. Archie's box of condoms rest on the shoulder of the table. They're unlubricated—strange choice. Next to the condoms I find a tube. Hold it up in the faint light of the Centipede game. It's KY Jelly. For those of you from Wisconsin, that's a sex lubricant. Put the condom on, lubing it up. Veronica runs a dreamy finger along her breasts. . . down towards her abdomen. I turn her over, spreading her legs, leaning forward. I can fuck her as long as I want to—do anything I want. Slide inside her—

A motion.

Just a singular motion. Pull back—then forward again. Now I'm fucking her from behind. I glance down at her thighs, her ass, back. . .lean over, placing my chin against the nape of her neck. She's wearing a new perfume now. Irv must've bought it for her. Jam—pressing deep—hate fucking--they call it. I pull away from her neck, feeling the dark cool air around me.

Just stopping time.

Faster—faster--Veronica moans. Goosebumps rise along her back—like a bolt of electricity moving through us. Yes. You can own someone so completely that you can control their mind, their heart, their body. Like an oriental despot, you shut them down--take them completely--banish all memory at your whim and command. Oh shit! Liquid lightning rushing up my spine.

Roll over. Then I feel it. . . a sensation I've not felt for an eternity. I'm sleepy. Completely exhausted. The world spins. My forehead suddenly hurts. Did I rip open the scab? I don't even bother feeling it. No more thoughts. The endless barrage of sensation, even the light of The Centipede game fades into the darkness. After two endless weeks of insomnia ridden nights, pain no one should ever have to endure—

I sleep like a baby.

Thirteen

$\mathbf{A}$ knock at the door.

I awake in my bedroom, sheets curled around my feet. The air smells fresh. I feel renewed, as if the memories of sleepless nights--the unbelievable exhaustion was the dream and this is reality. Knock—knock—knock--it continues.

"Hello?" I call out.

No one's downstairs. Derek's door is locked, no typing sound ringing out through the air. Silence punctuated by--knock—knock—knock--sunlight blares through open windows overlooking the city. Wander up the stairs--feet cold against the stone steps. My eyes haven't adjusted yet. The brilliant sun reflecting off the white walls makes me squint. Upstairs is empty too--knock—knock—knock—slow and steady as it echoes off the walls. Someone's at the front door—

"I'm coming," I cry out.

Derek or Archie must've forgotten his keys. Or perhaps it's the mailman with a hand delivery? Before I reach the door, it swings open and—

It's Veronica.

She's dressed in one of those French maid's outfits with the black top and lacy apron. A wide beaming smile on her face, she holds the sky blue French duster in her hands. I ask what she's doing here? She simply puts a finger over supple red lips, gesturing for me to be quiet as she steps into the doorway and--

I awake.

The Carlsberg beer lamp overhead. Sit up on my elbows. I'm still on the pool table. Someone threw a plaid blanket over me. Through the open doorway, a column of sunlight beams into the game room. Stretching arms out, I feel calm and refreshed. From reflection in the glass window of the centipede video game, I notice the rings have disappeared from under my eyes--face beaming with a smile.

In the shower I can't stop smiling, the facial gesture fills me with euphoria. Ever try smiling for an hour? I begin whistling. Flash—me fucking Veronica. Derek must've taken her home. It almost feels like a dream. Wow, the things we take for granted, like a good night's sleep. It's as if a horrendously long day has finally ended. Life's returned to normal.

No. . . better than normal.

You know how confident you feel when you're getting laid? Multiply that feeling times a hundred. On the way to work, I can't stop smiling--full of energy, brimming with confidence. I don't think Hal ever violated me—nothing could violate me, nothing could hurt me. At the red light on La Cienega, I throw my hands in the air, singing along with the radio. I don't give a shit about what that man in the Saab thinks. Wander into my work cubicle by noon, spreading open the California State Bar examination books with fearless impunity. I'm a sponge—click—click—click--hanging up on callers as I absorb the information. Better than I've ever been before--and no, it's not because I've forgotten how normal feels. Look at me, ripping through the sheets of this book like a genius with a photographic memory.

I'm Superman.

During afternoon break I snack on a Twinkie. It's the best thing I've ever eaten. Honestly. Licking my fingers clean with a smile, I return to work to find the light over my desk buzzing on and off. Standing on my chair, I try to fix it. Then I stop. Look down—do you see it too? The rows of cubicles looks like the walls of cells and the people inside them like trapped rats. This whole room is like those maze puzzles you used to do as a kid. But I'm no longer a rat. I've escaped the maze.

Did last night do this to me?

Is this what the Viking warriors felt when they marauded the coast of England for a thousand years? They sailed in, took what they wanted in treasure and flesh. C'mon, rape, pillage and plunder is the oldest occupation--the stuff of history books. My phone rings. I sit back in my cubicle, ready to hang up when I hear

Derek's familiar voice. Under the blinking florescent light, I cradle the receiver to my ear.

"Hey mate," he smirks, "sleep well?"

"Yeah, great," I feel the smile forming on my lips, "better than great."

"I want to meet you and Archie tonight."

"I'll be home at--"

"No. Meet me at 8:30 at Mr. Chow's--"

Click.

I've never eaten at Mr. Chow's.

So it takes a few minutes to find it. Mr. Chow's is where all the big players at ITM dine. Inside, giant black and white circles of leather obscure the ceiling. A black and white tiled floor flows through booths crammed full of execs and penguins and flamingoes. I spot Derek and Archie at the bar having a drink--notice the Tsingtao beer already waiting for me, a ring of condensation around it. Look at them grinning ear to ear as they watch me—as if only they know the punch line to some secret joke.

"How ya feeling?" inquires Derek behind his grin.

"Great," take a sip of the beer--the best I've ever had.

Derek glances around, making sure no one is within earshot before he says, "I asked you all to come here because I think we're going through the same thing."

Just then a flamingo saunters into the restaurant-- tight red top, a waist that's the girth of a garden hose. She strolls towards a corner table where an old man with thick, black glasses sits, surrounded by a cadre of flamingoes. He reminds me of an old spotted owl— precariously close to extinction, surrounded by a colorful cadre of flamingoes. As she saunters by, every male from the bartender to the Mexican valet staring through the front door eyes her.

I turn back to Derek who puts his hands together in a praying position, tapping the end of fingers against his nose, "Historians call this sensation the aphrodisiac of power."

"Look that up too on the internet?" jokes Archie.

But Derek's dead serious, "In politics, men in power speak of being intoxicated with energy, able to work longer, harder, quicker. They become hypersexual like a Kennedy or Clinton screwing everything in sight. The rush is addictive."

"You can say that again," I sit on the stool, relaxed with everything around me-- no fear about school debt, my career. It's not that I'm ignoring things. But fear doesn't exist anymore. Flash--I return to a naked Veronica laying in the darkness on the pool table. There is no challenge in the world I can't overcome.

"I felt it with the girl Hal brought home," Derek spills out his heart, "I mean--I did it as a practical move to get her out of the house. But the next day, I felt imbued with this psychological power. I was stronger. I was scared of myself—or sharing this with anyone else," he turns to Archie, whispering, "and maybe I helped guide the events with you. I needed someone else to see it. . . to validate, to tell me I wasn't going crazy," Derek turns to me, "what happened with you was accidental. But none the less, we've all crossed over."

"So why are we here?" I ask, sipping my beer.

"Look around this place--have to be successful to get a table," glance around-- suit and tie clad execs, successful penguins. . . the gray spotted Owl in his mid 60's, flat eyes blinking, surrounded by three flamingoes. The spotted owl slides his aging hand down the back of the flamingo with the tight red top, "look at them all," Derek's voice framed against their chatter of laughter, clink of glasses, "this is the watering hole of the Alpha wolf. These fools are just renting it."

"The Alpha Wolf?" wonders Archie out loud.

I, ever the walking library of animal knowledge, answer, "In a wolf pack--or most any other communal mammal group, there's always one leader—the one who makes the decisions--has first dibs on the females--the Alpha Wolf."

The manager approaches Derek, "Mr. Van Horn, your table's ready."

We stroll through the restaurant, all eyes turning-- discerning if we're important enough to merit a second glance. My mind reels for a moment, the question burning through me: are we rapists? All eyes on me. Do rapists saunter right through Mr. Chow's? I guess they don't have to be an alleyway lurking derelict in an overcoat. The manager leads us upstairs to a private dining room. The door shuts and we're alone. I notice the security camera mounted in the corner--

"Never mind that," Derek tells me, "things only on when they close up at night. So," he continues the conversation, "humans are a social animal and we have our own Alpha Wolves. In the animal world it's physical prowess. In our society, power is money—young or old, if you're rich and powerful you can get chicks," I think of it in my terms: to the flamingoes, it's about nice cars, clothes, meals, "but the reality is that for both of them, it's about passing on a gene code--"

"Hold on, Dr. Seuss," Archie waves his hand, "I'm not looking to procreate. I ain't nobody's daddy—at least I hope not."

"On your free nights," counters Derek, "what do you do?"

Flash—Archie going to bars, drinking tap water— Archie considering hanging out at a frozen yogurt stand to pick up women—Archie eyeing every girl in the room—

"I use a condom," he adds, "not lookin' to be somebody's Daddy."

I sip my beer, silently listening to Derek, "But you are! You're fooling your body--mock reproducing. From the yard man to the CEO of IBM, when it comes to sex, generalities stand. You see an attractive woman, your heart speeds up--blood rushes to your genitals. On average, males fantasize about sex every 90 seconds."

"Yeah," I interject, "but we're guys."

"Women," he banters on in his clipped accent, "their vaginas lubricate at the sight of an attractive male, nipples standing erect."

Archie and I flash a look of disbelief.

"Fine," adds Derek, "remember downstairs when the girl in red passed by us?"

Flash—the sauntering ass in the tight pants, red top framing turning, eyes wide as we watch her, recording her with our eyes--the same question passed through our minds:--"Would I fuck her?" Derek gives words to my thoughts, "could I fuck her? Is she better than what I'm fucking? Is she worth it?" he slaps a hand against the table, bringing me back, "like we're tuned into the same radio station--all of us thinking the same thing!"

"So?" my question hangs in the air.

"Our greatest fear as a race is to accept our true, animal nature," he sighs, "sex, the most powerful instinct. The feminist movements created the new age guys like Hal-- Gap wearing, effeminate, weak males. You think Hal could fight a world war, save his family from Indians?" his eyes bore deep into me, "we've already gone farther than the Hals of the world could ever dream. Let's finish it, break the seal--see what lies beyond."

"You mean . . .do it again?" I ask.

"I'm proposing that we conduct our own social experiment," Derek's thought the thing out, "we have to be careful. If the police catch on--it won't be in any papers."

"Why?" I ask.

"Cops won't publicize what they believe to be serial crimes--unless the press gets wind of it. They want to keep out copycat types and conceal vital clues. It would take awhile before they'd be forced to make the public aware. So even if the coast looks clear, it isn't. We have to be very cautious," he explains how we'll do this by using unlubricated condoms, no spermicides that leave traces in our test subjects. KY Jelly will be the only safe lubricant--absorbed by the body, leaving no signs of physical trauma. We'll employ surgical gloves when we touch the subjects. With air cans, the type you use to clean your computer, we'll blow off any foreign skin residue or pubic hair from their genital areas. No kissing, no saliva—nothing to leave traces of DNA.

"You realize," I add, searching for the words, "you're saying that we--that we. . "

"Rape them?" Derek fills in the silence. Then squinting like a philosopher considering some scholarly point, he says, "yes and no. We'll consider only the rudest of women as test subjects. And even then, we're not inseminating them--no bruises--no signs of our presence. They're left on the beach, martini in hand. We're aiming to conduct a social experiment, gentleman, not to traumatize."

"Still sound awfully misogynistic to me," I mutter.

He explains it's the perfect opportunity: his house is secluded. Hal's away for the next two months. Archie and I have always been able to make Thursday night gatherings-- so that will be the night we'll do it.

Derek holds his wine glass up.

No words are spoken.

Nothing more need be said. But I know that in toasting, I'll enter into a pact, a promise that can't easily be broken. I stare down at my beer, tiny bubbles racing through the golden liquid. I'm a nothing tech support supervisor—my career ruined by a demented actress. I'm a man who's entertained dreams of peering into Aston Martins and VIP tables, to see what others couldn't.

But this could be madness?

Still, something's building in me, like the bubbles inside my beer—like the way the parasites grows in the stomachs of hippos—I saw it on the Discovery Channel. Except this thing makes me feel happy as it overtakes me, spreading its tiny tentacles through my body. Maybe it's the real me—my inner Alpha Wolf. Shit, haven't done such a good job so far. Maybe I should let the Alpha Wolf run things for awhile? But hell, this deliberation's just a waste of time—

Because I made my decision last night.

I raise my glass.

"To The Clan of The Alpha Wolf," grins Derek, the grandest wolf of them all. The clink of glasses. He finishes off his wine and hands us tiny silver pins he's fashioned with wolf heads on them, "every clan has to have a shield," glancing down at his watch, he taps the table "it's Thursday gentleman. We start tonight."

Fourteen

Hover over the dance club.

Below you, the rhythmic throb of music, fog rising up to the rafters. From up here, the sea of black clad bodies sway like grain in a pyrotechnic wind. Do you see us-- our tiny silver wolf's head pins on our collars? I follow Derek as he parts the crowd like Moses at the Red Sea.

Zoom in.

I know I look a little out of it, distant eyes staring into nothingness. The whole room pitches and rolls around me like a boat in a storm. My heads throbs, notice how I lightly touch the band aid on my forehead--where Veronica cracked me with the frying pan. This place is a dance club called "The Garden of Eden". Do you smell the stench. Unless Adam and Eve had some serious b.o. issues, it's an ill chosen name.

In the corner, a camera crew films the bar and dance floor, passing right across us. But I'm not worried about being recorded. Notice the MTV logo on the camera. They're here to film the dancing--probably for some stupid show.

"There's one," Derek eyes a fit oriental girl with pigtails and explosively perky tits. Take away the black stretch top and she's The Secret Life of Suzie Wong—an old movie with William Holden. Jesus, don't you ever watch old movies? As we pass, Suzie chats it up with two black guys in those bright, tacky oversized FUBU jackets.

Archie's pick is a brunette, Audrey Hepburn lookalike in an out of place, black evening dress. Standing at the bar, chatting with the bartender, bright blue eyes and an engaging smile--could almost pass as Holly Golightly.

Archie is the first to try. Waiting for the bartender to return to work, he squeezes in next to her. A moment of tense conversation and she spins around on her bar stool, the zipped up back of her dress is his only response.

"Says she only dates producers," he shrugs upon his return. But he's smiling—a real smile. Because now there is no fear. Now the ego isn't on the line, it's just a game.

"Yeah!" Derek screams over the music, "put her on the candidate roster!"

Look at us.

We still don't have drinks because the bartender doesn't notice us. The women won't take notice of us. But I feel real, like everyone else is just a mirage. It's like they're all black and white and we're the only three people in color, strong and fearless--

How can you fear illusions?

When it's my turn, I cut through the sea of birds like a knife through butter, pushing penguins away, not even bothering to apologize. Nobody dares to bother me. I see a woman who catches my eye--blonde with an oval face and long, penetrating eyes cloaked in cute horn rimmed glasses. She's older than me, mid-thirties I guess, short cropped blonde hair. For some reason I suspect she's Russian.

And no, I can't explain why.

"Hey," I approach, been a long time since I played this game, "how ya' doing?"

By the look on her face, you'd think I'd just urinated in her drink. I never find out if she's Russian. Adjusting her horn-rimmed glasses, she saunters across the dance floor, disappearing into pyrotechnic smoke.

Who cares? She's just a fucking illusion. After a few passes, we're not even trying to break the ice, just spouting cheesy pick-up's, aiming to insult. If I were a screenwriter, I'd fashion a whole bunch of quick jump cuts—the three of us talking directly into camera--and then pan over to the women, registering their reactions:

```
INT. BAR — NIGHT

Pointing to his pin, a half drunk Cullen
says:

                    CULLEN
         The big bad wolf's come
         to eat you up.

Blonde 2 walks away--

                              SMASH CUT:
```

<pre>
                    ARCHIE
               (with intensity)
          You're   ugly...but   you
          intrigue me.

Brunette 2 slaps him--

                              SMASH CUT:

Derek's already said something to SUZIE
WONG TYPE GIRL.

                 Suzie Wong
          Eat Me!
                   Derek
          Be   careful   what   you
          wish for.

Suzie Wong type SLAPS him—
</pre>

Then I notice her.

From the far end of bar, a girl stares at me. It last only a second. She turns away, scrutinizing a tall, yellow Galliano bottle over the bar. Who ever drinks that shit? But her eyes were on me. Remember how the rest of the bar looks gray? Well this girl has color--short cropped dark hair, a black biker jacket. But what I notice most is the mole on her cheek, like Marylyn Monroe's. I think I saw her before at--

"Voting time," Derek laughs, walking back to our huddle.

The vote is cast and recast because it has to be unanimous. Derek keeps tossing in the dissenting ballot, "C'mon," he squirms like a kid whose friend's won't take the game seriously enough, "half the girls you're voting on are in groups. We need loners!"

Finally, the choices are made.

Derek hands out the pills with as much glee as Jim Jones stirring up a batch of Cherry Kool-Aid. We separate, negotiating the sea of gray, colorless bodies-- tiny green pills pressed between our sweaty thumbs and index fingers. No second thoughts, no sudden injection of morality. It takes me forever. Finally I spot her in the far corner chatting it up with a guy. Well, not really chatting. Because she shoots him down and is once again alone. The time is right and--

Flash—I bump into her, dropping the pill in her drink.

Flash-- Archie plops his into Holly Go-Lightly's tumbler.

Flash—Derek snaps the pill off the top of his thumb. Three milligrams of Rufinol flip and turn, plopping perfectly into Suzie Wong's glass as she turns, swaying, staring out at the dance floor.

Fade out.

Don't you love the way that sounds? Screenwriters almost always end their script with those two words. Don't you think it would look cool as we fade out to a black screen? It suggests time's passed. Then we fade back on Derek, discovering pigtailed Suzie Wong, confused, trying to negotiate her way to the bathroom. Archie finds Holly Go-Lightly slumped down, asleep in her chair. He rouses her, quickly escorting her towards the door. Laughing, giggling, girls in arms, the two of them meet up as they stroll out of the club with total impunity, out in the open for all to see!

And me?

I'm still wandering all over the place--no idea where Glasses Girl went, but she ain't here. Guess we'll never know if she was Russian. But, I console myself, I did what the old Cullen would never have dared--the old Cullen, paralyzed with fear, the post-feminist coward who couldn't defend himself.

Fuck him.

After helping stuff the two test subjects into Derek's Volvo, I lean against the next car, catching my breath. That's when the gods smile down. For who do I see in the next car, but the tall blonde with glasses, slumped over the wheel of her Saab convertible, mumbling incoherently, car keys at her feet. Then it's back to the pad. Spare me your morality. You know you're just as excited as me to see what happens next.

Foo Fighters blasts over the stereo.

Bourbon and gin overflow into tumblers, splashing onto the floor. The snap of surgical gloves. We're fucked up in the game room, pool table—Centipede game--drawn curtains, spinning around the three clothed beauties laid atop the pool table as white lights explode--

"Give it to me baby!" screams Derek, "c'mon!" he presses the button—snapping pictures of them--the hum of Polaroids sliding out, "Cullen, could you fix her?"

Holly Golightly's eyes have rolled into the back of her head. I slide her dark sunglasses back on, hiding the sight from view. Suzie Wong keeps giggling. My girl with glasses stares at the camera flash, fascinated by the explosions of light.

"Now," Derek waves the developing photos in the air, "we'll know if we've put the wrong clothes on one--or forgotten a detail. Alright, let's get to it."

Hands pull back stretch fabric, fumbling with button clasps. The stretch fabric's hard to pull off. Tug hard--the pants from Glasses Girl flies off. I fall back on the floor. Laughter. Unbutton the black strapless bra of the near sighted beauty who wouldn't give me the time of day. Full pendulous breasts tumble out over her chest, tight round nipples, beautiful scoops of skin and flesh. My eyes trace down her abdomen--a lake of milky white skin, totally still without a ripple of fat. I pull back the black lace panties and now as for the girl who wouldn't speak to me--

I own her ass.

"Well now," Derek chuckles, "we definitely know she's a real blonde."

He sips Armagnac from a large, crystal snifter. Holding one of his girl's pigtails to his mouth like a telephone, he jokes, "Anyone in there?"

She giggles out an endless stream of laughter. He pours a few drops on her breasts, licking it off her nipples, carefully tracing around the pink aureoles with his tongue. The sugary, brown liquid runs along her abdomen, coursing between her legs. His tongue follows behind, lapping it clean, disappearing below her waist.

Her giggle turns to a moan.

"Gentleman," Archie's already dropped his pants, lubricating his condom, "are we ready to go where no man has gone before?" he maneuvers between Holly Golightly's legs, anchoring hands on her slender hips as he hums the Star Trek theme.

Derek continues lapping like a cat.

"Spock," Archie berates him, "you're wasting precious time! Hey, let's dim the lights."

"No," Derek presses, "turn the lights off—you can't see anything."

The lights stay on.

Kick off your shoes. Unbuckle your belt--drop pants and boxers. Take the condom--rip the foil—strap on and lubricate it. You're ready to go. Derek's still eating out the oriental girl with pig tails. Her hands swarm around his head, fingers running through his hair--

"Ten," Archie calls out like mission control, "nine. . . eight. . .Derek get your head out of her crotch--don't know where that girl's been-- seven. . . six—"

Almost expect to hear a drum roll as we scan the three women laid across the pool table--blonde, brown, and black hair falling atop green felt. Towering over the three of them, we laugh and giggle. Could almost be a Beach Blanket Bingo movie if it weren't for the nudity. . .and the condoms. . .and the fact that none of us could fuck Annette Funicello--I mean, c'mon, she could be our mom--never mind, bad analogy--

"Three," screams Arch, "two. . . one--"

"Oohhh!" the blonde with glasses sighs as I enter her. She's wet. I didn't need the lubricant. Grab her ass which tightens under my grip. I draw her close so I can go deeper. She's looking back at me with this expression. Wow! How do you explain the look? Like she was never made for anything else but fucking, for pleasing me, for supplying my every wish and desire.

I almost blow right then and there.

The power to own, the power to control. I understand why society's made this so taboo—it's fucking intoxicating! Energy coursing through me as if her very soul is moving through her, rushing into me. Maneuvering in and out, I lay my head across her breasts, feeling her swelling breasts rising and falling, heartbeat pounding.

"Party! Party! Party!" Archie charges back and forth, pounding into his brunette—pounding with all the raw hatred and anger he's stuffed behind that smile. On the far end, Derek takes his time, moving slowly as he pours himself more Armagnac, resting the sifter on the ledge of the pool table.

I keep going.

Faster and faster.

Her neck tendons throb, glasses moving up and down over her eyes as I shift her back and forth. Her red lips part, eyes rolling around. Put my face near the base of her neck, taking in her scent. . . faster and faster. The other girls moan. I hear my thighs smacking against the edge of the pool table--the Centipede game buzzes—Foo Fighters sing until the highest octave is reached—

Climax.

"Da!" my girl moans, "Da! Da!"

For those of you from Arkansas, *da* is Russian for yes.

"Hey," I scream to the others, "she is Russian. She is Russian!"

Laughter.

Hearing us laugh, the girls join in too.

That night I have a dream.

In it, I'm stumbling through the rooms of Derek's home, calling out for my buddies. But they aren't there. Creeping upstairs, I find Veronica, still clad in a French maid's outfit, silently dusting furniture. A martini on a silver tray is thrust into my face. Turning, I see the Russian girl with glasses, also clad in a maid's outfit as she serves me my drink. Sipping my Martini, shaken not stirred, I watch The Animal Planet on the flat screen as they silently cook and clean. We're alone just the three of us—

One big happy family.

In the real world, the party continues.

It's like living in a film noir movie. Imagine one of those movie montages with racy music and lot of quick cuts as the weeks roll by—all bright lights and laughter. The three of us in Derek's car, lights of La Cienega and Sunset reflecting off the polished hood. One Thursday we dress like Sinatra's gang, dark suits, black ties, sunglasses. Gay Bear's don't dare stop us--we just cross the velvet rope. It's attitude as we drink and laugh in our group. We're not here to make friends.

The endless typing from behind Derek's locked door. He's working when I leave for work and still at it when I get home--tap—tap—tap—ding!

More naked girls on the pool table. Plop plop fizz fizz—oh what a relief Rufinol is. They're on their backs moaning in throes of ecstasy--

Tap—tap—tap—ding!

"Cullen," Hal leaves a message on the answering machine, "why won't you call me back?" I'm passed out next to the machine, sprawled across the living room couch, sleeping like a baby—

Tap—tap—tap—ding!

My dream is always the same. I lounge around the house, surrounded by more and more of my test subjects, all clad in French Maid's outfits, an army of mute women to service my every whim and command. There's plenty of sex and burritos and beer. See me now. That's why I'm smiling in my sleep--

Tap—tap—tap—ding!

We look like Sinatra's gang in Ocean's 11. Strutting in slow motion, you see the three of us walking side by side--dark sunglasses, tossing martini glasses carelessly over our shoulders. The glass shatters in our wake--yeah, that's what it's like—

Tap—tap—tap—ding!

Trunks slam—cars drive—liquor flows--pick up lines ring out-- slaps across our faces, huffs of indignant despair. The snap of surgical gloves—Derek's Polaroid shots--hiss of air cans spraying. There are so many of them, flashing so quickly, you barely notice the details of their faces--blondes, brunettes, red heads, Orientals, Dutch, Latin Americans, Jews, Catholics, Protestants, we take em all.

She slaps me—

I'm fucking her on the pool table.

She laughs in Archie's face—

She's on all fours over the corner pocket.

She shoots Derek the finger—

He playfully rubs the eight ball between her legs.

Tap—tap—tap—ding!

Milky white flesh, tan skin, short hair, long hair, trimmed vaginas, shaved stuff like an infant, big tits, supple hips, small tits, luxurious hips, tan lines, no tan lines. We fuck em all—a cacophony of laughter and moans and sighs—

Tap—tap—tap—ding!

"Cullen, I'm pretty pissed dude," Hal leaves another message on my phone, "why are you not returning my calls? What's wrong?"

Tap—tap—tap—ding!

Then we see Archie and a girl on the pool table, Carlsberg Beer lamp swaying over his head. Then we see it—he yawns, bored with the whole thing. The music fades and we suddenly hear Archie say:

"Guys?" he asks, "you listening?"

We're gathered around the television. It's Sunday morning. Even though I know they won't write it up, I scan the newspapers for rape articles. All I find are violent gang rapes in South Central. Lounging on the living room couch, empty plates with remnants of the scrambled eggs sit on the glass table as we watch an ancient episode of the old Dating Game on TV Land. A girl in bell bottomed jeans and a sweat shirt is partitioned from a Guido Disco guy. The camera zooms in on the girl, sky blue Duke University sweatshirt visible as she says, "I want a guy who's sensitive--"

"Give me a fucking break," Archie throws his napkin at the TV.

"C'mon," squirms Derek, "Duke's my Alma Mater."

"I want a guy who likes walks through the park," the female contestant spouts off her ideal man over the TV, "quiet, romantic meals--"

"That chick's probably dead by now," I add, "anyway, I don't think Duke admitted girls back then."

The camera pans to all six other contestants, probably gorgeous by 1960's standards. They sit on stools in front of a velvet curtain: six young women tanned blacker than George Hamilton at an equatorial Club Med. Look at their hair. Probably started the hole in the ozone layer with all that hairspray they've consumed.

"I'd do her," Derek points at the Asian girl on the far end.

"What about your alma mater?" I jest.

"Nah," he sighs, "not my type."

"I never thought I'd say this," Archie finally explodes like a balloon, "but I'm fucking bored."

"We can change the channel," I add.

"Not that!" Arch winces.

Derek says nothing, his face bathed in the sunlight from the open window.

"I mean," Archie paces around, "I never thought it would be like this. I'm sort of sick of sex? I don't want to fuck them anymore," he points at the TV screen before walking over to the wall of windows, "even they make me nauseous."

"Arch," I add, "they make everybody nauseous."

Then it hits me. Maybe I am tired of the experiment too? I mean, this whole thing's starting to get old. It's just the same act over and over again. After awhile, their faces blend into one, "You know," I turn to Derek, "I agree with him."

"We've reached the first stage," he tells us, eyes still closed.

"What stage?" I inquire.

"An awakening," Derek settles deeper into the leather couch. A cloud passes by, the shadow playing off the lines of his face, "it's time to raise the stakes—to turn it up to the next level."

"How?" wonders Archie.

He opens his eyes, "We get kinky."

"Are you guys gonna have another beer?" the waitress asks us.

"Mind your own fucking business," I bark.

We fan out of the corner booth of the Barfly. It's a Euro-trash hangout, dim lights and dance floor—I know, after awhile, they all start to look the same. Working through the crowd, my one beer in hand, I see Archie get slapped by a tall, hot chick who reminds me of Sandra Bullock. For those of you from Alaska, she's the girl from that movie Speed. Derek sinks his teeth into a Japanese girl wearing the shortest mini skirt known to man. And me? I'm just wandering around, not very interested in the social experiment tonight--

"Buzz off," a voice says.

I turn, seeing only the back of her head. She doesn't turn to face me, but there's no one else standing around us which prompts me to remark that:

"I didn't say anything."

"You were about to," she says. Then I realize she's staring at me through the mirror over the bar. I glance up, my face like a sun rising over a jagged horizon of Johnnie Walkers and Grey Goose Vodka. Next to my reflection, I see her hovering like the moon--face soft and long, framed with short cropped, dark hair—almost black. I notice the mole on her cheek like Marilyn Monroe and realize that I've seen her before. I'm about to ask if we've met when she gripes:

"Told you, you were going to say something," she spins around, facing me--eyes dark, sucking back the dim light of the bar, "I don't want to know you, hear from you--anything," she turns back to the bar, holding a five dollar bill in the air, barking at the bartender, "yo McFuck, think I could get a drink?"

The fact that the bartender hasn't seen her endears her to me. There's something real about her—something, hell, I can't explain it. From the far end of the bar I see two Persian guys, slicked back hair and Members Only jackets--looked like they walked off the set of Break Dancing 2, The Electric Boogaloo—that's one you don't want to rent. They're laughing at me, thinking I struck out. I smile because I didn't strike out at all.

I just found my test subject for the night.

"No fucking way!" Derek demands when we cast the vote.

"Why are you always shooting down people?" I grunt, "she's alone—she's—"

"I've seen her around before--probably knows the bartender--"

"She couldn't even get a drink!"

"I don't like her," Derek's not negotiating on this point, "how about the blonde in the back. You like the blondes."

I concede. But when I move in to drop the pill in Derek's suggested candidate, I can't get close. She meets up with a cadre of girlfriends. The other guys have already left, getting the car. I don't have time for this crap. Then I spot the girl with the mole, still sitting at the bar.

Sometimes you have to improvise.

"Oh no," she rolls her eyes at the ceiling, "not you again."

I plop the Rufinol in her drink. From the corner of my eye, the pill dissolves in her tall beer glass. I try to say something. She puts her fingers over her lips, "Just shut the fuck up and go back to your little friends. . . or whatever you cretins do."

"Sure," I smirk, walking away.

The minute hand of my watch moves—tick. . . tock. . . tick. . . tock. . .from my corner booth I see her yawn. . . the second hand sweeps around two more times. . . she puts a hand over her face, slumping down over her glass of beer. I've gotten pretty good at reading the telltale signs. I'm up, negotiating through the crowd, wrapping a hand around her shoulder. As if she moves through syrup, she glances up at me, eyes crossed-- confused. The two nosy Persians in the Member's Only jackets flash me the thumbs up as I pass.

"Baby," I say to her just before the door, kissing her on the lips, pushing my tongue through her slack-jawed mouth. I can still taste the Grolsch beer from her tongue. The Gay Bear opens the door as we exit the bar.

I hop into the front seat.

We're in a hurry, driving back up to the house. As we prepare to unload the girls in the driveway, Derek explodes, "What the fuck's she doing here!"

"Why are you so bent out of shape?" I retort, "the other one was--"

"Everything," he's pissed, "is a unanimous vote. You know that!"

"Well not tonight!" I challenge—his bossiness is getting out of hand, "who made you the proctor of this social experiment?"

"Let's see," he counts off the tops of his fingers, "it's my house, my car, my—"

"What do you want him to do?" asks Archie, "bring her back now—all passed out?"

"I don't fucking care," Derek explodes, "take her somewhere. But she's not entering my house. And we are not talking about this anymore. Archie, inside the house!"

A girl slung over his back, Archie shrugs to me--not seeing what the big deal is. They enter the house leaving me alone.

For a long time, I sit in the Volvo.

Listen to the ticking of my watch--run my thumb along the burled walnut paneling of his door, I'm angry. I mean, why does Derek have to control everything? He's always shooting down our candidates? This isn't the fucking space program—we're not looking for the next generation of astronauts. All you have to do is lay on your back--moan a little—and shit, even that's optional!

A Land Rover passes.

Their lights reflect into my car, illuminating my girl's face in the rear view mirror. She's half sitting up in the back seat. In the dim light, her dark hair is black as night- - eyes closed. I turn around. She slumbers, peacefully silent. Turn to look. Her purse fell over on the floor— makeup, cigarettes, cellphone spilled out on the floor. I'm thirsty. Before I drop her at the beach, I resolve to get something to drink.

"That was fast," mutters Derek.

He sits at the kitchen counter, silently staring into a coffee cup. Passing, I peer into it--just coffee. I know he hasn't taken his girl. He's sulking. Somehow, back in his presence, I feel bad. It's amazing how he can intimidate or pull the self-pity out of you.

"I'm sorry," and I explain that, "I'm going to drop her off in a minute."

"It's my fault," he sips the coffee, "shouldn't have left you alone--won't happen again," he's despondently sad. I was just trying to prove I wasn't going to be anyone's bitch. I didn't mean to hurt him like this. I still don't see what the big deal is.

"Whoa!" Archie storms into the room, alternately wiping sweat from his brow as he adjusts his boxers, "anal sex doesn't really feel that different," he takes a beer from the fridge, "was thinking--if we keep turning it up a notch, we'll probably soon get to that shit they did in the cave, huh?"

"I doubt you'd ever get that far," a woman's voice says.

Fear.

This is where I almost piss my pants.

In the doorway stands my mole girl. Biker jacket slung over her shoulder, she's awake. Archie's knees give way. He falls down--beer spilling across the wooden floor. My hands shake as I rest against the counter. I saw the pill in her drink. Jesus, she must have found it, fished it out without me seeing! How would she know it was a sedative?

I turn to my last hope--to Derek. He remains calm, composed. In one second I give myself up to him. I will never doubt him again. I shouldn't have ever doubted him. Shit! Shit! Shit! How are we going to get out of this! Again my mind fills with images of federal correctional facilities, anal rape, Luther raving about Momma's Jambalaya.

"Lucky you didn't go all the way," she turns to me, "cause if you tried to fuck me up the ass, I would've definitely had to say something."

I'm paralyzed in shock.

She's not scared--picks the half spilled beer from the floor, taking a big swallow, "Before any of you pricks think about chucking me over the balcony," she holds up her cellphone, "I left a very detailed message on my answering machine with names, details, and addresses. Amazing what you hear when you keep your mouth shut."

More silence.

"But I'm being rude," she finishes the beer, crumpling the can in her hand as she lets out a loud burp, "my name's Charity. Pleased to meet ya'."

Fifteen

I fight to keep my legs from shaking.

Charity bites on the end of her short cropped hair, "What planet you guys come from? People've been using Rufinol for years."

"H-h-how," stammers Derek, "have you been using it?"

"Take a 2 mg dose," she rolls her eyes, "add a snort of coke--shot of tequila and you're toast all night--cheap girl's party ticket. Of course after awhile you gotta up your dosage."

"Two milligrams," Derek is thinking out loud, "had no effect—you were conscious the whole time?"

"You must be the Professor," she turns to me, "and I know you're Gilligan. You guys are always so sloppy--"

"You've seen us before?" asks Derek.

"She has," I remember two times--

"All over the fucking place," with her foot, she traces out a tick tack toe sign in the spilled beer, "kind'a hard to miss ya drugging all those girls, walkin' em right out the bar. When you finally came up," she turns to me, "I knew the score, pretended to fall asleep. Let me give you boys a pointer: even if you've drugged someone, never use your real names."

"So you. . . pretended?" I'm sure Archie's head is still jumbled with visions of anal rape in prison. He's having trouble focusing and working through the black cocks stuffed in his face.

"You're not the quickest one, are you darlin'?"

Silence.

Derek's and Charity's eyes connect. I realize why he's so calm. He's already figured out what I just now know. She has no intention of calling the police.

"What do you want?" he asks.

"That should be clear," she sits on the counter, legs swinging, chewing on another lock of dark hair, "I want to join the club."

Derek winces as if the mere suggestion of such a thing is too ludicrous to even consider, "What's your name?" he asks as if he missed it the first time.

"Charity. And don't think I'm stupid enough to give you my last name. If you want a full name—call me

Sweet Charity," she continues gnawing on this lock of hair.

"Could you stop that?" I finally interject, "animals die from hairballs--"

Charity coughs like a cat spitting out a hair ball. Holding a cupped hand over her mouth, she spits up something into it and tosses it at me. But there's nothing there. She smiles, "Nobody gets out of here alive."

Great.

As if things couldn't get worse, we're being blackmailed by a morbid, hair eating junkie with a bad sense of humor. And she wants to join the clan! Does she even realize what she's proposing? I see it now—Archie and I struggling as we haul some brawny Gay Bear to the pool table so she can--whoa, hold on. What the hell can she do to him?

"You know what we do here?" inquires Derek.

"Don't have to be Einstein to figure out that."

"It isn't exactly a two way street," continues Derek, "how do you propose to perform the act--while your male subjects are unconscious?"

"I've my methods," she sighs, "anyway, I'm not too picky about gender."

"Whoa," Archie snaps open a fresh beer, working through the fear, "this is starting to get interesting."

Remember the Frank Sinatra group shot?

The Rat Pack photo with the three of us, strutting in slow motion side by side--dark suits, silver wolf's head pins on our lapels, dark sunglasses, carelessly tossing Martini glasses over our shoulder like we've just finished a long night's gig at The Sands Hotel. Well now we have to add a chick with identical sunglasses and a smart business skirt as she struts towards—

Stop!

"I am not wearing this shit!" screams Charity in the backseat.

"That's the uniform," Derek says firmly as he drives.

"Uniform? We're not fucking Menudo!" she tosses the dress out the window, "and where's my fucking wolf's head pin, huh?"

From the passenger seat, I glance at Derek, lips pursed, blowing out his top lip as he restrains emotions. Calmly, he pulls the Volvo on the side of Mulholland Dr. and turns around, "you get it when I say you do."

"I didn't vote you President. Look at yourselves. Men in Black is so passé. And you better want to make me happy," she leans forward, immune to his probing stare, "or it's Sing Sing for everybody," silence. All I can hear after that comment is Jimmy Buffet's Margaritaville faintly chiming over the radio. Charity suddenly gets an idea, "now that you bring up the point, I think we do need a uniform."

That's how we wind up here.

Do you see us? Standing next to the barrel full of peanuts? How the fuck can you miss it. We're the three idiots in Hawaiian shirts, wolf's head pins on our collars, and Bermuda shorts. The cheesy sports bar is all wood with NFL banners on the walls. The place is called Dublins and yes, as you've already figured out, it is not your standard, trendy LA hangout.

"Isn't this great?" Charity alternates between eating peanuts and chewing off a strand of her hair, "real people here—salt of the fucking earth."

When I shut my eyes and hear her speak, there's a morbid, biting tone to her voice. You almost expect to see a chick with dyed black hair, sporting a lot of spiked leather apparel. Yet when you open your eyes, she seems so cheery, white bread, middle America—except for the hair biting bit. Her toughness is tom-boyish—like the kind of girl that likes football games--

"I fucking hate football," she turns away from the game spread across TVs mounted all around the place. Mashed remnants of peanuts stick to the end of her hair. I guess there's no figuring her out overnight.

"A psychiatrist can help you with that," Derek finally adds, looking totally unnatural in his Hawaiian shirt filled with Toucans and sail boats.

She tosses a quarter at him, "Put a song on the juke box, Buffet Boy."

As you can see, there's a tension in the air. Charity and Derek are definitely fighting for control of our little social experiment. But for now, he's trapped. Without a trace of emotion he walks over to the juke box, disappearing in a crowd of faces. And somehow I know that that's when you have to be scared of what he could do.

Once he's gone, Charity happily scoops a handful of peanuts into her hand, "You guys are too into the Hollywood scene. When there's a whole other side to this city. You want reality. This is reality--real people--"

Just then the crowd parts and out of the corner of my eye I see Derek on the phone, speaking frantically into the receiver. He's not hiding his emotions, anger turning his face cherry red. The crowd forms again, breaking my view.

Charity rattles on like the Energizer bunny, pontificating her views on drugs and rape--in a bar where we will probably drug and rape, "If you're really going to do it, forget about the actresses--bunch of anorexic, plastic titted air heads. Who're you kidding? Three fifths of our race live in dire poverty where fucking's the only form of entertainment. Wanna' break the seal, go down the dark path? Gonna have to get your hands dirty. We need to be the Franklin Delano Roosevelts of rapists--

fucking the common people, janitors, taxi cab drivers, the postmen of the world."

"I'll keep you in mind when I'm voting for President," adds Derek as he returns, "until then--shut the fuck up about what we do--"

"Zeig Heil!" she launches a straight arm in the air as if saluting Hitler, spilling peanuts from her hands.

The night plays out as chummily as a bachelorette party. We drink Budweisers and are forced to shoot "Lemon Drop" shots. Why is it that women only drink hard alcohol when it's disguised as candy? It's like what Derek said—how they disguise things, like shrouding sex under a cloak of romance. Finishing my shot, I can tell that Derek wants to call the whole thing off. But Charity wants to continue the experiment--with her own additions to the rules of course:

"I mean," she picks hair out of her teeth, "why do we have to be so rude to these poor girls? Can't we just choose one and go for it without the insults?"

"Because those are the rules," answers Derek, stern as a concrete cinderblock, "and if you want to change them—well then, you're operating alone. Because if you do, we're going home now--without you."

Just then, an ESPN camera crew passes beside us, canvassing the reactions of fans who've watched the end of the game on the TV's. The on-air host is this fat guy in a maroon blazer--

"Fine," Charity flashes fangs at Derek and turns, tossing her glass of beer in the host's face. He stops, totally shocked, trying to make sense of what's happening, "just get the fuck away from me!" she hisses like a cat. Still confused, wiping beer from his eyes, he stumbles away. She turns back to us, "well, put him down on the list."

"Oh that's great," Derek mutters, "get us all on tape. Police will love that."

"Why Don't We Get Drunk and Screw" comes on the juke box as we hit on Loyola Law students, paralegals, secretaries, UPS clerks, off duty bartenders, Virgin Atlantic cargo supervisors, nurses, and some poor schmuck who sells ad space in a Vintage Baby Doll collecting magazine. In place of the conformist black attire of the penguins, this crowd sports their hearts on their sleeves, "Divers do it deeper," T-shirts covered with corporate logos like "UPS", colleges teams such as "The Wolverines"—

It's like being in a room full of bumper stickers.

I stake out the best looking blonde in the room. A short, fit girl with too much of a tan and an overly tight Laker shirt. The kind of girl Latinos and construction workers gawk at. She reminds me of a small mountain cat. As we start talking she blurts out:

"Are you Jewish?"

Well that's a new one.

"No," I fumble for witticism, "I'm Pagan."

Cocking her head at an angle, the mountain cat squints, confused, "What kinda' pagan?" empty eyes staring back at me. It's like talking to a wall.

"I'm . . .Greek Orthodox Pagan--pray to the gods of mythology like Zeus and Apollo—"

"Oh yeah," she claps her hands, excited to add to the conversation, "that black guy in the Rocky movies is named after him!"

"That's right. We sacrifice to him twice a week, Tuesdays and Thursdays--slaughter goats and dogs and. . . cats. Our back alley's as clean as a Chinese restaurant."

This shoots right over her head, "I'm an aromatherapist--really into incense," no shit—go figure, "is there a temple in Hollywood or Brentwood I can visit?"

"Yeah, but, I'll be right back," I turn as if just to get another drink. I keep walking. Yes that's right. You heard it from this guy first. I've found—

The girl too stupid to fuck.

The evening continues. Votes are finally cast. Of course Derek takes his sweet time, vetoing almost everyone. Our night of slumming ends with three fairly nondescript women and—well—

"I didn't ever think I'd grow up to do this," I stare down with disgust.

Archie's winces, adding, "Man, this is some fucked up shit."

At the far end of the alley, Derek pulls in with the Volvo, the headlights illuminating this poor son of a bitch, legs and arms sprawled across the mountain of green trash bags. His Arizona Sun Devils baseball cap obscures his face. We put it like that, unable to deal with looking at his drugged visage.

"Why'd she drug him?" wonders Archie, "never knew a guy who refused a proposition from a good looking girl."

"You think she's hot?" I ask.

"I mean," he scrutinizes him, "wouldn't kick her out of bed."

"You wouldn't kick anyone out of bed."

"And neither will she," Archie points at her victim's acid washed, ripped up jeans, "I think those are the same Levis Madonna's wore in that Like A Virgin video. I mean, you'd think she'd have picked that other guy. At least he had a tight ass."

This conversation is getting way too weird for me.

"C'mon," barks Derek, pulling up with the car full of women.

Charity sits in the front seat smoking a cigarette, watching us trying to force her "test subject" into the back seat.

"He's too big," I moan.

"That's what all the boys claim," she jokes.

"Put him in the trunk," barks Derek.

"And where," I ask, "will we go?"

Archie and I maneuver into the backseat with three women crammed between us, on top of us, and below—there's more tits in this picture than a bad Ron Jeremy porn. Only a cop with Mr. Magoo's eyesight could fail to pull us over. Struggling to shut the car door, the car's warning sounds out: "The Door is Ajar. . . the door is ajar--"

"It's not a jar, silly," one of the subjects laughs through drugged dementia, "it's a door."

The night doesn't get much better.

"Fuck this shit!" Derek explodes.

The three of us stand in our Hawaiian shirts and boxers, three stripped down women laying before us—a sea of bad tit jobs and wide haul hips crammed together. Because at the far end of the table, this poor bastard is stripped, laying face down because that's how we left him on the table. All you see is this hairy ass falling out of yellowing Fruit of The Looms.

Archie shakes his head, "I can't do it while I'm looking at this guy's hairy ass."

"What do you think we have to look at all the time?" Charity, stripped down to her faded black bra and panties that say "Eat Me" and sucks on a cigarette, "you guys get smooth, hairless bodies. What do we get? Flabby, ungroomed pubic areas and a big smelly old cock. Does a guy ever think to shower before he gets a blow job? No. And let me tell you, it gets ripe down there."

"Well that was enlightening," smirks Derek.

"And--what am I supposed to do now?" she peers down at the back of The Fruit of The Looms, "rub up against his ass cheek?"

"I'm gonna chuck you over the balcony!" explodes Derek, rushing at her.

I force myself between them, like a ref breaking up a fight. "Ow!" Charity's nail swipes across my cheek as she takes a swing at Derek, "Everybody fucking calm down!" I scream, "we're all in this together now."

"Guys," Archie calmly offers up, "we came here to rape, not to fight."

The surrealist nature of that statement sends us all into silence. Outside I hear a police chopper cruising across the expansive valley.

"Why don't we turn some romantic music on?" Archie walks over to the stereo.

"How about a little Buffet?" requests Charity as she looks at the three of us in our boxers and Hawaiian shirts, "make a theme night of it."

Archie and I laugh. I'll do anything to calm Derek down. All I can think about is the pistol he claims he found under the floorboards of the house. Flash—I can see him putting a bullet through her head. As Archie flips the drugged guy over, he burps—breaking my train of thought.

"There goes the foreplay," mutters Charity.

I steal a moment, whispering to Derek, "Tomorrow, I'll have a talk with her—"

"You better."

"I'll calm her down, alright? Just cool off."

He stares silently at the floor. And it frightens me because I've no idea what he's thinking. But he doesn't continue. Once again he's in the kitchen, drinking coffee.

Charity never takes off her bra or panties. Somehow, to my shocked surprise, she manages to get an erection out of her subject, "C'mon guys," she notices our look of shock, "the wind blows the wrong way and that fucker's up."

Straddling his legs, she pulls back the bottom of her panties and climbs on board, motioning up and down. But the poor bastard keeps loosing his erection. She finally excuses herself and retires to the bathroom for a few minutes—to finish the evening. It's when she comes out of the bathroom, red faced and weary, that I ask her to lunch the next day.

That night I dream my dream.

Now I'm sitting on the couch watching animal programs, sipping my eighth Martini, eating a little Humus and pita. Around me swarm an army of maids— Veronica, the Russian Girl with glasses--all mute, all clad in French Maid outfits. They silently wipe up the table, wash the glasses with glee, constantly serving me half-filled bottles of beer. Since they're half filled, I keep requiring more and they bring it without a word, heads bent low in deference like Japanese maidens. I could piss on the floor and they'd clean it up with a smile.

Then I hear it.

Someone's banging on the window. Through the glass, I glimpse Charity clad in an identical French Maid's outfit. On the opposite side of the glass, she stands on the balcony deck, banging her feather duster against the window. She's red faced, screaming something at me. I can't hear what she's saying.

The other girls turn for a moment, curiously studying her. Charity's going to fuck up the party. Then she vanishes. A moment later I hear her at the door, ringing the bell over and over. Hands over my ears, I try to ignore it. But the maids, ever so proper, move towards the door. I fight to stop them--

The doorbell keeps ringing.

Charity and I meet at Pinks on La Brea Blvd.

It's this run down hotdog stand. We sit in the back corner as I try to eat my double chili cheese dog topped off with bacon sprinklings. It's her favorite and all the cooks know her here—she's a fixture. Now I don't want to be a critic or steer you away from this place, but don't delude yourself by thinking that this bacon ever had the pleasure of being part of a pig.

Charity pulls her chair close. Swinging around to grab a bottle of Tabasco, I notice the lighter roots in her dark hair. It's only dyed dark. Dousing the hot sauce all over her food, she laughs and bites her hair. I feel as if she views me as the most sensible member of the group and perhaps her closest ally. The truth is that--

Charity scares me.

"What are you thinking?" she asks.

I voice my sentiments, "That I have no idea what you're thinking--that until you become a team player, until you see what we've seen, it's just going to be a game. And if you treat it like a game, we'll all get caught."

"What's it matter? Nobody gets out of here alive anyway."

"And what's that about?" I squint, "I mean, alright—so we're all gonna die. I'd rather live out the next forty years of my life out here rather than locked up in jail because you don't take this whole thing seriously."

"I do take it seriously."

"What do you get out of it?"

Changing the subject, she eyes her double chili dog dripping in hot sauce, "Reminds me of my boyfriend in college."

I don't know what to say. I never know what to say to her. I'm the Alpha Wolf. I fear no one. But around this woman, I feel like a Hal.

"Alright," she sighs, "I'll lay my cards on the table, tell you why I'm here."

She puts down her double chili dog, her smile turning to a serious scowl as she leans close, her words hanging in the air:

"What would you think if I said I was going to kill Derek Van Horn?"

Sixteen

Silence.

Charity studies me with expectant eyes--double chili cheese dog hovering over her lips. I'd like to think she's kidding, but her look is so serious. I know they fight for control of our group, but why would she threaten to kill Derek Van Horn?

"I would say you're crazy," I finally break away, cautioning that, "we're all crossing some very serious lines already—so I don't take this kind of joke lightly."

"Who said anything about a joke?" she glances away, biting into her hotdog.

"If you're going to kill him because of what we're doing—well, might as well kill Archie and me."

"I'm not concerned with that. I've even participated—partly."

"Then why would you want to kill him?"

She responds with another question, "Do you think some crimes can only be paid for with your life?"

"I think you're just another crazy LA chick."

"Maybe it's just been a long time since you met a person with scruples?" she stiffens in her seat, chomping on her hotdog, "do you know why Alpha Wolves don't cry?"

Because they're strong, I think to myself, but decide not to answer her ridiculous questions, merely asking, "Is being crazy your primary occupation?"

"That's just my day job," she laughs, entertained by the witticism, "during the evenings, I'm an actress--been doing it for awhile. I'm up for a really big role this week. There, now you know something."

"That isn't jack shit!"

She smiles, wiping her prior composure away.

And this infuriates me, "I used to have a boss like you. His name was Mo Simon—whacked out Hollywood agent who'd go manic on me all the time, smiling, making outrageous, random remarks. Back then it scared me," I sip my Coke, "but now I realize he—like you, was just more scared than I was."

"Maybe you're right," she takes another bite of the dog, brushing it all away.

"No," I shake my head, "you can't threaten to kill somebody and then say--oh never mind."

Chewing her dog, she responds through a mouthful of food. I can't understand. She repeats as she swallows the huge bite, "Why isn't he your boss anymore?"

"He fired me."

"Why'd he do that?"

"Because I used to be this fear filled little prick, scared of my own shadow. I let egg heads like him intimidate me--fire me. That's how I wound up with this crappy job I have," I laugh, "or did you think my life's dream was to be a tech support agent?"

She squints, confused, "But you're not scared anymore?" her question hangs in the air followed by her loudly sipping the last remnants of her Sprite.

"No. I'm not scared."

"Well then?" she probes deep into my eyes. I know what she's thinking without her saying it—nobody gets out of here alive--the question begs an answer.

I know what I have to do after lunch.

"I'm sorry sir, you can't--"

"Shut the fuck up," I grunt at the security officer as I storm through the lobby of International Talent Management. The ridiculous Calder statue casts a long shadow across the open elevator doors. The heels of my shoes click hard on the marble floor—the partners spent an ungodly amount to fly this crap in from Northern Italy. Before the guards can grab me, the elevator shuts and—

I march down the long hall of doors—it's just like when I was looking down at the tech support cubicles. This place is one giant Habitrail—those plastic mazes of tubes and cubby holes you bought for your hamsters. Assistants and junior agents poke their heads out like mice, sniffing out the source of the excitement. Even the two adolescent kids from the mail room clutch their mail cart like demur rodents, staring in shocked amazement.

Behind me, the security officer screams, giving chase. They're mice too—tiny, insignificant.

I'm the only human in this place.

Nothing can hurt me.

Turning the corner, junior agents stand in line in front of the office door, little mice rolling calls on their remote headsets--chattering on like schizophrenics conversing with imaginary people. The chattering stops. I fling my arm forward, knocking the rodents out of the way. The guard turns the corner, pistol in hand. These agents could stop me, but they're too shocked by what I'm about to do. That's right—

I'm barging into Mo Simon's office.

The Madagascar lemur's got his back to me.

Dr. Evil bounces on his blue rubber ball--bald head sweeping up and down, momentarily hiding Sean Connery's face on "The Hunt For Red October" poster on the far wall. I slam the door shut, locking it a moment before the security officers arrive.

The Lemur puts his caller on mute and bounces around, to view this interruption. Upon seeing me, his eyes light up with sadistic pleasure, "Crack addict! Didn't expect to see you again," he snaps back on his switch box, addressing his caller, "sorry Sigh, gotta send an outcast to jail. Yeah, I'll call you back."

Without a word, I sit in the same chair he berated me in months ago. The stupid John Wayne, Franklin mint statue towers over a pile of unopened mail. Security bangs even louder on the door. A second later and they're calling on his phone. I imagine the alarms going off at the Beverly Hills Police Department, SWAT teams rushing to ITM.

"How's the unemployed life treating you?" Mo folds his hands together.

He knows that in less than a New York minute I'm going to be dragged off to the Beverly Hills jail. Then from Spago's to The Ivy, everyone will be talking about how he bravely faced down this crazy nut-ball. But Mo doesn't know the new Cullen Gersh--The Alpha Wolf.

The phone continues to ring.

He mistakes my silence for indecision, "Crack Addict, let's get this over with," he reaches for the phone--

In a single motion, I grab the John Wayne Statue by the legs, flipping it around, employing it as a club, bashing the phone system apart. Plastic and metal fly. Mo plants both hands on his desk to keep from rolling off his ball. A second later his severed headset wire dangles uselessly around the French cuff of his Hilditch & Key shirt.

In the reflection of the glass top desk, my face takes on this Satanic quality, eyes squinting, face red, lips sputtering on raw energy, "For once, you're going to shut the fuck up and listen," I lean forward, able to smell the Armani cologne on his suit, "you are going to hire me on Monday of next week as a full agent on the fast track to the head of the department. If you don't, no guard or cop in the world will get rid of me.

I am not a crack addict. I'm a magna cum laude graduate of NYU law school. I know how to legally stalk you, ruin your life, poison your cat, field-dress your dog, fuck your wife up the ass while your two daughters watch, and then impregnate them! I'll do it legally and you'll never be able to stop me. You'll never know another calm, safe moment in your worthless life," I hit this crescendo of screaming, "AS I SPEND THE NEXT TWO DECADES MAKING YOU MY FUCKING BITCH!"

Silence—

Except for my heart and the guards pounding on the door. Power drills start up on the other side of the door.

They're trying to drill the hinges off. The lemur's eyes never leave mine. To us, there's just a tense silence. . . then the strangest thing happens--

He smiles.

Now you may not think this is a big deal. But I and most of the staff of ITM have never seen Mo Simon smile in our entire lives. Look at him—looks like Mr. Clean, this big bald head framing that shit eating grin. He's about to speak and then stops, a cupped hand over his lips as he carefully phrases his response and then, "You got the goods!" he waggles a happy finger at me.

This isn't what I expected, but it's a step in the right direction.

Walking around the desk, he pats me on the back like a father to his son, "Never knew you had it in you, kid. You've got big brass balls racing in here. And that threat—well, fucking writers couldn't have scripted better lines. Make me your fucking bitch—it gave me chills. You were ready to donate twenty years to make my life miserable. That's fucking dedication!" he points to the black and white photo of the founder of ITM as he says, "Morris Lepke would be proud to have you as an agent--"

Just then, the door collapses.

The security guards and cadre of rubber necking agents are just as shocked as I am. Standing in the middle of the room, Mo Simon embraces me. At the sight of their shocked expressions, he suddenly laughs. Then I'm laughing. And this is how after 18 of the worst months of my entire life—

I become an agent at International Talent Management.

Things are going great.

I get my own office with a tiny view of Wilshire Blvd. After the first staff meeting, heads no longer turn. I'm introduced by Mo, arm still around my shoulder, the son he never had. He gives me a handful of starter clients. Next thing I know, I'm rolling calls like crazy, taking lunches, dinners, and drinks with up and coming managers and agents.

"Hey big shot," Derek telephones me midweek, "how's it back in the land of the living?" in the background rings the tap—tap—ding--strange to hear such things as I sit in the confines of my office, as if he's calling from another planet.

"Fine," I answer.

"Could you get me four tickets to a film premier next Thursday? Boarding school friends of mine are coming into town."

I think of a bunch of Abercrombie and Fitch guys in croquet sweaters--curiosity's peaked, never heard Derek talk about any of his friends, "Sure," I say, wondering if he'll let us meet them?

By Friday I'm swamped with work. It's almost like I never left—like I was simply promoted to full agent after a delayed sick leave. Now a new set of challenges materialize. Work sucks up my days—hours and hours of phone calling. I take a young kid from the mail room as an assistant--and no, I don't abuse him.

"Hey big guy," a knock at my office door. The room is still bare except for my desk, phone, and chair and a box of files on the floor. Claryssa sticks her head in, "too much of a big shot to take an alley break?"

Sun plays through tree branches.

Popping open a Coke, I peer down, searching for the line of ants Claryssa mashed under her heel. But they're long gone—even the cigarettes have been wiped away by the wind or a janitor's broom. It doesn't seem like the same alley.

Claryssa lights a cigarette, leaning back against the fence, frizzy black hair falling over her eyes. I realize it's not the alley that's changed, it's us. Claryssa's job once seemed so grand, an escape from the mailroom, an upward spiral towards agent. Now it's merely the purgatory between the basement and offices.

I'm now the superior figure.

"It's 'cause you're a guy," she exhales, blowing smoke rings through a beam of sunlight--the smoke curling and spinning in the God's light--a Hallmark card for nicotine addicts, "you get fired and then storm back in and make full agent. Most everyone thinks Mo staged the whole thing—to keep everybody on their toes," she laughs.

It's that sarcastic laugh you give to your friends--the one that conceals the knife of bitter feelings under a shroud of harmless humor. Sarcasm is the last refuge of the passive aggressive. Once again I think about what Derek said--how women hide everything.

Claryssa's nervous. It's not just my promotion. I'm different now, not that scared little kid running to her for strength and advice. Even my shadow towers over her, sweeping back down through the cool alley. I don't pull my eyes away, but play chicken-- my gaze locked with hers.

She turns away first, "So what's the secret?"

"To what . . . the job?"

"No, the whole thing," she sucks back on the cigarette, "you vanish, leave without calling—disappear. Now you're back with this new confidence thing?"

I grin. If she only knew the secret to my success, "Just have to focus on yourself and realize the rest is just an illusion."

Claryssa smiles, like she's solved some riddle.

It's one of those gestures that words can't easily describe. It's her way of getting the upper hand. I know that if I ask what's so funny, she's going to accuse me of becoming one of them--the rich fucks, another one of the morally bankrupt Mo Simons of the world. That's how she's going to write me off. But she doesn't get it. She can't distinguish between the fake and the genuine article.

I'm not going to let her grandstand.

So I just stay there, waiting as she smiles and smokes her cigarette. Flash—I imagine Claryssa, naked on the pool table-- her breasts, the genuine articles, falling over the sides of her chest. I bet she doesn't trim her pubic hair. Then I suddenly realize that I don't have those violent spasms anymore. My flashes are all sexual and reassuring as if--

A car alarm sounds in the distance, breaking my train of thought. This break has lasted far too long. I realize I'm never going to take another one with Claryssa.

That's all behind us now.

Charity and I start hanging out a lot.

And no--I'm not trying to screw her. Does everything with you have to be about sex? She's easy to be with. My job sucks up most of my after hours—Archie's working weekends downtown at Prudential—he got promoted. Derek's trapped himself in his room doing who knows what as we hear tap—tap—ding! She's the only member of the group I can spend time with. The next week, I get my first big paycheck. I turn around and write a big check to my credit card company who I owe more than what most Indonesian men make in four lifetimes. But there's light at the end of the tunnel. I know that soon, in the foreseeable future, I'll be able to buy that second beer.

"When I was a little girl," Charity tells me as she turns her car onto Sunset, "I hated the mole on my cheek— looked like an ungainly spot. I spent hours and hours trying to rub it out--to cover it up with my mom's makeup. I would've gotten a skin graft if I could've. But then one day, I woke up and, it was just a mole. . . just a mole on my cheek."

Silence---the air rushing through the open car windows.

"What the fuck are you talking about?" I ask.

"You could . . .dress a little nicer—that's all."

As if I should've figured that out from her demented little monologue. I study my pinstriped suit, "Looks fine to me."

"It ain't workin' buddy, unless you're gonna sell some used cars."

"If nobody gets out of here alive--what the hell's it matter how I'm dressed?"

"My son," she pats me on the back, "let me begin your education."

She takes me to Barney's men's department.

She instructs me on style. We study clothes—the fabrics, the weaves, but buy nothing. Now I know that looking at her black biker jacket and jeans ensemble, you wonder what she could she possibly know about fashion. But she knows a lot--taught me how to spot a hand-crafted suit from a machine made--for those of you with lesser sartorial skills, look for the stitching around the lapel and the real button closures on the sleeves. The word sartorial means "of or relating to tailored clothes". I can't tease anybody about that one—had to look it up myself.

"Where'd you learn about clothing?" I ask her.

"My Dad was a sharp dresser," she folds a piece of worsted English 100's wool in her hand and opens it, seeing how it holds the wrinkles. She says nothing more about him.

In fact, she divulges nothing about her personal life at all. She's as intriguing as Derek in many ways. Riding around in her beat up Volkswagen Jetta, the bumper crushed into the back of the trunk, I search for any clue about her background. But all I see are spent Marlboro Red cartons, a Homer Simpson key chain, and discarded Diet Coke cans--it's like Sanford and Son on wheels.

"So why don't Alpha Wolves cry?" I repeat the question she once posed to me.

She brakes the car at a stoplight, "Smart boy like you should've figured out that."

What a strange person she is—almost like I'm talking to a façade of a person who comes from wealth, trying her best to hide it. I wonder if I've met the real Charity. She is an ever changing puzzle of a person.

Person.

Notice I don't describe her as a girl or a woman? While we're at the light, she spots a cage full of puppies. Dragging me in, she hugs the puppies and kittens, cooing to them in a sweet baby voice, "Isn't this one cute?" she turns to me, snorting out her strange signature laugh.

I get nauseous. The pet store spins around me. I'm so uncomfortable I have to leave, grabbing a drink of water at the Starbucks next door. Then it hits me. It's easy to be with Charity when I think she's one of the guys, but to see her feminine side frightens me. I've been dehumanizing women into mere sexual objects for so long that to see any of them any other way is terrifying— especially a fellow partner in crime. Back in the car, she senses I'm troubled. But I don't talk about it. That pisses her off. She can't stand not being a member of the gang.

"I think you're the one who's afraid," she chews on her hair, a reminder of the unsteady nature of her personality, "afraid men and women are very much the same."

"What? C'mon," I get to roll my eyes, "you've never finished the act when you're with us! We're friends, but face it, you're a fish out of water when it comes to this."

The thought of her not being part of the gang infuriates her, "I get off seeing naked people—but not the way you guys do. And why? Because you were raised with titty magazines--guys getting off like dogs in back alleys. You're playing out rolls you've jerked off to—pure, socialized fantasies, my friend."

"Maybe it's biology?" I counter, "maybe a woman just can't understand because she's made differently?"

"I'm so tired of that crap," she rolls her eyes, "the bullshit argument that we're genetically different. History's shown that in countless societies, men and women cross gender roles. For instance, the Greeks were all gay--"

"But overall, there's commonality."

"Because little boys and girls are socialized differently from birth. We get pink blankets, you blue--we get baby dolls, you guns--doesn't mean we're born different. We mimic our parents—our culture," she gnaws at her hair.

"Where'd the socialization come from? Face it, Charity, it's biology. I mean women were made to be monogamous--men to spread their seed--"

"That's utter crap!"

"You're living proof of it. You never participate with us, never finish--"

"Fine," she slams her brakes, squealing to a stop in front of a fire hydrant, "wait in the car," she slams the door, disappearing into this store called 667 Santa Monica--the logo below reading "Just one digit away from hell." Peering through the front window I notice mannequins straddled over each other, decked out in leather and spikes with black strap on devices.

Seventeen

Thursday night, Charity goes nuts.

For the first time she sheds her clothes. We're now all naked, screwing our four test subjects on the pool table—a Latin girl and two brunettes. The room smells of sex—echoes of drugged moaning and our grunting, the slapping of testicles against asses—hands fastened tight around hips. On the far side of the table, Charity goes insane, moving and flexing her ass back and forth, grinding against her female test subject.

"Now that's what I call an improvement," smiles Archie.

All eyes are drawn to her--sweaty, red face as she leans over, sucking on her test subjects breasts. Her eyes are filled with emotion. She looks enraptured in the act and at the same time consumed with self-hate, maybe even guilt—like she's ready to cry and laugh at the same time. Despite this inner conflict, one thing is true. She's now part of the clan.

When she's finished, she turns to me, grunting angrily—as if I made her do it, "Take your biology and shove it up your ass."

The rest of them laugh. Because they don't see what I see--

Tap—tap—tap—ding!

So here we sit.

It's not like the Frank Sinatra shot, but pretty close. We're at Ago's restaurant, a trendy Italian place--all stone floors and exposed ducts and ceiling. Penguins and flamingos move in slow motion in front of you, shaking hands, hugging, trying to break the ice, bidding each other hello and goodbye. The sound's off. So you see their lips move, but all you hear is Beethoven's "Ode to Joy" flowing over the building's speaker system.

Then the crowd parts for a second.

You glimpse us, sitting at the bar as we watch them pass, our tiny pins reflecting back light--Archie, me, Derek, and Charity—matching dark sunglasses, pinstripe suits--and an evening dress for Charity. It's the only thing she'd agree to. We're the only ones in color as we nurse our single beer and stare through this illusion.

Look pretty tough, don't we?

A blonde hostess crosses our line of vision--freeze frame her, menu cupped under her arm—we could lay her under the Carlsberg Beer lamp. The brunette in the corner with the TV producer—freeze—we'd put her on all fours, fuck her up the ass. The brunette toying with her lover de jour at the bar—freeze—we'd pour Armagnac all over her and lick it up from her tits to her twat.

We drive our beat up Hondas and broke down Jettas, cracked windshields and crushed bumpers. We buy our suits on the sale rack at The Men's Warehouse and Barney's airplane hangar sale. We sport our one pair of black shoes every day of the week. With the exception of Derek, our bank accounts are empty--credit cards maxed out. We drink our one beer and can't afford a pizza. Yet to us, these women are the French Maids of my dreams. This is how it is at the apex. We can have, hold, fuck, suck, and do whatever we want to anyone in this restaurant. . . anyone in that bar next door. . . anyone in this city. . . anyone in the whole fucking world—including you and your mom and your sister and everyone else you know.

We fear nothing.

We are members of the most exclusive group in the world.

The Clan of The Alpha Wolf.

And the world is our bitch.

"So good to see you," the owner grips my hand.

You don't notice his wide face and gray hair—just that massive, red nose overtaking his face like that spore thing in Alien. His name tag reads "Rudolph". How ironic life can be. Dapperly dressed in a smart, Zenya chalk stripe suit, he greets each of the guests with a limp handshake as we enter the gallery.

"Hope he fucks better than he shakes hands," Charity giggles to me, "did you see that nose."

Look around.

It's one of those swanky art galleries on Rodeo Drive. One of our writer clients is also a painter. It's kind of required that all the junior guys show their face at this private showing. I know--your eyes are already following the red carpet into the crowd, trying to figure out where everybody got their little plastic cup of free champagne--

"It's amazing what these tasteless people out here consider art," mutters Charity like a baroness of style. I feel uncomfortable in this formal setting. But I can tell Charity's been raised around it. She moves through the crowd, unfettered and free.

She looks pretty good, huh? Wearing makeup and a real evening dress, she uses just the right amount of jewelry. Hair's straight and shiny, don't even notice the spot she's gnawed out--she's stunning in a modern, sort of urban way, like those dour, pale faced models you see in a Calvin Klein ads.

She catches me staring at her and stiffens--the tomboy who's suddenly realized her tits draw attention, "Don't get any ideas, buster. I still remember who was gonna rape me--"

"Jennifer," an older woman smiles, skin drawn tight--gray hair, emaciated--the veins of her neck sticking through skin as if some torture device lays beneath her silver and black evening dress. The wife of some wealthy guy—she is an example of what happens to the flamingoes in their autumn years, "how are you doing darling?"

Charity pauses for a millisecond, a computer loading a new program. Then there's a confused smile, "I'm sorry. . . but do I know you?"

"But Jennifer, darling," her voice sounds like Worth Avenue and Rodeo drive mixed into one.

"My name is Charity."

The woman opens her eyes wide as if awakening from a dream, "I'm so sorry," she giggles, "thought you were someone else—a friend of the family," she holds up her empty champagne flute, "must be the Bollinger talking."

"Funny old lady," Charity rolls her eyes as the woman leaves, the flowing gown hovering over the tiled floor as she disappears into the crowd. I wonder if Charity's lying—if she really knew that woman, "What?" she grins at me, "you waiting for me to start gnawing on my hair? I don't know her, Cullen," she sighs, "so go do your stupid Hollywood thing so we can get the hell out of here--don't have much time."

I glance at my watch, knowing that it's Thursday--we have about thirty minutes before we meet up with the gang at Il Picolino, an Italian restaurant on Beverly. When I look up, Charity's gone. A full band assembled on the stairs starts playing "I Did It My Way." I search for Charity amongst the faces, meandering through huddles of conversations and easel propped canvases. Charity taps me on the shoulder. I turn and--

My heart skips a beat.

It's not Charity.

"I'm sorry," she smiles. I'm staring at possibly the most gorgeous woman I've ever seen--tall, blonde hair swept up into this hairdo high over her head, "I saw you from over there in the corner," her words flow through me like electricity. I study her body without tearing my eyes from hers--admiring her sweeping neck and elegant evening gown. No plastic tits here--no implants or severe, shaved down mandibles. Just soft features, pure and clean. She reminds me of Grace Kelly in Rear Window.

"You look so familiar," she says, "did we. . . did we go to college together?"

"Where'd you go?"

"Vanderbilt," her voice smooth—like silk.

"Wish I did," I smile, "I went to Columbia--but my cousin went to Vandy. . .back in the 70's—so," I stammer like a fool, "guess you missed him."

"Interesting," she points at the silver Wolf's head pin on my lapel, "corporate logo?"

"Of sorts."

Sipping champagne from a long stemmed glass, not plastic, she suddenly reminds me of the woman in that old Tattinger poster--you'd know the poster if I showed it to you.

"So what brings you to this dreary affair?" she sighs.

"I—well. . . my firm reps one of the painters."

"Oh," her eyebrows rise, the look of interest, "you're an art agent?"

"Afraid not. I'm the one nobody likes--a motion picture agent."

She nods her head . . . if we were in the country, you'd hear crickets--

"But," I fight the awkward pause—the indicator of the end of the conversation, "I like art. I mean—well. . . I took art appreciation in college."

This makes her laugh, "And what do you think of this art?"

Scan the painting next to us, all this oil paint smeared across the canvases, "Looks like when my old Crayola crayons melted in the sun—no seriously, don't laugh. See the color here? That is definitely Burnt Sienna mixed with--"

"No, it's Sierra brown."

"Was that even a crayon?"

"Of course."

"Must be from the big pack."

"The one that had the sharpener?"

"Ah, El Grande. That was too rich for my blood," I chuckle, "and that sharpener was shit—just broke the tip off your crayons."

"But if you didn't have the big pack, you didn't get the flesh colors." Notice how her eyes wrinkle in the corner when she smiles—pretty cute, huh? "if you don't have the flesh colors, you have to color people in yellow. That doesn't work."

"Unless you're Chinese. Maybe in China, they don't ship the flesh colors?"

"I don't think anyone's that yellow," she giggles and extends a graceful hand. "But I'm being rude. My name is Eloise Preston."

"I'm Cullen Gersh," and then the weird moment--like we're meeting again. Because all the time we spent together thus far doesn't count because we didn't know each other's' names. Her champagnes almost finished. So I realize another way to keep the conversation going, offering to escort her to the bar for a refill.

My heart races as I navigate us through the sea of people. Eyes follow us, but they're admiring Eloise's striking form. I'm nervous as a schoolboy around her—where'd that come from anyway? Are schoolboys really that nervous? Screw it. I'm the Alpha Wolf, I remind myself, resolving to vanquish fear as we stand at the bar.

"This showing is crap," I confide to her, "never really been into art. But, ah, what do you do?"

"I'm an art curator."

"Wow--that's—well," my eyes never leave her. I have to rebound quick, "I just put my foot in my mouth. You know, I did take art appreciation in college—Italian classics and all."

"I like that you look me in the eyes," she confides, "most men don't. You have a lot of confidence--"

"Cullen," Charity, empty champagne glass in her hand, breathlessly charges in, "was looking all over for you!"

Talk about an inopportune moment. Eloise's smile stays planted on her face, but her eyes turn away from me, studying Charity, wondering if this is my girlfriend or wife. Charity doesn't help. She couldn't give a shit about what anybody thinks.

"Eloise, this is my friend," I stress the word friend as I add, "Charity."

"What a beautiful name," Eloise sips her champagne, "what's your last name?"

"That is my last name. Sweet is my first name. . . Sweet Charity. Sounds like a porn star, huh?" she makes that snorting sound again as she laughs. When compared against Eloise, Charity suddenly seems so loud to me.

I snap the valet card in her face, "Why don't you bring the car around?"

"Yessam'," she mimics some stereotypical, Southern black servant, "wanna' Mint Julep too, Massa Gersh?"

I'm relieved as she strolls away with the ticket. Turning, I explain that, "She's a friend of a friend of a roommate --spent some time in the rest home," I whisper, "we try to get her outside--fresh air and all. I don't want you to think we're dating."

She's still smiling, "You've made that pretty clear."

"So," the hands of time clicking away—I finally add, "are you alone . . . here?"

A pause and then, "Yes."

"Would you mind if I asked for your number? I know being a busy art curator--"

"Do you have a pen?"

"Sure!"

"Cullen's in love," teases Charity.

I turn the Honda onto Beverly, "Shut up."

"Didn't look so confident around her, did you--big Alpha Wolf?"

I try to look tough. But inside my heart's flying. Honest. I feel this lightness in my chest. My mind keeps returning to that first image of Eloise, the elegant woman—because she's not a girl, sipping her champagne. Champagne, how fitting is that?

Charity sings:

> "Cullen and Eloise,
> sittin' in a tree,
> r-a-p-i-n-g--"

"Do you think you're being funny? Because you're not," I'm suddenly hot. Turn on the air conditioner. Before I realize what I've done, the stench filled air rushes through the car, spraying drops of foul condensation all over us--

"Jesus H. Christ!" Charity covers her nose with her hand as she fumbles for the window, "what'd you do! Piss in the fucking vents?"

"It's the filter--need to change it."

I do need to fix it. I need to buy some of the clothes Charity picked out for me. I need them if I'm going to look good on a date--a real date which doesn't necessitate the use of pharmaceutical agents. I think of the myriad of points I will complete--as Eloise's number burns a hole through my pocket.

I call her.

OK. . . so you're not surprised. Before you start teasing me like Charity, let me stress that I waited three days before telephoning. I got her answering machine. Don't you love when that happens on a first call? It's always more casual, you can leave a message and get them to call you back—everyone's sort of prepped and ready.

Probably wondering how I can afford a date? It's true that my personal estate is about as liquid as M.C. Hammer's--won't be able to pay off my Visa card debt in time for a possible dinner, unless she's not free until next year. But hey, I'm the confident Alpha Wolf. I'll worry about that problem when I get there. She calls me back the next day. We talk about the only topic we share: the art gallery party. Turns out she left early. We're on the verge of resorting to pregnant pauses and discourses about the weather when I blurt out:

"How about dinner?"

"Dinner?" she pauses--my heart sinks--then, "I'm free on Wednesday."

"That'd be great. Where do you want to go?" I wince, hoping she doesn't pick Le Dome or Spago's. I'm on a shoestring budget.

"Well," she pauses, "you pick."

"LA's got a lot of places. I need some criteria to make the decision," shit! Why'd I say that? Just when I succeeded, I give her another chance to pick an expensive place!

"Just as long as it's under the stars," she says, "I'd like to sit outside for a change."

A smile covers my face, "I happen to know the perfect place."

That's how we wind up here.

Stop and take in the moment. Big band songs spread through the air like curling smoke. Stars dance through a reddish, LA night sky. Eloise smiles at me, beautiful with blonde hair pinned up high over her head. Her eyes glisten at me as she brings the straw between perfect red lips, sipping her supersized Coke.

That's right baby.

We're at The Mini-Mac.

Behind her, the boom box playing Mack The Knife skips a beat. The bum doesn't care, he's finally shut up about government conspiracies, pacified on the supersized fries I bought him. Above us all, the golden arches glow down on us--pretty sweet, huh?

Who said you had to be rich to be charming.

"I love this song," Eloise smiles.

"Why?"

"All my life at balls and parties, always found myself dancing to it. Then one night, I actually listened to the words. It's about a man who kills and rapes men and women, slicing their throats—dumping them into the river. I find it funny—all these society ladies doing the box waltz, oblivious to the gruesome words floating through their heads."

Eloise keeps talking. She's an art restorer at the Getty Museum. And no, she stresses, she never wants to be an actress. As I listen I try to place what animal she is, but I can't. She continues with her life's summary--after Vanderbilt, she attended graduate art school at the Courtauld in London, then a fellowship at a frame shop in London.

"So you're not from around here?" I ask before biting into my double hamburger.

"My dad was in international finance," do you hear that lyrical quality to her voice, "I was born in Manhattan--for the first six years, lived in The Plaza Hotel--"

"Hence Eloise."

C'mon, I hope you remember the kid's books.

"Yes," she plops a fry in her mouth, "it's true. I'm the only woman you'll ever meet named after a cartoon character. I was baby Eloise in the Plaza. Then I was Eloise in the Crillon in Paris, Connaught in London, Ritz in Madrid. Sounds very romantic, not exactly a place to raise a child."

"Get room service whenever you want."

"Always the new girl at the local American School—if you're lucky enough to have an American school. You never fit in foreign countries. You're a stranger in your own country. Foreign diplomats' kids grow up like that. They call them displaced lunatics."

"How'd you handle it?"

"Lost myself in art—easy to do in Europe where the past haunts you."

"Haunts?"

"In Rome, near the Borghese Gardens, we lived in a 600 year old apartment, built in the early 1400's—before Columbus discovered America. We lived there for six years. My parents owned the place, but I never felt like it was ours."

"But you traveled around a lot and--"

"No. It wasn't that," she stares through me into space, "as a little girl, I'd sit in my room ruminating on all the people that had lived and danced and died in those rooms. To me, it looked like Grand Central Station--filled to the brim with people of different dress and ages. And one day I realized I'm just one of them--a renter, soon to be consigned to the same dust. Haunting is the only word to describe it. History permeating the entire culture, emphasizing the fleetingness of our lives. I think that's why Europeans aren't as into money, why they stress the pleasures of the moment—eating, drinking, dancing."

I imagine a young Eloise, blonde haired and skinny legged, brooding in those dark rooms, alone and quiet. There's something very sad and endearing about it--

The bum behind us farts.

Suddenly I hear the squealing brakes and sounds of traffic, the beating police chopper streaking by overhead, returning to reality, "Yeah," I gesture to the plastic and brick cubicle of the Mini Mac, "this is probably the oldest landmark around here—not much to haunt you."

"That's what I like about America," Eloise wipes her lips with a napkin, "I wonder if we aren't lucky not to have all that history? We invest an importance in the now that really doesn't exist. I mean, this is the future."

Don't know about you, but, "You just lost me."

"Look out your bedroom window sometimes--a sea of buildings, gravel roofs, satellite dishes, billboards--skyscrapers in the distance. In the sky, jets make final approaches. Sometimes, for a second, I see this world as someone from my apartment back in the 1400's would—as the wondrous, futuristic, wild future we live in and just consider as the present."

"You have this way," I tell her, "of making everything. . . I don't know--poetic."

"You're kind—the first nice man I've met in this town."

Suddenly her smile and laughter don't seem so euphoric, but more like a protective façade. I sense she spends a lot of time alone in her apartment in LA just like in Rome. She's almost created her own universe out of antiques and archives.

"You've been hurt out here?" I ask.

She silently nods her head.

"How?"

"I've never seen men behave the way they do here--come up, boasting about their jobs as producers and directors and writers. When the truth is they're all a bunch of poor, struggling kids trying to look rich."

"That would be me too."

"No," she's serious, "I moved here because I was engaged to a lawyer who lives here. Then I found out he was screwing half the town, perpetrating at bars that he was a movie producer. It's so clichéd an outsider wouldn't believe it's true. I hated myself for being so dependent and stupid."

"Everybody sort of falls in love with someone?"

"My mother always said a woman is nothing without her independence."

"Well there are other guys out here."

"How about this? The night I break up with him, I'm driving around, panic stricken. I call a girlfriend of mine who pleads with me to stop at a bar--place on Sunset where she's going. We'll meet and talk. I'm standing there, crying, trying to drink a beer when these two weirdoes approach. The first one introduces himself, shakes my hand and then licks it," I imagine this little grease ball penguin licking his hand, "when I turned away, the other one wraps his hands around my neck, telling me how he could strangle me. So I'm crying and then to make matters worse, this third guy starts rubbing against me. I yell at him and he's about to hit me--that's a night out on the town in LA."

"It's why you hesitated when I asked you to dinner?"

"It's one of the reasons why I'm moving as far from here as I can."

"You've had some bad experiences."

"I'm not the only one. Have you ever met a girl who wasn't 23, wanted to be an actress, and had been out here 6 months? They all have the same story. Where are the 25 or 27 year olds? They're not here. Because this town eats them up and spits them out on a monthly basis."

"Never thought about it that way."

"The cliché of the greasy producer, the nasty lowlife movie guy with gold chains who wouldn't get into a bar in New York, he lives here. LA is the zoo of walking clichés. These young girls from the heartlands are thrown into the mix. So broke they have to pay the rent with nude photos or soft porn in the Valley."

"It's not easy for a guy either," I stop--I'm walking on thin ice, "but I see your point. Let's talk about happier things."

That night we walk along Ocean Avenue.

Palm trees punctuate a splendid view of the ocean. Everything feels different when I'm with Eloise. All those stupid romantic plots screenwriters construct in melodramas seem so real—my heart actually feels light. Dropping her off at her apartment, she agrees to a second date.

"I'm going on a business trip to the MET until next Monday," she says--for those of you from Montana, The MET is the Metropolitan Museum of Art—for those of you from South Dakota, that's in New York City. I can't believe I'm going to have to wait another week. We agree to go out that following Tuesday.

I turn to give her a peck on the cheek. I guess she was expecting a kiss on the lips. It's an awkward moment as my lips wind up touching near her ear. Only as I skip down the steps, does it hit me. Being around her really is like being in a movie.

Eighteen

I'm walking on air.

The next day, I wear the same suit just so I can smell the remnants of Eloise's perfume against the cloth. I feel empowered and euphoric at the same time. It's like nothing can hurt me now. I feel more complete than I've ever felt in my entire life.

That night we go to Lush.

A nightclub in Santa Monica--you know the drill, same dim lights, penguins, flamingoes, gay bears, and overpriced drinks. We straggle in, pins on our collars-- The Clan of The Alpha Wolf, on the prowl.

"This is getting so tiring," Charity moans, "where are the common people of the world. All I see are the same clubs. If we keep it up, we're gonna wind up raping the same people."

"For now, we keep it here," Derek is firm, "I'll work on new venues."

"I have an idea," Charity's eyes suddenly sparkly, "why don't we break convention? I'll share a girl with someone--"

"I'm in!" Archie throws up his hand.

They set off as a duo, looking to get slapped by a flamingo after asking if they can "share her". Derek runs through the Asian constituency in the back corner, slaps and drinks flying. When asked to pick a candidate, I don't go for a blonde, but chose brunettes. Derek raises his brow at this:

"I feel like a little variation," I say, "just turning things up a notch."

"I can't fucking believe it," bemoans Charity, "Arch and I didn't get shot down once. What? Is this whole fucking city bisexual?"

They finally find a heterosexual flamingo who refuses to be broken. And me? There's something germinating inside me, so small that words can't describe it. Do I feel conflicted as I hit on these women? No. I see my life as a simple compartmentalized landscape. I'm the Alpha Wolf, building my strength, doing what makes me great. Then why don't I pick a blonde? Do they remind me of Eloise? I don't know why. Hell, most of the time we don't know what we're feeling or why we do things.

She laughs at me, curling her lips—as if to say: if we were the last two living organisms on earth, she would not consider me. Little fucking bitch. I smirk, walking away, already able to picture it:

"Yes! Yes! Yes!" she moans.

She really is beautiful with strikingly rigid features and short cropped black hair. Her breasts are large and fake—notice how hard they are to the touch. And she didn't bikini wax her patch of pubic area—a mound of hair. Still, I can't get over how tight her waist is, running my fingers around her like a connoisseur admiring art. When I slide my fingers around her anus, she moans with glee—so I keep doing it and then put something else in-- the smell of her perfume wafting through my nostrils.

"Yessss," she moans, face pressed into the pool table.

Usually when I'm doing this, my mind is clear—devoid of thought. But tonight I wax poetic as I stare at her face, pressed sideways against the pool table. Where are you, I wonder? Our perspiring stomachs make that farting sound. Run my hand under her chest, caressing her breasts. She shudders--was that an orgasm or an exclamation? Questions flow. Where are you now? Are you with your boyfriend, your boss, your professor—or is it darker—are you with your father or girlfriend or some faceless fantasy?

Or are you with me?

"Tell me my name?" I whisper in her ear as I push in and out of her.

The response is only rushed breathing--her beating heart against mine. A final thought enters my head as I finish--maybe you're just alone in darkness?

"You're only supposed to have one," I say, "always keep the beer half filled."

Charity probes me with concerned eyes, "Listen sport," she points at her empty Corona long neck, "it's empty—so I'm gonna have another."

We're back at El Torito, the old Beverly Hills stomping ground Archie, Hal and I used to visit. The smell of nacho chips and chimichangas fill the air. The bar, a favorite of the just after 5 crowd, is now completely empty—the handful of waitresses on the far end of the bar, staring at us with weary eyes. I wave to them. They don't respond:

"Friends of yours?" inquires Charity.

"Not quite," then I explain the tradition of one beer and all the free chips and salsa you can digest.

"Tradition is the crowning of kings--that's just plain cheap," she rolls her eyes, "you guys must've been fat woofing down all those carbs."

Turning, I glance at the bar across the street. It's not Thursday—the women we used to watch aren't there--the table now filled with three middle aged guys in suits. How long ago that life seems now, I muse. Glancing down at my one beer and plate full of chips, I realize how stuffed I am. Pretty good for $3.75, huh? And yet a new energy runs through my veins. I'm so excited I can't restrain myself:

"I've never been this happy," I explain, "I have a place for lust and another for--" I catch myself and stop.

"Love," Charity accuses, "you were going to say love."

"No, I wasn't."

"What then? One place for lust and another for-- conveniently holding your one Corona?" she finishes off her beer and winces at me-- a painter searching a portrait for a flaw, "is this where we start playing the romantic French music?"

"I think it's where you tell me that you don't believe in love."

"Bullshit. All people believe in love--five seconds before they cum," she giggles, "suddenly Cullen's in love.

Most of the time, you guys don't know what you're feeling."

"Must be our biological programming," I return to our old debate.

"Ugh," she rolls her eyes, "not that again."

"And you're enjoying yourself with what we do?"

And again, for a single moment, I glimpse the conflict within her, "Never in my wildest dreams did I expect it to feel the way it does," I feel that this is coming from the heart: "it's like being in a beautiful restaurant, but the food is bland."

"And Confucius say, he who eat crayons, fart in Technicolor," I guffaw.

"No, serious—there's some excitement to it, but the test subjects are drugged—lights off, no one home. Nothing to share. It's like fucking a hole in the wall."

"What about the power of it?"

"Big deal, so you control someone. So what? Are women like charging bulls that can't ever be captured? No. Hell, they're at those clubs to meet guys—they're looking for romance and love. What we do has the same amount of power as killing a deer."

"You've hunted Bambi?"

"My dad was a gamesman. I've trophy hunted. Let me tell you, it ain't too sporting. You're eight feet from a deer, rifle pointed at him. The deer's staring back at you, cause he's a deer—doesn't know what your gun is or what you're gonna do to him. There's no valor in it, barely a sense of power. The odds aren't the same—fight isn't equal. It's more like shooting fish in a barrel."

But that's what I find so exciting! No strings attached, no responsibilities, no one to answer to--like prowling through your own dream world, living in your own porno--

"Don't get me wrong," she sighs, "I like it—find it interesting because I can study the enemy, see how the male mind's been socialized to work. . .it's like entering the mind of a killer. . . or rapist, I should say," then she polishes off her beer and the conflict disappears under a façade of smiles, "Jesus, can't you get a fucking drink around here?"

The waitresses ignore her until she's half standing in her stool. In utter shock, one of them brings her a second beer waiting to open it until the order's confirmed. Then the waitress smiles--and doesn't give her that tipping isn't a town in China shit.

Sucking back on the fresh Corona, she continues, "But I see nothing good coming from us living out a fantasy."

"What's your point?"

"You can get lost in dreams. We use an artificial device, the Rufinol, to create an unreal environment of drugged women. Yes, it's intoxicating—we're drawing the boundaries of our fantasy world into physical reality. We become Oriental despots--Lord Emperors of the body and mind. Someone insults you at a club? You can devour them whole. But the dream ends--the control ends when you drop them off at the beach," she gnaws worriedly on a lock of hair, "I'm afraid some of us are forgetting where the dreams end and reality begins."

Drum beat against the bar counter, "Translation, please!"

"Derek's pushing the stakes higher and higher like no one can stop him. Archie's crazed with power and you— you're suddenly in love," she peers deep into my eyes, "I'll make my offer once. If you refuse it, there's no second chance, no going back—because I won't believe you."

"What is it?" I expect some wild comment.

But she leans over, staring at me—her eyes a mixture of conflicting emotions: anger and hatred and sadness and a horrible fear of what she's become as she says, "We must stop this now."

"No way!" I scoff, "Charity, everything's that happening to us is good."

Her offer is over as she smirks, "Know where you are, Cullen Gersh," she winks, spreading her arms to the bar around us, "right now, are you being a cheap ass at El Torito in Beverly Hills or the El Torito in your dreams? Betcha both feel like reality," she clinks her beer bottle against mine, "either way, your one beer's always half empty."

On Wednesday, Eloise and I meet for our second date.

We dine at a Cuban dive on La Cienega. It's got the two things I like in a restaurant--cheap and tasty. All the guys from ITM order number 7A on the menu, flattened chicken breast with a garlic seasoned sauce and onions--you get fried plantains and rice and beans too. But stay away from the Cuban soft drinks, they suck. We eat and laugh. It's easy talking to Eloise, beautiful in a white top and black pants. Her hair's pinned up again and she has this great scarf tied around her neck—Hermes probably. As we talk, I'm still amazed that she doesn't care about the entertainment industry.

"You promise you wouldn't want to be an actress?" I ask.

She nods her head no.

"Even if you could star in the biggest movie in town and kiss Mel Gibson?"

"I don't even go to the movies," she sips her wine.

"But they're great. How about TV?"

"I like Different Strokes—those cute kids adopted by Mr. Drummond."

"That whole cast wound up blowing guys for crack."

"More than I needed to know. And what about that one with girls who are all close friends?"

"Uh. . . that could be any one of a hundred shows."

"You know—ah. . . it's on the tip of my tongue! They're all buddies in a prep school--"

"The Facts of Life?"

"That's it! I always thought the blonde, Blair, was hot."

"Hot—as in a sexual way?"

"No, hot as in she had a fever," Eloise shows her sense of sarcasm, "what do you think?"

"So," I lean forward, ears perked, "you wanted to get it on with Blair?"

"I find some women sexy, maybe even arousing. Doesn't mean I want to fuck them."

There's something sexy about hearing her say the word: fuck.

"So," I ask, "do you have any shows you've watched since sixth grade?"

"I read a lot."

"You realize all the shows you like are about loners nurtured in a family setting?"

"Maybe so."

Flash--I'm reminded of that mental image: a tiny Eloise, all blonde hair and skinny legs, alone in that apartment in Rome, playing solitary games, imagining the dead tenants of eons past.

"Since pop culture holds so little for you," I ask her, "what do you like?"

"I'll show you."

On the way back to her apartment, she turns my car radio to one of those classical stations that's so far down on the band-with, you only find it when you're searching for NPR news. Suddenly this beautiful classical music flows through my car. The city lights cruise by, showering light on her sweeping neck and blonde hair pinned high over her head. For a second I forget I'm driving a piss stenched Honda. I'm somewhere else—somewhere more special than any movie I've ever been to.

I'm alive.

"It's Mozart," explains Eloise, "Piano Concerto number 25 in C--allegro maestoso."

"Show off."

The tension rushes through me when I drop her off at her door. I still hear Piano Concerto number whatever the hell singing through my head as our lips grow closer to each other. Then we're kissing, her lips soft against mine--scent overtaking me. I open my eyes.

Ever done that when you're kissing?

The other person's eyes grow together--looks like you're kissing a Cyclops. She opens her eyes too--a massive, blue eye dotting her forehead like one of those weird purple things Hindus worship. I sink into the still blueness of it. And no--I don't try to screw her. Why is everything about sex with you?

We just make a date for Saturday night.

I know, this is turning into a habit.

Again, that wonderful feeling.

Long after our date, I still hear remnants of that piano concerto. And I also have a cadre of beautiful women at my disposal. I have one compartment for lust, the other—perhaps--for love. Maybe it's my animal and human side in their individual realms? I ponder such thoughts as I return home that Thursday--

"You're late," Derek barks.

"It's still early."

The whole gang is assembled in the kitchen. They're all dressed up—

"I left a voice message this afternoon," Derek says.

"My assistant must not have given it to me."

"Plans different today," Derek straightens his tie, "put on a fresh suit. Let's go."

Lights flash through Derek's Volvo.

"We're going to pump up the volume," Derek explains on the car ride out.

We're clad in these dark, double-breasted suits. It's James Bond Theme night. Charity's clad in this sleek, black jumpsuit—tits perking through the stretch fabric-- the same sort of thing Veronica wore to The Ballet of Chestnuts. Then I see the blinking lights of the theatre marquees and realize that it's the film premier I got Derek's four friends tickets for.

It hits me.

"No!" I shoot out of my seat, "we're not going to drug girls at a film premiere!"

"Don't be ridiculous," Derek winces, "we're going to drug them at the post party."

I turn to Charity for help, but she simply shrugs. She made the one time offer to me at El Torito and I refused it. She doesn't believe I would ever stand up to Derek--to stop him.

"This is fucking crazy!" I rant, "people I work with-- people I know will be there!"

"Then you won't feel alone," his eyes tear into me.

"No fucking way!" I explode, slamming my hand against the dash. I tell them that the experiment's gotten out of control—it's reckless, it's—

"Can't you see it now?" Archie's sticks his head between the front seat, his eyes bordering on madness, "out there march an army of secretaries, models, unemployed actresses, low fat yogurt stand patrons, P.T.A. mothers, Swedish au pair girls, generals, cocktail waitresses, totalitarian world leaders—all waiting to be raped--to be rendered equal and meek in the eyes of the world. Fuck communism, socialism, democracy, dictatorships--this is perfect social harmony," slamming a hand against the roof, he howls like a wolf on the prowl, "Party! Party! Party!"

"Hey," Derek shrugs at me, "you were the one who wanted to turn up the tempo."

My eyes trail behind the red carpet.

Paparazzi camera flashes explode. Reporters extend microphones into the walkway. In front of me, Charity poses for the cameras, followed by a bright eyed Archie. Camera men take photos first and see who it is later. Derek hands the four tickets I got him to the usher at the door.

Throughout the movie, my mind swims. What the hell are we doing? This is the most high profile place to snatch a girl. I turn to Archie and Charity, munching excitedly on popcorn as they watch the movie. Then I catch Derek staring at me. Once again I have no idea what he's thinking. These people feel so distant from me now.

In the darkened theatre, my mind returns to Eloise—to the two slobs in that Hollywood bar—the first licking his hand after shaking hers. The second wrapping his hands around her beautiful neck, the third fucker rubbing against her and then threatening to hit her--I could kill him! I imagine tears trickling down her cheeks. She came here because she broke off her engagement and is waiting for her friend. She doesn't need this. She's alone, fed up with men, fed up with the whole fucking town.

Just like I was.

After the movie, we're herded into the post party which is in a tent behind the theatre. Everything's white—white tent, floor, waiters in starched white uniforms. A whole spread of sushi is laid out on marble slabs. Wines flows liberally.

"This is fucking great!" Archie stuffs his face with Ahi tuna rolls.

"Funk Soul Brother" pounds over the speakers, the beating rhythm vibrating the walls of the tent. We're huddled in the corner, my associates eyeing their potential prey with the excitement of a wolf at his first kill. What are we going to do--keep raising the stakes, until we've raped the whole fucking world?

"I told you this would happen," whispers Charity, intrigued by the change of scenery.

"So what are you now—one of Derek's henchman."

"Hey," she pokes me, "said it already—everything happening to us is all good," she turns, watching a tall, brunette waitress with a bare mid-drift and tray full of drinks.

"What happened to the whole common man shtick?"

"Relax, she's a waitress."

"I can't believe you're going for this."

"Spare me the morality speech. You wouldn't care if we were at anything other than an entertainment party. I'm not going to be the first to act unless it's putting a bullet in his head. And for that, I wait until the time's right."

"You know you feel conflicted," I tell her.

But she's all smiles as she turns, staring at Derek Van Horn. When I turn back to continue the conversation, she's gone—vanishing into the crowd. So I hide in the corner watching my associates get slapped and berated. Charity's right. I wouldn't have a problem if we stuck to the original plan—low profile. Look at me, as I stand here, three agents from ITM walk up and talk to me—while my friends are all around us, staking out rape subjects!

"And who's this?" Charity wraps a hand around one of the talent agent acquaintances. I must look like I'm going to kill her because they all leave. Then she just leans over giggling, asking why I can't take a joke.

By the time voting time rolls around, I'm really pissed off. I use my vote to strike down every candidate—it's my turn to stress the fact that our moves are unanimous.

"Do you have a problem?" Derek's hisses.

"I don't think any of them are suitable candidates."

"Why?" his eyes tear into me.

"Because this could get me fired or send us all to jail!" I fight to keep my voice low.

All their eyes are on me—Charity, Derek, Archie-- who silently shrugs. The fucker's got no damned spine. I suddenly hate them all. I feel trapped, left behind, shocked and confused by their insanity.

"We are not leaving this party without subjects," presses Derek.

"I'm leaving."

As I turn to leave, Derek grabs my arm in a firm grip, "You're going nowhere."

Flash—Derek raping the Viking Girl--telling me he'd kill Veronica--working in that fucking room day and night the same tap—tap—ding! like a fucking lunatic.

Charity's eyes follow the both of us. What's she thinking? Why doesn't she say something! She said she'd kill him. I jerk my hand away, weaving through people as I try to leave. The tent spins around me. There's only one exit and--

Snap! Snap! Snap!

Camera flashes explode as I stumble along the red carpet exit. Paparazzi fire off shots first and then figure out who it is. As I cross the gauntlet of press reporters, it hits me. Forget my friends seeing us. Those camera crews are going to have photos of all Charity, Derek, and Archie walking out with their rufeed test subjects--photos that could be discarded or used by police investigators if--

Jesus Christ, what's happening?

I can't face going home. No, I need a place I can think--a place to regroup. I think I'm hyperventilating. Aren't you supposed to stick your head in a brown paper bag, or something like that? I grab a cab and flee to the only sanctuary I know.

"Are you alright?" Eloise asks.

Her hair is tied up over her head, makeup off. Still, she looks beautiful.

"I'm sorry," I say, "I know our date isn't until Saturday," I sit on the floor beside her, my chest sweaty against my shirt, "had a rough day--wanted to see you."

I want to feel clean. I want to shed all the dirt and guilt and whispers that are getting louder and louder. How bad can I really be? Here I am with this beautiful, kind woman in a room that smells of flowers, Mozart's "Figaro" playing over the stereo.

See, I did take music appreciation.

She brings me over to where she's been sitting—in front of her fake gas-lit fireplace. Next to her rests Dante's Divine Comedy.

"Do you ever do light reading?" I try to smile.

Under her leg, she produces a Vogue magazine she's been reading. Spreading it open in her lap, she smiles, "I'm happy you came over," she takes one of the perfume samples out, rubbing it on her wrist--the smell floats into my nose, "I didn't want to wait until the weekend to see you. And look what I went out and bought." She points to a TV in the corner.

I smile, "We could watch The Facts Of Life on TV Land," and then it just comes out of my mouth, as if my Id suddenly decided to speak, "I know it sounds weird and corny and far too soon to be speaking about feelings but--I love you."

She presses a finger against my lips, silencing me. Oh, just to be near her. What Veronica had on the outside, Eloise has on the inside too. She's the most special girl in the world. I peel back the top of her nightgown. On her bare, perfect shoulder, I notice a birthmark in the shape of--

"I know," she giggles, "looks like Texas."

We kiss again, falling back on the carpeted floor. And I'm thinking that I would never have met this wonderful woman if the experiment hadn't been going on. I'd be some derelict trapped in a tech support room feeling sorry for myself.

It's so hard to figure out what I should be?

Am I to play the considerate, silent, studious, weak-willed Cullen Gersh? Or am I going to continue to be the self-confident, tough, never get hurt Alpha Wolf? The Alpha Wolf who led me here, to this West LA apartment with this woman. But he doesn't care who he hurts or what he does. His pack is over at a film premier party, drugging their rape victims right now. Jesus, what seemed so elementary is so complex and confused. You could write endless volumes on the spaces between the two identities.

Eloise's nightgown comes off, discarded on the floor beside her. My heart races as I peer down at her naked body—real handfuls of breasts that aren't massive and hard to the touch. Soft nipples and a firm abdomen flowing down to milky white hips. My lips trace across a tiny birthmark on her shoulder blade. . .caress her breasts, tongue tracing down her stomach until my lips are between her legs. It's like kissing her again, I think as her hands play through my hair—her stomach suddenly tight, pressed against my head.

Finally, she pulls me away, whispering, "There are condoms in my night-table."

The fire dances across her body as I enter her. Her eyes wide, staring back at me, hands tight around my shoulder as I move in and out of her.

Flash—all those women on the pool table.

I caress her lips.

Flash—kissing those women in the game room.

I cradle her ass in my hands.

Flash—slamming my hands around their bottoms.

Who am I? What am I doing? How can I rape and make love? Then the thoughts fade away and for a few more minutes, I'm clean and new and reborn to the world. If it were a movie, I would fade out on the two of us making love against the fireplace. I'd skip the sweat and our stomachs pressing together, making that farting sound and the fact that she orgasms five minutes before me.

But this isn't a movie or a book, is it?

"Was it good?" I ask.

She looks uncomfortable, suddenly pulling Dante's Divine Comedy out from underneath her thigh, "that's what was poking me."

"You didn't answer my question."

Tossing the book in front of the fireplace, she asks, "Why does every young guy think it's a competition?"

"Older ones don't?"

"Only a guy under 30 asks how it was."

"I'll remember that," I smile, "so until I'm 30, I want to know--how was it?"

"I don't know--can't remember the others."

"If I made you forget all of them, must be pretty good," I notice the tiny birthmark on her upper back.

She catches me staring at it, "I know--it looks like the boot of Italy."

"No," I kiss it, "more like the state of Maine," rolling over, I flip through Dante's Divine Comedy. "Why'd they call it a comedy anyway. I never found it very funny."

"A comedy didn't mean the same thing back then."

"It was boring--that's all I remember," I flip to a random passage where a character is describing how everyone wound up in hell:

> *"My son," the gentle master said to me,*
> *"All those who perish in the wrath of God*
> *assemble here from all parts of the earth."*

I imagine us on the boat to hell.

Charity, Derek, Archie, myself, Hitler, Genghis Khan, Vanilla Ice, and the guy who invented the Chia Pet— why? Have you ever smelled one of those things? We all sit in the decrepit boat as the skull faced boatman, Charon, cloaked in black robes, rows us across the fiery river towards Hades. Archie's blaming Derek for getting him into the whole thing. Derek's busily typing on his typewriter—tap—tap—ding! trying to finish the last lines of his masterpiece. And Charity? She's beating Charon over the head with his ore, swearing and threatening to kill him unless he turns around as I try to tell her repeatedly that Charon is already dead--

"I love that book," Eloise pulls her beret away, letting golden hair tumble down.

I flip through the glossary, "Had to read it in college."

"Do you know who burns in the deepest fires of hell?" she asks.

"Who?"

"The liars," she says.

"And well they should," I smile, putting the book down, glancing up--

My heart skips a beat.

"What's wrong?" she asks.

I think I'm going to pass out. A buzzing sound fills my ears--throat goes dry. I'm going to dry heave. This was the last safe refuge I had in the world. Glancing up at her long hair, shimmering like golden silk around her shoulders, I realize it.

How could I have been so blind?

I think back to poor Eloise in that bar, crying as the first man licks his hand, the second throttles her throat, and the third bumps into her and then threatens her life. I hadn't slept in two weeks, mind totally clouded. Still, what a fool I've been—so fucking stupid! At the gallery she even came up to me--asked if we went to Vanderbilt together--said I looked familiar. Because—

Eloise is the Viking Girl.

Part Four

In The Shade of The Forbidden Tree

"Of Man's first disobedience, and the fruit
Of that forbidden tree whose mortal taste
Brought death into the World, and all our woe,"

-John Milton's *Paradise Lost* (1667)

Nineteen

"Cullen, are you alright?"

Her words rip through my soul. I fight to hold a look of composure. Beads of sweat dot my forehead. The fireplace spins around me. My head feels so light—like a balloon ready to deflate--shooting through the room at any second.

Her hand touches mine.

I fight to stop the recoil. I stare back at her face, hoping that I'm wrong. The long blonde hair falling along her fine featured face--pop a helmet with horns on her head and she's ready to sing some Wagner--

The Viking Girl.

Flash—when she called me an asshole at North, I thought she wore Veronica's smug look. But Eloise was just frightened, scared. Remember the two guys moving away from her as Hal and I wandered up to the bar? Those were the two sons of bitches who scared her. And her engagement had been called off that day! Then I wandered up, bumped into her and--no. Slow down. I never meant to hurt her. But how different it looks from the other side of the mirror. How did this get so confused?

Derek raped her.

Flash—hover over the game room, peer down at Eloise, drugged and naked. My little baby is naked as Derek, pants at his ankles, thrusts in and out, her legs gathered around his shoulder--oh fuck. I flee to the bathroom. Lock the door—flush the toilet as I puke, harsh bursts of brown fluid, singing my throat and mouth. When the storm passes, I press my forehead against the cold porcelain, nausea shuddering through my body.

"Cullen," Eloise inquires through the locked door, "are you--"

"I'm fine," my voice faint, "must be something I ate."

Turn the faucet on, bathe my face in cold water. Look in the mirror. It's like staring into the face of a stranger. Those aren't my eyes. Where have you gone, Cullen Gersh? From the depths of my mind, I hear the whispering. I shut it off before I can hear the words.

I'm the Alpha Wolf. The old Cullen never had the confidence to meet Eloise. The old Cullen was a pandering, whining, insomniac, weeping and yawning in his cramped tech support cubicle. In less than two months, I've accomplished more than that weak willed boy would have in a lifetime. Yes, there are casualties-- always will be. Who said the world is fair? I'm going to go outside this bathroom. I'm going to continue being confident, strong—I didn't mean to rape her. It's not my fault. It's just--

"You sounded sick," Eloise is waiting in the living room, cup of tea in hand.

"I'm fine now," I search for my coat.

"Are you going?"

"I've a long day tomorrow."

"Was it something I said?"

I realize I'm being crass. I stop, taking the cup of tea from her. The click of porcelain on wood as I set it on the side table. I hug her, arms tight, holding back tears— her hands against my back, fingers tightening.

"I've got to go," I finally say.

She presses to know when we'll do something again. I tell her we'll grab a late lunch on Saturday afternoon. She says she'll be up in Hollywood and can pick me up. I want to leave--I jot my address down and leave.

The car ride home passes in a dream.

I'm not ready to go home. Hell, I don't even have a home. I drive aimlessly down Sunset, cruising through the unlit roads of Bel Air and Beverly Hills, snaking through neighborhoods, delaying my return to the Hollywood Hills. Tonight, it would be better if they already took the girls to the beach when I arrive.

It's drizzling.

The musty smell of rain fills my nose.

Rain drops tip tap against my windshield. Do you know how sometimes the world seems so simple? You feel like you can control anything. Then you realize how lost you really are--frightened by the crowds of people, mass of traffic making you feel small and alone. You want to hide in a basement or a dark closet where no one can touch you. Because the truth is that we see only what we want or what we need. The rest fades away like the imperceptible buzz of your air-conditioner. There's complexity in everything--an unpredictability in the way that the car next to us will accelerate or the patterns the ripples will make in that puddle in the street.

But maybe some things are simple? Flash—Eloise, peering into that fake, gas lit fireplace, "Do you know who burns in the deepest fires of hell?"

"Who?" I ask.

"The liars."

Am I a liar?

I pride myself on tolerance--on being able to get along with practically anyone. You probably do too. But who am I? Who are you? We're trapped inside ourselves, never able to get the bird's eye view. Yet we are afforded the inside view. We know how differently we act in varied circumstances, how our personality changes around different people and it makes our own self-image too blurry to understand. To the quiet one, we're loud—to the introverted, we're the extrovert. And around that loud guy, we're the shy one. Are we the sum total of our actions? Or is there one role that defines us?

Hell, maybe I'm full of shit?

Maybe you know who you are. Maybe it's just me. But I can't believe I'm the only one who feels like this. All my life, I've tried not to rock the boat—ever that quiet kid creeping into mom's bedroom for movie money, hoping my footsteps on the wood floor won't wake her from the barbiturate sleep. My dad never taught me how to act or dress or speak. He's a fleeting memory, a gallery of idealized snapshots long since tinted sepia yellow. I never challenge the moral majority when they're wrong--never stand up for my beliefs. Hell, beyond my generation's commitment to tolerance, to a sensitive guy, post-feminist passiveness.

No.

That's the old Cullen talking. I'm strong. I'm the Alpha Wolf. Nothing can hurt me. I can have my pie and eat it too. I didn't mean for Eloise to get hurt and I'll protect her forever. Sometimes things happen—things beyond our control.

They're still having a party.

I stand wet from the rain. The air in the foyer is cold and dry, burning my eyes as I silently watch them at the end of the dark hall. In varied choices of underwear, Archie, Derek, and Charity congregate around the kitchen counter. A dirty ashtray, bottle of Cuervo Gold, and half-filled shooters rests between them. Through the open door of the game room, I know there are three sets of open legs.

I turn away.

"One hell of a film party," Archie says as he and Charity toast.

"This is still bullshit," Charity gripes, "I still want the common man. Ya know what? I want to fuck a postman—real salt of the earth."

"You are not going to do the postman," Derek makes it clear.

Charity sees me first as I enter the kitchen. Everything goes silent. Then Derek asks if something's wrong--steel blue eyes stabbing like daggers. Glance down at the bottle of liquor. I'm intimidated by Derek, aren't I? He's not taller than me, but thick and possessing an intensity I could never have. He would devour me if I crossed him. Still, I feel so close to him. Like he's a lover or a brother who's so close that his anger, although unjustified, hurts me.

"How you doing?" I know he's looking up at me.

"Hope none of my friends are in there," I point towards the game room. Without looking, I descend the stairs towards my bedroom.

Do you know how sometimes the world feels different? In an almost imperceptible way everything feels different, like I'm not really in Derek's house, but a different house, almost the same except for some tiny flaw my subconscious picks up on. Sleep doesn't help it.

When I wake up the next day from restless sleep, the bedroom still seems different. Stand at the wall of windows, hand pressed against the glass as the sun glistens over the steel and aluminum skin of Los Angeles. The wind blows, whizzing on the other side of the partition. I can see Sunset Boulevard and downtown beyond, but it's like being in another city.

Brushing my teeth, I stare at my reflection and it looks different. My hair is crazy from sleep, but there's something else—something different. A finger against the glass, I reach out, touching my reflection. It doesn't look like me. That's how I feel when I go to work, sitting in my office. I know it makes no sense and I can't explain why. But I want to make sure these phone calls I'm rolling aren't fake--that this office isn't merely a conflation of plywood and fake furniture.

After lunch, I'm on the toilet.

What? You don't think protagonists in a story take a crap? We all burp, fart and go to bathroom just like you-- well not quite the same. Agents often use remote headsets when they're on the toilet. As you scan the ITM bathroom stalls, you see a line of Italian shoes and dropped pants as the chit chat of a thousand conversations echoes off the walls.

In the last stall, I'm rolling calls on the can, muffling the mouthpiece with my hand to hide the cacophony of other conversations. The feeling is actually starting to wear off as I loose myself in my work when--

"Gersh," another lit agent who wouldn't give me the time of day when I was in the mail room, sticks his hand underneath the divider, "getta' load of this."

It's a Playboy pictorial called "Passions and Fantasies"—no articles, just naked chicks--probably get it with your subscription. I open it up. The inside cover shot is a brunette with massive, pendulous breasts. She lounges behind a blonde, perfectly airbrushed body, stomach sucked in, laying across a bed, eyes closed. Her eyes are closed, hands on the bed—almost as if she's drugged. It's a familiar pose I've seen many times under the lights of the Carlsberg Beer lamp. I share a private smile with myself ready to hand the magazine back when it hits me.

Photos like this used to feel exciting. I think men find power in what they can see. Glimpsing a naked woman is empowering--as if you've stolen something from her. But now it just seems hollow and stupid--

"Toss it back," the agent beckons as he flushes his toilet, "I gotta go."

"Wait a second," I hold the magazine sideways, focusing on the blonde's face.

Flash—the older Russian woman with glasses and sandy hair that I brought home from the Garden of Eden on the first night of our experiment. Holding the Playboy pictorial close, I peruse the face of the sleeping girl in the picture, laying on the bed. Flash—the Russian woman screaming Da da da! Could it be the same person? I hold it closer until the face fades into a storm of tiny printing dots—like some Seurat painting.

"Hey," he bangs on the door, "I'm going Gersh."

I return the magazine.

Maybe she was a playboy model? Most of those models live in Los Angeles. But there's something—some thought I can't quite put my finger on. Almost as if—

"Cullen?" I hear my assistant's voice through the divider.

"Yeah?" I say.

"I gotta call on the office line for you."

I tell him to have the guy call back. I hear my assistant's feet shuffling on the stone floor and then he says, "He says its urgent. . .says his name's Irv Hirschberg."

I'm nervous.

Heart pounds--why the fuck would Irving Hirschberg call me? You remember the last time we met—his naked ass pumping back and forth as he fucks my ex-girlfriend. Damn, even that feels so far away now. My feet race along the gray carpeted hallway. Wild thoughts dance through my head--has Mo turned on me? Crossing his open door, he waves at me, bald head moving up and down as he bounces on his blue ball—

Doesn't look like he has a problem.

Returning to my office, I tell my assistant I want no interruptions. Then I lock the door, rush to my desk and stop, finger pausing over the phone set button. A deep breath. I pick it up.

"Gersh?" the loud New York accent attacks my ear.

"Yes," I cringe, lowering the volume control.

"I was. . ." a long pause--my heart races, "we can't find Veronica. She's been missing for a couple of weeks. Parents called me and got the fucking police involved. Cause the little--" he catches himself, but I know he was going to say bitch, "girl is missing. I got cops crawlin' up my ass."

I laugh uncaringly. Who the hell cares? Big deal, Irv's got one less girl to fuck--

"So," Irv's voice brings me back, "you haven't heard from her?"

Then it hits me. Irv's never even apologized for fucking my girlfriend, "Of all people, you know we don't speak. She's your problem now, Irv," I take pleasure in using his first name so informally.

"Don't have to beat me over the head with it," he breaths deep wheezing breaths like an old dog. Still no apology. I wonder what he's thinking right now. I hope the cops crawl right up his ass and make his life a living hell, "if ya do hear--gimme a call."

A few minutes after the call ends, as I'm waiting for my assistant to connect me with a writer in New York, a troubling memory hits me. I remember the first night I spent at Derek's home. We were by the fireplace and he turns to me, smiling that wolfish grin as he says, "You'd like to kill Veronica right now--wouldn't you? You'd like me to kill her. I'd do it--"

I'd do it.

"Cullen," my assistant comes over my headset, "A Derek Van Horn calling on line three?"

"I'll take it," speak of the devil.

"How you doing, mate?" he asks gingerly, the whispery voice in my ear.

"Fine."

"With work and all--haven't seen much of each other lately. Wanted to invite you to a party at my parent's house on Thursday night. To be honest, maybe it's more of an invitation for me. I don't think I can take another of their bloody parties alone."

Silence.

"So?" I realize he's waiting for an answer.

"Yeah. . . sure."

Hang up the phone. Is it just me or does Derek Van Horn always invite you to stuff just after he's done something very wrong? Irv's words echo through my mind. Veronica just leaves without saying anything to anyone? Derek's inviting me to parties—trying to keep an eye on me. He's done a lot of things and—I smile. Listen to me. Irv probably got in a fight with his sweetie and she ran off and decided to make his life hell. As if Derek Horn could ever kill someone!

Ridiculous.

That night, I procrastinate in calling Eloise.

You know how you do that? You say you'll call in an hour or so. Then you're busy and before you know it, it's too late to call. I collapse in my bed, the strange feeling still about me. I crave sleep.

But the same dream continues.

I'm back in the house. Charity continues pressing the doorbell—a loud blast of sound rumbling the walls of the house, knocking over the half-filled beers scattered on tables and chairs. I fight to keep the French Maids from opening the door. Charity starts pounding at the door. This can't go on forever--I have to open it. My hand grips the knob—which is hard to do because the door's shaking so much from Charity pounding on the other side. Then the door opens--

It's a smiling Eloise.

She's in a French Maid's outfit.

And it's the most horrifying thing I've ever seen—

Wake up.

Tap—tap—tap—ding of Derek's typewriter rings out through the house. The sky is dark. Roll over, wiping sweat from my forehead as I glance at the clock. I've only been asleep for an hour. This is the first time in ages I've had trouble sleeping. The whispers beckon again from the dark alcoves of my mind—just like they did in Eloise's bathroom. I hear them whispering through darkness:

"So wrong. . . so wrong. . . so wrong--"

"You up?" I hear another say.

I shoot up like a schizophrenic hearing a new voice. In the open doorway stands Archie, silhouetted in the light from the hall.

"Hey buddy," he wanders into the dark bedroom, "thought I heard you rolling around."

"Can't sleep too?" I ask.

"You'd think I'd collapse? I got a promotion—lots of new special projects and work. You know, what we're doing's really given me strength."

Archie feels the rough texture of my sheets, "Jesus, this is crap. There's a great sheet sale at Macy's right now—Egyptian cotton. Lots of linen sales this time of year."

This is classic Archie, combing his mind for a tidbit or trifle of humor to introduce some troubling point.

"Why don't you just tell me what happened," I cut to the chase.

He smiles, appreciating the sentiment, "I came home from work early yesterday-- I know, first time in weeks. Anyway, I sort of saw something--something we should talk about. I mean it's probably nothing, but--"

"Arch," I glance at the bedside clock, "I gotta go back to sleep. What is it?"

Archie tells me a story. He comes home early yesterday, wandering through the downstairs hall, the sounds of Derek's typewriter's tap—tap—ding! in the air. As the typewriter clicks away, Derek opens his door, about to step outside. Archie happens to be right there. Through the open door, he sees a red flag--the same one I'd seen months before. But Archie manages to see the entire thing, including a symbol on the far end of the flag.

"It was a swastika," he winces, "a big, fucking black one."

Flash—the swastika covered forks. What are you going to say now? Did old Grand-Dad loot half the fucking country during the war? Or is it something more insidious, something darker? Is Derek one of those militia guys who cream over gun shows and fantasies about blowing up Federal buildings? Have I moved in with a lunatic? Maybe I wouldn't normally react so strongly--but lately, hasn't taken a lot to throw me off balance.

"I saw it clear as day," continues Archie, "and Derek was standing in the hall, but his typewriter was still going—how can that be? What's he working on in there? Been locked up every damn day since I moved in. Don't get me wrong," he holds up his hands like he's stopping traffic, "don't want'a rock the boat. I mean—best time I've had since I've been here. Hell, best time I've had in my life. But I'd be lyin' if I didn't say this Nazi shit worries me."

Looking at Archie, I wonder if my friend feels the way I do? I even think about asking him, but decide to remain silent. Maybe there is no substance under that pretty boy face. Archie's got a mind for numbers and processes, maybe, I think, he knows the how, but not the why. Hell, maybe he just doesn't care about the why. After all, his life's going great—got promoted. So did I. My life's going great too. Maybe it's just the whole Eloise thing that's got me a little freaked out.

"What do you think we should do?" presses Arch, looking for direction.

"I don't know," I sigh, "but I know who can help us."

"So, you fuck her yet?"

The next day, I phone Charity, telling her we have to meet at lunchtime. I pick KooKooRoo's--this healthy chicken and turkey chain. All Charity wants to know is if I've bedded Eloise. By the time we order our sliced turkey dinners, the joke's old.

"So tell me," she leans close when we sit down, her breath smelling of cigarettes, "is it different—you know--

not raping and all?" she explodes in snorting laughter. But now it feels like she's stabbing at me.

"Chew your hair and shut up."

She rolls her eyes, "Cullen, I'm just yankin' your chain," she spoons half the turkey into her mouth, "alright, what's so serious that I had to miss drama class?"

I tell her the whole story about Derek and the Nazi crap, finally ending with Archie discovering the flag in his room. I tell her that these are signs that Derek might have gone mad—that he must be stopped.

She rolls her eyes when I'm done, "Warned you about dreams getting confused with reality—"

"Do you want me to beg? I'm sorry I refused your offer. I was a moron. I've seen the light--I need your help peaceably stopping Derek," I cautiously ad, "without blowing his head off."

"Why do you need me?" she thrusts a proud fist into the air, "thought you were the Alpha Wolf?"

"Fine," I plead, "I'm begging for your help. I see things clearly now--"

"No you don't. You're pussy footing over Nazi flags and typewriter sounds--"

"Derek's been locked away in that bedroom for months—day and night the tap ding of his typewriter. It's only natural I'd be curious. And now I think it's a clear sign of his insanity."

"Derek's raping women and you're concerned with typing?" she rolls her eyes.

"I think it proves he's nuts!"

"No. You're just curious about what he's working on."

"We hang out together—it's only natural I'd be curious too."

"Bullshit," she retorts, "we hang out all the time--never wonder about me."

"If nobody gets out of here alive, what's it matter?" then I sigh, "you won't even tell me your real name," then I throw out what the old lady called her, "Jennifer."

"Nice try," she says, never missing a beat.

"Fine," I moan, realizing we're not going to get anywhere unless we talk about her, "how did that acting thing go--said last week you were trying out for some role?"

"I'm on a second call back," she smiles, unconsciously gnawing at a lock of hair, "thank you for asking."

"Nice roll is it?"

"Troubled adult girl. She's smart though, does what she wants. Like--if she wanted to know what Derek was doing in that room, she'd just break in."

"He's got a numerical lock on the door--probably deadbolts too."

"Sure he has a window. And I know for a fact that tomorrow night he has to show up at some party at his parents' house."

"He invited me."

"Me too—figured we could show up late."

I shake my head negatively.

"He's also gone on Saturday afternoon--spending the afternoon at some club."

"What are you," I smirk, "his personal secretary?"

"I just listen," she huffs, "could do it then—we could wear black Ninja suits, deadbolt the front door and crawl around the back--" she proceeds to discuss the details of the proposed breaking and entering as if it were a tea party.

"No," I finally say, "I'm not breaking into his bedroom."

"Pussy," the roll of the eyes.

"I thought you didn't care."

"You've peaked my interest," she shrugs, gnawing on a fresh lock of hair.

"Then do it yourself."

"Right. So when I see all the dead bodies inside, you can say I made it all up."

I put an end to the conversation. You know I'm dying to find out what he's working on. But he's my friend. He's been there for me when I needed him. In a way he brought me to Eloise. And I am not going to invade his privacy. But still my mind races as I return to work. Veronica's missing—Nazi flags—Archie said the typewriter was tip tapping even as Derek stepped out of the room. The suspicious thoughts I laughed down yesterday now seem all the more real.

Could Derek Van Horn be a madman?

Twenty

Derek Van Horn's parents live in the Alamo.

Seriously. It's a fortress of aged stucco and exposed timbers, nestled atop the hills of Bel Air. How do I know this? Because on Thursday, Derek invites us to his parents' house for that party.

"I really appreciate this," he apologizes as we walk up the driveway crammed full of cars and Mexican valets, "you know how I feel about going to these stupid things—always helps to have company in hell."

Flash—the four of us in Charon's boat, slowly being rowed towards hell.

He stops me, allowing the others to continue, "You alright, mate?" his clipped accent like flowing champagne.

"Yeah," stare down at the grass.

A hand to my chin. He lifts my face up, our eyes locking, "Nothing's wrong?"

"No," I stare into his cobalt eyes. Are these the eyes of a killer? Does a killer grow up at homes like this, high in the hills of Bel Air? "I just don't like parties."

Derek sighs, "Better get used to it," he pats me on the back as we draw closer to the house, "no man ever made it in the world without mastering the art of cocktail party conversation—like trying to smile in hell--first one to flinch loses his testicles."

But this is far from hell.

The party is beautiful. The kind of beauty I filled my childhood dreaming about—a peek into that reserved booth--cut from the same cloth as Mo Simon's Aston Martin leather interior. The yard is filled with bougainvillea and roses. TV news reporters stand gathered, interviewing guests for the evening news. But just like the car, I don't feel like I belong here. Finding a corner in which to hide from the crowd, I feel cleansed by the gathering's charm and laughter. Killers don't go to places like this—right? Killers—listen to me.

Hide my face. Mrs. Van Horn bounces by like Tigger after a chocolate espresso bar. The song "Manhattan" flows through the air. Women laugh. Hands pick at the exquisitely prepared hors-d'oeuvres spread across countless tables. As the crowd parts, I catch sight of the band standing on an elevated stage in the far corner.

This is The San Juan Capistrano for middle aged flamingoes. A place for the old and divorced to gather, dripping in pearls and diamonds, as anorexic as concentration camp victims, maneuvering through the tents--their legs aren't quite so spindly fit, but the silicone breasts still defy all laws of physics. Around them old spotted owls chit chat over the smoke of fine Cuban cigars.

"Having fun, mate?" Derek drapes an arm around me.

"Sure. What is this exactly?"

"Party for the Mayor's reelection campaign," he frowns as if the mere sight of the party pains him.

Across the way we spy an emaciated brunette in her mid-forties, decked out in a ruby ensemble, glancing about--making sure no one sees as she picks up three Godiva chocolates, stuffing them into her mouth.

Derek and I laugh. It's like old times as we watch her walk away. The thoughts and suspicions I harbored only hours ago fade away with the music and wine. How could I have ever doubted him? Derek Van Horn is my best friend in the world. Perhaps that's just the liquor talking, but just give him the benefit of the doubt--look at him smiling congenially, patting me on the back. He's about to tell a joke:

"So," he catches his breath, "want to fuck her?"

I spit up champagne, golden drops flying everywhere.

"Whoa," Derek chuckles, "calm down."

Wipe my mouth, "Y-y-you can't be serious."

He points with his eyes. In the corner, Charity starts a conversation with a woman in her early forties, sandy brown hair done up above her head with feathers and jewels. Archie's in the corner, arm against the tent's wall as he chats with a socialite. Just behind him is one of the news reporters interviewing the Chief of Police. It hits me—they knew. They all came here, knowing what they were going to do—waiting for me to get sauced.

I point to the news camera crew just behind Archie, "Reporters are here!"

"Relax. They're interviewing the chief of police."

Well that's really reassuring.

"Why didn't you tell me?" I grit my teeth.

The same smile covers his face, but it's just his war mask, "Would you have come?"

"At your mother's party!" that gurgling sound is my stomach. I'm going to be sick.

"Relax," he spins around, surveying the thick crowd of old flamingoes and owls, "they're so loaded by now—don't know what's going on. Hell, I know most of the divorcees without escorts," then he pats me on the back, "Cullen, have to admit, we're turning things up a notch. And I have something extra special planned for later."

Then he disappears into the fray.

I stand against the tent wall, scared and alone as the wolves meander through the crowd of middle aged women, capitalists, entertainment types, and political lackeys--laughing, making small talk, getting shot down. Archie gets slapped by a woman in her late forties in a taffeta and black evening dress. I cringe—and not just because of the taffeta. The police chief is standing right behind him!

Fear grips me.

I race into the house.

Hunched over the toilet, I vomit up the rest of the champagne. Jesus—we're all going to be caught! Derek's lost his mind! When I can't puke anything else up, I flee through the halls of the Santa Fe style house. I just want to be alone. The place is all cotton burlap couches, Santa Fe art, Hopi rugs, and locked doors. I finally find safety and seclusion in a dark hallway.

As my eyes adjust to the half-darkness, I realize I'm standing in a hall chocked full of framed family photos. . .

baby Derek on a swing. . . teenage Derek playing rugby—probably in England. . . the Van Horns at the pool. At young Derek's feet are two young blonde haired girls--can't be older than four. At first I think one of them is his sister, then I remember he has no sister. I focus on the second girl, all sandy blonde hair--maybe they're both younger cousins or family friends?

"Hiding?" Charity discovers me in the hall.

"This is madness!" I rant, "we're all going to jail!"

"Cullen," sighs Charity, "gotta rape em' first. Anyway, Derek knows these people—who we can take safely out of here," she gnaws at her hair, adding "you know, from the yard, I saw his dad through a window."

As if I fucking care.

"Shades were closed," Charity yawns, "but you can see him--passed out at his desk with Johnny Walker," her eyes adjust and she squints, scrutinizing the wall of Van Horn memorabilia.

"Fucked up," is all she says.

"Damn right it is."

"No," she points, "the photos. Look at them all—how they're spaced?"

Scan the walls of pictures--birthday photos at the roller rink--out in the front lawn--at the beach, the Van Horn's always smiling, but no one's touching anyone. It's eerie, no hugging, no holding. They're all distanced from each other--as if each is surrounded by an invisible force-field that--

One of the waiters enters the hall, dragging a bucket of empty wine bottles. He eyes Charity and I as he crosses us.

"C'mon," she pulls me back towards the party, "don't want to look like a suspect do you?"

I leave the party. At first I try to walk home, but realize I've a slim chance of making it to Sunset Blvd. by midnight. So I sit in Derek's Volvo and wait. The minutes tick away. Thoughts of murder and rape dance through my head. A cold sweat bathes my body. I'm on a rollercoaster that won't slow down. Then they come, stumbling down the dark driveway, silhouetted shadows framed against the trees and parked cars.

Watch them move in slow motion.

Derek like the pied piper, playing his imaginary flute as he dances about, all smiles. The dark muse Charity follows, spinning around and around in her dance, arms flying, dress thrown outward. Archie, ever the fool, cheering out his war chant, "Party! Party! Party!" Around their arms, supported and guided by hands, the victims walk and stumble, eyes crossed to the impenetrable void, lips parted—laughing, giggling, drugged--possessed like those enslaved children wandering amidst the piper's false tune.

You can imagine what happens next.

"Oh yes! Oh yes!" she cries.

This time I cannot see her—could be any one of the handful of socialites at the party decked out in dresses and pearls. She's merely a voice now, moaning through darkness. This is the new surprise Derek Van Horn has in store for us. Each of my associates take their test subjects to their respective bedrooms. Charity is given the game room to play alone. Derek takes the pool house—

Individual "laboratories" he calls them.

The dark home is now consumed with distant moans and sighs floating on the hilltop winds--creak of wood, giggles, spilling of champagne. I shut my window to block out the sounds, but still I hear it. The rapings are longer, far deeper than a rushing thrust to orgasm. No more the clannish gatherings, no more the physical sex, the Alpha Wolves have brought the event to a new psychological level.

Each alone with their test subjects.

Without control—the eyes of others upon us, we pick our nose, fart, and burp at will--doing things we would view as disgusting in anyone else. But when we're alone, social convention fades away. And what of them, my associates? Do they engage in taboo acts, licking and touching and feeling places untouched--unseen? When you reach the point where there's no more fantasy to fulfill, no more places to violate, no more taboos to trespass, what then? What do they do behind those locked doors? Do they practice acts perceived as perversions--things never to dare do with the eyes of another upon them? Because they truly are alone now-- aren't they? Perhaps they just break the ground-rules, leaving behind DNA evidence, kissing with bare lips, running bare hands along their subject's skin, whispering in their ears? Because they fear nothing anymore. Because they're starting to believe the whole thing—that they are different—that nothing in this world can affect them.

It's not even the police I fear anymore. I know they are extremely careful in who they chose—women who arrived without escorts. And yes, there were hundreds of people there and Derek vetoed half the place. What Charity said about dreams makes sense. I'm afraid because we're drifting into uncharted waters—far beyond the realm of reality. Beyond these walls--

My friends are fucking figments of their imagination.

And me? Look down, do you see me curled in a fetal position, pillow half over my head? Shield the moaning. I used to be an insomniac who needed the moaning to sleep. Now the moans won't leave me. Everything's become so confused. Toss and turn—thinking of reaching out for the only secure thing I have left.

Calling Eloise.

But I don't. It's like I've drifted so far away that phone lines can't even connect this place back to the physical world. I need a rocket ship to take me back to reality. Press the pillow against my ears, trying to make it all go away.

That night, my dream spins nightmares.

In it, I'm running through the house. It's night, moonlight spilling across wood floors. The French Maids wander, lost in the dark, bumping into couches and tables, tumbling down stairs. Bumping and moving around them are flamingoes—their long legs silhouetted in the moonlight. I force my way through bodies in the half darkness, but they don't see me anymore: blind, deaf, and dumb. The wall of windows overlooking the city and deck below are cracked open, bloody bodies floating in the pool below.

"Eloise!" I cry.

In the darkness, it's impossible to discern her from the others. The silent mutes continue, bumping into lamps, knocking over tables, breaking glass, wandering sightless and confused. The wind howls through the open wall of glass. In its wake I hear the haunting whispers, faint voices of my female test subjects floating through the ether:

"Where am I?"

"What have you done to my body?"

"Cold. . . so cold."

"Scared. . . scared."

Somehow I find Eloise, collapsed on the couch, forehead bleeding all over her black and white French Maid's outfit. The blood looks black in the moonlight. I try to comfort her, but she can't speak. Her eyes float through me like a blind woman. Tears trickle down her cheeks. Her lips move--but no sound. Only the whispers of the wind fills my ears. Around me now, human forms have vanished. I can only see birds, French Maid's outfits falling off their forms as they stumble through the house, crashing, falling, searching for their souls. For the souls I have stolen.

I awake.

Tangled in sweaty sheets. The lights of jets landing at LAX blinking out like false planets. In the other room Derek's—tap—tap—ding! rings through the air. I stumble to the bathroom, turn on the light, spill cold water against my face. Glancing up, I see my reflection. How weird it is to see a stranger's face in the mirror. Then I look down—do you see it too? My hand is shaking, a constant, quivering shake. What the hell is going on? I have to talk to someone.

Then I know who I'll tell about the dream.

"You're fucking nuts!" Charity laughs.

"It means something--"

"Yeah," she scoffs, "that you have some strange fascination with tropical birds."

On Saturday when I tell her I want to talk, she actually invites me to her place. She lives in the penthouse of an old Hollywood apartment building just off Sunset—all stucco Spanish and red tile. Burning with curiosity to see more, I can't wait for the elevator to open.

I should've known.

"I think Freudian dream analysis is crap," Charity bemoans, her voice echoing off the blank white walls of the two level flat. The only objects in the living room is an Apple laptop resting on a box of old movies-- Wuthering Heights, Love Story, From Here To Eternity. She tours me through the bedroom—bare walls, a wrinkled sleeping bag on the floor, and a Mickey Mouse clock resting atop enough boxes of Marlboro Reds to buy yourself the Russian presidency.

"So you're a minimalist?" I mutter.

"Like to keep mobile," she ushers me into the kitchen.

Cupboards empty. I almost wonder if she lives somewhere else--just rented the place to fuck with my head. We eat microwaved Pink's hotdogs on paper plates, paper napkins--an utterly disposable meal. Light creeps through the shades drawn over the majestic floor to ceiling window. This place has to cost at least a few grand a month--

"I keep having the dream," I mutter, "keeps progressing like a story."

Charity bites into half of her dog, muttering through food, "Spare me the Freudian crap. Maybe all those French maids is your subconscious telling you to clean your room."

"Or how wrong we've all been?" I lead in gently.

"I'm just beginning to find the experiment intriguing."

"Charity," I lean close, "this raping is reaching perverse—no," I correct myself, "unreal proportions. We're enslaving women."

"I don't see any slaves around," she scoffs, the bitter scent of double chili cheese and cigarettes on her breath, "how many women have you raped? Don't give me that look. When you strip all the bullshit away, raping's what you do--so how many?"

"Too many."

"So," she sucks back her Coke with a loud sipping sound, "you're screwing all these girls--building your confidence. Everything's going great. Then you fuck Elise--"

"Eloise--"

"Who cares?" she rolls her eyes and gnaws at a lock of hair "get in Elise's pants--the thirst is quenched. After getting what you want, you suddenly have a conscience."

"It's not like that at all--"

"Hypocrite," her eyes bore into me, "never heard you talk this way before you screwed little sweetie. And now," she stops gnawing on her hair, pointing the lock of hair accusingly at me, "want to ruin the party for the rest of us. On The Love Boat when the couple fell in love early, Captain Stubing didn't let them off early, did he? They cruised around until all the passengers got their rocks off."

"This is not the fucking Love Boat!"

"For you, it is," she turns upward, blinking her eyes like a star struck girl, clutching her heart as she speaks in an overdramatic, dreamy voice, "and for me, somewhere out there is my man or woman. . .or both. . . preferably together, waiting beyond the golden horizon for all of us to get buck naked and fuck. And you," she points a finger at me, "want to steal my chance—all the passengers chances at true happiness."

"What do you want from me—to roll over--let this continue? I'm the voice of reason here!"

"Fine. Let me put a bullet in his head!"

"Not that La Femme Nikita bullshit again? Are the voices telling you this? Forget to take your lithium today?"

"Hahah," she cracks dryly.

"If you really wanted to kill him, why does my permission matter?"

She jabs a finger at me, "Because dipshit, I don't want to spend the rest of my life locked up in some dank jail. I want no questions--no police. Archie's a push-over. But you, I'm not so sure. You've already said you won't let me kill him."

"What about your one time offer--"

"It's too late for that. Some crimes you pay for with your life," she stares into space and I have no idea what she's thinking or talking about.

"If he deserves to die for raping—then we all do," I stress.

Then I see a tear trickle down her cheek. She wipes it away, sighing, "I know," I glimpse the conflict inside her. Is it because she's a woman? Is it because she identifies with these test subjects? "like you said--we all got good things from this."

"What did it do for you?"

"That movie role I was trying out for? Got it. After three years, I got a part in a great film," and the tears and sadness leave her. She's smiling—a new façade to conceal the person underneath, "they shoot next month. I got it because of what we're doing."

I distill this conversation back to the hard, cold point: "This can't continue. Help me stop it."

"As a little girl I always wanted to make a difference. But I was missing that extra something--until now. This experiment has helped me. I've been a loner who's spent her life in emotional development drama classes, searching for an inner child that isn't there."

Probably find a hairball though. She isn't listening to me!

"I decided to start watching people," she ignores me, "that's when I saw what you guys were doing, I was intrigued. When I realized Derek led you all down that dark path, I thought I'd found a way to make a difference in the world by killing him," then she stares off into space, "but now," she hesitates, "to be honest—I'm not so sure. I think this is an experiment. . . I find what we're doing important and intriguing."

Jesus, I've lost her. She can read the sad look on my face. Jumping up, she saunters onto the living room rug, "Let me tell you about the acting role I got. When my character's a little girl, she sleeps over at a friend's house. The girl friend tells her not to wear panties to bed. My character thinks it's weird, but complies. Later that night-

-door opens," she points to her open bedroom door across the majestic living room.

"I don't really have time for this," I'm ready to go.

"Try something different, Cullen, like shutting up and listening," she rolls her eyes, "where was I? Oh yeah--the door opens," she points at the open bedroom door, "and in walks this shadowy character. Now the two girls are sleeping on their beds," she points down around her and races to the door, playing the shadow covered stalker, "and he walks in-- the friend's older brother."

"So this isn't a movie of the week."

She ignores me, "He creeps through the room, looking at the sleeping girls, wrapped in their Holly Hobby bedspreads. He starts getting it on with his own sister. This little kid's sucking serious dick," she mimics fellatio by poking a thumb at her cheek and poking at the other side of her mouth with her tongue, "it's twisted. They've been doing this a lot. Then the friend, who's too young to know what ejaculation is, tells my character she likes it when her brother pees in her mouth."

"I don't want to hear any more of this!" I'm about to stand.

But Charity acts out her narrative with chilling force, drawing my eyes back to her, "He climbs into my character's bed," she huddles in a fetal position on the floor, "she's crying—waves of emotions, confusion, fear, curiosity--tears trickle down her cheeks. He doesn't leave, arms wrapping around her," she arches forward in pain, "the brother and sister cajole me--laugh like it's nothing," fear covers Charity's face as she acts quite convincingly, "she's afraid—afraid of being young and stupid—afraid that this is just a normal thing adults do—afraid she'll be the fool. Then the pain! Where she's never felt pain before. She screams! The sister puts her hand over her mouth, muffling the sound! Struggling, grunting," she wiggles around on the floor, "she attempts to throw him off--saliva bubbling over my friend's hand. The friend tells her it'll soon feel good. He keeps fucking her--all she feels is the blood dripping onto the sheets--"

"I've had enough." She's a fucking lunatic--this mad woman who talks of perverse acting roles and finds gang rape fascinating! I stand up. "I'm tired of this shit. You lose yourself in fiction. We're living in the real world, Charity, where you now admire Derek," I space the next sentence out, speaking slowly, "you aren't even going to help me stop him, are you? All your talk about guns is bullshit."

"Now who's being dramatic?"

I decide to tell her that Veronica is missing.

"Yeah?" she says, "and someone shot John Kennedy too--doesn't mean Derek Van Horn was on the grassy knoll. He's a rapist—not a murderer."

"He has a gun--former owner left it in the house."

"Have you seen it?"

"No."

I refer to his slaving away in his locked bedroom on his supposed masterpiece. I question what the hell that could be? I claim he does nothing in there, like Jack Nicholson in The Shining--tapping away at his typewriter, writing the same lines over and over.

"So let's go," she wipes her lips with a napkin, "we know he's gone for the afternoon with his parents. Archie's working overtime all weekend. Want me to help you stop him--without putting a bullet in his head? Prove to me he's crazy. Cause until then, Cullen, you're just wasting air--blabbing on and on, putting a hole in the ozone layer."

"Fine," I stand up resolutely, hyped into a frenzy, "let's go!"

Twenty One

You can't see through Derek's window.

A tiny rectangle of frosted glass lingering amongst the shadows. Down here, the sun is obscured by bushes and undergrowth. Charity stares at me through a black Halloween mask, hiding her face. The masks were in her trunk. She thinks it's romantic to dress like a prowler.

I refused to wear mine.

We stand on a steep, dirt incline plunging down to the lower level of the house. A few moments ago we threw the deadbolt on the front door, exited the home through the sundeck sliding door, carefully scaling around the cliff set house. From the front drive, this incline is masked by bushes framing the sides of the split level home. Standing here, I'm not even sure if this window leads to Derek's bedroom.

"Maybe he doesn't have a window?" I wonder aloud.

"No," Charity mentally triangulates our position, finally pointing above, "the kitchen window is directly above this patch of bushes above. This is it."

Derek would kill us if he knew what we were plotting. Peering up through thick foliage at the top of the dirt incline, I assure myself a third time that his Volvo is gone-- he's off with his parents. I'm burning with curiosity to see what lurks beyond this window--is it stuffed full of Nazi paraphernalia or will we discover the grand masterpiece he's laboriously constructed?

Employing a credit card, Charity's deftly picks the catch on the window, "Used to date a burglar," she smiles around her black mask as she opens the sliding window-- her body blocking the window.

"What do you see?" I stumble along the dirt incline, trying to peer around her. Then I realize the window's obscured by fabric hanging in front of it—maybe a rug?

"Guess we gotta go in," Charity rolls up her sleeves.

Pushing her feet through the tiny window, she maneuvers herself, wiggling like a cat through the tiny frame. I follow, dangling legs through first. I doubt I'll be able to fit. The panel grinds into my hips, but somehow I make it. Charity supports my hips as I let go of the rim and fall.

"Ow!" I land on the floor with a thud, fabric covering my face, something poking me in the ass. I note the scent of citrus air freshener. Pushing and pulling, I struggle to free myself from this Indian blanket covering the wall. Then my eyes adjust.

The bedroom is smaller than mine. The inside of the metal door also has a numeric lock. The walls are white--a frameless mattress on the wood floor surrounded by a set of free weights. A roll top desk sits in one corner, a stereo in the other. But my eyes are suddenly drawn to the massive Nazi flag, the red flag I once glimpsed, covering the entire far wall.

"See," I point at it.

"Big deal—ouch!" Charity stubs her toe on a free weight dumb-bell, sending it rolling into the closet door.

I reach for what's poking me in the butt, producing a pistol. I'm holding it by the barrel for her to see. It's the first one I've ever held. Read the markings, it's a Berretta Centurion--the words .40 caliber spelled out in thick, white print atop the barrel.

"There," I say, "what more evidence do you need? He's nuts. Let's go."

"Hold on Tonto," Charity holds up her hand, "you said it belonged to the old owner of the house. Derek just found it—doesn't make him crazy."

I motion to the writing desk. Atop the bureau is a dust covered picture of a four year old Derek, his parents, mother still youthful, Dad still grim, at their feet is a baby toddler. But Derek's an only child--

"Will you open the desk," Charity blasts, "suspense is killing me."

Pulling back the roll top reveals an old typewriter-- ancient mechanical frame with a clean sheet of paper inside. Next to the typewriter rest two stacks of paper. On the left is a fresh pile of unused sheets--the other side is dog-eared pages, shuffled face down. This must be his masterpiece--too thick for a screenplay. Maybe it's a book? I lift the stack, searching for the title.

The cover sheet is bare.

Scan the second sheet—blank--flip through sheets—all white, shuffled, ragged, but totally empty, "See!" I cry, "he's more nuts than Jack Nicholson. At least in The Shining, the guy typed out a sentence over and over--"

"Tap—tap—ding!" I drop the papers in shock--the sound thundering through the room. Glance down at the typewriter. I haven't touched it. The sound thunders through me—tap—tap—ding! shaking the walls. I cover my ears and turn to Charity who stands at the stereo tape player. She presses the stop button.

The sound stops.

"Ah," she sighs, "the soothing sounds of the typewriter. A little more mechanical than the sounds of the ocean."

Holding up the blank pages, I say "He's not typing shit—playing the recorded sound."

Charity doesn't seem too concerned, frowning as she picks up one of the dumb-bells, "Maybe he doesn't want us to hear him working out? Or whacking off?"

I examine the Nazi flag covering the far wall. Motioning towards it, I realize that every door simply leads to another closed door when it comes to Derek Van Horn—

"Ding dong!" the doorbell resonates through the metal door.

We freeze.

With her black mask, Charity silently mimes the word: Derek?

Shit.

Could it be Derek? The front door's locked from the inside—to buy us time if this would happen. Charity races to the metal door, but it requires a code to open it from the inside! We set everything back as we found it—

Ding dong!

Racing up the incline, our knees covered with dirt, we're ready to sprint around to the sun deck door, reentering the house. Pushing through foliage, sunlight breaks against my face—blinding me for a moment as I turn, ready to scramble to--

"Cullen?"

I freeze. Ten feet away I see him. My eyes adjust. I see the rusting car in front of the garage. And there he stands, red faced, worried, upset—emotions rushing through him. But it isn't Derek.

Hal has come home.

"Why haven't you answered my calls?"

Hal doesn't want to drink the coffee I've made him. Steam rises from the "I Luv Mom" mug. Gathered around the kitchen table, he interrogates me, eyes burning like beacons on his wide, flat face.

"I've been really busy," I glance away.

"Busy?" Hal squirms, readjusting his Tulane cap. He suspects something. I've avoided him for two months-- who wouldn't suspect something, "heard you got fired."

"Got rehired—actually promoted. A lot's changed since you left."

"Could Batgirl leave us alone?" he grunts.

"You can address me directly," stings Charity as she takes her black mask off, "I'm right here. Might as well know--I'm privy to everything that goes on here."

Hal cups his face in his hands. He's worked up-- probably been rehearsing this moment ever since he was sent down to Mexico. Jesus, to him this story stopped after that first night. And look how worked up he is over just that. If he finds out what we've been doing since he left--

"I don't want to be here any longer than I have to," even though I can't see it, I can smell the faint odor of Hal's Purell in the air, "take a few days to find a new place. I didn't do anything, but I'm still thinking of going to the police--not going to stay in the same house as a rapist."

Charity giggles.

He turns to me "Who's she?"

"Boy are you in for a surprise," she explodes into snorting laughter.

"What surprise?" his flat cheeks turn red.

"Shut up," I tell her.

No one says anything more. But Hal and I know each other. He now sees a confident Cullen--immune to imposed morality. He knows many things have changed. He senses more than that--

"Oh no," he stumbles back, stool falling away. This is the first person outside our clan to glimpse the truth, "there are more?"

"Hal," I hold up my hands, "slow down."

"A lot more," Charity sighs. Reading my shocked reaction, she simply shrugs, "was gonna figure it out anyway."

Hal is frightened. He doesn't know the whole story, but knows enough to be very afraid. Scared people do drastic things. Eyes scanning the counter, he focuses on the cordless phone. Before he lunges for it--we collide! His frame is small, but he hits me hard, knocking me against the counter's edge. Tumble to the floor, Hal clawing at my face.

"Get the fuck off him!" Charity slaps him on the head.

"You lunatic!" Hal screams at me, spit flying as he claws my face, "you let him keep raping! You should all go to jail!"

I block his swings. But he keeps going, arms flailing, saliva and sweat raining down on me. But I spin around, tossing him back onto the floor. He kicks me hard in the stomach. Anger rushes. I crack him in the face. He collapses, a quivering heap of flesh. Charity's just standing there, shocked at this grown man crying.

"Get something to tie him up with!" I scream.

Madly throwing open drawers, she finds a roll of speaker wire. That'll work. Slamming him into a chair, I hold him down as she spins the wire around him—tying off his wrists, securing his chest and thighs to the chair. His nose is bleeding, trickles of red blood coursing down his flat cheeks, mixing with the tears from his cheeks.

I hear Derek's voice in my head saying that this type of man is what we revolted against—the effeminate male, the monstrous abortion of the feminist movement. The antithesis of the Alpha Wolf—a cherub's face, not a single stubble poking through. His frame tiny--weak and small--one punch, he's down for the count—

No. I banish Derek's voice from my mind. Run a hand through my hair--I feel so dirty. I just hit my best friend and tied him up! But what really gets me is that I know Hal's not crying from the pain--

He's crying for me.

He's crying because he's lost his best friend in the world. Around him, I realize how much I've changed. I forget about him possibly violating me. This man is too good to ever do that. Look at him, pale and small—like some guardian angel. We went through college together—shared a place in the City for four years--

The doorbell rings.

"What the hell is this?" gripes Charity, "Grand Central Station?"

We came in through the sundeck door so I never released the dead-bolt on the front door. I can only hope that it's Archie or Derek, locked out? Charity hedges her bets, dragging his chair behind the counter. From the foyer you can now only see his pale, round head. Then she grabs a meat tenderizer hammer from another drawer, holding it precariously over his testicles—like a railroad worker about to drive a spike:

"One move and you sing Bee Gees forever."

I open the front door.

It's Eloise.

Clad in jeans and a white top, the sun plays with the outline of her blonde hair falling around her shoulders. Shit! I forgot about our lunch date! I try to look calm--composed.

"Great place," she steps into the foyer, sees the hints of others beyond me--in the kitchen, "didn't know you had company."

I attempt to block her face from Hal's view, "No, was just about to step outside--see if you were here," thoughts race--I have to get her out of here! Can I leave Hal alone with Charity? I damn well can't let Eloise stay. Wrapping an arm around her, I casually walk us both out the front door--smiling, "was just leaving, myself."

"Slow down," Eloise says, almost tripping on the steps.

Alright, maybe I don't look so casual.

"Have a good time," Charity waves from the kitchen.

For a brief moment, Hal sees Eloise—a face he has not forgotten during those months of replaying in Mexico. His face goes white--this is just too much. The last thing I see before I shut the door, is his head falling over--

As Hal faints.

Once we're in the car, Eloise isn't hungry.

Sometimes women can sense things. But then again, maybe the perspiration drenching my brow or the fact that I haven't called her in days is a clue. I drive us to The Planetarium at Griffith Park--where James Dean had that fight in Rebel Without a Cause. We sit on a bench overlooking the entire valley. It's smoggy, we make out faint hints of skyscrapers and an iridescent glow in place of the sun.

"You haven't called all week," she starts, "did I upset you?"

"Nothing you did," I peer through the smog, "just tired from work."

"I don't want you to think I'm being clingy--we don't have to go to lunch. I mean—you don't have to do anything. I'm leaving LA. I promise I won't suffocate you--wouldn't do that to anyone."

"I know," I smirk, trying to calm my racing heart, "independence and all."

Her face glistens against the smog--the way Ingrid Bergman looked in the fog in Casablanca. Her beauty is so ravishing that my pulse slows, my mood calms. In place of guns and screaming is the mere whistle of the wind. Do you ever stop and wonder how you've arrived at a certain place in your life? I feel like that right now. Of all the people in the world, all the things happening—we met each other. She's everything I ever wanted in a woman. The words come out naturally--not the way they did at Veronica's ski lodge.

"I love you."

I want to lay my head in her lap, confess the whole thing--weep like a child. I should. For I've become Veronica, acting, pretending. I feel weak, like I can't be the Alpha Wolf anymore. But I've done things—things I can't explain to her. So what does she love? Some concept of me. If I love her, I must tell her the truth-- who I really am.

But not now--not just yet.

I just want a little more time with her. Stroking my hair, she says it too, "I love you," then she laughs, "of course this should happen as I'm leaving—already turned in the 30 day notice on my apartment."

"You could break it, maybe lose your deposit," then for no particular reason I ask, "why did you wear your hair up with me on our first dates?"

"My mother thought when I wore it up--made me look ugly."

"Now you don't mind looking good?"

"I have a fear," she sighs, "of being beautiful."

"You're not just beautiful--you're well read, the most educated, wonderful person I've met out here who--"

"I'm not asking you to stroke my ego. There are things you don't know about me. For instance, I'm well read, but I can't afford to lose my deposit. Then I'd have to ask my Dad for money."

"You guys don't get along?"

"We haven't talked in over four years," she sighs, "he's a bastard--cheated on my mother all his life. The reason we were dragged around the world was part business--part personal--but all him," little Eloise, silent and alone in her Roman apartment come even clearer into focus, "ever the proper woman, my mother found a husband at the bottom of a bottle of Tanqueray," Eloise pauses for a moment, "I always think of her looking at herself in that bedroom mirror, pulling back her skin with her hands, trying to stretch her way back to the youthful girl."

"Is she dead?"

"No. My story's sad--not dramatic."

The wind blows.

"At my age," Eloise smiles, "my mother was more beautiful than me—should see the pictures, blonde hair, long, skinny legs, black boots, short miniskirts. In New York, when she walked into Trader Vick's, every head turned--every eye on her. She thinks she was too beautiful--married far too young. Before she knew what life was about, it was behind her."

"So she gave you this independent streak?"

Eloise sighs, "Beaten into me. Always support yourself, never be a slave to another. But it's more than that. When I walk into a bar, hair down, makeup on, I feel like my mother--all black boots and miniskirts. The heads turn--eyes focus--what most women wish for, but it fills me with dread. Because in the spotlight of their gaze, I sense the power, but I know how fleeting beauty is. Soon it'll all be gone," she glances down at her hands, "the hands wrinkle," she looks at me, "I'll be a middle aged woman, gray skinned, whose ass--no matter how much I exercise, will always be a little too flabby."

I shake my head disbelievingly.

"Cullen," she sighs, "you're charming, but smart little girls learn what's in store for them," her eyes take on this dreamy quality. "Getting old isn't good or bad. It's the way it is. Whether nature or life dictated it, it's part of the human condition."

"So you wore your hair up cause you're afraid of being addicted to youth?"

She nods in agreement.

"And now you're not?"

"Around you, I'm not afraid of it," she scratches her back. I notice the tiny Italy shaped birthmark on her scapula—poking just out of her shirt.

The thought explodes through my mind—this is the Viking Girl! Derek raped her. What would kind hearted Eloise, stroking my hair and loving me, think if she knew the truth—that I was an instrument of her rape--that my best friend is back at my house with a meat tenderizer between his legs. Who knows what will happen when Derek gets home.

The tension piles on, turning my neck muscles to concrete, sending my heart racing. Flash--Irving called—flash--Veronica's missing--flash—Derek says he'd kill Veronica—flash—Hal will not back down—and then a new image. My friend's life is in danger. Derek pressing his Berretta pistol to Hal's head and pulling the trigger—

Stop.

I have to break our lunch plans. I have to get the hell out of here and back to the house before Derek gets home. I stand up, telling Eloise I have to leave.

"When will I see you again?" she asks on the drive

Twenty Two

"What?" frowns Charity, "didn't think I could take care of him?"

Sprawled across the couch, she nurses a beer and winks at me. I shake it off, no idea what she's trying to communicate. She flips the channels on the flat screen TV while she tries to whisper something to me. Before I figure out what's happening, I hear Derek's voice echoing through the room:

"Charity did a damn good job."

Turning, I catch him exiting the game room. Charity rolls her eyes, amazed that I didn't understand her winking thing. Derek approaches, dragging one of the living room chairs to the center of the room--just underneath the black security monitor. He's wearing a large black pin with red print that says: "Pornography Is The Theory, Rape Is The Practice."

"Anything worth watching on there?" he asks, calm and composed. As if someone isn't tied up in another room—as if we're all just going to lounge around and watch old Dating Game shows.

Flash—I imagine Derek pulling out his pistol, blowing Hal's head off.

He knows what I'm thinking. The way I see it, we have two alternatives. We can kill Hal, lock him up forever and flee the country, or let him go to the police— I can't allow any of them. Jesus! How did everything get so twisted—so confused! But Derek just whistles to himself, as if nothing's the matter.

The front door opens and in steps Archie, short sleeves and jeans--he's been at Prudential all day, "What's the emergency I had to get back for? Had to leave a system audit."

"Good," sighs Derek, "we can begin."

A minute later, Hal sits in the chair.

It's a scene out of one of those Arab terrorist movies. Tied up with speaker wire, he sits in the chair in the center of the living room, a brown paper bag over his head. In the second chair next to him sits Derek. Behind him, the flat screen TV projects a college football game, sound muted—angry players silently colliding as--

Derek pulls off the bag.

Hal squints, eyes adjusting to the light. We sit all around him, like a silent tribunal. The central air-conditioner switches on, the sound making him jump. Over his shoulder, a wide receiver scores a touchdown.

"What do you all want?" asks Hal.

The TV breaks to another Budweiser beer commercial with talking frogs.

Derek smirks, "The question, Hal, is what do you want? To send me to jail?" his hand sweeps across us, "send us all to jail? And I do mean us," leaning close, he produces the vial of Rufinol from his pocket, shaking the half empty bottle in Hal's face, "I couldn't have used all of these by myself."

Hal turns away.

Derek tosses the vial over to Charity. I see her quietly lift a couple of pills for herself, quietly stuffing them into her pocket. When she sees me looking at her, she makes a cute face: the little girl with a hand stuck in the cookie jar.

"What gets me is you were stupid enough to put your name on it," he points to the prescription label.

"In Mexico, it's legally given with a prescription."

"Why'd you get an illegal--"

"I was on spring break in Cancun during college--wanted something to help me sleep."

I vaguely remember Hal complaining after a spring break trip with some of our buddies. I didn't go with them, but he returned to school griping about the crude drinking and womanizing. Flash--imagine Hal, locked in a condo bedroom, sedated as his rowdy friends drink and carouse on the other side of the secured door--

"I think you've drugged people," Derek accuses.

"Bullshit!" Hal explodes, his eyes imploring Archie and I to action. We both stir, glancing away. What am I supposed to do? Let Hal call the police and toss us all in jail? That's no way out, "Rufinol," continues Hal, "is the most commonly prescribed sleeping pill in Europe and—

fuck you!" his face turns cherry red, "don't have to tell you anything, you degenerate!"

"You don't," answers Derek, "but if we're going to go down--the cops will know you gave us the cache of drugs in lieu of rent. Another tip, if you're going to dispose of drugs, flush em down the toilet—not in the trashcan--"

Hal tries to speak.

But Derek raises the tone of his voice, charging on, "Believe me, we will all testify to that fact. And we have the vial with your name on it. I'm sure the authorities can go south of the boarder--dig up the prescription record with your name on it. Now, I am a man of my word. I once invited you into my household and I will insist you make this your home for awhile—until we've all had time to cool."

Hal's chest rises up and down, seething.

"But if you're thinking of opening that big mouth to the police," Derek points to his wolf's head pin on his t-shirt, "all of my money will go into our legal defense and you will take the rap," Derek's face becomes almost satanic as he leans close, ranting, "AND GO TO JAIL FOR THE REST OF YOUR WORTHLESS FUCKING LIFE!"

Hal sits frozen with fear.

A long silence. There really is no way to stop him, is there? He has so much money. O.J. got off, why couldn't he? And anyone who defies him goes to jail. Charity turns to me, our eyes locking. She raises an eyebrow--as if to signal me to some kind of action.

"Well," Archie sighs, "guess that's that."

The cuffs are unlocked. Slowly Hal scans us, realizing just how far we've gone without him. If he could, he'd empty a bottle of Purell into his hands, but the speaker wire holds his wrists firm. Hals' now the kid who missed a year of school, static and unchanged, now surrounded by others who have grown up. Still I wonder--have we regressed? So concerned with staying out of prison, I've procrastinated--refusing to face the horror of our actions. Maybe Hal's the only moral character here?

"I'll be in the hospital all week anyway," he stares down at the glass table like a beaten dog, "then I'm out," but his threat is hollow—Charity would call it senseless blabbing. Turning to me, our gazes lock--in his eyes I see something I've never seen before—

Pure hatred.

I glance away, looking up at the black orb overhead, part of Derek's elaborate security monitors. In the black, round sphere I see all of us reflected back, twisted and distorted, like we're being photographed through a wide angle lens. I'm dazed, confused, spinning around and around. What am I supposed to feel? How am I supposed to act?

Charity looks at me again and I feel so distant from her. Turn to Derek, he's my only hope to ending this thing. The Clan began with him and me. Maybe it can end that way too. I tap him lightly on the back, "Derek-- think you have some time this week?"

We agree that he'll pick me up on Monday after work.

Derek is half an hour late.

At dusk, the shadow of the Calder statue stretches across the sidewalk in front of ITM. Derek pulls up in his Volvo and we drive down La Cienega for a long time.

"We going for a drink?" I inquire.

"Of sorts," he smiles cryptically, snapping in a Crosby Stills and Nash CD.

We drive forever, heading through Korea town-- towards the distant skyscrapers of downtown. The traffic is thick and the neighborhoods sketchy. Downtown LA is a ghost town after five o'clock—wind whipping down empty streets. You'd expect a tumble weed to float by.

It's the kind of place you don't drive to without a reason. Wild thoughts race through my head. Is he going to kill me--leave me out here to die?

You can see the look of surprise on me when we drive up to the Staples Center. All blue neon lights and slick glass, it's the flagship arena for the city. The car is dropped off at the V.I.P. parking center. We're ushered through a private entrance up escalators to a sleek hallway of dark walls with individual doors.

"My family has a skybox," Derek opens the door.

The skybox is immaculate. A large room with a bar and wall to wall mirrors overlooking seating area for fifteen to twenty spectators—place is totally empty. Where the front wall would be is an open expanse peering out on the massive sports arena. Down below, two Hockey teams duel it out over the ice, their faces projected on massive TV's lining the walls.

"Here," Derek hands me a beer.

We sit down at the front of the box, the crowd cheering below us. Derek's eyes follow the players. I can tell he likes Hockey. But I'm not here to watch a sports game. I choose my words very carefully, replaying them over and over in my mind before I say, "Derek, the entire thing has to stop."

"It's an experiment," he smirks, eyes still on the game. Down below two players are beating each other with their sticks and the crowd's going mad, "experiments always end—just not yet."

"Sooner or later a test subject," listen to me dancing around the truth, "a girl--a victim," I stress that word again, "a victim is going to go to the cops--if she hasn't already."

I think the opposing team's player got thrown in the penalty box. Because the crowd screams as Derek answers, "Hasn't made the papers yet."

"C'mon!" I explode, "you—yourself said they wouldn't print a serial killer in the paper unless they absolutely had to! They know about all of them—we've got half the city waking up at the damn beach. People catch on. And," run fingers through my hair, "it's more than that—what we're doing is wrong."

"Cullen, you getting moral on me?"

"Maybe so," I sigh, "I'm not pointing the finger. I did everything by my own freely made decision. But I see things differently now—I can never see things again the way they were."

Derek smirks, "Reminds me of a story my Grandfather used to tell—you know, the one who looted the silverware--"

Another story is not what I need right now. But he presses on:

"In the last days of the European war, he was on a scout mission overrun by Germans," Derek tells me how the Nazis interrogated the man, finally tying him to a tree in front of a firing line. They draw their guns and "in the final moments of his life, he feels the hands of death upon him. It's not icy, just paralyzing. He shuts his eyes, bids goodbye to his life. The German guns fire. And nothing--just the sounds of the soldiers laughter!"

The crowd cheers as a player scores a point.

"My Grandfather gave himself up to death," continues Derek, "bid goodbye to everything he had, all that he loved. He was naked, divested of all things . . . but when the smoke cleared, he was alive. They fired blanks at him. But he had died--notwithstanding the facts, psychologically, he went to the edge and returned to tell the tale. He said he was never the same after that. That's what we're doing."

"Derek, we're gang raping women."

"That was just the beginning," he lifts a cautious finger, "we're just beginning the next stage of the experiment. Do you know that with certain psychotropic drugs, we could actually converse with test subjects for hours and they could answer in lucid, clear responses? They would be comfortable around us, engaging in conversation, no fear of us--no memories of any of it when they awake."

"This is fucking madness!" I stand up.

Two more players are at it on the ice, fighting and clubbing each other to death as the crowd chants excitedly. A collective roar of energy filling the vast auditorium.

"We've already sailed farther than any could imagine," Derek turns to me, sucking back the last of the beer, "Masters and Johnson never even got their feet wet. The Marquis De Sade never left the safety of the cove. None of them could've imagined the horizons we've already navigated! Think of the distant shores to discover—ports of call at the epicenter of our species— beaches hidden from even ourselves."

Flash—all four of us on Charon's boat, sailing across the river of fire towards hell. Chills rush down my spine. Down below, two more players club it out down below, red blood on white ice.

"How could someone from your background, with all the privileges of life, do such horrendous things?" I ask.

"Don't even pretend to know what my life's been like," he shudders, "you have no idea what I've been through," the façade drops away for a moment, "you've no idea how twisted and pained it all was."

"Then just tell me why?" I sigh, "why are you doing all this?"

The crowd cheers.

"Because you're such a great protagonist," he jokes.

"Fuck you!" I explode, tossing my wolf's head pin at him. It's the first time I've ever challenged Derek Van Horn. The pin falls to the ground without a sound, "this is like some Nazi experiment--submerging children in ice to see how long it takes for them to die. We've broken so many codes of decency, I've lost count!"

"You were there with us, Cullen—with us all the way. When you came to me, you were nothing. A kid who crept softly across floors, afraid to wake his mother. You wanted to be a writer, but became an agent—full of fear and self-pity. Now you stand up to me? I've given you all this—more than you could ever imagine."

I remain firm, "It has to stop."

He grows silent, turning back to the game.

I don't care. Because I realize that at that moment, I hate Derek Van Horn—hate him more than anyone I've ever met. He's the puppeteer at the strings. He's the Pied Piper, luring us on with his music. If he hadn't raped Eloise, none of this would've happened. And no, I don't blame him for everything--I take responsibility for my own actions. But it must end. That is all I know—it must fucking end! We're not going to be able to end this peaceably. Do I get a gun? Do I go with Charity's first plan? No. There must be another way. But how do I persuade my fellow wolves to stop killing--when the taste of blood is so alluring?

I leave the skybox.

I go back to work.

My office is the only refuge I have left. It's almost nine o'clock. I shut off the lights and sit in my chair, staring out my window at the traffic on Wilshire Blvd. I just want to clear my mind, squinting my eyes until the stream of traffic grows into two endless streaks of red and white light—

"Am I disturbing you?"

Turn around. Claryssa stands in the doorway. The light from the hall casts a long shadow across my office. We haven't spoken since our alleyway break. She shuts the door behind her and turns on the lights. I see a look of worry across her face.

Pulling the headset from my ear, she sits down, saying, "Saw you leave earlier," a car alarm rings outside, "you were with Derek Van Horn."

"Yeah," why's it any of her business?

"Been hanging out with him a lot?"

"We're roommates."

She shudders, "When you asked me about the Van Horns--that day in the alleyway, I warned you to stay away."

"I don't always do what people tell me, Claryssa" I try to appear strong, "we've become good friends--"

"Derek and I were at Harvard," she picks at her eye, "did you know that?"

The TV dating show flows through my mind, "Derek went to Duke."

But her expression never changes as she repeats herself, "Derek and I were freshman together at Harvard. And without all his money, he would've gone to jail--"

"Spare me the dramatics—what's your point?"

"Have you really changed that much, Cullen Gersh?" then she says it. Once again, I feel the ground fall out from under me. Suddenly the .40 caliber pistol and Nazi paraphernalia and threats on Veronica's life and discussions on morality are turned upside down as Claryssa's words reverberate through my head:

"Derek was arrested for brutally beating and raping a girl."

Twenty Three

The verdict is in.

Yes, he's fucking nuts! Remember how he professed his naiveté at Mr. Chow's, that it was the first time he ever did such things. Bullshit! And forget about the detached psychological allure he invested in his "social experiment". This man's already violently beat and raped someone, scarring them for life! Claryssa says the poor girl lost teeth and had her nose broken. Who knows how many women he's destroyed over the past years? He probably got bored raping alone—needed partners.

This changes everything.

We never psychologically scarred anyone, taking pleasure in their pain. Derek never navigated us into uncharted waters. He lured us into his own ocean of pain and madness, a place he knew quite well. Yes, he masked it all so carefully, cutting out the violent elements as he tailored the horrendous act for our tastes. But he was truly like some pied piper possessing us with his music.

How stupid I am.

Stupid! Stupid! Stupid! I race my piss stenched Honda down San Vicente Blvd, trying to escape it all. In my mind's eye I observe Derek Van Horn with his jeans in an imaginary t-shirt that reads "If You're a Rapist and You Know It, Clap Your Hands." Peer into the eyes of a lunatic—the fucking Boston rapist!

Remember our conversation back at Mr. Chow's-- him confiding about all those feelings of empowerment he garnered from rape? Yeah, like he'd never done it before in his whole life! When in reality he's a Charles Manson type, inviting us into his house because it's not fun to rape alone.

No.

Rumors. There's no proof other than Claryssa's accusations. Maybe he pissed her off in school? Or better yet, he never said anything to her. You know how she hates rich people. She's always gossiping too. Shit, she's the Soviet bear--the hater of all the rich and powerful. When I ask her if the story is documented in the Boston newspapers, she claims his family dispatched a league of lawyers to Cambridge to quash the whole affair. She can't quote names or places. The only substantial evidence she offers is that she thinks a friend wrote the sordid affair up in The Crimson—that's Harvard's campus publication.

So right now, it's mere conjecture made by a total gossip monger.

Then why am I here?

Stop the car--strange to be back in this once familiar environment. I locate a vacant parking space right in front. Getting out of the car, I stop, examining the stucco building, tiny balconies crammed full dying plants and rusty bicycles. Veronica's apartment building hasn't changed a bit. Search for the spare key underneath the cupid statue in the pile of mud constituting a flower bed.

It's gone.

Just then a tenant, college girl in a UCLA sweater, leaves the building. I walk in before the door shuts. Glance at the mailbox--Veronica's name's still on it. Stroll into a large open atrium, notice that in the cement, you can see the outline of a swimming pool--like so many, filled it in for insurance reasons. A security light near the stairwell faintly illuminates her front door. It's locked. Check the living room window facing me--she never keeps it locked.

It slides open.

I make sure no one's watching. Why am I here, the thought racing through my head. Claryssa broke the dam and I'm awash in Irv's call, Claryssa's accusations, Eloise's face—I'm acting crazy because I'm losing my mind!

I climb into the apartment.

The place smells musty. Turn on the light in the kitchen. Dishes still in the sink. Open a shelf, breakfast cereals, Triscuits—everything in order. Enter the bedroom, meager light creeping through the window from the apartment balcony next door. Her Gone With The Wind posters are on the wall. I notice the space on the desk created by the jewelry box I stole. Open the closet, clothes intact. Turning to the bed, I stop--certain something's wrong. The pooh bear is still in her bed.

My legs wobble.

In my mind, I hear Veronica, "I could never leave Pooh Bear--he's my little Rhett Butler. We've never spent a night apart."

Derek killed her! The bastard chopped her up, served her back to me and called it chicken! I mean, everything tastes like chicken, right? Remember that week where all we ate was chicken--No. Calm down—be cool. I can discern human flesh from chicken—right? It has to taste different. I think I'm going to throw up! Rest on the edge of the bed, bed-frame creaking under me. Deep breaths. Maybe I should get a paper bag and—ah, never knew how that worked anyway. Jesus, I'm trapped in a nightmare.

What should I do?

Boy does that question carry a lot of luggage. Like-- what do I stand for? Am I a moral person? Shouldn't I suffer. The list gets longer every time I think about it. And then the final thought, a whisper from the depths of my mind:

You've raped women.

I know! Let the whispers tell me something new. I know I'm a fucking worthless degenerate. You know how you have those wacky dreams sometimes? Wouldn't it be great if I just woke up now and it was all over. Stare at the phone. I'm not in a dream. I must accept the consequences of my actions. I must call the police--

Then I see Eloise's face.

Tears coat my eyes, burning and salty. She would fade to black. I'd go to jail-- never to see her again unless it's through a Plexiglass wall. Who can root for the bad guy, let alone love him? She goes on with her life, marries a man, has kids, meanwhile I'm grabbing my ankles in San Quentin, trying not to clinch my sphincter as Luther sticks it to me, drawling on about Momma's Jambalaya.

That's where morality will get me.

Grab a Kleenex.

With tissue paper, I wipe my prints off everything and leave. Back in the car, I resolve to get the article—to align Charity and Archie with me. That's what I have to do—get documented evidence of the Boston rape.

UCLA's research library is pretty good.

It's open until eleven, so I'm afforded a few hours to try and locate the publication. Do you see me in the corner? Tie loosened, sleeves rolled up, gnawing madly on the pencil as I tap on the computer keys. The Boston Globe has all their back issues archived online. Claryssa and I are the same age, so I know the year to check. Scrolling through papers, I find no mention of Derek Van Horn or a rape at Harvard. Then I remember The Harvard Crimson. It's highly doubtful the UCLA library would have an archive of them. From a library search I discover that they're not even archived on the internet. I get a phone number for the editor's office. No answer. It's late on the East Coast.

I'll have to call tomorrow.

On the way home, I'm tired.

With drowsy eyes, I almost drive right into the back of a parked post office jeep. It's parked right around a bend in the road near our house. Slamming my foot into the breaks, my Honda stops inches from the back bumper, the huge Post Office eagle logo illuminated in headlights.

I'm still shaken when I enter the house.

It's dark. I open the door, creeping through the living room. Charity's asleep, legs sprawled across the couch as an infomercial for an abdominal machine casts strange light through the room. I continue creeping when I see it on the kitchen counter--

"Holy fucking fuck!"

That carefully worded exclamation should give you an idea of how shocked I am. Passed out on the kitchen counter is a man in his mid-thirties, blond hair, US Postal Service shirt still on, pants at his ankles, satchel at his side. Laying on his stomach unconscious, the bright blue dildo rises out of his ass like a beacon. Charity turns to me from the couch, yawning. Our bodies reflect against the black, security unit overhead.

"You--" I struggle for words, "you drugged the mail man?"

"I told everybody I was itching to do it," she yawns.

"You don't fuck a Federal postal carrier with a dildo!"

"Oh," she sighs, "that was really all Derek."

"Listen to yourself. Did you know Derek brutalized a girl at Harvard, beat her senseless--raped her--"

"Was that while he was up on the grassy knoll," she rolls her eyes, "and I guess you have no proof of this either."

"I'm going to get proof!"

Tap—tap—tap—ding! flows through the air, the faint sound coming from downstairs. I imagine Derek in his room, broadcasting the fake typewriter sounds over his stereo. What the hell is happening.

"You're all fucking mad!" I scream.

She shrugs, unable to see what the big deal is, "Chill out. You're so afraid of everything," how far she's drifted from me. There's such a distance between us. I search for the only face I can trust in this mad house, "Is Hal home?"

"Nope," she mutters, "I think he sleeps at the hospital now."

I gesture back to the dildo rising out of his white ass at a forty five degree angle-- like a leaning tower of Pisa, "This guy could go postal on us!"

"I can protect myself," she yawns, staring idly at a Thigh Master infomercial on TV, "guy had a cute ass. But he was so annoying. I bring him in and all he does is yap yap yap about Scientology. Of all the postmen in the world, I get fucking L. Ron Hubbard. Told him I had to go back to work too—bastard wouldn't leave. You two would get along, both got diarrhea of the mouth--"

"You fucked the postman," I'm still trying to reconciles the moment.

"Relax. I dropped it in his beer real quick," she fiddles with the TV remote, unsuccessfully trying to turn off the Thigh Master commercial, "which reminds me—they're not supposed to drink on duty. You're a lawyer, isn't that a Federal offense?"

"I'm sure butt-fucking one with a dildo is!"

"I told you, that was Derek's handiwork. He got pissed when he found the guy on the counter. I just wanted the bastard to shut up. But Derek screamed that since I'd gone this far, I had to go to town on him. He was just pissed that someone did something without his permission. You guys just don't get it," she turns, eyeing the dildo, "this really isn't how women think of rape. We're not just men with tits--"

"Thought men and women were all the same in your book?"

"No. I specifically said we could be socialized to act differently--"

"I'm not having this conversation now!" I cover my ears.

"You started it," she rolls her eyes, "anyway, I'm going to stuff our mail back in his bag, leave him down the hill. And don't start bitching. Archie'll help. The guy won't remember a thing."

I point back at the blue shaft of plastic, "Don't you think his ass'll hurt?"

"We're not sadists," she rolls her eyes, "used lubrication. Anyway, take it from someone who's been there—doesn't hurt as bad as you think."

There's a subtext to our conversation, isn't there? So I just say it, "You're lost aren't you. . .lost in those dreams," fucking postmen--more reckless and crazed than I ever thought to imagine.

What's happening to us all?

"You're still full of shit," she smirks, "on Saturday when Derek ripped Hal to shreds, I sat there, watching you. Eyes downcast, you were the obedient school boy. But that was the time to act, wasn't it? While he tore your best friend to shreds. We were all there. Archie would've said nothing. I would've gone with you—you know that. I even had a gun."

The ranting of an insane asylum patient.

"You did nothing," she rolls over, "maybe Derek's right? Maybe the powerful always win. That's why I'm not going to do anything," she points to the dildo, "that's the truth. What we're doing makes complete sense."

First thing on Thursday, I call Harvard.

While on hold with one of the staff members, the same question rolls through my head—did I miss my opportunity? Shit, I never even saw the opportunity. Or maybe, like a pussy, I tried my best to ignore it. Charity's right. The moment was in my grasp—the moment to end it all between us, strictly within the clan. Even effeminate Hal had the courage to face Derek. But me--

I blew it.

"You still there?" the woman at Harvard breaks my train of thought, "we had a fire in our archives center. Those articles burned up."

A sick feeling in my stomach. No evidence. Walk to the window and set my forehead against the glass. Tears trickle down my cheeks. Look at my reflection—like looking at a stranger. I hate this job—I hate this office—I hate this world. I want my life back! I want the old insomniac, weakling, pussy ass Cullen Gersh. But there can be no peaceable terms. Charity has already drifted from me. The Crimson article is destroyed--I've no evidence to persuade her or Archie to my side. I see Eloise's face fading into darkness--drifting farther and farther away from me. There's no way out of this except--

"Sir," my assistant speaks over my headset, "you're late for your lunch with Mo Simon."

I'm not very talkative at lunch.

We eat in a window table at his favorite place, a restaurant called The Mandarin on Camden, just down the street from our old watering hole, El Torito. In this elegant Chinese venue, we dine on Chicken in Black Bean Sauce and Beans Szechwan, interrupted every other moment by producers, directors, actors, wanna-be's—all coming to pay their respects to this bald headed uber agent of ITM. My stomach gurgles with nausea. I stare at my plate of food, thinking that it is merely an illusion.

All this must be taken away from me.

"So," Mo finally says--the tendons around his bald head flexing as he bites and chews, "looks like you're doing fine--" he talks business for awhile. But I'm not thinking about that crap right now. Looking at the waiter, bent over as he scrapes up a broken glass, I imagine myself bent over as Luther slaps my ass in some dank San Quentin prison cell.

My bowels gurgle.

"Listen Cullen," light reflected off the chrome bumper of a Land Rover cruising down Camden cuts across Mo's bald head, "there's some hot independent film floating around town. I know your buddy--that pecker head, Irv Hirschberg's trying to snatch it."

"Uhuh," I'm going to go to jail—I've no time for work. The tension kills me. My stomach is on fire--intestines are like a snake, slithering through my body.

"I want you to find out more about it," continues the Lemur, "snatch it up for our Indy film department. I want to broker this project. It's some kind of Truman Show shit. Same old, same old—scripts supposed to be great, but barely anyone's seen it—shot on a shoestring budget. I'll have a buddy of mine at Paramount call you with details."

"Sure, Mo," I mutter, "no problem," but I'm really wondering how I'm going to break the news to him—that his young protégé is a Ted Bundy serial rapist who's about to turn himself in to the authorities. My bowels flare and distend. I press my legs together, trying to hold it all in, but I can't hide it--my body revolting under the stress.

I fart.

Mo and all the industry types around don't say a thing—silent and complacent as they dine. Only two Midwestern tourists grunt in displeasure. How do I know they're tourists? Look at their plaid and khaki ensembles-- fell out of an old Ralph Lauren ad. I cover my face, embarrassed.

"Yeah, that's right," Mo turns to them indignantly, "he passed gas. What? You gonna sue him?"

They turn away, fanning their nose with napkins.

"Fuckin' out of towners," he resumes his eating as if nothing's happened.

My body has fired the first revolutionary shot. I must end this—my suffering must begin. You want me to suffer. Hell, I want me to suffer. So let's just get to it.

After lunch, I'm turning myself into the police.

Mo gets a phone call as we finish eating.

Turns out some lawyer needs to see him down the street. He asks me to drive his car back to ITM. So here I am, once again, back in the hunter green Aston Martin, It's fitting. One last ride—it's like the last meal they serve prisoners. I bathe in the smell of the green piped cream leather. Drop the roof, roll down windows, grip the walnut inlayed wheel, crank up the music—he's got Beethoven's 9th in the CD player.

I'm driving to my death sentence.

Turning onto Wilshire Blvd., Beethoven in my ears, I think upon the weak willed child who drove this car three months ago. How much has changed since then. Back then this car was the manifestation of all I did not have. It was the reserved booth in the restaurant, the hotel suite I couldn't afford, the party I was never invited to. And now I've peered beyond the curtain, seen what others could only dream of. The price I paid was in human bondage—hurting and crippling people—Jesus, sounds like some Dostoevsky morality tale. I hurt all those women—and for what? So that I could realize that the only allure of the reserved booth is the fact that you're not allowed to sit there. Hey, c'mon, it's not made of gold—it's just another fucking booth. I mean look at this car—it's just stupidly overpriced and a bitch to fix.

Stopping at a light on Wilshire, I notice three blonde flamingoes, Gucci and BCBG bags in hand, standing on the south corner of the street, the Beverly Wilshire Hotel behind them. They probably enjoyed an outrageously priced lunch of mixed greens and water. By now, you know the drill--

Take it in slow motion.

Lips purse, pupils dilate, sunglasses drop as they take a closer look at me in the Aston Martin. I fumble at the stereo, lowering Beethoven's symphony. The shortest one waves, "How you doing?"

Screw this. If I weren't in this car in this suit, they wouldn't even notice. It isn't even worth doing in slow motion—it's not worth any time at all. I'm going to drive back to the office and call the police and tell them everything. I'm going to end this madness.

Just then the taller of the girls leans forward. She smiles flirtatiously. There's something familiar about her—hell, she looks like all the other flamingoes. With a flirtatious grin, she whispers something to me. It takes me a moment to realize what she's said. She's already spun around on her heels as I replay the words again:

"Just drive away."

Her confused friends watch her walking away from them. They call out to her. Then they turn back to me as if I said something to cause this reaction. But you saw me—I said nothing! Only as she enters the Beverly Wilshire Hotel do I place her--

It's the Russian girl with glasses who screamed "Da!"

The one in the Playboy pictorial. But how could she recognize me—was she like Charity? Was she immune to the—

Slam my foot on the gas.

"Sir, you can't park--" the valet barks--his sentence sliced off as I race into the lobby of the hotel. Eyes dart. I spot her, a storm of long legs and blonde hair, racing to the bathroom.

It's deadly still.

Perfume hangs in the air. The marble tiled bathroom is as big as my bedroom—totally empty and still. Bend down, peer under the stalls. The toilets all start to flush, making me jump—I catch the hint of a shoe in the last stall. Someone else is surprised too. Walking up to the door, I knock--

"Go away!" I hear her say through a thick foreign accent, "just go."

"You know me?"

"Go away—or I call police!" she threatens. I hear her sing song tones of cell phone buttons being pushed.

Fine, do me the favor.

"You were in the Playboy pictorial—weren't you?"

No answer.

I bang on the door.

She chatters on in Russian—some foreign language. I'm about to rip the door off when security charges in— two burly Gay Bears in black suits. Grabbing me, I'm pulled out of the bathroom. Maybe it's my suit or the car or the fact that I chased a hot blonde into the bathroom-- they think this is some kind of lover's squabble.

"I just need to get back in there," I protest on the street, "I have--"

"You're trespassing," the Gay Bear shuts his eyes, "now drive on."

Hear me out.

She recognized me. She must've remembered something about that night. Now if you bumped into an assailant who drugged and raped you, I could understand the running away—the hiding bit too, but why would you ever ask the criminal to just drive away? And if he's chased you into some bathroom, you're frightened, you've got a cell phone. Why would you threaten to call the cops? You'd have already called them! Screw that. You'd run to the hotel security guards, begging for them to protect you, pleading for them to catch the assailant who's chased you into the lobby--you'd do everything in your power to stop me.

Another red light.

Two down and out Mexicans in cruddy jeans motion across the cross walk. An idea! Maybe she's an illegal immigrant, a Russian hooker who smuggled her way into the country—doing skin pics for money while she searches for a fat cat boyfriend in the LA clubs? Maybe she can't contact the police because it'll mean instant deportation.

How awful is that? To be raped, to be violated, and you can't tell anyone. How awful we've been. We never stopped to think about the women, waking on beaches, martini glasses and bottles strewn around—feeling of violation inside them—I flush the thoughts out of my mind.

I can end this.

Pressing the gas, the car gracefully accelerates. I drive into ITM's underground garage, exchanging Mo's sleek sports car for my poor excuse of an automobile. My mind races as I drive away. Charity's right--can't waste any more time. Driving down Santa Monica Blvd., I spot the white marble building rising majestically over the low skyline.

There's no open spots around the place. I stop in front of this short, squat Mexican guy clad in a Taco Bell T-Shirt that says "Just Drop The Chalupa", sitting gray faced on a public bus bench.

I toss him the keys as I leave my car forever, "It's all yours," won't need it again. Confused, he tries to return the keys, but I walk away assuring him that, "It's yours."

Then I consider warning him about the A.C. filter, but I don't speak Spanish. Hell, he'll find out soon enough. The worn soles of my shoes click against the marble steps. But I don't hear that. Rather, Beethoven's "The Ode To Joy" blasts German song into my very soul. In a way, I feel joyous--at peace with the world. Turning back, I glance at the sky for the last time with the eyes of a free man. I can answer those whispers now—I've done wrong, but I shall repent and now I shall suffer.

"The Ode To Joy" continues.

And before you say it, I didn't come here because I think it's cushier than Los Angeles. I came because it's close and I know how to get here without getting lost. I remember it from the Eddie Murphy movie. That's right.

I'm giving myself up in Beverly Hills.

Twenty Four

They must be pissed.

I tell my story to the reporting officer--the whole thing, blow by blow as I sit in a room of gray faces and police uniforms. They usher me to an interrogation room—just like in the movies—big light glaring down. I sit there for almost two hours, sounds of cops and dispatchers flowing through the closed door. They're pissed about the postman. C'mon, be realistic, even if we were lucky enough that no girl contacted them, you just can't butt-fuck a Federal mail carrier and expect to get away with it.

I stare down at the Styrofoam cup of water they offered me after the first hour. Ripples course across it as the door finally opens and two of them enter, their Old Spice aftershave overwhelming. The second one drags a chair close, the crinkle of his belt and holster as he sits. It sends a second shock wave of ripples across my water.

I glance up.

There are two of them. The first one is older, thick gray mustache concealing his lips as he speaks. His eyes are black, framed in leathery, beef jerky dried skin-- reminds me of a weathered bull, "What is your occupation, Mr. Gersh?"

The second one is young, reminds me of a sheep—all baby face and smooth white skin as he pulls out his tiny note-pad, ready to scribble notes.

"I'm a feature film agent at International Talent Management--ITM," I answer. Then I point to the dossier in his hand, "I told all of it to the reporting officer."

I know they're going to go through a litany of questions again and again and again—just like on NYPD Blue. But I decide to make it simple. I'm here so I can go to jail for the rest of my life. I'm not going to fight it:

"We left them all at the beach—every last one on the sand," I spill out my soul--tears welling in my eyes. It's a horrendous confession of sins and injury. By the end, I'm sweating profusely as I stress that, "I want you to know-- we didn't hurt, physically--didn't hurt any of em."

They say nothing. The bull merely winces, mustache still as the water in my cup. The sheep jots a final note or two in his pad. More silence. Maybe I was so complete that they don't even need to ask questions? So I place my hands on the table, waiting to be handcuffed as I murmur, "Well—do I go to a holding cell now?"

Then they laugh.

The leathery bull grins, lips peeking out beyond the mustache, "That's a funny one, Mr. Gersh."

"What?" am I losing my mind?

The bull holds up his hand like he's stopping traffic, "We had this one guy-- William Morris agent--all pumped up on heroine, claiming he ran over Donald Duck on Roxbury and Little Santa Monica. Funny part was, son of a bitch keeps talkin like Donald, saying," and the bull blows air along his cheek, imitating Donald, "book me! I'm a menace to society!"

The sheep laughs.

The mustached cop smiles, "I been at this twenty years kid and it never ceases to amaze me," he leans close, Old Spice ever present, "got a little too coked up after lunch, huh? Look," he puts a hand on my shoulder, "LAPD gets their kicks busting actors humping hookers on Sunset Blvd. In Beverly Hills, we pride ourselves on our sense of equanimity. So just go home, get some sleep-_"

"Didn't you read the report!" I point at the file, my entire story typed out by the reporting officer, "it's all there! Every detail. I know you don't print the details of these rapes in the newspaper—so how could I know all this stuff unless I'm guilty?"

"Mr. Gersh," the bull strokes his mustache, "we are not idiots. Over the past 24 months, there has not been one reported rape victim who woke up on any beach in LA county."

"But it's true!" I demand. I've been transported to the fucking Twilight Zone!

"Even if these women didn't remember a thing," the bull continues, "one of them would've contacted the police or at least have been spotted by the beach patrol--"

"You have to put me in jail!" I stick out my wrists.

"Kid," the Bull takes a deep breath. The joke is tiring him, "unless you got some coke you haven't blown up your nose, you're going home. And don't even think about bothering the guys down at LAPD. We already informed them about this crank story."

"What about Veronica?" I stammer, "Derek killed her!"

"Yeah," the bull grimaces, "we spoke to this Irving Hirschberg. He tells us she's some flaky actress. He just heard from her. She's back in town. Turns out she got some commercial in Fiji and is now shacked up with the director--"

Flash--Veronica's chattering on about a Pert Hair Products commercial she's trying out for, "Shoots in Fiji in a few weeks. They don't give a lot of warning--just call you and poof--you're on a plane to the islands—real remote, no phones or faxes—it's like The Blue Lagoon."

Well, I feel like the village idiot.

The sheep turns around, "Mr. Gersh, I've been sort of writing a script—crime drama that's much grittier than your baby talk story."

Great.

Of all the officers in the world, I get the screenwriter.

The bull winces at his partner, "What are you talking about—grittier? His story's laughable. Who would ever leave their rape victims on a beach? He'd get nabbed before he could begin."

Silently, I listen to the sheep reply:

"Not if he used different beaches?"

"And what? Cruise the 405 with drugged girls? Not too sound a plan."

"Could drop em at a theme park like SeaWorld," he turns to me for a reaction, "lots of people there. That'd be real cinematic. They never put theme parks in films."

"What about the one with Donald Southerland?"

"The roller coasters one," he winces, "that sucked--nobody saw that."

"Or how about Vacation--remember Wally World?"

Alright, this isn't working.

I give them a business card with my priority phone line—they can call me when they get their heads out of their asses. As we leave the room, the sheep asks if he could drop his script by ITM. I don't even bother answering him. Fuck it. Fate has mandated that I handle this myself. Well that is exactly what I'm going to do—going to drive up to the house and put an end to all of this tonight—before any other women are raped! Only after I march out of there, racing down the marble stairs, fuming and angry, do I realize that I have no car.

I take the bus.

Now I don't know if you've ever used the LA bus system.

But let me tell you, it is not an easy thing to do. Forget about having exact change--the fucking driver doesn't even speak English! You should see the route map too--faster flying to London and back than to get from Beverly Hills to Hollywood on the stupid thing.

To spare you a lot of time and anguish, I wind up back at ITM. Before my assistant can read off the ten page list of calls and faxes, I tell him to rent me a car. He moans. After working late--this is the last thing he needs. So I'm locked in my office, staring at the mountain of faxes and papers that have piled up over the afternoon. I search my mind, trying to figure out what I'm going to do next. Just because Veronica isn't dead, doesn't mean Derek isn't a murderer. He has a gun. He's stronger than me—but somehow I must face him. Yet this can't just be a suicide mission--I can't just die.

I have to stop him.

My private line rings. It's the Beverly Hills P.D.—they've verified the story and are ready to take me in. But I'm wrong. When I pick up the phone, some guy I've never spoken to before blurts out, "Golden Poon!"

"What?"

"The film distributor's Golden Poon," a pregnant pause, "Mo told you about the movie, right? Those punks are talking to some nobodies called Golden Poon who--"

I hang up on him.

Taking a deep breath, I vaguely remember Mo telling me about some independent movie he wants me to procure—hey, you just don't listen real carefully to your boss when you're about to go to prison for the rest of your life. This must be Mo's contact at Paramount. Hell, I don't have time for business. I have to think who can help me in ending this ordeal. Derek is mad. Hal won't help me. Charity'll barely speak to me. Who do I have left to aid me in this great task?

Archie.

I call information and get the number to Prudential's Dividends department. Using their electronic switchboard, I dial Archie's extension. The line rings forever. Archie's been working overtime and weekends for over a month and this night, of all nights, he goes home early!

"This is Ralph," a voice yawns over the other end of the phone.

"Is Archie there?"

"Archie?" a long pause, "who's calling?"

"Cullen—his roommate."

"I don't think so," Ralph suddenly grows surly.

"I'm his roommate," I stress.

"Yeah, right," he yawns again, "nut ball was fired a month ago. His roommate would know that, don't you think?"

Fired? I almost drop the phone.

"You credit card people need to quit calling here," reprimands Ralph, "already told you--he's no longer an employee of Prudential. I'm sure he's screaming and yelling at some boss somewhere around town. I warn you, kid's gone nuts."

The experiment did it.

Derek did it.

Archie acts so empowered, probably shot his mouth off to his boss, talking back, being insubordinate—flash—remember Archie in my room, feeling the rough texture of my sheets? "Jesus, this is crap," he says, "there's a great sheet sale at Macy's right now—Egyptian cotton. Lots of linen sales this time of year."

I imagine Archie driving off in the early morning, idling his days away in shopping malls, wasting the hours away watching movies, eating cheap meals at the Panda Express in the food court. He knows all the right sales—all the bargains. Wandering amidst stores, waiting for a week to pass, waiting for his drug--to get the rush of that Thursday night hunt, to chant his war song, "Party! Party! Party!"

Someone knocks at my door.

My assistant looks at me like I've gone mad. His lips move and it takes me a moment to realize that he's telling me that my "Rental car is downstairs," adding that he, "collected the keys and left some pressing documents on the passenger seat for you."

Pressing documents—hah, like I care. Grabbing the keys, I leave the office. The rental car is an old Ford Tempo—that cheesy type that only exist in rental car fleets. I fire it up, racing out of the garage.

I must face my destiny.

I'm living in a nightmare, I think on the drive home. There's no way out. No way to make it—to make me, right—whole again. What am I to do? I'll make it up as I go along. Turning onto Sunset, I spot Derek in his Volvo, driving the opposite way. I don't waste a moment, spinning around, following him.

He's racing at top speeds down La Cienega, turning onto Santa Monica Blvd. I dart between cars, trying to keep up. He turns onto Fairfax and I lose him. I drive up and down Fairfax for a few blocks, passing countless bars and pizza stands—no Derek. Just as I'm about to turn around, I spot him entering Cantor's Delicatessen. I stop my Tempo in front of a red zone on the opposite side of the street.

At the door, he's greeted by a thin, dapperly dressed man in a three piece suit. Even from this distance you can see the man's two front teeth poking through his upper lip—like a ferret. The ferret and Derek seem to know each other and talk for a moment. Through the glass window, I watch as the ferret escorts Derek to a corner booth where two men are waiting—a tall skinny Indian and a fat Chinese guy.

Look at their body language.

The way they one arm hug and sit close, joking and smiling. Derek speaks--the men laugh. Yes, he knows these people. From their expressions, the conversation quickly turns serious. The Indian man shakes his head no. Derek turns to the ferret and they both stand up to leave. The fat Chinese man grabs the ferret's arm, shaking his head yes.

Derek sits back down.

The Chinese man looks around before pulling a sleek, aluminum attaché case out from under the table. They stare at the case for a moment. Derek opens it and for a moment, I see the stacks of money--neatly lined together. Derek smiles. The four of them shake hands and he and the ferret quickly leave, each going their separate way as they exit the deli.

He has a gun. He rapes. He talks to ferrets and collects briefcases of cash from shady men in corner deli booths. Jesus Christ, I'm living with a character out of The Sopranos! I'm going to physically confront him? What nefarious things is he up to? There isn't much left. We've done just about every nefarious act possible.

I've become soiled.

Tears trickle down my eyes as I sit in the car. I've done such horrible things. I must repent. I must suffer. Then I get to thinking—thinking thoughts I haven't considered before. Going to the police is almost too easy—letting them clean up my mess. Letting them face my victims. It's too easy. If I'm going to be a man, I not only have to deal with Derek, I have to first tell Eloise.

I have to tell her everything.

"I knew you were going to drop by," smiles Eloise.

Her door has one of those plastic Pumpkin decorations on it. As it swings open, I notice that her TV is on, an old Happy Days show playing in the dimly lit living room. It sit on a pile of boxes. Most of her apartment is packed up. She clears a pile of candy from the couch which is already wrapped in plastic.

"Movers are coming tomorrow," she explains.

"Munching out?" I look at the candy.

"It's Halloween, silly," sighing, "guess kids don't trick or treat around here. You're the first to come by."

She invites me to sit down. A glass of red wine rests on the coffee table. Before I can say no, she darts off into the kitchen to pour me a glass.

Scan the pile of framed photos on the floor, waiting to be packed away--snapshots of Eloise with foreign looking friends in foreign looking places. In the pictures, her smile is like Mona Lisa's, a sense of sadness and joyful exuberance mixed into one—a living contradiction. How wonderful this girl is, everything I've ever wanted. Why couldn't I have met her at one of those frozen yogurt stands Archie talks about--or in the frozen foods section at Ralph's Supermarket?

The funny thing about our lives, is that we think they're drab. We pray for the excitement of movies and TV. But the endless good and bad of our everyday lives is the stuff of drama. How ironic that I must tell her the truth—that the first woman I've truly loved with all my soul, must leave me forever. I must be a man.

I must make the wrongs right.

"Eloise," I place the wine on the table, taking both of her hands in mine. Her skin is soft, scent sweet, "I've been working on a project—something we have to talk about."

"Seems like that's all we do," she giggles. Seeing the look of seriousness on my face, she stiffens, "is this where you tell me we can never speak to each other again?"

On the TV, Ralph laughs it up at Al's diner. Grabbing the remote, I turn it off. Just the sounds of Brentwood traffic fills the room. We remain silent.

"You're not going to want to talk to me again," I tell her, "ever."

"How can you say such things?" her long hair falls around her shoulders, glistening off the light of her halogen lamp.

My mind races, but there's no proper way to phrase it. How do you tell someone you love that you were an unwitting instrument of their rape? Some things, all the wily diplomats in all the world, can't explain.

I reach out, running my hands through her hair—like golden flax. The way comes to me, "Why did you wear your hair down that night?"

"What?" she cocks her head to one side.

"The night you broke up and went to North--to meet your friend," shut my eyes, this hurts so much, "you wore your hair down."

"No I didn't."

Her mind races, she still doesn't know what this is about. I bathe in the moment—truly the last moment we will have together. After this, everything will be different—everything changed.

Then I say it, "When I bumped into you, your hair was down."

Her mind is far away, the words I hear are her speaking to herself, "Wore it up. . . until the weird man grabbed my neck, knocked my beret off and. . ."

Tears gather in her eyes.

She shudders.

Keep going.

"It was still down when you woke up at The Jonathan Club."

Electricity! She jumps away--hopping back along the couch, slamming into the side arm. Eyes wide, lips shaking. A lifetime of things pass and change. The sound of brakes squealing out on the street bring me back. And it has gone—it has left us. . . just emptiness in the air.

I am suddenly a stranger in her apartment.

"Oh fuck," she keels over, coughing. Rushing out of the room, she collapses over the toilet, vomiting--back arched, face submerged below the toilet seat--vomiting the same way I did not so long ago.

Falling back, she slams against the bathtub, her face as red as a wilted rose—eyes bloodshot. My body grows heavy, like my feet are filled with concrete. Her lips tremble as she watches me standing silently in the hallway.

"I didn't hurt you," I mutter.

She wipes back tears, dry heaving again, but nothing comes out. Then she weeps again and finally gathers the strength, "All this time--all this time you don't tell me— you knew what I did."

She doesn't make any sense now. Tears trickling down my cheeks. But I stand solid in the hallway, knowing that she doesn't want me to draw nearer.

"I can't believe you wouldn't tell me," she sighs, "it explains why you're ending us."

"I'm sorry," I turn, heading to the door.

The last thing I hear is Eloise saying, "Overdose--"

The closing door cuts her off. I feel like I'm going to pass out. I race down the stairs to get out of there.

The Ford Tempo is a piece of shit.

Roll down the windows as I gun the accelerator-- thing barely tops sixty down Sunset Blvd. The pile of papers my assistant left on the passenger seat fly around in a maelstrom as I twist and turn along the hilly road, racing towards the Hollywood Hills. A cop car rests on the right shoulder, sirens flashing as he writes a ticket to a girl in a green BMW. The driver's wearing a Chicken suit. I race by them like a stranger about to leave this world. Only as I weave into the side streets in the hills do I remember it's a holiday.

Thursday.

And Halloween.

I pass a child on the street corner dressed up as a Devil with a little horned cap and pitch fork. Who burns in the deepest layer of hell? The liars. And what a liar I've become. It is time to say things as they are.

I am a rapist.

My associates are rapists.

We've only broken laws, violated taboo, and trespassed basic tenets of our humanity--all of these things imposed in a society to keep us all decent to each other. Because once you begin raping, how do you stop. Because power corrupts and changes you forever. Only now, in the darkest seas uncharted by any other, do I truly understand that morality does exist. It's not a morality based on society or religion, or anything other than treating each other kindly. Because we're the consummate predator. Yes, we can build cathedrals and send a man to the moon. But that same mind can perpetrate mass genocide and do things to others of our species that no animal would ever think to do.

Now I can answer Charity's question:

Alpha Wolves don't cry.

Because Alpha Wolves don't think.

They are wolves operating like most animals, reacting off basic programming. Animals eat and hunt and screw and care for their young and die. They don't feel sorry for themselves. They don't bury their dead. They don't record their history. They don't commit suicide.

And I am not a wolf.

I am a human being—a mammal capable of doing things beyond any other mammal. We think. We love. We do as many horrible acts as wonderful. We hurt those that we love more than those that are strangers. We weep for dead parents. We grow sad for no reason at all. And we become joyous at a whim. We fall in love with memories and fantasize upon dreams. And without a moral code, we degenerate into monsters.

Alright I've been pontificating. I hate it when people lecture me, but I want you to understand what I'm thinking. Long after I've killed myself tonight, I want you to know that I was a good man. If you won't give me that, then at least believe that I tried. Yes, I committed horrible acts, but know that I tried to set wrong right. At least know that I gave up my own life in doing so.

Stopping at a red light, I glance down at the mass of papers scattered across the seat and floor. I notice the fax, recognizing the seal on the cover sheet. I pick it up, reading the text. Pull over to the side of the road, flipping through the pages over and over again. The bright neon light of the Kinko's beckons from across the street. Yes, I take a deep breath. I have the power to end this thing-

Twenty Five

I stand in the dark foyer, watching them.

Gathered around the kitchen counter, Archie, Charity, and Derek converse, empty plates scattered on the table. The smell of cooked food lingers in the air. They finish the last of their drinks, eyes darting towards the baseball game on the flat screen TV.

The meal before the hunt.

Creeping down the hall, I watch Archie wipe his lips, dropping the napkin on the table as he tells a joke. Derek fingers his "Pornography Is The Theory, Rape Is The Practice" badge pinned over his breast. It's become a fixture now. Charity takes a sip of chardonnay. How far I've drifted from these people—these total strangers. I grasp the package in my hand—

"Tonight, we turn it up to the next big notch," says Derek.

"Hall!" I call out, marching into the loft area, the package tucked behind my back.

All eyes turn to me.

"He's at the ," he turns to me, English accent smoothing out the corners of his words, "so the prodigal son's come to lecture us," he fingers my wolf's head pin in his hand.

Without a word, I pull the package from behind me, handing out the stapled two page article. It flutters and falls in front of Charity, Archie. I leave a fourth copy in the middle of the table.

"More words?" Charity rolls her eyes.

"Read it," I bark.

She picks it up, eyes glancing across the page--

Derek Van Horn was arrested by the Boston P.D. in charges of rape and battery stemming from a Saturday Night party. The charges made by an unidentified female student purport that Van Horn drugged her at a party at Lowell House and then-

"What are you up to, mate?" Derek grabs the pages, instantly noticing the seal on the fax cover sheet.

He turns, mind clicking, trying to figure out how to take the articles from them. But they're reading, eyes streaming across fine print. Archie picks up the Xeroxed article, flipping through them—

Tied her down to his dorm room bed. When she resisted, Van Horn allegedly beat her about the face and neck, breaking her nose, and dislodging teeth. He then proceeded to—

Archie pulls away, silently looking up at Derek.

The flashes of images in their mind is violent and bloody—mean and gritty—filled with a woman begging to leave and a man who refuses to do so. It's a violence not found in the esoteric cover of Derek's rationalizations. What happened to the great social experiment? The intellectual pursuit? This article documents violence, animal brutality at its worst. Charity glances up at me before continuing to the next paragraph—

Raped her repeatedly, ignoring cries of help. The unidentified girl was admitted to Mass General Hospital with a cerebral hemorrhage and—

"You beat them?" Charity finally asks when it's over.
Silence.
"We've been doing this for months," Derek stammers, "this changes nothing."
Flash—Derek holding her down, beating the girl, knocking that tooth out--
"Yes it does," Charity boldly presses, "we drugged our subjects—never psychologically doing anything."
Derek smirks, "This coming from the girl who raped the postman. You all loved it—couldn't get enough of the power. You wanted to see the animal within you—the Alpha Wolf? Think wolves are kind to each other? They

rip each other to shreds on a daily basis with a force humans only reach in war."

"You had it all planned when you bought this house," I accuse, "went to Irv's Ballet of Chestnuts to collect candidates for your little game," turn back to them, "and it keeps getting turned up a notch until what? When we're beating them and hurting them—until we've become little Derek Van Horns!"

"C'mon!" Archie angrily tosses pages into the air, "I would never beat anyone!"

"How'd you spend today?" I probe his eyes with the same force that Derek used on me, "at the mall, checking out a white linen sale?"

"Stop it! Stop it!" his face glows red.

Wide eyed, Charity stares in shock as emotions well within him. Archie's like a balloon expanded too large—I just need to add that final ounce of pressure:

"Lost your job over this," I sigh sadly, but I'm really trying to speak to Charity and Archie—to gather them behind me, "your whole life has changed. But is it good? I look in the mirror and it's like staring at the face of a stranger. We've all become monsters."

Hands clap. Appearing totally bored, Derek applauds with a complacent face, "Bravo," he compliments, "what a nice--"

"Archie," I bark—no more time for idle talk, "call the police."

Motioning to the phone, Archie picks up the receiver.

"I'd wait a moment," Derek reaches into his pocket. I expect him to pull out his Beretta pistol, but it's the TV remote. Push a button. The baseball game flashes off, replaced by a fuzzy green screen and--

"I gave her a 1 mg dosage!" Hal's voice rumbles through the room, shaking the very walls. It's so loud you want to cover your ears, "for someone who weighs her weight, she'll be out for at least 16 hours!"

Hal isn't here. But I see Archie, lips closed, face ghostly white—hands opening, the phone dropping to the floor between us. He stares at the TV. The fuzzy green screen is now the green texture of a pool table, shot from overhead. Upon it, Eloise lays sprawled, blonde hair against green felt--painted in a thousand high definition pixels. Around her, we stand—deliberating, voices blaring across Derek's surround sound speakers mounted around the room:

"That ain't till about noon tomorrow!" roars Archie.

"And she'll have no memory of this?" thunders Derek.

"None," Hal's recorded voice is so loud over the speakers that it shakes the walls, hurting my ears, "probably no memories up to thirty minutes prior to ingestion either. Chances are she won't even remember Cullen or I or when I drugged her beer."

Derek hits another button on the remote.

Another shot from the same overhead lens--same pool table. Now we're all crammed on it, life a lifeboat in a dark sea. Watching myself engaging in sex with the Russian girl with glasses is like watching a stranger rape an unwitting victim. Then another shot with Charity and us together, raping.

Charity honks out her snorting laugh, impressed with Derek's ingenuity.

"I'd hate for loved ones to see this stuff," he winces to us, "very compromising."

Flash—I remember returning home during one of my first days in the house--found Derek fiddling with the security monitor in the game room. I must have caught him installing a camera in the location in place of a motion sensor, "You put that camera in before any of the rapes occurred--had this thing planned before we did anything!"

He makes a face—as if the accusation doesn't even merit a response.

"Planned it all?" Charity is very impressed.

"Is it true?" presses Archie, "you wanted me to drug that. . ." his voice trails off into silence. Then his eyes open wide, "doesn't matter. I don't want my mom seeing that shit on Hard Copy!" he jumps to his feet, knocking the chair out from under him as he speaks to the crowd—but really to me, "we'll be vilified. All that shit recorded!"

"Let's quit blabbing," Charity rolls her eyes, "nobody wants this shit getting out," she turns to Derek, "what do you want?"

Derek sighs, "One more night--"

"No way!" I explode.

"One more Gathering of The Clan of The Alpha Wolf. After tonight we all leave this house forever," he says, "but this night, we're not going to choose our victims merely because they weren't nice to us. Everything up to now's been party lines and lies to make the truth palatable."

Flash—Derek talking about his Nazi silverware, telling us that a man can talk people into anything—

"Now we see it as it really is," continues Derek, "going to take men and women we know—that we hate, bring them here one last time. Then I destroy the tapes. It ends."

I scream out my opposition.

But they're not listening to me. The social experiment once so seemingly simple is now unveiled as complex— too complex for anyone. No one cares to sort it out, they just want it gone.

"We don't really have an option," admits Charity.

I tell them he can't be trusted. But they're still thinking of what it will look like when that video plays on the 5 O'clock news. Even Hal is silent—still the beaten dog. So I rant on about the foreign men and the briefcase of money at Cantor's deli. Derek's eyes grow wide as he fingers his badge pin, surprised that I followed him—shocked that I discovered his secrets.

"And," he retorts, using my point as the final nail in the coffin, "do you know what those men will do to your loved ones? I'm asking for one last night. I hold all the chips. Violate me, tape's all over press tomorrow while your loved ones, like the Viking girl, float in a ditch."

"DON'T THREATEN HER!" I scream.

He says nothing.

Because he doesn't have to.

He knows my mind is filled with gruesome snapshots of Eloise floating in some ditch, the fat China Man and shady Indian man looming over her. Remember the night we discovered the Nazi silverware? Derek told Archie and I how to corrupt people: "Countless good men have done more evil things to save their family or loved ones."

I should've warned Eloise to leave town for a day or two. Instead, I set us both up. For one more night, he will be the leader. But it isn't a clan anymore. It's a chain gang and he towers over us, weapons of leverage in hand.

"So how does it work?" asks Charity.

Derek points at Archie, "This time, we don't use test subjects who meet a criteria of being rude to us in the first few minutes. We pick people we know well. Arch, you were fired by a bitch of a boss at Prudential, right?"

He nods his head.

"Cullen, you were hurt by Veronica."

I can't believe this is happening.

"I have someone special in mind for myself," he says.

"And me?" inquires Charity.

"We both know who you want?" he smiles.

"What are you going to do?" I stammer, "add kidnapping to the list."

"No," he winks, strolling over to the game room door, ushering us forward "already taken care of everything."

He opens the door.

There they lay.

Three bodies on the pool table--naked legs protruding over the table, the rest of the bodies disappearing under the white sheet. I struggle to reconcile this image. They're on the stomach, heads to the side. A mountain range rises through the sheets from the outlines of their heads--endless valleys of their noses and cheekbones under the white cloth. It's so still, you can hear the buzz of the Centipede game.

What have we become?

"They were taken this evening," Derek runs his hands along the back of a milky white calf. It's a woman's leg, but I can't imagine who, "since we were dealing with people we knew, I had to resort to professionals," he points to me, "the foreign gentlemen you saw me with at Cantor's Deli. They drugged and took them from their offices, homes, apartments—each administered 2 mg of Rohypnol."

Administered.

What a great way to paint it.

When really they burst into the dimly lit Prudential office. It's after hours, only janitors cleaning up as hands wrap around her face, arching her back in the seat, stuffing the pill into her mouth—

"So they have no memories of the break-ins," continues Derek, "and will be returned this evening—not to the beach, but back to their initial or nearby locations--
"

Veronica comes home, tossing keys on the table. Strolling into the bedroom, they're waiting. The faceless demons of our own creation. Dark hands wrapping around her—

"They were all cased for a week, to make sure we could take them without complications. And no problems arose."

A third body rests under the sheet. I wonder if it's Derek's or Charity's test subject. Then I remember he told her he knew exactly who she wanted. Perhaps they're sharing. Jesus, this is so deranged.

Derek draws up the corners of the sheet. We stare like frightened school children at the backs of six milky white thighs. The cloth hides the buttocks of the proposed victims. Can't even tell what sex they are. I look up to the fish eye reflection of this demented scene in the black security monitor.

"Stand against the table," orders Derek.

He ushers us forward, directing Archie to the far side--myself to the middle. No space for Charity. She says nothing, simply standing at Derek's side. Archie looks at me before motioning forward, unbuckling his belt. I remain near the door. The Centipede Game sings out it's little promo song, luring children into depositing a quarter as it shoots missiles up the screen, destroying imaginary monsters.

"C'mon," the monster sighs, "let's finish the experiment."

Flash—Eloise laying in a ditch.

I step forward.

My hands tug away my shoes. Then the belt and pants--dropping to my feet. Eloise floating dead. Is this how it is in Hell? Is it not so easy to recapture one's soul after it has been sold? Stand at the pool table--cold wood frame against my pubic area.

Without surgical gloves, Derek spreads the legs open in front of him. I look down. He's erect, ready to enter his test subject. And he isn't wearing a condom.

"What are you doing?" I'm shocked.
"No condoms tonight."

Twenty Six

Derek Van Horn is the devil!

Even has horn in his name. Those piercing cobalt eyes—knows everything I say before I say it. And how does he do that? Because he's a writer? C'mon, he's lured us in his hellish nightmare by saying all the right things—until now! Now the elegant cloak is cast away and we see him as he really is—just some crazy, perverse fucker, unholy and wrong. I fight to reconcile the words I'm hearing. Has he just lost his mind or was he always this mad? We all stand around, silenced by the shock. What will this prove? How is this the grand finale to his perverse social experiment?

"Without condoms," Archie stumbles with his words, speaking to Derek as if he doesn't already realize, "you're gonna leave DNA evidence."

"Can only find DNA," Derek responds, "if you know who to look for. We're each fucking another test-subject. Cullen isn't being asked to screw Veronica. Archie, you aren't fucking your boss. It's two degrees of separation. Even if they were to realize what's happened and get DNA testing, they'll never be able to link back to us. They won't know who to look for!"

"No," I moan, "this is madness. I'm not going to impregnate anyone."

"This is the way of nature!" lectures Derek, "what do you think sex is? Just mock reproduction! We control our bodies, regulate and stymie fertility--trick our minds. But to our bodies, we're doing what we always have—reproducing! The wolf scars his bitches for life. And tonight we shall cross the borne and become Alpha Wolves."

"You've miscalculated on this one," I step back, "there's only a small chance we'd knock them up. A lot of them could be on the pill--they could have abortions or might even have venereal diseases, Derek. These are human beings, not dogs!"

"When you peer deep into the truths of sex," the cobalt eyes flow, "it's all the same. We will do exactly what the animals do. We will let nature handle those points. An Alpha Wolf doesn't use gloves or condoms or--"

He's gone mad! "We aren't wolves, Derek. We're people!"

Glance at Charity, shocked and wild eyed. She's perfectly still—not even gnawing on a lock of hair or rolling her eyes.

"No," I forcibly pull Archie back, "we won't do this-"

"Thank you for the political disclaimer," smirks the wolf, "but there's no decision to be made. YOU WILL IMPREGNATE YOUR TEST SUBJECT!"

"No!" I explode.

Derek sticks his hand into the corner pocket of the pool table, drawing out the Beretta Centurion pistol—black gun metal--the one from his room. He thrusts the barrel in my face.

"C'mon Derek," pleads Archie, "put the gun down."

Gun at my head, Derek repeats himself, "you will continue or THERE'LL BE TWO BODIES IN THAT FUCKING DITCH! NOW DO IT!"

I look down. The sheet on his test subject has been drawn back, revealing only the upper shoulder of the girl. I see it clearly:

The birth mark in the shape of Italy.

Oh fuck, it's Eloise.

No more images, no more thoughts—just energy flowing through me, hate filling every void of my body. He wraps a finger tightly around the trigger. Death creeps upon me. Flash—Eloise in the ditch. Rush forward, colliding into him--swing my arm, knock the gun a millimeter over my head as it explodes—

BANG!

The gunshot rings out through the room. We're falling down, colliding--hitting each other. I'm on the ground. No words—no thoughts. Two animals tearing into each other—two wolves ripping each other apart. He cracks me backwards. The room spins around us and then I see the end of the barrel in my face. Death is here. This is the end—my life measured in the milliseconds of time as he pulls the trigger and--

BANG!

Muscle and bone splattering all over me. A piece of bone rips through my eyebrow. Blood and tissue scattered across the floor. Hand at my chest, my face, waist. Derek's gun falls to the floor, smoke rising from the barrel. But he must've somehow missed.

I'm not hit.

"Holy shit!" cries Archie, grabbing his head, rolling around on the ground, screaming in a panicked howl, "holy shit! Holy shit!"

Look down.

Derek lays on the wood floor, gurgling up blood, gun laying in his open, blood soaked hand. But how? Look up. Do you see it or am I just dead and dreaming?

Charity's got a gun.

Can almost hear Aerosmith singing that line, huh? Her finger turns white, wrapping around the trigger of her tiny revolver—smoke rising from the end of the barrel. Her pistol's smaller than Derek's—a symbol that her amusing threats were so very real.

She shot him.

"Holy shit!" Archie continues to howl, "holy shit! Holy Shit!"

"Never said you had a gun!" I rush back, knocking my head against the pool table.

She fucking shot him!

Shot him right through the chest. He's going to die right here. Look at all the damn blood flowing out of his body, spilling out onto the wooden floor, creeping into the cracks between the planks as--

Laughter.

Derek chuckling as buckets of blood drain out of his mouth and body. A big smile on his face, flashing red stained teeth as he stares at me—eyes wide. It's a different Derek—now at rest, at ease with the world, a pressure lifted.

Tears race down her face, streaming makeup across her cheeks. She drops to her knees, blood soaking deep into the fiber of her pants, to the waistband where she concealed the weapon, "How long did you know?"

"Since. . . beginning," he coughs a violent wave of blood and fluid—eyes going blank as he glances at both of us, "just. . . waiting. . . for. . . it--" lips stop. One final spasm, arms in the air and then down as if some final volt of electricity has left him.

It's a joke—right? It's a fucking joke. Feel his pulse. Derek's dead.

"Holy shit!" Archie howls again, "holy shit!" turn to him, crumpled half naked under the pool table. Covering his face, he curls into a tight ball, spine flexing through skin as he mutters senselessly. Jesus, we're in deep shit--

"What do we do?" Charity turns to me, weak and deflated.

Suddenly I'm the boss?

The usurper's become the leader? Look at this mess. The room spins as I attempt to plot the next move: I've got a bloody corpse, three drugged people, and a sidekick having a nervous breakdown under a pool table--wish I could make a funny joke to lighten the mood for you, but--

There's nothing funny about this scene.

Think!

Glance at my wristwatch, almost midnight, "They were abducted pretty early today so we don't have that much time before they wake up."

Look at her--blood all over. Charity looks like she just walked off the set of Carrie. She nods, making it clear that she at least understands my words.

I gesture at the shrouded figures on the pool table--can't bare to look at them now, to see Eloise's unconscious face. Hell, I'm barely holding my fucking mind together! One more inch and I'll get under the pool table with Archie, "We get rid of them. We'll need a big car—Derek's Volvo," I fish through Derek's corpse's pocket for the keys. My knees sink into blood--more blood than you've ever seen in movies. You'd think this place was a slaughter house--

"Derek's parents are going to come looking for him," Charity kneels beside me, gnawing nervously on her hair, "they know you and Archie and--"

"Give me a fucking break!" I'm going to hyperventilate, "one step at a time," maybe I need to breathe into a bag. Shit, he doesn't have his keys on him.

I stand up.

"Where are you going?" she's panicked.

"To get the fucking keys!"

Charity doesn't want to be alone and follows me into the living room. I slam open the drawers before I realize I'm leaving bloody handprints everywhere. Shit! My fingerprints in blood all over the white Formica. Then I spot what looks like a spare key in one of the kitchen drawers. Hold it up to the light. It's a copy--no logo, not sure if its for the Volvo.

I sprint out of the house. Charity follows. Mind racing as I press the key into the lock. We'll drop them separately at the beach and then—shit, Charity's right. His parents are going to come looking for him! People just don't vanish—no questions asked. The key fits. At least that's working and—

BANG!

Holy fuck. Another gunshot. It's from inside the house, reverberating through the half open front door. The neighbors had to hear that! Charity and I glance at each other before we dash back to the house.

Archie holds Derek's Beretta in his hand.

Sitting cross legged on the floor, legs covered in Derek's blood, he holds the Beretta to his head, barrel still smoking. Shit, he must've tried to shoot himself in the head and pulled away at the last second--

"No, Arch," I plead from the doorway of the game room.

He swings the gun up at me, "Stay away!" his blood stained hands shaking, eyes wild "raping people . . . we've been. . . raping?" this horribly pained look passes across his face. He drops his head, stuffing the barrel of the gun into his mouth--

"No!" I scream.

He pulls the trigger.

The flash of muzzle fire—BANG!

Nothing.

Just a white faced Archie, cold sweat trickling down his brow as he sits, gun still aimed squarely into his mouth.

No bullet wound.

No wound.

What the hell's going on? Archie collapses, gun clamoring on the floor beside him. Carefully I draw nearer to him. He huddles in a fetal position under the pool table, the legs of the drugged test subjects hanging over the edge, casting him in shadows. Charity whispers to him, trying to nurse him back to reality. He isn't even talking anymore, just shaking and babbling senselessly to himself, hands over his face.

I pick up Derek's pistol, stand up and aim it at the floor, firing--

BANG!

The gun kicks--gunshot rings in my ears. But no hole in the floor. Derek's gun has blanks. Flash—I think of Derek's grandfather, lined up in front of that Nazi firing line--what the hell is happening? Glance at the gaping wound in his dead body. Charity's gun sure as hell didn't have blanks. Then I remember, Charity asked him how long he knew something—

"What did he know?" I ask her.

"Who I was," she answers without saying anything more.

"What?"

"Now's not the time to--"

"WHAT DID HE KNOW!" I explode, holding the gun with blanks.

"The acting role I told you about in my apartment," she says, voice trailing off, "I am the friend."

"The dark haired girl," I whisper.

Flash—the photos of the Van Horn family the two little blonde girls holding hands—the violent reenactment of the sex scene in her apartment. Charity is the sister's friend, the other blonde girl who slept over at their house--Derek crawls into the bedroom--

"The story you told was real?" I whisper, lips laced with the metallic taste of blood.

She silently nods, "Felicity Van Horn died of a heroin overdose eleven months ago. I'd not seen the Van Horn family for almost fifteen years--spent time away—in therapy. Felicity did not. She hung herself in a Reno hotel room."

"You decided to make your mark and wandered into us," which begs the question, "what the fuck were you waiting for?"

"To see how it would end--maybe I was stalling—confused," remember her eyes, so full of conflicting emotions, "afraid that I'd become the one thing I hated. Curious to peer into the mind of the creature that ruined our lives, wondering why--wondering if I could really kill him. In the end he made it easy, wanted it—begged for it."

"What?"

She reaches into her pocket, unfolding the Xeroxed copy of the Harvard Crimson article, "The night of the postman, he must have heard our conversation. He bet you'd be in such a hurry that you'd never notice it. But I trust nothing."

"What're you talking about?"

She drops the paper to the floor, "Read the byline."

Glance down, scanning the header of the Crimson article--

By: Derek Van Horn

Of course, Harvard told me the fire destroyed all their archives. Charity and I discussed the article in the living room the night I found the postman. Derek heard us somehow and created an article. But why would he create a forged article about a rape? Glance down at his dead body. Why would he drive us to do this? Another thought. I shoot up, staring down at the bodies under the sheet. Slowly I draw back the white cloth, revealing the stranger's faces. Three attractive women, laying ghostly still and—

I've never seen them before in my life.

"Do you know these people?" I grab Charity, yanking her up.

She nods no.

Run my hand along the upper shoulder of the girl with the Italy shaped birthmark. It smears to my touch— makeup. Grabbing Archie, I force him out from under the pool table. He fights, refusing to look at the girls. I slap him, barking for him to: "Point out your old boss!"

But he won't open his eyes.

What the hell's going on? Glancing back at Derek, I notice that his "Pornography is the philosophy. Rape Is The Practice" pin has been jarred loose by his fall. The top's come off, revealing a black lens inside a metal casing. Leaning over, I notice a black wire poking out from around his shirt. Pull back his clothes. More wires leading down to equipment taped to his chest. A sea of black wires set against one white electrode pad over his heart—the thingamajig they stick on patients during EKG's.

"What the hell's that?" Charity winces, leaving the shaking Archie.

We don't have time for this crap--Derek's gun has blanks. He wears an EKG pad over his heart, has people we've never seen drugged on the pool table. He knew he was going to die—told Charity he was wondering what took us so long:

"Charity," I grunt, "take the guns."

We head downstairs.

I'm ready to break down Derek's door.

But it's unlocked. Push it open, revealing the dark bedroom. Half expect a suicide note on the bed. Turning on the lights, the room is as we saw it last--unmade bed, free-weights on the floor. Touch the play button on the tape-player—tap—tap—ding! thunders through the room. Charity sorts through the stack of blank white pages, her blood stained fingers leaving fingerprints everywhere.

Jesus, what a fucking mess.

And I'm just as confused as you.

Collapse back on the bed, running fingers through oily hair. Then it hits me, "Charity," I stammer, "remember all those internet articles Derek would look up?"

"What?" then I realize she wasn't there when he showed us all the articles on Rufinol, "what's the one thing missing in this room?" I ask her.

She turns puzzled.

"There's no computer."

He played the tap—tap—ding! to keep us from hearing what he was really doing. We both glance towards the large Nazi flag covering the side wall. Side by side we stroll towards it—Swastikas growing ever larger. I reach out, drawing back the massive red flag revealing—

Another room.

A long, narrow workspace stretching back thirty feet, crammed from top to bottom with computers and monitors and chairs and strange equipment. I recognize the Avid equipment on the side console—

"This is an editing booth," I tell her.

At the end of the room, against the center wall is a large 21 inch computer monitor. Push away the roller chair in front of it and stare at the screen. There are two open video windows on the monitors—like two tiny movie screens. One is shooting the game room from an overhead shot—the same one Derek used to tape us. But the second angle is on the floor because I can see Archie huddled in the frame and hear his whimpering over speakers mounted above us.

"The badge pin he wore," whispers Charity, "it's another camera and there's a lot more."

"How do you know?"

She's pressed the power button on four other monitors. Each screen is divided into four panes—each with a different room in the house. Every one of those black orbs is a camera. Through the living room unit, he watched Charity and me talk about the Harvard Crimson article. And there's more. She turns on a few other screens—still frames of us, not in the house—but at a bar, The Garden of Eden—

"What does this mean?" Charity asks in panicked tones.

Turn back to the monitor in front of us. At the corner of the computer screen is a bar graph—the type you see when you email documents. The slots are slowly filling up—really big file. Oh shit. He's emailing a document to someone—by the look of the graph, it started 12 minutes ago—about the same time Derek died. I think of the EKG pad, probably linked to his heart.

"He set the footage to email if and when he died! Probably emailed pictures of us killing him," I cry, "we've got to stop it!"

We try and fiddle with the keyboard, pressing buttons, turning knobs--but it has no effect. Shit there are ten keyboards in here and I've no idea what controls what equipment.

"Can we just unplug it?" asks Charity.

I'm about to smash stuff when--

I hear Archie scream, his voice blaring over the speakers in the room. Glance back at the monitor. From two different angels I see him sitting up—and I see—oh shit, there's movement in the game room—legs and arms hanging over the frame are moving!

"Oh no!" I cry--the test subjects are starting to wake up.

We turn, rushing upstairs.

Take this in slow motion.

Because I don't know what to do—so I need time to think. The poor drugged women are waking up. Archie's freaking out. Derek's dead. The house is covered in blood. My prints are everywhere. And the video footage of us killing the son of a bitch is probably being emailed around the world. Racing up the stairs, I'm as freaked out as you.

There is no way out of this.

Everything moving slowly, like in syrup. I glimpse the white light flickering at the top of the staircase. Stepping into the living room, blinding light pours through the still half open front door. A car is running in the driveway, headlights on. I pray it's Hal.

Then I see the silhouette of a man, walking in slow motion into the living room. It's the baby faced police officer—the sheep, smile disappearing from his face as he sees us covered in blood, lit up in the headlights behind him. A look of shock slowly fills his face. His gritty crime drama screenplay that he's brought by falls from his hands, moving painfully slow through the air as it falls to the floor. Instinctively his hand swings back—near his gun, as his mind tries to make sense of what he's seeing.

Nobody gets out of here alive.

That's what Charity always says. She and I stop at the top of the stairs, staring at the police officer. From our angle, we can see into the game room, glimpsing things that the officer won't see until he draws closer. Jesus Christ! The naked test subjects are sitting up on the pool table, Archie cowering beneath it. The three naked women have the white sheet around them, covering their breasts and genitals as they take foam plugs out of their ears. They point at Derek's blood soaked body with wide, curious eyes, admiring the corpse. And—

They're laughing.

Part Five

Truth Beyond The Garden's Gate

"All nature is but art, unknown to Thee;
All chance, direction which thou canst not see;
All discord, harmony not understood;
All partial evil, universal good.
And, spite of pride, in erring reason's spite,
One truth is clear. Whatever is, is right."
Alexander Pope's *Essay On Man* (1773)

Twenty Seven

Three of them are naked.

Hair golden against hunter green felt. You break them down, finding fault. But these three women are perfect .. . etched faces, modern day works of art. We stuff Mona Lisa's half assed grin in the back of *The Louvre*, but hang these beauties on every magazine cover in every checkout line in the free world—as you've probably realized, we've returned to the beginning of our little tale.

It's called a circular narrative.

And right now, you're supposed to be confused.

From overhead, we peer down at the naked nymphs which began this book—three beautiful women you'll now easily recognize: the Suzie Wong look-alike, the short brunette who slapped Archie, and the Russian girl with glasses. Our first catch from that first night at the Garden Of Eden. Completely naked, the three women lay sprawled across the pool table, eyes half crossed, thick soupy smiles. Then Derek leans forward, face buried between Suzie Wong's legs--

"Spock," Archie jokes, "you're wasting precious time! Hey lets dim the lights."

"No," Derek rumbles in THX sound, "turn the lights off—you can't see anything."

The audience giggles.

Turn to them. The faces around me, their flesh lit up by the movie screen--white ovals against the blackness of the movie theatre. A few people turn to me. I attempt a smile, really just getting as far as a smirk. Watching myself on the screen now is like watching a complete stranger.

Suddenly the scene with the postman flashes on screen, blue dildo sticking out of his ass. I don't even remember the events of that evening. The memories now are simply the conflation of camera angles, the rousing sound-score, and quick snap cuts on screen.

"Relax. I dropped it in his beer real quick," Charity's voice rattles your ears in THX, "which reminds me--what kind of postman drinks on duty? You're a lawyer. Isn't that a Federal offense?"

I can only reply that: "I'm sure butt-fucking one with a dildo is."

The audience explodes in laughter. The old owl next to me slaps his knee--laughing so much it sends him into a coughing spasm. His young flamingo hands him a fresh Kleenex.

It's been over two years since that evening happened, so I've had plenty of time to reflect on this phenomenon. When you drape the postman scene in a shroud of fiction, the horror undergoes a metamorphosis into comedy. The audiences' eyes open wide, laughing because it's so uncomfortable, because such thoughts have passed through their minds, because it's the stuff of dreams-- totally unreal.

We're now at the Van Horn's cocktail party.

Amongst the chit chat of the party goers for the Mayoral soirée, Derek and I discuss the madness of him trying to rape people at the party. For the thousandth time, the socialite sneaks Godiva chocolates into her mouth. And for the thousandth time, the audience in this movie theatre and countless other theatres, see it. I don't know if she's an actress or a real person--

But they laugh all the same.

I think back to things not on film.

The memories that are still real and visceral--that haven't been transmuted into camera shots and sound scores. Memories that are still only mine: Charity and I, covered in blood, stand at the top of the staircase, my heart racing as the baby faced cop draws his gun on me. Let me tell you, the LAPD needs only five minutes to march an entire army into your backyard. Right after the sheep radios in, police helicopters buzz, spotlights sweeping in through the wall of windows. A legion of LAPD police officers--SWAT soldiers isolate through each room. Through the front door, neighbors and reporters crowd the narrow hill-side street with vans and spotlights of their own.

Everybody's carted down to LAPD.

It's not that nice Beverly Hills holding cell. I'm locked alone in a tiny interrogation room with a puddle of urine in the back corner. And the pisser definitely ate asparagus—room fucking reeks. All I can think is that I'm happy my parents are dead-- only because they won't have to hear what I've done. Thoughts of suicide dance through my mind. But handcuffed to a metal bolt on the wall, I'm helpless. This is the end of my life as a free man. They're not going to let me die, forcing me to be violated by Luther in some penitentiary until I'm this toothless old man who mumbles to himself and cares for pigeons.

The clock ticks away.

After twelve long hours, they come, silently leading me down a back hall into an alleyway. It's noon. The alley warms to the sunlight creeping over tall buildings around me--smells like rotten eggs here. Glance down at my handcuffs, turn to the two grim faced cops and trash dumpsters--so this is corporal punishment? A bullet in the head in some back alley? I saw something like this during a PBS program on Chinese capital punishment.

My life passes before me--images of me opening my mother's medicine cabinet—Veronica's face in the blinking falafel lights—my father telling me to look for the green flash—Derek handing me my wolf's head pin—Hal and I drinking in college--Charity laughing— and Eloise. . . it rips me apart to see her face staring lovingly back at me as--

The cuffs are unlocked.

They push me between two dumpsters. I'm waiting for the bullet. Then on the far side of the trash cans, I spot the sleek, black limo running idle--thin fog of smoke rising from its exhaust. Silently, the officers gesture me to enter the limo.

I'm alone in the car.

Privacy guard raised between me and the chauffeur, I try to fiddle with the control console as we cruise out of the alley. I can't lower the partition. Turning in front of the police station, I glimpse the sea of reporters gathered around the news stations' vans with orange satellite antennas raised. Only then do I notice the white terry cloth bathrobe on the far side of the couch. On top of the robe is a hand scribbled note:

CHANGE

Cruising through early morning traffic on Little Santa Monica Blvd., I discard my bloody clothes on the floor, hoping to change out of it all—to be clean—to go back to that innocent insomniac. If only it were that easy. Changing into the white robe, I note The Peninsula Hotel logo on the breast pocket just as we pull into the hotel.

A smiling manager in a tan suit opens the door, "Mr. Gersh, the others have arrived. Here are your room keys."

"What the hell is going on!" Charity screams as I enter.

The manger shuts the door, leaving us alone. The room is elegant--fabric covered walls, clean sheets, brass fixtures—like you or I care. Focus on the line of tiny liquor bottles on the dresser, caps unscrewed--empty. I open the minibar, grabbing the last bottle left—Cointreau. Tastes like orange peels, but I drink it, hoping it'll help calm me.

"So what is happening?" Charity demands again.

"Where's Archie?" I grunt.

She points to the connecting door, "In the other room--under the fucking bed, babbling. Now what's going on!"

"I don't know!" I explode, "we should be in jail now. Not here."

"I need a cigarette," she mutters--

There's a knock at the door.

Charity opens it.

"I am Simon Arthur, Derek Van Horn's corporate attorney," I hear. Then Charity steps back as he enters. And I instantly recognize him. Ignore the three piece suit and elegant attaché case and notice those two massive front teeth protruding under that tiny button nose. It's the ferret--the strange man I saw Derek meet at Cantor's Deli—those teeth seem ready to gnaw a tree down or whatever the fuck ferrets do, "where is the third member of the project?" he asks, glancing at me.

"Resting," Charity gestures to the connecting room door as she lights a cigarette with shaky hands.

The lawyer gestures for us to sit at the edge of the bed. He sits in the accompanying chair, placing his briefcase on the table before stating that: "I know that for performance reasons, some things were concealed from you. I just want to assure you that everything's been taken care of," he nods his head with frustration, "the only reason the officer was there," with his eyes, he points to me, "was to tell you that a Mexican man was found in a car bearing your registration. Which in no way explains his screenplay found on the floor of the house."

"And?" I press.

"We filed permits in triplicate to all pending municipal offices," the lawyer shivers, "but who ever imagined Mr. Van Horn would do. . . well what he did," a long pregnant silence, "I assure you, if we'd known, my firm would never have assisted him."

"Why are we not in jail?" asks Charity.

"Mr. Van Horn scheduled a morning delivery to the LAPD with his video tape confession," replies the ferret, "which precluded you all as suspects. They know the whole thing was a suicide."

A suicide?

Did I hallucinate everything? Am I losing my mind? Is this going to be like that season of Dallas where Bobby's death and everything else was just a dream? Derek is dead! I saw Charity blow his head off in the middle of the game room.

The ferret taps his two front teeth against the bottom—a clicking sound--before he smiles to Charity, "Darling, it's alright. Mr. Van Horn confessed in his tape that he purposely substituted real rounds into your revolver. The LAPD knows you didn't mean to kill him."

Glance at Charity. I remember testing Derek's gun. It was filled with blanks. From her look I can tell that she never confided to Derek that she had a gun.

The ferret interrupts our shared stare, "I know this has been an in-depth creative process, but I assure you," he leans over whispering—like he's sharing some secret, "there are no cameras here. As you saw in his editing booth, the project was cut and emailed out last night."

"What project?" I ask.

"The film," he answers in a matter of fact voice.

"What film!" I explode, hands over my head. I can't take much more of this shit.

Silence.

"You did sign these?" I hear him open his briefcase. He hands us a stack of papers. I can smell French scented soaps on his hand. Scan the papers quickly—employment contracts with confidentiality clauses. At the end of one contract, I spot Archie's signature—on another, Hal's signature. I stress, "we never signed any--"

Flash—Derek's home on the first night. He tells me: "If you don't want to feel like you're imposing, I'll charge you an unreasonably small rent--even draw up a nice little rent document--you can sign it. Very legal." I sign the agreement--a lot of clauses and fine print--hadn't slept in ten days when I perused it. Glance down at the next contract--my signature is shaky—

But it's my signature.

"I didn't sign one of these," Charity emphatically declares.

"You didn't have to," the ferret sighs, "you're the major beneficiary and stockholder in the production entity."

"What production entity!" I scream.

"The reason for your delay at the police station," the ferret rambles on, "was because the police tried to stick us on fine points relating to the corporate structure and the remote surveillance--"

"Remote cameras!" Charity chokes on her cigarette and snuffs it out.

"Two at Mr. Chow's before you were involved--one in the bar area, another in the dining room where they had the Clan of The Alpha Wolf scene. All disguised as surveillance cameras."

I remember surveillance cameras in the private room. Even raised the point with Derek. He told me not to mind them. They were turned off--

"Even the mobile film crews were properly licensed," the ferret explains, "cost a fortune. But Mr. Van Horn was insistent on shooting all over the city. And working with Los Angeles, Santa Monica, West Hollywood, and Beverly Hills can drive anyone mad. Each one requires different paper work! Getting the camera set up in the Staples Center was nearly impossible--"

"The Staples Center?" I interrupt, "as in—where Derek and I met?"

"Yes," he sips his sparkling water, "expect you wouldn't notice it. Was well concealed behind the suite's two way mirror. We would've used the regular remote camera crew, but the stadium refuses us access due to broadcasting agreements."

"Regular camera crew?" I'm at the edge of my rope.

Silence.

"How did you think he was recording everything?" the ferret looks at me like I'm crazy. What he says next blows us away, leaving us in silenced shock, "we disguised them as an MTV camera crew at the Garden of Eden—cutting the logo licensing deal with MTV was nearly impossible. And the others--"

Flash--the crew filmed us the entire time at the Garden of Eden.

Flash—the crew disguised as an ESPN news team filmed us at Dublins. Remember? Charity even spilled beer on the host dressed in a Chicago Bulls jacket.

Flash—at Lush, the camera crew recorded our ever move.

Flash—at Derek's mother's Mayoral party, the news reporters filmed us.

Not to mention the hidden remote cameras hidden in the bushes, the fixed cameras inside every room of his house, the camera mounted to Derek's pin badge that says "Pornography Is The Theory, Rape Is The Practice". Our entire story serendipitously documented on film—

Stop.

I hold my hands up, "How'd he record us talking? There were no sound booms-- no microphones."

The ferret reaches into his briefcase, producing the silver wolf's head pin. The pins Derek gave each of us. The pin I wore until I tossed it at him in the skybox.

"A high tech sound mic," I whisper to myself, answering my own question.

The ferret nods, "Yours were top of the line. Base models were issued to the day players."

"Day players?" Charity stops, eyes wide, "they were actors?"

"If you want to call them that—actresses, a handful of strippers—all gathered from Mr. Van Horn's talent agency," he drops another stack of contracts on the bed. Charity picks them up, madly flipping pages--

Remember that first night, Derek called over girls. When I asked him how he did it, he said: "With some inheritance money, I bought part of a casting agency. I go through the book of head shots--pick a few every so often—just to relieve the stress."

"They were all actresses," Charity drops the papers between us.

I don't know whether to scream or cry or beat my breast or just lay down like Archie and babble as the ferret smirks, "Of course, despite the mandatory sexual protection, they were all screened for a clean bill of health prior to hiring. They knew they were to have no contact with you outside of the film. Although I'm aware of a small problem at the Beverly Wilshire," his eyes point to me.

"Just drive away" the Russian girl with glasses told me on Wilshire Blvd. That was why she hid from me—ran to the bathroom of the Beverly Wilshire, threatening to call the police. And I even saw her in a Playboy nude spread, doing what she normally did for money.

What a fool I've been!

"I was assured the film would be discretely edited," explains the ferret, "my firm does not work on pornography. I assure you, each day player signed a very solid confidentiality agreement to protect—well," he whispers blushingly, "to conceal the explicit sexual nature of their compensated duties. As per Mr. Van Horn's request, I'm leaving you copies in triplicate of all day players' general releases for your files. We keep the originals at my firm downtown," he's packing up his attaché case like it's time to leave.

"Wait one damn minute! They agreed to be drugged?" I'm still on the previous point. No way. This poor attorney's been misled. We drugged those girls—all those pills dissolving into drinks.

He smiles demurely, "There was a $30,000 bonus for each successful performance. But I assure you, no matter what they signed, it would be illegal to drug them."

Actors.

Planted at the bars for each of us. An entire charade put on to test our reactions? I still can't believe it. No way. Charity doesn't believe it either, focusing on the immediate matter at hand like:

"Who paid for these rooms?"

"Golden Poon."

"Golden what?" I wince.

"The film distributor, Golden Poon," the ferret replies, "purchased the Hong Kong right to the film. You witnessed their actual transaction at Cantor's Deli. Monies from that sale were set aside for your room and board as well as PR and marketing budgets," he puffs up like a proud peacock, "I assure you my firm, entrusted to broker the domestic rights to the film, will sell to a major studio. Which means more money for all of you."

Oh crap, Golden Poon—the Paramount caller—lunch at the Mandarin when I puke on myself as Mo rattles on and on about a particular project.

This is the indie movie Mo wants.

Time flows.

The audience laughs. Before you know it, we're almost at the end of the film--

"Put your hands in the air!" screams the sheep on screen.

On the movie screen, the .40 caliber semi-automatic trembles in his hands as he steps over his fallen screenplay. Frozen, Charity and I stand at the top of the stairs—eyes wide, face wet with blood--

"Oscar material," someone whispers in the audience.

The sheep almost drops his gun as he silently stares in the game room.

The audience now peers into the game room. From a low angle shot, Archie huddles under the table screaming, Derek's dead body beside him. Above them, the three naked women huddle, sheet gathered around their wastes as they giggle—a strange, haunting laughter filling the entire screen, bringing me back in time to--

"This can't be true!" cries Charity.

The ferret has left. We're alone in the room now—Archie's whimpering floats through the half open connecting door. I stare out the hotel window to the garden below.

"They were paid to be drugged!" Charity throws her arms in the air.

I can't deal with the situation and decide to check on Archie. He's lying in the bed, sheets to his neck, back to me. I would've expected him to be the strongest, cracking jokes and jesting. I guess you never know what lurks beneath a smile. I try to imagine him during the past months--aimlessly strolling through malls, checking up on sales, studying people from the serenity of his bench. Did he smile?

Or was he crying even then?

What is happening to us? How can this be a fucking movie? And a movie half the town's dying to find out about. Doubt strikes, prompting me to wonder if, "This is a sting. Maybe the cops are fucking with us?"

"I've got it!" cries Charity.

Returning to her room, I find her ripping through her purse, tossing cigarette cartons, cash, old Kleenex into the air, "I knew I had it here!" she holds up the three green pills--the Rufinol pills she pocketed from the vial when Derek berated Hal.

Silently, she hands one to me, holding another in her open palm. No words need to be spoken. There's only one way to find out. Put the pill into our mouth. The moment it touches my tongue I taste it. We exclaim in unison:

"Fucking sugar!"

He switched the pills. C'mon, he showed us the bottle and we were so intrigued—no questions were asked. So we were giving sugar pills to actresses—day players getting $40,000 a pop to take a sugar pill and play possum.

"In all those clubs and parties," Charity works it out, "Derek always vetoed girls--declining anyone who wasn't one of his. . . planted girls."

Remember him at Dublins? Frantically on the phone, calling up his planted actresses and camera crews waiting at another location, telling them to high-tail it over to the sports bar--one of the only nights his simple plan was complicated.

"Must've thought it was all over when you went home with me," says Charity.

I remember how angry Derek was—adamant that I not use her, screaming that I bring her right back to the Barfly. Why? Because he knew she wasn't one of his planted girls! Charity swallowed the pill in her drink and thought nothing of it. She'd used Rufinol for years and therefore 2 mg had no effects and--

She was immune to sugar pills.

"So we never raped anyone," Charity collapses onto the bed, silent for a long moment as she lights another cigarette, "Jesus, don't know if I should feel elated or hang myself in the bathroom. All those people were actresses," then she begins to chuckle—the chuckle growing into laughter. The laughter of waking up from a horrible nightmare and realizing it's just a dream, "fucking amazing what people will do. That mailman took a dildo without a peep."

But the darkness hits me, "I raped Veronica. . . my old girlfriend," I give her the blow by blow--how we struggled on the floor, her face illuminated in the ghostly red light of the oven. She hits me with a frying pan in the head. Then Derek brings the first girl into the car and in the dark game room, I raped her.

Rifling through the carbon copied contracts, Charity pulls out one with Veronica's signature. I hold it to the light, searching for a flaw, but the signature's real. She accepted the role. Hell, why wouldn't she—got to hit me with a frying pan, but:

"She would never have agreed to screw me on screen," I retort.

"C'mon, this is the same girl who fucked the diaper guy--"

"She'd do the role for exposure, but I know her. She'd never agree to real sex on camera."

"Looky here," Charity hands me another copied release.

The actress' name on the contract reads Jill Simon. Her role is described as VERONICA STAND IN--

"You were an insomniac, hadn't slept in almost two weeks," Charity continues, "had a head wound, and were in a dark room. Derek knew that having Veronica there would force you into the whole thing. It was the only way to draw you into the story. So he sets her up and switches the girls--"

"Then she left town for a commercial shoot," I mutter to myself. It really is like waking up from a bad nightmare. I didn't rape Veronica! Didn't rape any of those women. I didn't rape anyone! Then when did he plan this charade?

Flash—I remember what he told Mo Simon about his next project—in Mo's office, the first words I ever heard Derek Van Horn utter,: "It's sort of a reality based film, no real script, let it flow--in the vein of Truman Show meets Cops--"

Flash—on the first night together, he gave me a hint about his masterpiece, "I'm looking for some great neorealistic film, but we've pushed the envelope so far, there's nothing left to shock--"

"He never had a plan," I whisper to Charity, "just got us to sign releases, mounted cameras--was going to bring together real people and see what happened."

"How ironic," Charity lights another cigarette. Nothing more need be said. What she means is how ironic that fate forced him to confront a topic that haunted him.

One memory strikes me so forcefully that I remember it more vividly than any other. The two of us at the Staples Center skybox, I confront him, asking: "Just tell me why? Why are you doing all this?"

"Because you're such a great protagonist."

Charity stares blankly at the sugar pill. She's free of it all. She's done horrible things, killed a man who haunted her all these years. She's attained revenge and everything else—and she gets it for free. I remember Charity asking me if some crimes are so horrendous that they can only be paid with the person's life.

"He wanted to die," I whisper to myself.

Flash—on that first night at his home, chuckling Derek says, "Sometimes everything seems so complex that I want to just shoot myself dead--I'd do it too if it could somehow benefit somebody or something--suicide is so damn selfish."

"Somewhere along the line," Charity says to me, "maybe after he was shipped off to England--away from the madness, he realized the horror of what'd he done to her--"

What he did to his sister.

I think back to Charity playing out the events of that horrible evening when she explained her new acting role. I remember Derek's parents' party for the mayor, his Dad locked away, drunk in his study. Mrs. Van Horn, the stoic mother with a lioness façade, chattering on. How many locked doors are there in the Van Horn mansion? Inside this mad world, they created a monster. Somehow, Derek broke out, realizing the horror of what he'd done. Maybe when his sister killed herself, he was unable to live with himself.

"When he went to that Ballet of Chestnuts," I say, "he was ready to kill himself--just looking for a swan song to leave behind. Running into you made it easier."

"Murder in movies is always more popular than suicide," mutters Charity.

Then she silently weeps. So we sit, Charity and I struggling to reassemble our reality, flushing out the illusions, the fake mirrors and hidden cameras of Derek Van Horn. Now the sunlight seems brighter, the buzzing in my ears is gone—I think for the first time in months: I have a whole life ahead of me. Then I realize it, one final problem, one final bug in the well-ordered plan:

"Charity," I whisper, "one person was raped."

"Who?" she asks.

"Eloise!" Hal and I drugged her before Derek could've even hatched the idea! Hal used his own drugs in his own privately planned agenda--

Rifling through the contracts, she glances up, "No Eloise Preston here," then she adds, "wait a minute. Derek walked into the kitchen and said he raped her, right?"

I nod my head yes.

"So no one saw him? You knew he wanted her out of the house--all he did was zip his own pants up and walk in the kitchen. No one saw her violated because she wasn't."

It's true. We only saw him zip up his pants. And he was in the game room for almost no time. When we went back into the game room Eloise was almost totally clothed, he bothered pulling her pants down to her knees—that was it.

"So," recounts Charity, "Hal really uses his Rufinol on you—your chick accidentally takes it. You guys drag her back to Derek's house. Derek wants her out--pretends that he rapes her. Then later that night, he gets this idea for his film--"

All night he's in his locked room—tap—tap—ding ringing out as Hal bangs on his door. I imagine Derek sitting at his computer desk, formulating his movie idea, downloading internet articles on Rohypnol, working out all the details like switching Hal's medicine bottle, using his talent agency models and--"

"Oh no," shoot to my feet, "I have to go!"

Twenty Eight

Eloise.

There's only Eloise. That's what I think, leaping out of the taxi, sprinting across the street. I don't even think about the fact that I'm barefoot and clad only in that white Peninsula Bathrobe. Her apartment door is unlocked. Opening it, I call out her name. The empty walls give my voice an echo--stray packing boxes in the corner. She's left. I race back down to the street, but there's no moving van in sight.

She's gone.

I never even asked for her forwarding address. Why would I? Thought I'd be dead by sun up. The taxi runs idle in the street. Dejected, I climb back in:

"Where to?" the driver inquires.

But I'm not thinking about where I'm going. All I can think is that after all the people I've met in my life, I let her slip through my fingers. Hell, why would she ever want to speak to me again? I'm the guy who drugged her—who lured her up to Hollywood and dumped her on a beach. But I thought, maybe if we could talk, I could explain it all. There has to be hope. Because after all this soul searching and suffering--

No one raped her.

"Hugh Hefner!" gripes the cabby as he looks at me in my bathrobe, "we going to the Mansion or you getting out?"

Great.

In all of LA, I get a cabby who not only speaks English, but one who has a sense of humor. But where do I want to go? She's gone and I know that even if I could find her she's never going to speak to me again—

"Today please?" the Cabbie demands, "I want to go to lunch."

His comments sparks the idea. I give him the location.

My Mini Mac is busy.

Noon time diners stand in line, waiting for their double hamburgers and Big Mac's. In the back corner, the homeless bum rants on about the government and some Mormon conspiracy. Eyes turn as I step out of the cab in my white, terry cloth bathrobe, people parting around me like Moses at the Red Sea. Then I see her. Over there in the back corner--she sits, teary eyes staring down at a full carton of fries and a burger. I knew she'd come here one last time before she left. So distressed she doesn't even notice me.

Standing over her, I try to be witty, "You could've super-sized those fries."

She hesitates. Hands still cradled over her face. All eyes are on us. In a movie this is when we kiss. But there aren't any cameras here. Derek Van Horn is dead. The movie is over. This is real life. I'm a guy dressed in a bathrobe standing in front of a beautiful, teary eyed girl. But deep down, I know this moment is important— maybe the defining point of my life. Then it hits me:

I don't think she's going to turn around--

The audience applauds.

I'm sure you want to know what happened at the Mini Mac, but you'll have to wait. Because the sound of hands clapping breaks my train of thought, bringing me back to the movie auditorium. The film's over, but the lights haven't gone up yet. Credits float by, bold print against a black screen. In Los Angeles, especially at a film screening, no one leaves until every last credit has been shown. The names of the principle cast pass first. The audience is still clapping as the names of the supporting cast--the day players, follow--take a look for yourself:

RUSSIAN GIRL WITH GLASSES
CLAUDIA SLOVIKI
SUZIE WONG LOOK ALIKE
MARGARET CHANG
RUDE BRUNETTE
LEE S. CHARLOTTE
RUDE RED HEAD
KIMBERLY CLARK

RUDE BLONDE 1
JENNFER TAMBURIN
RUDE BRUNETTE 1
ANNE BOURGEOIS
RUDE ORIENTAL 1
NANCY TATE REEVES
RUDE T-SHIRT GIRL
VICKY SEINGRAM
RUDE FILM PARTY GIRL #1
TABATHA BAFLOFF
RUDE FILM PARTY GIRL #2
VANESSA POLOWSKY
RUDE FILM PARTY GIRL #3
MONICA B. SORBELL
RUDE SOCIALITE #1
SYLVIA MARSHAL
RUDE SOCIALITE #2
ASHLEY THURGOOD
RUDE SOCIALITE #3
WENDY WASSENSTEIN
DRUGGED DRINKING GUY
CORT RICHARDS
DRUGGED POSTMAN
ALLEN T. CUMMINGS
ESPN ANNOUNCER AT BAR
FRANK SCHMIDT

Ferrets speak the truth.

From the middle aged socialites to the postman--all paid actors. Most of them struggling, the same type that strip or agree to nude photos in order to pay the rent while they wait for their big Hollywood break. For them it was a day job with a little extra pay at the end. Although I think I'm safe in saying--

The postman got paid double.

Then comes the production credits chocked full with Derek Van Horn's name—directed by--produced by--sound mixed by--edited by--scored by. In Hollywood it doesn't look good for someone to get so many credits. People don't believe it's true. But the magic of this film is that Derek Van Horn didn't make it for anyone but himself, his last tribute, his final fuck you to the world. Another thought fills my mind--

On that first night at his house, Derek sizes me up as a possible candidate, asking me: "If you had total freedom, what would you like to do with your life?"

And I reply: "Always wanted to be a writer."

The final screen credit flashes on screen:

WRITTEN BY CULLEN GERSH

I fight hard to keep my eyes from tearing.

A secret gift from him to me. Then the lights come on. People staring at me as I stand, straightening my tuxedo jacket, filing out with the crowd of black tie clad patrons as we exit the plush theatre. It's the screening room for The Academy of Motion Pictures—that's why there's all this movie memorabilia on the walls—hell of a lot more than Irv ever had.

Reporters wait outside the building, spotlights flashing all around the red carpeted walkway. Stepping onto the walkway, a barrage of microphones are thrust in my face. Reporters I've never met bark questions to me--addressing me by my first name, as if we know each other:

"Cullen, how has your life changed over the past two years!"

"Gersh! Over here—photo spread for People!"

"How do you feel about the film's record sales overseas?"

I silently stroll down the walkway and into the limo.

The post party is at our old watering hole.

That's right--the same El Torito Archie, Hal, and I used to frequent, nursing our one Corona long neck as waitress grimaced. Post parties with a campy feel are very popular these days--so the Hollywood rank and file think nothing of it. They're too busy trying to get through the pack of Gay Bears and enter the Mexican restaurant before all the free food and booze run out.

The place is done up with banners and lights, barely recognize it. On the walls are productions stills, still photographs from the movie. These are the shots Derek took on his Polaroid camera. A big band blasts dance tunes from the back of the restaurant, lyrical songs floating through the air. The place is packed with gay bears in leather jackets and headsets, working security--oblivious to the countless flamingoes, massive tits on spindly legs. I told you they were gay. Between them, countless penguins waddle as a handful of old, spotted owls blink from the far corners of the room, trying their best not to go extinct.

Glance through the window, peering across Camden Ave. at the cigar bar, remembering the three Amazon bitches who insulted Archie so long ago. The place is now a Pack and Post shop.

Things have changed.

This special movie screening and post party marks the two year anniversary of the general release of "Rufinol and The Modern Art of Dating." The film, funded on a $65,000 budget swept across the United States, breaking sales records, generating—yeah, like you really care. Anyway, I promised we'd never talk too much business--

But I will tell you this: when polled on the Rufinol phenomenon, as it was termed by Time Magazine, audiences claimed to love the film because it seemed so real, people had trouble believing it was just a film. Feminists groups and ill-informed religious leaders still picket theatres and video rental stores, thinking the film is real adds to the mystique. Of course no one takes mind of these skeptics. They're the same people who think wrestling is real and politics are fake.

Cruising towards the bar to grab a Corona, I inevitably make the rounds, passing faces I now know so well: Claudia—that's the Russian Girl with glasses from the Garden of Eden. The one I chased into the lobby of the Beverly Wilshire Hotel. We've gotten to know each other since we flew to the British premier of the movie. The girl waving to me from the end of the bar is Sylvia Marshal—one of the rude debutantes. In her older forties, she's a riot. Tells dirty jokes and is an aromatherapist in the evenings. Keeps offering me a free session, but I hate smells.

Sipping my beer, I smile a hello at Margaret Chang, one of Derek's countless Chinese girls. Mo, the white Madagascar lemur stands in the far corner, winking at me as he continues telling some story to Irv Hirschberg and his new Hollywood girl fresh off the bus—excited to be here. I wave to Vicki Seingram—the girl I took home from Dublin's. Behind her stands Alan Cummings, clad in all black, discussing something very passionately with someone. I wince. As far as I'm concerned, no actor should ever play that pig thing in Deliverance or that postman--

"Cullen!" near the door, Veronica waves with her beau de jour in hand--this short Polish producer with one long eyebrow.

She didn't make much of a presence in Derek's final cut of the film and has struggled ever since to break into the business. I still see her on TV. She's that annoying girl in a grass skirt doing those Pert Hair Care commercials.

She calls my office every so often, trying to set up a dinner date. Derek would find that funny. He'd also smile at me never returning them.

So there's a lot of empty hellos and quick nods of the head as I navigate through the sea of black ties, slowly cruising towards the rear of the restaurant.

Then I pass Archie.

Sitting in a corner booth, a facial tick causes him to blink endlessly. I hear he's easily fatigued—maybe due to all the drugs they have him on. Well, you know how I feel about pills. He's like a shell shocked soldier who never gets better. Maybe when you strip away all those smiles, he was always like this—extremely vulnerable? I don't know.

We don't talk much anymore.

I only see him at these post parties. He refuses to attend the screening—don't think he's ever seen the completed film. I find the movie cathartic in some strange, indescribable way. One day at lunch, Mo said that he thinks Archie fakes his vague symptoms, passing on film roles in order to drive up his asking price. I'm sure others feel the same way. The studio keeps supplying him with a wheelchair, hoping he'll use it--see it just outside the booth. That would really elevate the mystique.

And notice the girl nursing him.

That's right. The Suzie Wong look alike—Derek's girl from the Garden of Eden. Mothering him, she feeds Archie his chicken burrito, cutting it into tiny bite sized portions for him. They met at a post party last year. Now in her Gucci ensemble she bought with his Platinum card, she'll soon get bored and tell him she's ready to return to the Bel Air home she picked out with some of his proceeds from the film. His agent tells me he's talking about marrying her. The TV rights to the wedding were already auctioned off to some sensationalist news show.

Archie smiles as I pass.

It's a strange smile: the longing attempt for comradery--when in truth, the sight of me makes him want to curl up into a ball and die. There's too much memory in my face--too many secrets between us. Because as agents, execs, guests, hangers on, and sycophants compliment us on our movie performances which seem so real--only you and a few of us know the truth.

This is why my face sickens Archie.

You probably think I'm rude not saying anything to him. At a press party six months ago, I tried talking to him—that sent him into convulsions. There are no scars or bruises on his skin, but he is sick--I know, I'm waxing poetic again. Who knows? Maybe his girlfriend, wiping salsa from his ghostly white cheeks, can help? Archie finally got his LA girl.

At least until the money runs out.

As I pass, he mimes the words: I'll call you soon.

 Life is fucked up.

Seeing Archie makes me think of Hal. Weaving through guests, my thoughts return to a time when we could barely afford that one drink here. I've not seen Hal since Derek died. My calls and letters go unanswered. I used to think he'd go to the police with the truth, but you've seen how that would work. Hell, the studio would probably parade him around the country, letting him rant and rave about what we did. No one would believe him anyway—just add to the hype. Someone from UCLA said they heard he moved to Thailand--another thought it was Fiji. Hal never struck me as the beach type.

But their comments have created this imaginary image of Hal that fills my mind. It's the portrait of a man haunted by memories, genuinely disappointed in society. In my imaginary scene, he walks tormented across some tropical beach. If I were a novelist, I would write:

Rubbing his hands madly, he wandered alone on windswept beaches, a stone's throw from coral reefs and rainbow fish. Sometimes natives, dragging in nets of star fish and octopus, watched him with cautious eyes. His gait carried an intensity to it: sharp, well-appointed footprints in coarse sand. He arrived on the beach near sunset, flat, full face bent downward, offering greetings to no one, as if searching for some lost jewel. He disappeared around the bend by the time the moon took flight over a dark horizon. The locals thought he was possessed by a spirit. They were frightened by the foul smelling plastic bottles found along his path. They refused to walk in the faint whispers of his footsteps, waiting until the next day when they were refilled and the Purell bottles washed away by the warm and inviting sea…

I know what you're thinking.

Don't quit your day job.

I wave to Claryssa, sitting in a booth, lecturing to a fresh cadre of young trainees. She still hasn't made full agent, but has enough opinions to fill ITM. In the booth behind her sits Cort Richards--the guy we brought home from Dublins. He holds hands with Frank Shmidt, the remote camera crews chief--disguised as an ESPN announcer at Dublins. I guess they're dating.

Spilling into the back room filled with tables of longnecks, chimichangas, burritos, and tacos, I notice the cadre of flamingoes flashing eyes at me. It's like a bread line of massive tits propped on spindly legs, holding plastic plates with salad greens. They don't excite me anymore. Don't want to sound arrogant, but this happens a lot.

Look up.

Pretty impressive, huh? Supported from the ceiling on wires, the four identical black and white photos of Derek Van Horn loom over all of us. His bigger than life image peering down on the guests. In a way, this is like his funeral, isn't it? Even now, you find yourself drawn in by the mere photographic reflection of his presence. Only one thing can drag you away—

Do you see her?

She's winking at us from the center of the room. Her hair is done up in this feather thing--don't know how to describe it. She's in amazing shape, has this serious trainer in Brentwood. Clad in an elegant, black Prada evening dress, she's stunning—no, more than stunning. Striking in a very Audrey Hepburn way with a thin, lithe frame. She grins at me, eyes glistening--perfect white teeth.

Now you realize who she is.

Hell, you've seen her in most of your favorite movies, including that other big one. So in the end, you know her name now—her stage name at least. Don't feel too bad. I only know her as Charity. But then this is Hollywood, truth and fiction always get confused.

Just as Archie suffers, Charity thrives--like a sick patient whose fever's broken. The buzz is that she's taking the best actress Oscar home this year for that movie with Mel Gibson. I guess the ghosts have left her. Just look at her hair—doesn't gnaw on it anymore.

She's dating an Italian racecar driver--the guy over at the snack table, stuffing his face full of shrimp quesadillas. She sees what he's doing and turns to me, shrugging as if to say: what can I do? I gesture as if I'm writing in a note pad, signaling we don't get together often enough. I had to break our dinner last month. She was stuck in Italy after that. Her eyes point towards the bathroom.

I understand.

"About the only place they leave me alone," she apologizes for our meeting place as we stand, hidden in the tiny alcove just outside the women's bathroom, "those reporters follow you everywhere."

"You look great," I say as I protectively shroud her from the view of people moving in and out of the bathroom. Around Charity, I feel like a big brother—maybe we share a bond stronger than family. I don't know, never had siblings.

"Thanks," she sighs, "can't do lunch until next month. I catch the late flight tonight to Paris."

"I'm booked up all month--" then I pause, smiling. It's one of those moments in your life when you're suddenly afforded a moment of clarity, stepping outside yourself.

Charity and I have done pretty well. I'm now the head of motion picture literature at ITM, on the fast track to senior partner--Mo Simon's golden boy. He still can't believe that I worked on the film during my hiatus from ITM. He also doesn't know about the lucrative writing offers I've refused from the studios. Although I will admit that during late night working spells, I still consider getting out of the biz and writing books. But right now, I'm an ITM man. C'mon, we both know I never wrote any movie.

"You know," sighs Charity, glancing up at the posters, "even in death he has to rise over everybody and hog all the attention. Like the eyes of Dr. Eckelberg staring down on us all."

"Who?"

"The Great Gatsby," she rolls her eyes, "this from the head of ITM's literary department."

"Motion Picture Lit," I correct, adding, "the script never passed my desk."

She chuckles in her strange honking laugh. Then a somber look fills her face, "It's funny. I find myself missing him. . . thinking about things a lot."

"Like what?"

"All that crap he spouted--kind of ironic now," she glances over my shoulder at the crowd, "don't you think?"

"What do you mean?"

"There isn't enough Rufinol in the world to get us as many offers as fame has," she rolls her eyes.

"I'm sure you actors always get more than agents."

"Don't tell me you're not an actor," she doesn't need to say anything else. What she means is that our film performances everyone loves is really us and ever since the film ended, we've been acting.

"Do I note a hint of regret?" I add.

"Just a craving for a double chili cheese dog," she smiles—that distant look still in her eyes, "I was at a gala for the Getty--read this quote in an exhibition. It was from some painter—don't ask me who because you know how horrible I am with names. But he said: if artists were to portray the world as it really is, no one would believe them," her eyes move through me, focusing on the crowd beyond.

"Charity, once again," I smirk, "I've no fucking idea what you're talking about."

"Guess it doesn't matter if you get it or not—nobody gets out of here alive," she leans close, lips against my cheek as she kisses me, "don't change, Cullen Gersh. That puzzlement is what I love about you."

Then she weaves around me. Wandering back into the crowd, she's all smiles and grace. How many dimensions people can possess--or maybe I just never really knew her. I follow a few steps behind Charity, just in time to see her racecar driver boyfriend polishing off the last of the quesadilla and starting on the chimichangas. I stand in the corner, so the reporters and fans and penguins and flamingoes and gay bears gathered around Charity won't notice me.

She shoots a final fleeting glance back, eyes glistening. I guess things have worked out pretty well, huh? When Derek Van Horn found me, I was a whining, lost, insomniac and she, a hair gnawer—or whatever you call them. Then through a series of demented events, we wind up here--at the pinnacle.

Life goes on and people are forgotten.

But not a day passes when I don't think of Derek Van Horn--when I don't feel him glaring down on me as he does now from the posters hanging overhead. He's forced me to excel--to try to be happy. You could write volumes about him. A boy who grew up in such a demented house that his parents never exclaimed bitter outrage over his suicide. They knew it was coming. Who knows what dark things happened to him, a child raised behind the brutality of false smiles, perpetrating the most heinous act, driving his sister to suicide. Yet he felt remorse, finally giving up his life for what he'd done. For me, he was a great friend and bitter enemy, don't know whether to love or hate him. But he forced us all to confront ourselves. He can't be held responsible for our reactions to our true selves. He made me who I am.

If I were a screenwriter, I'd wrap it up like this:

INT. RESTAURANT — NIGHT

Through a sea of fans, Cullen, tall, dark, HANDSOME turns to Charity.

They raise their drinks to the poster of Derek Van Horn overhead…they share a private moment, toasting…

CULLEN & CHARITY
(at the same time)
To Derek Van Horn.

The camera turns upward, sweeping over them
all, moving closer to the massive poster of
Derek, until his face is all we see as we...

FADE OUT

I really love that phrase—fade out. It's so lyrical and--
"Daydreaming again?" she asks.

Her hand wraps around my shoulder as she whispers
in my ear. C'mon, did you really think we'd end like that?
I'm happy to see her at the party. I'm happy this is reality
because I don't think a movie would've left someone like
me this happy. So who is this phantom woman? Let's get
back to that Mini Mac and—

I'll tell you what happened.

Twenty Nine

Eloise.

I stand over Eloise.

The patrons of the Mini Mac watch me, this strange barefoot man in a white terry cloth robe. The bum in the back corner continues rambling on about a Mormon conspiracy. I want to say a thousand things. But before I can speak, Eloise turns, wiping tears from her eyes:

"I owe you an apology."

"Why would you apologize to me?" I sit down.

She takes a deep breath before beginning, "The one thing a woman hates is the myth of the perfect woman. All our lives, we're haunted by these vision of airbrushed sex objects and perfect mothers we'll never become."

"I like you," I say, "don't care what you are."

"I've been lying--pretending to be that perfect woman. You were the boy at the bar," she wipes her eye, "and I lied, trying to seem so good. Because I was afraid to show how weak and wrong I am. I knew my fiancée was cheating and did nothing but ignore it. Even went to a psychiatrist and was prescribed sedatives to calm me. No friend asked me to meet at North on that particular night. I went by accident."

"I don't understand."

"I came home early that day and changed to go out to dinner. Only then did I accidentally catch him in the pool with one of his women. I lost it--not at him, but at me, for allowing myself to fall into such a situation. Over love, I moved here, created a life around him. Only then did I realize it: I was my mother, falling for a philanderer just like my father, shutting my eyes to it all. Frantic, I drove--"

La Cienega Blvd.—Santa Monica Blvd.—Wilshire Blvd.—streetlights and stop signs flashing by in a dream, like that Miami Vice promo. Sounds familiar, huh? She's out of her mind, fiddling for the vial of sedative pills in her purse. Her hands shake madly--

"At the intersection," adds Eloise, "this car runs the light, forces me off the road. I plow straight into a concrete bus bench, totaled the car—"

Flash—as we drive to North, I remember Hal saying, "Look at that accident," open my eyes. Someone's driven their BMW right into one of a concrete bus bench-- front end smashed, windshield shattered, engine smoking.

"It was the last straw," with a McDonalds napkin, she wipes her eyes, "I was out of my mind—car totaled. I'd have to call my fucking dad and he'd just laugh, thinking like mother like daughter. I was crazed--"

Crying, she takes another sedative, stumbling out of the car. She's on the corner of Laurel and Sunset. The responsible thing is to wait for the police. But she's so distraught, so out of it—she stumbles away, heading to the bar.

North is just across the street.

She enters the nightclub, ordering a beer, trying to calm down. Her whole life has fallen away. She's given up her job in Europe and everything else to come to LA for the man she's had a long distance relationship with for two years. She wore his engagement ring until tonight. And now it's all over—her life is over. She needs a drink.

But she's picked the wrong place.

Standing at the bar at North, her hands still shakes. The sedatives aren't working. She has a third and fourth pill—anything to stop the screaming in her head! Sipping her double Vodka martini, the two goons approach-- gesturing to meet her. She obliges only because she hopes they'll leave. The first one licks his hand after touching hers. She turns away, the second mockingly throttles her, knocking her beret off. Hair falling around her shoulders, she's deep into an anxiety attack, her mind, a vortex of confusion. She lives across town, has no car no fiancée no life! Her mind grows woozy but the thoughts won't stop and her damn hands won't stop shaking! Wiping back tears, she downs the martini and orders an Anchor Steam--

Hal and I stroll in.

I graze her. She screams at me. I scream back. She's on the edge of her sanity. She downs the entire beer just as the dizziness overwhelms her. The bar starts to spin and everything seems distant—far away. She feels nauseous.

Stumbling, she makes it to the bathroom, locking the door. She remembers the doctor telling her something about mixing sedatives with alcohol—it can be fatal. Her heart slows. Bathroom spins faster--ground rushing up at her. Did the floor just become the wall--did she fall down? Her mind floats back to that little girl alone in the endless Roman apartment of brooding shadows. The spaces between her heartbeats fills an eternity. Time to cross over, to play with her ghosts. No more heartbeat. Eyes close one last time, darkness enveloping her as--

I break down the door.

"You saved my life," she wipes more tears away with the Mini Mac napkin, "you pumped my stomach, got rid of the sedatives--"

Flash—Hal and I burst into the bathroom. Eloise lays sprawled under the toilet. Hal opens her eyes--eyeballs roll back in her head. She's semiconscious. He tries to maneuver her head over the toilet, but she's too big. Turning to me, he pleads for: "Help!" We position her head over the toilet. He jabs his finger into her mouth, pressing down on her tongue.

Eloise starts vomiting. I turn away. Neither Hal nor I see the pills floating in the toilet basin: Hal's Rufinol and her four partially dissolved sedatives. Hal keeps choking her with his finger and in a panic, flushes the toilet, washing away any evidence.

So we never drugged her!

Hal's Rufinol pill didn't have time to even enter her system! She was drugged on her own sedatives and would have probably died from an overdose if we hadn't intervened--

"I know my identification didn't have an LA address," continues Eloise, "so you left me at a safe location on the beach," she sighs, "you knew all along, didn't you? If you hadn't broken into the bathroom at that particular moment on that particular night, I'd be dead—another LA drug overdose on some bathroom floor."

I'm dumbfounded.

"We didn't know you'd taken the sleeping pills," I explain, "Hal tried to drug me and you accidentally--"

She presses a finger to my lips, "I don't care. I don't need to hear it all. I don't care if you were there to rob the bar. If you hadn't barged into that bathroom, I'd be dead."

The entire Mini Mac stares at us.

She leans forward, kissing me long and passionately. Her smell and her presence and everything that is Eloise Preston fills my soul. It's more than any movie or film or book or word or sentence could ever try to capture. And I say it this time—the words carrying so much energy it sends shivers down my spine:

"I love you."

Someone explodes in laughter.

It brings us back to the present, to the post party. Two penguins waddle through us, charging headlong into the bathroom. Eloise rolls her eyes, she hates anything to do with the movie business. Charity and her press junket have floated into the front room. Only the Italian racecar driver remains, digging through an empty tray of tacos. Most everyone is in the front now. It's the end of the party, banners torn down, plastic champagne glasses discarded on the floor as Derek Van Horn stares down at the room.

"Honey, can we get out of here?" Eloise flashes a devilish smile, "I'm in the mood for a little sex."

"Let's get the car," I fire back.

We exit through the back.

It's a quick two blocks walk to the garage. I took the limo. Eloise drove separately since she refused to go to the screening--hates movies and especially dislikes this one. She can't believe I ever offered to act in such a film. But even more than that, she can only shake her head at the fact that the entire world loved it and--

It made my career.

Eloise doesn't know the truth about the film because she isn't in a single frame of it. Yet that one night of reality was what hatched the idea in Derek Van Horn's mind. Eloise doesn't ask questions about that night at North because she's embarrassed about her actions. So she sees it simply--I was her knight in shining armor.

I saved her life.

Standing in the cold evening air, I'm happy she had the foresight to use this valet garage. Now we don't have to wait in line as the press cavalcade down the street harasses us with questions. Just the two of us: a tuxedo clad agent and his beautiful fiancée waiting for their white Volvo, hey, it's lot more reliable than an Aston Martin—

Even if it is a bit boxy.

"I just don't get it," she furls her brow, "why do men love seeing naked women in those movies?"

I keep quiet, simply smiling.

"What are you grinning about?" mist rises from her warm breath as she pokes me playfully.

"Nothing."

"Well Mr. Silent," Eloise kisses me before motioning into the lobby, adding, "I'm going to the bathroom."

So it's just the two of us.

Was hoping this would happen. Now we can end our little tale just as we began it. I guess at the very end, you realize that our lives are drama. Last week on the Discovery Network, I saw a show on human evolution-- said our minds evolved to focus only on things relevant to our day to day existence. The moment we realize the moth is harmless, it goes unnoticed. I guess that's why with time, you no longer notice the buzz of that loud air-conditioner or the rattle in your car door. We perceive only the new and take everything else for granted.

Maybe that's why we grow bored with our perfectly fine mate or perfectly fine job and fanaticize about lovers and things we can never possess? Maybe that's why we fail to realize how beautiful and dramatic our own lives really are--why we turn to books like this and films and TV and racy magazine pictorials.

But I don't fantasize anymore.

You and I have crossed through the barrier of dreams, journeying into that fantasy world. As you've seen, most of the shit you dream about is only exciting because it's taboo or beyond your reach. When you've crossed the fence and done everything your perverted little mind can conjure up, the grass may be soiled, but it's no greener than your own. So you cross back over—returning to where you began. But maybe this time you don't take a woman like Eloise or your boyfriend or your girlfriend or your whole life for granted. You realize how wonderful all our lives can be--how fleeting and precarious it all really is.

That's why you can't just do anything you want.

That's why no one should do what we did. Our lives are compromise. Since you and I were born, we've been rationalizing our way out of feeling guilty for our actions, talking ourselves into believing that what we did wasn't so bad. Well, after all this, you see where rationalizations get you--might find yourself behaving like me. Although you might not film it--

That's been done already. Critics praise our performances for their genuine edginess and intensity. Audiences from New York to LA flock to see it, fascinated with the subject matter. Derek Van Horn generated hundreds of millions of dollars by feeding a neo-realistic obsessed audience the one thing they'd never had:

Reality.

Of course, only the five members of the Clan of The Alpha Wolf know that fact. Probably surprised after all this time that I can admit this gruesome fact. Well, you were there for the entire thing. That's why you're the fifth member of the Clan. Come visit me at ITM. It's the building on Wilshire with the fucking soup spoon in front of it--tell the gay bear at the front desk that you're there to see me.

I'll give you your very own Wolf's Head pin.

Because we are rapists.

Despite my subsequent feelings of guilt, my desperate attempt to pay for my crimes with my life, I knowingly violated all those women. You're guilty because you stayed and watched the entire thing. More than just Nazi monsters have dined off Derek Van Horn's silverware. The fact that none of it was real shouldn't make it any better. But it does. And don't think for a second that I don't realize that in our minds and yours, we raped those women.

But without such things, I would never have met Eloise. Maybe without the social experiment, I would not truly love her with my entire existence. Because my nocturnal dreams aren't haunted with stumbling French maids. My day time fantasies aren't filled with Playboy pictorials. That's why I said nothing when--

"Honey, who are you talking to?" Eloise shuts the lobby door.

"Uh. . . nobody."

The valet drives up in the Volvo. I open Eloise's door. She shivers, hopping in. Tip the valet a few bucks and he races back to the warmth of the lobby.

This is our very last moment together.

So while I've got you here, let me leave you with one last thought. A few minutes before, when Eloise made that comment about not understanding why men loved to see naked women--I grinned and said nothing. I smiled because for a split second, my fiancée, the woman I love and know so well, seemed so distant.

You've felt that before, staring into your lover's face or hearing them say something so unpredictable--that for a moment, they suddenly seem like a total stranger. It's a reminder of how complex we really are. For even as you make love to that other person in your arms, reflecting on how you completely know them inside and out and have grown bored because of it—the truth is--

They feel the same about you.

Because you both stand separated, peering at each other from across the infinite chasm of your own secrets and lost hopes and fantasies and wild perversions--things you'd never explore or share with another individual. The difference with us is that we did journey into those dark caverns. In many ways we're better people because of it. So explore the dark places of your soul—whether that means role playing Little Red Riding Hood with your lover or asking that little slut at The Sunglass Hut to keep bending over to pull out Ray Bans so you can stare down her blouse—

But don't hurt anyone.

Or you'll find you're unable to live with yourself.

And that's the worst state of all.

Unless of course you're some fucked up weirdo. And in that case, you ought to be locked up for the rest of your life—sick pervert. But you're not a weirdo, are you? And how am I so certain of this? Because you and I have been through hell together, the best of times and the worst of it all. I've gotten to know you.

Because my name is Cullen Gersh.

And you and I, my friend, are very, very much alike.

SIRI
ENTER

CHINA ENTOMBED THE WORLD
NOW HUMANITY FOUND AN
ESCAPE

BY 2059 Chinese manufacturing pollution triggered the worldwide flood predicted to last 7,000 years. Plagued with COVID-19 and restricted within flood-walled-zones, humanity prepares to perpetually online on Dreamspace, a digital diversion platform that's as real as life. To play the perpetual game, users must first find a compatible game-mate in the dating module. Once merged, the couple's minds are immersed online permanently gaming with each other, while their offline bodies are maintained in medical body-vaults.

Before the worldwide drop, FCC Web Agent Ray Kemper must solve the murder of a beta-tester who may have met his killer on Dreamspace's dating module. The web agent must date the anonymous users his victim dated in their exclusive worlds, luring each into a digital-kiss to unmask their identity and catch his real-world killer.

The mystery unravels as the detective falls for a suspect who could be the love of his life on the end of it, forcing him to question whether our species is worth saving if doing so means giving up the very thing that makes us human.

"Davlin is the only living American auteur"
-DENNIS HOPPER
Actor, Writer, Producer, Director

"The most important sci-fi story ever written."
-GLEN A. LARSON
Creator of Battlestar Galactica

"Over-the-top finale would be right at home in a De Palma movie..."
-VARIETY MAGAZINE
Review of Davlin's prior work "Memory"

CENTERED AMERICA BOOKS
www.centeredamerica.com

Also available as an ebook

ISBN 9781735873633

$24.99 US
$32.65 CAN

FROM THE INTERNATIONAL BEST SELLING AUTHOR
DREAMSPACE
ESCAPE C19
ENTER
BENNETT
JOSHUA
DAVLIN

THE UNION 57 PETROCHEMICAL REFINERY OUTSIDE NEW YORK CITY IS OVERTAKEN BY TERRORISTS WHO WIRED IT TO BLOW UP, POSSIBLY TRIGGERING A CHAIN REACTION OF NEIGHBORING CHEMICAL PLANTS TO RELEASE A POISON CLOUD IMPERILING MILLIONS IN AMERICA'S MOST CONCENTRATED POPULATION CENTER. FBI AGENT TOM GRANT IS SENT TO NEW ORLEANS TO INTERVIEW A MYSTERIOUS FIGURE NAMED YVES ALEXANDER DUSSANT, A LONE PRISONER IN A SECRET JAIL CONSTRUCTED TO HOLD ONLY HIM. BECAUSE HEARING DUSSANT'S VOICE WILL INSTANTLY TURN A PERSON INTO AN UNWITTING SLAVE TO THE PRISONER'S TWISTED WILL THROUGH A PSYCHOLOGICAL CONDITION THE GOVERNMENT TERMS "CONTAMINATION". WHILE DUSSANT CLAIMS TO BE THE MESSIAH AND THE FREQUENCY OF HIS MANIPULATIVE VOICE CARRIES THE POWER OF GOD'S OWN. FBI AGENT TOM GRANT FEARS DUSSANT IS BEHIND THE UNION 57 TAKEOVER AND FOR HIS HELP, TOM MUST SHARE DETAILS AND SECRETS ABOUT HIS OWN LIFE, LEADING TO A SECRET THAT NO ONE COULD'VE IMAGINED.

If Constantine's Catholicism, which altered the unchangeable Hebrew Bible's Sabbath times and ways were true, then this book would depict the Messiah.

CENTERED AMERICA C/A CLASSICS

CENTERED AMERICA BOOKS
www.centeredamerica.com

Also available as an ebook

$19.99 US
$26.50 CAN

UNION 57

BENNETT DAVLIN

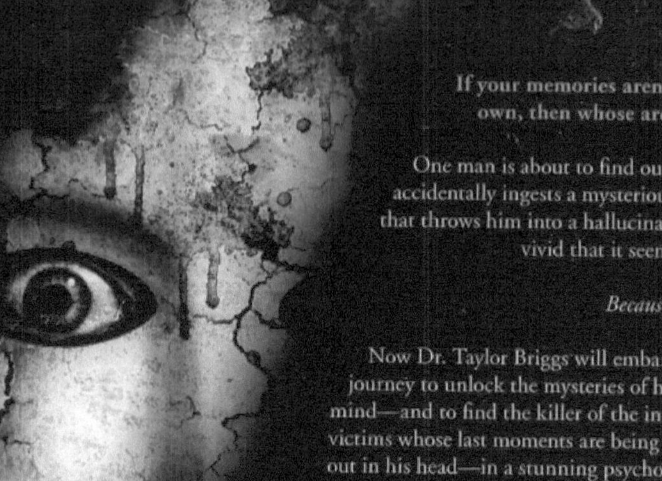

If your memories aren't your own, then whose are they?

One man is about to find out, as he accidentally ingests a mysterious drug that throws him into a hallucination so vivid that it seems real.

Because it is...

Now Dr. Taylor Briggs will embark on a journey to unlock the mysteries of his own mind—and to find the killer of the innocent victims whose last moments are being played out in his head—in a stunning psychological thriller that explores memory, its crucial role in our consciousness, and its power to deceive...

NOW A MAJOR MOTION PICTURE
Starring

BILLY ZANE   ANN-MARGRET
and
DENNIS HOPPER

AN ECHO BRIDGE ENTERTAINMENT IN ASSOCIATION WITH 3210 FILMS AND PARADOX PICTURES PRESENTATION OF A BENNETT DAVLIN FILM BILLY ZANE ANN-MARGRET DENNIS HOPPER MEMORY TRICIA HELFER AND TERRY CHEN CASTING BY CANDICE ELZINGA & JACK GILARDI MUSIC SUPERVISOR MICHAEL LLOYD DAVID STREJA & CHRIS MOLLERE MUSIC COMPOSED BY CLINT BENNETT & ANTHONY MARINELLI CO-PRODUCED BY BARBARA KELLY COSTUME DESIGNED BY KAREN MATTHEWS PRODUCTION DESIGNED BY STEPHEN GEAGHAN EDITED BY ALLISON GRACE DIRECTOR OF PHOTOGRAPHY PETER BENISON, CSC EXECUTIVE PRODUCED BY ROBERT J MONROE BRANDON HOGAN PRODUCED BY BENNETT DAVLIN JESSE NEWHOUSE & ANTHONY BADALUCCO BASED ON THE NOVEL BY BENNETT DAVLIN SCREENPLAY BY BENNETT DAVLIN & ANTHONY BADALUCCO DIRECTED BY BENNETT DAVLIN

COPYRIGHT 2006 MEMORE LLC
CREDITS NOT CONTRACTUAL

NOVEL
www.penguin.com

$14.00 U.S.
$17.50 CAN

NOW A MAJOR MOTION PICTURE
STARRING
BILLY ZANE,
ANN-MARGRET,
and
DENNIS HOPPER
NEVER BEFORE PUBLISHED
MEMORY
a novel
BENNETT DAVLIN

WIDESCREEN
BILLY ZANE
DENNIS HOPPER
ANN-MARGRET
TRICIA HELFER
MEMORY
SOMETIMES MEMORIES CAN KILL
BASED ON THE BEST-SELLING NOVEL

JACKIE CHAN
LEE EVANS   CLAIRE FORLANI
THE MEDALLION
TRISTAR PICTURES PRESENTS IN ASSOCIATION WITH EMPEROR MULTIMEDIA GROUP A GOLDEN PORT PRODUCTIONS LIMITED PRODUCTION
A JACKIE CHAN PRODUCTION JACKIE CHAN LEE EVANS CLAIRE FORLANI THE MEDALLION JULIAN SANDS AND JOHN RHYS-DAVIES
COMING SOON

GOD BIRTHED SCIENCE ON 11/10/1619
SCIENCE WAS USED TO CREATE CONTAGIOUS CANCER*
AND GOD REVEALED IT ALL THROUGH HIS PROPHETS

JEREMIAH gives the **WHAT**
an incurable plague for our sins born from nonbelief

DANIEL gives the **WHEN**
2020 AD, after the 2,625-year-long Israelite punishment begun in 605 BC when Israel was first conquered, proving their blood sacrifices were no longer rightful

605 BC ◄—— THE 2,625 YEAR PUNISHMENT ——► 2020 AD

and **WHERE**
The plague originates from the world-ending beast of "Ten Kingdoms" from the Land of 10 Kingdoms, Mainland China's historic name

EZEKIEL gives the **WHO**
China's King whom God codenamed Gog, launched the plague masked as an act of God, hence his codename so close to God's own

and **HOW**
Gog invaded with splendidly-clad soldiers dressed as "passengers" on "ascending chariots", airplanes, spreading his lethal, viral cytokine "storm"

JEREMIAH gives the **WHY**
God placed hooks in Gog, and when His people are powerless God will annhilate Gog and Magog and no one will ever profain His name again

"BE STRONG, DO NOT FEAR
BEHOLD YOUR GOD WILL COME WITH VENGEANCE...
HE WILL COME AND SAVE YOU"
ISAIAH 35:3-4

*JAHANKHANI, K., AHANGAR, F., ADCOCK, I. M., & MORTAZA, E. (2023). POSSIBLE CANCER-CAUSING CAPACITY OF COVID-19: IS SARS-CoV-2 AN ONCOGENIC AGENT? BIOCHIMIE, 213, 130–138. HTTPS://DOI.ORG/10.1016/J.BIOCHI.2023.05.014

CENTERED AMERICA BOOKS
www.centeredamerica.com

Also available as an ebook

ISBN 9798988146605

$24.99 US
$32.65 CAN

B. JOSHUA DAVLIN

The Conclusion of Ellen G. White's The Great Controversy
& The Solution to Daniel's Riddle

GOD'S GUIDE TO THE END OF THE WORLD WHEN EVEN YOU CAN BE SAVED

ISBN 9781735873688
90000
9 781735 873688

FROM THE 2020 DEMOCRAT PRESIDENTIAL CANDIDATE
OF THE NON-TREASONOUS WING OF THE DNC

HOW TO
WIN
THE WAR
The plan to save the U.S.A

BENNETT JOSHUA DAVLIN

WATCH THE 14-MINUTE SHORT FILM ADAPTATION OF THIS BOOK AT
WWW.CENTEREDAMERICA.COM

FROM THE 2020 DEMOCRAT PRESIDENTIAL CANDIDATE OF THE NON-TREASONOUS WING OF THE DNC

"...I next critized the sex-abuse cover-up scandal, protected for ages by the top elites of their (Catholic) bureaucracy. I disclosed that many of my male homosexual friends, once reaching middle-age, disclosed that they were raped when young by Catholic priests. This wicked conspiracy along with the wrong Sabbath showed the wickedness wrought from the nonsensical Papal infallibility.

I then revealed that my wife and I would never be in a meeting with Catholic Officials except for one, critical fact: **The archangel Saint Michael visited me in the presence of my wife on October 27th, 2017, and altered our lives, bringing us here.**"

- SAINT MICHAEL STOOD UP, PAGE 94

AT THAT TIME (SAINT) MICHAEL
SHALL STAND UP,
THE GREAT PRINCE WHO STANDS WATCH OVER THE SONS OF YOUR PEOPLE: AND THERE SHALL BE A
TIME OF TROUBLE,
SUCH AS NEVER WAS SINCE THERE WAS A NATION,
EVEN TO THAT TIME.
AND AT THAT TIME **YOUR PEOPLE SHALL BE DELIVERED,**
EVERY ONE WHO IS FOUND WRITTEN IN THE BOOK.

-(DANIEL 12:1)

CENTERED AMERICA BOOKS
www.centeredamerica.com

Also available as an ebook

$24.99 US
$32.65 CAN

SAINT MICHAEL STOOD UP

China is Gog

BENNETT JOSHUA DAVLIN

SAINT MICHAEL STOOD UP

China is Gog

BENNETT JOSHUA DAVLIN

Born in South Central Louisiana, Bennett Joshua Davlin began making films at the age of 5 and completed his first novel at 10. He attended Semester at Sea, London's City College, and graduated from *Tulane University*, later attending *Tulane's A.B. Freeman School of Business's* graduate MBA program. Davlin was a former war correspondent in the 1990s Yugoslavian conflict. He has worked in the oilfield sector and in structured and international finance. As a young CEO, he turned around the largest manufacturer of high-end American decorative goods, after which the policies of then-president Clinton forced him to offshore his manufacturing to China. He lived in Hong Kong and Communist China through various periods in the past 30 years. Davlin became a Hollywood studio screenwriter, penning such films as the Jackie Chan blockbuster *Medallion* for Sony, Columbia & TriStar Pictures. He wrote the international best-selling novel *Memory* published by The Berkley Imprint of The Penguin Group and translated in multiple languages by Sony Books, Blanvalet, and Random House. Davlin wrote, produced, and directed the adaptation of *Memory* into a feature film theatrically released worldwide by Warner Bros. and EBE. He served as a keynote speaker at The Tennessee Williams Festival and as a guest lecturer at NYU and other universities. In television, Bennett and his TV producing partner, Randy Douthit, co-creator of CNN's *Crossfire* and *Judge Judy,* work on projects under a *first-look* deal with CBS Paramount. He is also a government policy thinker and philosophical essayist on the site *Centeredamerica.com.*